GLENROWAN

GLENROWAN

AIDAN PHELAN

Australian Bushranging

This text depicts moments and characters based on actual historical events and people. It is a fictionalised representation and not a factual account. Similarities with recorded fact are intentional, though artistic interpretation has been applied in these instances.

For more information go to: https://glenrowanthenovel.com/

To contact the author's email: glenrowannovel@gmail.com

Second edition, published in 2021

Printed by IngramSpark

Glenrowan
Phelan, Aidan

ISBN 978-0-6489572-4-9
Libraries Australia ID 67988913

Edited and formatted by Aidan Phelan
Original illustrations, logo and cover artwork by Aidan Phelan

*This book is dedicated to the memory of all
of those swept up in the events of June 1880
&
To my son Dashiell*

Contents

PROLOGUE

1 Loyalty   50

2 Ned Kelly's Masterplan   129

3 The Devil's Elbow   185

4 To and Fro   210

5 Sunday Morning   228

6 Round Up   254

7 The Wait   273

8 The Train   311

9 Besieged   338

10 Death in the Night   362

11 A Deep Breath   388

12 The Last Stand   398

13 Last Rites   415

14 The Ashes of Glenrowan   445

15 The Rule of Law   468

16 The Last Days   499

EPILOGUE

AFTERWORD

Supplementary Material   551

*Next to a lost battle,
nothing is so sad as a
battle that has been won.*

Prologue

In a patch of the country cursed with perpetual dryness and clouds of dust kicking up whenever the wind would blow, smooth hills undulated clad in yellow grass that flicked about when tickled by the breeze. A creek trickled through this land, cutting through selections - those poorer quality blocks doled out by the government to those struggling to keep a roof over their head, let alone prosper. Farmers would work themselves to death clearing and fencing the land, trying to make something - *anything* - grow in the dust. The days blazed and the nights were frigid, and it was during one of these cold nights that Maggie Skillion and her husband Bill took some time after putting their children to bed to be affectionate. "Attending to country matters," they called it.

Maggie went into the sleeping quarters to get ready for bed, but found her hands would not co-operate, the knuckles having become swollen and stiff due to a chronic, and as yet undiagnosed, condition.

She called out, "Bill, can you give me a hand with the corset, my fingers are playing up again."

Bill Skillion was not anyone's definition of a perfect specimen of man. He was short, chunky and tended to slur his words. Still, he was Maggie's husband and had given her a home of her own and two beautiful children, Ellen and Jim. He entered the partition that concealed their bed and with his stubby, muck-ingrained fingers he fiddled with the hooks of his wife's corset. As he peeled the garment away and tossed it on the bed, with his free hand he grabbed Maggie's breast.

"Not so rough, dear," Maggie complained. She shed her slip and skirts, shaking her bare shoulders against a draught. She had barely felt the prickling of goosebumps rising up to meet the chill when she saw her husband throw his trousers across the room in a dramatic arc, his male parts ready and rearing to engage. Maggie considered how much easier her life would be if she was the one wearing the baggy trousers and Crimean shirt.

***

There was a knocking at the door just after nine that caused Maggie to sit bolt upright. She pulled a slip on and padded across the dirt floor to answer it. Hesitantly she drew the latch back and eased the door open. On the other side, barely visible in the moonlight, was a policeman.

"Margaret Skillion?"
"Yes."
"I'm Sergeant Steele of the Wangaratta police. Is your husband in?"
"I know who you are. What do you want him for?"

As if on cue, Bill wandered to his wife's side, dressed in his trousers and a sweat stained undershirt.
"What's up, Sergeant?"
Steele produced a pair of handcuffs and pushed the door open, sending Maggie stumbling backwards.
"William Skillion, I am arresting you for aiding the attempted murder of Constable Fitzpatrick."

***

Only a couple of blocks away from the Skillion selection was the Kelly selection, where Maggie's mother Ellen had made sure her younger children were tucked up in bed. As midnight approached, she nursed her two-day old daughter Alice at her breast and hummed musically. The father had long gone but Ellen's responsibilities remained. Another mouth to feed was simply her lot in life but it was a burden she took on with good grace as she looked down at the pink face suckling at her.

The peace was shattered when she too had a knock at the door. Her fourteen-year-old daughter Kate, bleary eyed, stumbled out of the sleeping quarters.

"Who is it, ma?"

"Can you check for me, dear; I have the baby."

As Kate opened the door, she let out a scream as Sergeant Steele pushed his way in. From under the brim of his helmet his piercing eyes stared the girl down. In his hand he brandished a Webley revolver, a heavy and clunky police issue firearm. He levelled it at the nursing mother.

"Where are your sons?"

"They're not here," Ellen scowled.

Steele gestured to the constables behind him and they rushed in. One grabbed Kate and pushed her in front of him as a shield as he went into the sleeping quarters. If there were men hiding there, they would have to shoot the girl first. The other constable rushed into the kitchen and began hurling the provisions out of the larder, upsetting a milk dish that shattered in the dirt. Baby Alice wailed at the disturbance. Steele's walrus moustache twitched.

"Shut it up," he snapped. By now Ellen had a gutful. The fire in her belly roared.

"You come into my house; push my daughter about like a stray sheep; destroy our food and now you have the gall to tell me to shut my baby up, you vile article!"

Steele called his men to him and once again produced his handcuffs and passed them along to his subordinates.

"Ellen Kelly, I am arresting you for aiding and abetting your son Edward Kelly in the attempted murder of Constable Fitzpatrick."

"You can put those damned darbies away. Let me pack my things for the baby."

"There's no time for that. Your daughter can bring them to you at the lock-up."

Ellen was escorted outside where a buggy was waiting to take her into town. She took a last look at her house and her sobbing daughter and then was spirited away.

SHOOTING A CONSTABLE.

Several members of a notorious family of the name of Kelly and a kindred spirit named William Skillian have committed a serious outrage upon Constable Fitzpatrick at Greta, near Benalla.

According to the information which has reached Melbourne, the constable went to the Kellys' house for the purpose of apprehending one of the sons for horse stealing. He found the accused at home and placed him under arrest, but allowed him to have something to eat before marching him off to the local watch house. Whilst the prisoner was regaling himself, a brother, his mother, and Skillian entered. The brother fired at the constable with a revolver, but missed, and the mother struck the policeman on the helmet with a shovel. Whilst the constable was defending his head with his arm from another blow by the mother with the shovel; the brother again fired and shot him in the wrist. Skillian also presented a revolver at him. Fitzpatrick was then overpowered and disarmed of his own revolver, but eventually made his escape. His injuries are said to be not dangerous.

Warrants will be issued for the arrest of the offenders, but it was found on Tuesday that they had disappeared. The Kellys were intimately connected with Power the bushranger.

The Greta and Wangaratta police have arrested Mrs. Ellen Kelly, a man named Williams alias Benckley, and William Skillian, for the outrage which was committed on Constable Fitzpatrick at Greta on Monday. Two of the Kellys are still at large and are supposed to have gone to New South Wales.

THE AUSTRALASIAN (MELBOURNE), 20 APRIL 1878.

The Victorian police had ramped up their search for Ned and Dan Kelly in the weeks since the convictions of Ellen Kelly, Bill Skillion and their neighbour, Brickey Williamson. Typically, the papers had gotten much wrong in their reports and Constable Fitzpatrick had twisted the narrative into a pretty bow to suit his own ends, backed up by his colleagues who weren't there. The Kellys had come to expect the traps to look after their own kind, of course, even at the expense of justice.

The genesis of the drama was that sixteen-year-old Dan had agreed to go with Fitzpatrick, who claimed to have a warrant, despite knowing he was innocent of any charges, and the boy fully expected to be let go in the morning. A scuffle broke out during which Fitzpatrick wrestled with Ned, whose pistol was cocked and ready in hand. It was a foolish move to rush in with a weapon ready to fire, but even more foolish to grab a cocked revolver, and it was nothing short of miraculous that Fitzpatrick was merely shot across the wrist.

Ellen tended the wound and Ned allowed Fitzpatrick to leave so long as he said nothing about what had happened. Dan had protested that Ned was a fool to let him go and the first thing he would do is tell his superiors, but Ned trusted the constable to stick by his word. Fitzpatrick held no feelings of loyalty for Ned. In fact, his prior fraternising with the infamous Kellys had all been a scheme of his to infiltrate the notorious family and uncover any dirt on them, however minor, to lead to arrests and convictions. What better way to climb the ladder in the police force than by stamping out the Kelly nuisance?

After the calamity, Dan had brought Ned up to the spot on Bullock Creek where he had taken possession of an abandoned miner's hut from which he prospected for gold in his spare time. They planned to get some quick money from prospecting to fund the court case. Ned also had the idea of distilling *poitín* in order to supplement the income. After six months of waiting for a result, the accused had been thrown in prison. Three years for Ellen, six years apiece for the men. Word had reached Ned that the judge, Sir Redmond Barry, had privately claimed that he would have given Ned fifteen years.

On October 25th, a police party had ridden out from Mansfield into the Wombat Ranges, intent on catching the fugitive brothers, and making £100 in the process. Ned had been told by his bush telegraph that there were three police parties coming in total, armed to the teeth and carrying belts to sling corpses over a packhorse. Ned was not in a position to test the veracity of the claims; to tarry could be a death sentence. His discovery of the tracks of police horses in the morning had put him on high alert and he had sent Dan out to find the police camp, which he located by Stringybark Creek. Ned spent the night on sentry in case the police came upon them in the night.

***

Ned Kelly was twenty-three years old but looked much older. His young body, tough and sinewy as it was, had finally demanded rest just as the sun was creeping up. The stronghold was a curious building that sat in a small clearing in the bush. It was a small, squat construction made of thick logs that intersected at the corners. There were no windows save several small holes just the right size to aim a gun through. The door was made of heavy steel from a ship's ballast, thick enough to withstand most bullets. It slid open and Joe Byrne, a tall man two years Ned's junior, emerged. Both had line-etched faces despite their youth and wore long beards.

Ned's dark hair was complemented with a beard the colour of red velvet cake, a genetic inheritance from his long-departed father. Meanwhile Joe's autumnal locks merged with a fluffy golden beard forming a wispy lion's mane. Both were strikingly handsome and had caught the eye of many a young lass in the towns but the lifestyle here in the ranges had aged them prematurely, not helped by their habit of washing their faces and hands in kerosene to get at ingrained dirt.

Ned cracked open an eye as he awoke to Joe holding a pannikin of tea out for him, from which steam coiled into the cool morning air. Ned immediately gasped and straightened.

Joe smiled, "Easy; there's no traps about. Here, this'll wake you up."

Ned accepted the cup and sipped the drink, which numbed his tongue from the heat. The steel pannikin warmed his chilled hands. Joe sat beside him, plucking a bottle of whiskey out from under his arm. He bit the cork and yanked it out with his teeth so he could add whiskey to his tea. Ned looked at his mate with bemusement.

"I barely slept a wink meself. I'll pay for it later, I'm sure," Joe continued. He spoke in a peculiarly clipped way.

"Whatever happens here, I don't want you and Steve mixed up in it. Maybe you ought to clear out while you can," said Ned.

The Steve that Ned referred to was Steve Hart, a nineteen-year-old jockey from Wangaratta and Dan's best friend, both of whom were asleep in the stronghold.

"We're your mates, and mates stick together. No matter what. You wouldn't walk away from me in my hour of need," Joe said. He paused to sip his tea-infused whiskey, "Besides, good luck splittin' up Tweedledum and Tweedledee in there."

Ned squinted at the sunrise. "Suppose we could just let the traps pass by, but if I run today, they'll only keep chasing. If I don't make a stand, they'll run me down for the rest of my life. What sort of life is that?"

***

That afternoon the report of a shotgun echoed through the bush. Ned and the others stood to attention.

Steve Hart became agitated and jittery, "That was them bloody traps!"

Next to the rest of the gang, Steve was completely out of place. He was weedy and walked with a limp from an old injury to his right leg, and patchy clumps of facial hair dotted his round cheeks and jaw. Yet, despite his physical shortcomings he had notable strengths. Joe Byrne nicknamed him "The Whippet" for his build as much as for his speed when hunting 'roos; a favourite pastime of the gang.

Ned stomped into the stronghold and scooped up his sawn-off carbine, which was a rickety old weapon with a skewed barrel barely held together with wire and waxed string, He jammed a pocket colt revolver into a crimson sash around his waist and quickly re-emerged.

"I'm going to take a look. You lot stay here."

"Bugger that, we're coming too," barked Dan.

The younger Kelly was stout with long black hair and soft moustache, dressed in hand-me-down clothes far too big for him. In the pocket of his waistcoat was a fob chain made of scavenged coins wired together attached not to a watch or fob ornament, which he couldn't afford to buy, but an old conker that he had often used when trying to amuse himself in the quiet spaces between chores. He was much shorter than Ned and as he had matured had begun to resemble his mother's violent brother, Jimmy. The resemblance irked the teen and had prompted him to grow out his moustache and oil his long hair with black boot polish to mask the resemblance.

"We're comin' with you, Ned. That's the end of it," said Joe.

Ned knew he could either accept the help or risk the others following him into trouble without his consent anyway.

"Alright; but you do exactly as I say at all times," replied Ned donning a Sydney soft crown hat and pulling the chinstrap under his nose in the larrikin fashion. The others fetched their weapons. Dan collected his hunting rifle, Joe took up an old Sharps rifle, while Steve grabbed his shotgun.

The gang moved as swiftly and stealthily through the bush as dingoes, but slowed down through a swampy patch dotted with tall clumps of spear grass and lush ferns. The four young men hid in the bush to watch the police camp from a safe distance.

A thin, severe looking man with beady eyes and a long neat beard sat beside a roaring fire preparing food. The other trooper, a stocky man with a long salt and pepper beard and retreating hairline, was busy reading newspapers by the tent.

"I can only see two. Should be more. I counted four yesterday," Dan whispered.

"They may be asleep in the tent. These might be sentries," said Joe.

"D'you recognise them?" Dan asked Ned. Ned nodded.

"I'd bet that's Strahan over by the horses, and I'll be damned if that's not our old mate Constable Flood by the fire."

"Flood! I'd like to skin that bastard," Dan said with a sneer.

Ned gestured for the others to come close. "Right, we'll bail them up, take their horses, provisions and guns. Send 'em back to where the bastards came from tomorrow morning. Agreed?"

The others nodded. Ned moved forward through the spear-grass and the rest followed, spreading out to create a semi-circle around the camp.

The police horses began to stir as they caught the scent of the bush-rangers. The stocky policeman donned his pistol belt then grabbed a double-barrelled shotgun, scanning the bush.

"Something's spooking the horses. I'm going to move them up a bit. Keep an eye out, will you?" he said to his companion in a Sligo brogue. The orders fell on deaf ears as the other man was clearly more interested in his cooking.

Ned and Dan split from Joe and Steve, moving ahead of them. Ned settled behind a large tussock and made careful note of the movements of the men. The stocky policeman returned, placing the shotgun against a large tree stump opposite the fire. He warmed his hands by the flames as the thin policeman stirred a bubbling billycan with a fork.

Ned patiently waited for the right moment. When both men's backs were turned, he signalled for the others to advance. The four young men rushed forward quickly, breaking their cover and entering the clearing, all weapons raised.

"Bail up! Throw up your hands!" Ned screamed, his eyes burning like wildfire. The two police showed little concern at first, until they turned and saw the bushrangers emerging from the bush like vengeful wraiths, echoing the screams to surrender. The thin policeman stood up and extended his arms straight out at waist height. As the gang approached, Ned realised it was not Flood at all.

The other trooper he had identified as Strahan ran backwards for the cover of a fallen tree, tugging at the flap of his holster. Ned spun and fired. The blast pushed a perforated ball from the barrel of Ned's mangled old carbine. The projectile split into shards and hit the retreating trooper. Shrapnel shattered his right eye socket, sliced his temple, pierced through the left forearm and lodged in his thigh. His head jolted violently on impact and he whirled. Blood gushed from the eye wound. The policeman clasped his face and crashed to the ground.

"Oh Christ, I'm shot!" he shrieked reflexively. He crawled a few paces, writhing in agony and confusion as a jagged piece of lead tore into his brain, pulverising it. He gasped several breaths, heaved and then collapsed. Ned drew his revolver and went to the fallen man.

The others moved in with guns fixed on the remaining captive, who trembled in terror.

"Oh, God, my time has come!" he exclaimed.

"Not if you keep those hands up! Check the tent, Danny," Ned barked.

Dan ran to the tent, snatching up the shotgun as he went. He pushed the muzzle through the flaps carefully.

"Come out of there, you bloody bastards!"

"There's no-one else here," the thin policeman interjected.

"Where are your mates?" asked Ned.

"They're out."

Ned stood over the body of his victim, which lay face-down in a pool of blood. Dan ran to his brother's side, twitching and blinking rapidly. He let out a nervous laugh.

"Plucky bugger. Did you see how he went for his revolver?" Dan said wiping the sweat from his palm on his oversized jacket. His breathing was shaky.

"Why did the fellow run?" Ned said to nobody in particular. He felt like he was floating in a dream and his blood ran cold in his veins.

"Who is this man?" Ned asked.

"It's Constable Lonigan."

"No, no; that's not Lonigan. I know Lonigan well enough to look at him," Ned said. He used his foot to roll the body over. The heavy corpse flopped awkwardly. Ned winced at the horrific sight of the sunken, bleeding eye socket awash with blood and brain fluid. Ned realised it was indeed Lonigan.

"Is he dead?" Steve asked.

"He's dead for sure," Dan answered. The sight of the corpse confused him. He had seen dead bodies before, death was nothing new, but he had not seen anything quite like this before and it didn't seem real.

Ned and Dan re-joined the rest and shared a moment of stunned silence. The gravity of their situation began to dawn on them all.

Ned shook his head. "Well, I'm glad for that. Lonigan once gave me a hiding in Benalla and nearly ruined me for life."

"Won't be locking any of us poor buggers up again, will he?" Dan said bitterly.

"Where's your revolver?" Ned asked his prisoner.

"In the tent."

"Keep him covered," Ned instructed Joe.

Ned patted the man down, checking his coat and boots for weapons. Satisfied, he signalled for the man to lower his hands.

"What's your name? Where are you from?"

"Thomas McIntyre. From Mansfield."

"Where are the others?"

"They left at dawn on patrol looking for you. They said they'd be back here before dark," McIntyre sputtered.

Dan waved a pair of handcuffs he had found in the tent at Ned.
"Here, put these on the bugger."
"What's the use in that?" McIntyre asked, indignant. Dan glared at McIntyre and went to speak but Ned stopped him and tapped his rifle.
"We have something far better than handcuffs here."
"The bastard would just as soon use them on us, y'know," Dan grumbled as he stomped off. He did not trust McIntyre and sensed that he would make a break for freedom at the first chance. If he did, and he raised the alarm, it would be curtains for them.

Steve emerged from the tent carrying handfuls of rifle ammunition.
"Look at this, Ned; and there's more of it in here besides."
"You came out here to shoot us, didn't you?" Ned snapped.
"Of course not, only to capture you," McIntyre insisted.
"I know what capture means to you lot. You meant to riddle us."
"Those are for hunting."
"Aye, hunting," Ned scoffed.
"What's done is done," Joe interrupted, "Now, we'll take some of that tea and some dinner."

* * *

Half an hour elapsed and the shadows grew long. McIntyre smoked his pipe with Joe Byrne while Ned fiddled with shotgun cartridges, plucking the wadding out and replacing the shot with bullets.

"What do you plan to do to the others? If you're going to shoot them,

I'd rather be shot myself than tell you a damned thing about them," McIntyre protested. Ned smiled.

"Well, I do like to see a brave man. I would not shoot any man who surrenders himself. If they give up their firearms and horses, they'll walk away free."

"What if they don't return? Will you shoot me?"

"I'd have shot you half an hour ago if I wanted that. Just do as you're told. If I do let you go, you will have to leave the force. It's a shame to see such strapping fellows in a lazy, loafing billet like the police."

Ned stood up before McIntyre, to whom he seemed like a looming ogre.

"I'll do it gladly. My health is bad anyway. I've been thinking of leaving and my life is insured," McIntyre blurted, his eyes darting around. Ned smirked; he took a strange amusement in his hostage's nervous ramblings.

"You faithfully promise you won't shoot them, if they surrender? Nor will you let your mates fire at them?"

"I promise *I* won't shoot them. The others can please themselves," Ned replied. Joe let out a chuckle at such inappropriate humour. McIntyre remained unamused.

"Tell me of your companions," asked Ned.

"Their names are Kennedy and Scanlan," McIntyre said with a laboured sigh.

"Kennedy and Scanlan. I'll remember that," Ned said nodding. "At first I thought you were Constable Flood. If you were, I'd have roasted you on this fire. There are four men in the police that if ever I lay my hands on, I will roast them alive: Flood, Steele, Strahan and Fitzpatrick. Don't know Kennedy, but that Scanlan, I have heard, is a flash fellow."

Ned checked over his weapons and paused in thought. "I suppose, one day, some of you fellows will finally shoot me. But I will make you suffer first and Constable Fitzpatrick will be the cause of all of it."

"You cannot blame us for what Fitzpatrick did to you," McIntyre said, tipping the ashes out of his pipe.

Ned went to reply when he heard something approaching from downstream. "Lads, quiet - listen!"

He noticed movement through the trees ahead. Kennedy and Scanlan were returning after their scouting mission.

"Take your places!"

The gang scattered into hiding spots. Joe and Dan took up position behind the tussocks of spear-grass. Steve crouched in the tent and crossed himself as he closed his eyes. Ned pressed his finger into McIntyre's chest.

"Remember: you get them to surrender, or they're dead men. You alarm them or run off, I'll put a hole through you as well."
McIntyre nodded and sat on a log facing the direction the riders were approaching from. Ned jumped over the adjacent log, nearly landing in the fire, and kept low. He had the shotgun to hand as well as a fowling piece from the police tent. From his hiding spot he was able to watch McIntyre and the arrivals.

Kennedy and Scanlan rode through the bush into the clearing casually, Kennedy atop a handsome chestnut mare, Scanlan a bay. The gang remained hidden, ready for a fight. McIntyre stood and approached the two riders nervously, unsure of what to say to induce them to give up their arms without alarm.

"Sergeant," McIntyre began. Kennedy took no notice of McIntyre's tone or body language.

"Good thing we made it back before dark, Mac, there's rain coming, I think," Kennedy said.

"Sergeant, I think you had best dismount and surrender yourself. The camp is surrounded," McIntyre blurted. His heart raced and his vision started to grow fuzzy. Kennedy chuckled at the remark, unsure of what to make of the bizarre statement as he could see nobody else. He placed his hand on his holster.

"That so, is it?"

Kennedy and Scanlan scanned the camp. Scanlan was first to notice Lonigan's foot poking out from the other side of a log. He immediately made a move to unsling the Spencer repeating rifle he was carrying slung over his shoulder. Ned saw this and pointed his shotgun straight up as he stood, blasting a warning shot into the air.

"Bail up, you wretches!"

The gang immediately burst out of hiding, weapons aimed, all screaming for the police to surrender. Scanlan whipped the Spencer around and fired from the hip as his horse bucked and bolted. The shot whizzed past Ned, who instinctively returned fire, hitting Scanlan in the ribs as his horse wheeled around. Scanlan groaned and slumped forward on his horse's neck causing it to rear. He slid back and tried to dismount, woozy with adrenaline, blood gushing from under his arm.

At the same moment, Kennedy dismounted, taking cover behind the saddle and firing over his horse's rump causing it to bolt. The whole gang opened fire, a shot from Joe hitting Scanlan in the hip. The wounded constable tried to move for cover but collapsed to his knees unable to breathe, his lungs punctured by Ned's shot. His horse charged off. Kennedy ran for the cover of the bush while firing at Ned. Absolute chaos reigned by the banks of Stringybark Creek.

Dan fired at the struggling Scanlan, hitting him in the shoulder and bringing him to the ground, just as Kennedy's terrified mare moved through the crossfire. McIntyre in a fit of panic grabbed the horse by the reins and swung into the saddle. He kicked in his heels and the horse lunged forward.

"Shoot that bugger! Shoot him!" Dan screamed.

Joe fired his rifle at McIntyre as he disappeared into the bush at top speed.

"Ned, the bugger's getting away!" Dan shouted to his brother.

"Get after him then!" Ned ordered.

As Joe and Steve ran after McIntyre, Kennedy lined up Dan and fired. His shot struck Dan in the shoulder. The boy staggered and dropped to the ground, clutching the wound with a groan. Kennedy quickly retreated into the bush, saw-edged leaves slashing at his hands and face as he pushed deeper into the wilderness. Leaping up from the camp, Ned followed hot on his trail.

Scanlan, on his hands and knees, shrugged the Spencer rifle off his shoulder with the last of his strength, but the pain from his wounds was too much. His punctured lungs refused to work. Dan got to his feet, keeping his revolver fixed on Scanlan with a trembling hand, in time to see the constable collapse to the ground, gracelessly planting his face in the dirt.

Kennedy ran for his life through the bush trying to follow the path McIntyre took on the chestnut mare.

Ned Kelly kept up a strong pace in pursuit. "Stop running, damn you!" Ned ordered.

Kennedy saw him darting through the trees toward him rapidly like a hound chasing a fox. He fired at his pursuer and the shot cut Ned's chin through his beard. Ned clapped a hand to his face as he took cover behind a tree.

He quickly examined his hand to see blood on his fingers. Ned growled with rage and, as he peeked out from his cover, saw Kennedy running. Ned took off again, determined to catch the policeman one way or another, his heart and lungs straining.

Kennedy ducked behind a gum tree and aimed again, but his revolver misfired. He doubled back to another, heftier tree and sank to the ground, quickly checking the pistol. Ned moved forward carefully and took cover to reload.

"You surrender yourself and I won't shoot you; you have my word," Ned called out.

Kennedy replied, "How can I trust the word of a bloody murderer?"

"I don't want to shoot you, but I will if I must!"

"I have a better idea; you surrender to me and I swear I'll let you live long enough to hang for what you've done," Kennedy barked back. With his gun finally unjammed, he leaned out and fired again before taking off. The bullet tore through Ned's sleeve as he rose to his feet with a freshly loaded shotgun. He grunted with effort.

Daylight was almost gone as Ned cautiously reached a heavily wooded area with little undergrowth. This part of the bush was home to a sea of thick blue gums that filled the forest all the way past Bullock Creek, where the stronghold lay. Ahead of him Kennedy waited, hidden behind a tree. The sergeant checked his revolver - one bullet left. He listened to the crunching underfoot as Ned approached.

"You're game, I'll give you that," said Ned.

Kennedy quietly cocked the hammer of his Webley then stood out ahead of Ned and fired. The bullet cut Ned across the ribs. He reflexively raised the shotgun and fired back. Kennedy was struck under the arm and groaned. He stumbled backwards, tripping on branches and roots, but miraculously kept his balance, scurrying off out-of-breath and clutching his armpit.

"Surrender, damn you," Ned called after him.

As Kennedy lurched out of view, the pain of his wound was unbearable, like fiery tendrils spreading through his chest. His fingers were weak and he dropped his revolver and stumbled on for a few more steps. Knowing he was defeated, Kennedy slowly stopped and turned. He began to raise his arm in surrender, just as Ned came around a tree at top speed. He saw Kennedy standing with his arm outstretched. He flinched and fired again. The blast hit Kennedy in the chest, punching him violently backwards. He sprawled painfully. He was winded.

As the smoke dissipated, Ned took out his revolver. Then he hit something with his foot. It was Kennedy's pistol. It dawned on him that Kennedy had been surrendering.

"Oh, Christ," Ned muttered.

Prone on his back, Kennedy gasped, blood filled his lungs. He lay passively, no more fight left in him, only pain.

"You've killed me now, boy," the policeman gurgled.

***

That night in the stronghold, the Kelly Gang sat by a fire while outside it rained heavily. They had been joined by Tom Lloyd, cousin to Ned and Dan. Tom was equipped with a rifle and stood by the partially open door, peering into the gloom with the cold air pushing in through the opening. He was a handsome young man of twenty-one with a soft beard, pouty lips and stern eyes.

As Tom kept watch, Dan nursed his wounded shoulder and Joe sucked a whiskey bottle dry. Despite being closest to the fire, Steve could not stop quivering and was wrapped up in a quilt.

Ned stood back reading a rumpled note. It was a letter written by the dying Sergeant Kennedy. The text was incoherent, the page smeared with blood. In his left hand Ned held a gold fob watch - Kennedy's most prized possession.

All the gang had looted the camp and the bodies of the dead men in an effort to grab anything of value – the spoils of war. Joe took rings from Scanlan and Lonigan as well as Lonigan's watch. Dan had taken Scanlan's watch, which had been damaged in the assault. Ned now wore Kennedy's wedding ring on his right hand. It was a plain band, but elegant in its simplicity.

Without a word, Ned threw Kennedy's letter into the fire. He reasoned that it was too disturbing a memory to leave a widow with, even if he was ever able to get it to her. Ned pocketed the watch. One day, if it was safe, he might return it to the widow, but there were more pressing things for him to consider. He turned to his gang with a haunted expression.

"We leave first thing in the morning. We're on borrowed time now."

Mansfield, Thursday, 1 p.m.

Intelligence has just been received that the body of Sergeant Kennedy was found within half a mile from the camp where the outrage took place, at eight o'clock this morning by a searching party, headed by Mr. Tomkins, president of the shire. There were three bullet wounds in the body. Marks of bullets were also found in a tree close by.

1.40 p.m.

Sergeant Kennedy's body when found was covered with his own cloak. It was scarcely recognisable, the face was so covered with blood, and so badly decomposed. It was found near the road along which Constable McIntyre returned. Kennedy is supposed to have been shot during the affray. The search party is very poorly armed.

7 p. m.

Sergeant Kennedy's body was brought in this afternoon, but it was only recognisable by its general appearance and clothing. His face was quite blackened, and the nose was partially gone. There was one large hole in the breast, as if a rifle had been put close to the body and fired after Kennedy had fallen. The clothing round the wound was burnt, and the right ear appears to have been cut clean off, as if with a knife. There is also a wound under the right arm. The volunteers had met parties of police, who believe they are on the track of the bushrangers. The police complain of being badly equipped. They are not sufficiently armed to cope with bushrangers. The police from Greta had no rifle, but one which they borrowed, coming along the road. The seven constables in search have but four rifles between them. The complaints are bitter against head-quarters for this shameful neglect. All pursuing parties are disheartened at having to go out and meet well-armed ruffians, while they themselves are so poorly provided with weapons. Messrs. Tomkins, P. W. Bromfield, W. Collopy, and Constable Orr deserve special mention for the part they took in searching for Kennedy. The inquest on Kennedy and burial, will be held to-morrow.

BENDIGO ADVERTISER, 1 NOVEMBER 1878

While Sergeant Kennedy was being buried in Mansfield, the rain belted and lashed the fugitives in the Wombat Ranges. With their rations tied up in gunny sacks slung on the back of the stolen police horses, they made for the mighty Murray River. Where it had been flowing gently through the hotter parts of the month, suddenly the river gushed and gurgled, swollen by sudden torrential rain.

The gang arrived in the vicinity of Bungowannah, where Ned and Joe had previously shifted stolen horses and cattle through, *en route* to New South Wales. They knew of a punt that could take them across but as they came in close to the bank and Ned gazed across to the opposite side, barely visible through the sheets of rain, they realised the punt had sunk in the floodwaters.

"We can't cross here," shouted Steve.

"We have to cross. If we stay here the traps will be on us like flies on dung," Ned shouted back.

"The horses won't make it, I know a spot further down where we can find shelter until the rain gives up," Steve insisted, gesturing emphatically. Ned begrudgingly accepted that Steve was right about the danger.

"You'd better be right about this, boy."

Sure enough, they found a lagoon by some dense scrub that would provide adequate shelter until the rain died down. They led the horses into the scrub where the canopy provided some protection from the rain.

Ned took a moment to look at his companions. Each one was sopping wet and exhausted from lack of sleep and being on the move for a week, trying to stay out of reach of the police. Dan in particular appeared ill; the bullet wound in his shoulder caused him much pain. The wound was deep enough to require stitches but they were in no position to seek a doctor.

Ned made his mind up to craft a humpy for them and ordered Joe to accompany him with their hatchet to strip bark off nearby trees. A bark shelter would at least provide a little protection and camouflage while they rested; and rest was what they desperately needed.

***

The following morning a short distance from their camp, Steve Hart and Joe Byrne monitored the road, while Ned and Dan went further up in the opposite direction.

Not long after midday a farmer by the name of George Munger came riding along the riverside heading towards Barnawartha. Immediately upon spotting the arrival, Ned produced the Spencer repeater, stolen from the corpse of Constable Scanlan, and levelled it at Munger.

"Bail up!"

Munger halted and raised his hands, "What is this?"

"Shut up! We need provisions," replied Ned, "deliver up the goods you have or I'll throw you in the bloody river!"

Though the gang had stolen eight days' worth of provisions from the police camp, it had all been soaked through in the rain, ruining it. The fugitives were starving and desperate, Dan in particular suffered bouts of wooziness, not helped by his wounded arm that was beginning to fester.

"I don't have any provisions. Who are you?"

"Never you mind who we bloody well are," Dan snapped, "just do as you're told!"

Munger was yanked out of the saddle and ordered to sit on the ground. The grass was drenched and Munger was uncomfortable as his trousers were soaked through.

Presently, Joe and Steve came up to see what the commotion was. They arrived to see Ned rifling through Munger's saddle bags, and Dan reclining on the grass nearby looking like death warmed up.

"We just turned a couple of young fellows back down the road," Steve said to Ned, "should we think of moving now?"

"Move be damned, you ought to have bailed the buggers up," said Ned.

"It would have been fruitless, old man. They didn't look to have a fadge between them," said Joe. "Who's the seedy cove by the water?"

"I didn't stop to ask his name. Keep him covered or look in the other saddlebag, would you?"

Three hours elapsed with no other arrivals. Finally, Ned elected to turn his prisoner loose.

"Alright, you can go. Mind you say nothing of this. If I hear you've said anything to the traps, I'll find you and blow your brains out. Understood?"

Munger nodded his comprehension and promptly mounted and rode straight towards Barnawartha police station. He dug his spurs in once he was out of earshot of the bushrangers and his horse pounded the dirt like its life depended on it.

Back by the lagoon the gang had already begun taking down their camp. Dan scowled at Ned as he struggled to roll up his swag with only one hand. Once the horses were ready the gang began to ride towards the Woolshed Valley.

***

Gunshots rang out above the Sherritt farm just after sunrise. There was commotion within the homestead and Aaron Sherritt, a tall and strapping twenty-four-year-old, soon mounted and rode up the ridge that looked down on the farm. Here the Kelly Gang waited for him, sleep deprived and bedraggled. One look at Joe Byrne, his closest friend, confirmed the rumours that police had been killed and he was involved.

"What do you need?" Aaron asked.

"We're out of food and we need iodine and bandages for Danny," Joe answered.

"Alright, wait here. I'll be back and then I'll take you to the rocks. You'll be safe there," said Aaron.

As Aaron whizzed around the house gathering supplies, he did not stop to explain what was happening beyond a rushed statement that he would be back in a couple of days.

The five riders with their three police horses moved slowly through the bush and headed up towards Native Dog Rock. Up above the canopy was a fortress that had been formed naturally by the rocks that curiously had a sapling growing in the middle towards a gap in the roof. In less desperate times Aaron and Joe had camped here when shifting stolen animals.

Once the gang hobbled the horses and ascended to the cave, they laid out their swags. Dan stripped off his coat and shirt, revealing the wound in his shoulder. The flesh was torn where the sergeant's bullet had sliced through it, and was puffy and red. In the wound the tell-tale signs of infection had begun to manifest: sticky yellow pus and an unpleasant odour. He took the bottle of iodine, soaked a cloth with the liquid and wiped down the wound. He clenched his teeth and let out a stifled cry as the iodine burned the already angry wound. After it was cleaned and bandaged, Dan curled up in his swag and sobbed himself to sleep.

That night Aaron and Joe kept watch for troopers while Ned and the others snatched what little fitful and restless sleep they could.

"Why did you do it, Joe?"

"The traps came after Ned and Dan. If it were you in that position I'd have done the same. I didn't expect Ned to go off like he did. The bastards never stood a chance excepting the sergeant."

Joe went quiet and looked pensive.

"If Danny and I hadn't pushed Ned to get a move on that sergeant would have been much worse off. Ned put him out of his misery. Still, I don't think I'll ever forget the look on his face once he realised what Ned was about to do."

Joe went quiet and gazed into the valley with a thousand-yard stare. His only perceptible movement was the action of swigging from a bottle of brandy. Aaron had never seen Joe like this and looked down at the trio asleep in the cave. He worried about what this would mean for Joe but swore to stick by him, even if it came at the expense of the Kellys and Hart.

The legal formalities prescribed by the Felons Apprehension Act have been complied with in every particular, and the Kelly gang are now outlaws by act of Parliament, and may be shot down whenever and wherever found within the limits of the colony. The Crown Solicitor yesterday appeared before the Chief Justice in Chambers, and produced affidavits showing that the terms of the act had been complied with, that advertisements had been inserted in newspapers throughout the colony under the hand and seal of the Chief Justice, requiring Edward and Daniel Kelly, and two men whose names were unknown, but whose descriptions were given, to surrender on or before the 12th November; and that they had failed to surrender. The Crown solicitor, on these materials, asked his Honor to adjudicate and declare these men to be outlaws under and by virtue of the provisions of the Felons Apprehension Act 1878. His Honor signed a formal order declaring and adjudicating them to be outlaws according to the terms of the act. Subsequently a meeting of the Executive Council was held, at which his Excellency the Governor signed a proclamation setting forth the adjudication and declaration of the Chief Justice that Daniel Kelly, of Greta;

Edward Kelly, of Greta ; and two men whose names were unknown, but whose descriptions were given, were outlaws within the meaning and provisions of the act. This proclamation appeared last evening in a supplement to the Gazette. No official intelligence came to hand yesterday, and the only information received from our own correspondents in reference to the Kellys and their companions is the following ; —

MANSFIELD, 16th November. — Nothing new has turned up regarding the Kellys' gang, beyond a report that they galloped through Mansfield at two o'clock this morning, to the disturbance of the residents. People here are living in a state of dread, as they all know that there are no police to protect them if anything disagreeable should take place. There are complaints coming in from Doon and Jamieson because they have not a policeman at either place.

THE AGE (MELBOURNE), 16 NOVEMBER 1878

The news that the four fugitives were proclaimed outlaws by act of parliament had been a shock. There was no precedent for such legislation in Victoria and the speed with which it was implemented demonstrated a rare unanimity in parliament. The newly-minted outlaws were in a bind as to how to proceed.

From his time as Harry Power's errand boy, Ned knew the value of a cashed-up network of harbourers. Now, he figured, given that he was no longer protected by the law he had no obligation to follow its restrictions. If he could not fund his sympathisers through money gained legitimately then there was nothing to stop him doing so through illegal means.

Prior to discovering their escape into New South Wales cut off by floods, Ned had entertained the notion of robbing the bank in Howlong. Now he began to revisit that idea. While the plan was still formulating, Ned knew that above all else there was to be no bloodshed in this endeavour. He refused to give the press and police further reason to label him a murderer.

Steve Hart still had not been identified, while the gang's ill-advised signal to rouse Aaron had given away Joe's involvement. This meant that Steve was still able to perform reconnaissance for a bank robbery without arousing suspicion. Ned also knew that Steve's sister Ettie would readily assist in this measure.

In the months leading up to the Fitzpatrick incident Ned and Ettie had become an item. Ettie was five years Ned's junior, dark-haired and classically beautiful; nobody would suspect her of being the sibling of a notorious outlaw much less the lover of one. Though she did not approve of his lawless occupation at first, she had found a certain thrill in such audacious behaviour and had taken to scouting for Ned, Joe and Aaron when they passed through Wangaratta with their ill-gotten gains. Ned knew that it would not take much to convince her to help him find the perfect target for a robbery.

So it was that on a mild summer afternoon, the township of Euroa was visited by a mysterious horsewoman dressed in black with a dark fly veil covering her face. She rode up and down all of the streets in the heart of town, taking mental notes of the placement of key buildings in relation to the bank.

She then rode up into the Strathbogie Ranges. After navigating the rocky climb, she found a small camp. She dismounted and approached; the swishing of her hips with each step demonstrating the femininity of the rider as she came close to the fire. Suddenly Ned emerged from behind a boulder and grinned at the new arrival. Ettie threw off her hat and smiled broadly at her beau.

"You're in luck, my love," Ettie said.

"How so?"

"A boy named Bill Gouge was killed in a riding accident. The funeral is only a few days away. If you get your timing right, almost the entire town will be there. The town will be empty."

"No witnesses."

"Exactly."

Ned pondered and then nodded to himself. He kissed Ettie enthusiastically.

"Euroa it is."

Melbourne, December 11, 2 a.m.
The following telegram his just been received from Euroa :— The wires have been cut three miles from here. The National Bank has been robbed, and the Manager, clerks, family, and servants taken away. At 4.30 p.m. they were driven in two vehicles to Mr. Younghusband's Faithfull Creek Station, and there locked up with about twenty others (!) until 11 p.m., when they were all liberated without injury. The Kellys stuck-up Faithfull Creek Station about 2 p.m. yesterday and have been about the vicinity since. One of them dined at De Boo's Hotel to-day. They brought in a vehicle belonging to Gloster, a hawker, for the purpose of removing the occupants of the Bank. They are supposed to have gone in the direction of Violet Town.

EVENING JOURNAL (ADELAIDE), 11 DECEMBER 1878

Night gifted the Strathbogie ranges a peaceful seclusion and the victorious outlaws a cloak of darkness. They dared not light a fire and risk being spotted or start a bushfire, surrounded as they were by tinder dry grasses and dead wood. Instead, they lit a solitary lantern in a dusty clearing by which they could begin the task of counting the takings from the Euroa bank.

Ned opened the sack that held the spoils and pulled out a wad of bank notes. He began to count them, placing them on the ground in stacks with a stolen gold nugget as the paperweight. Opposite Ned, Dan counted the coins; they glinted in the lantern light as he stacked them.

The gang members were now completely transformed. Having raided the wagon of the hawker James Gloster, each wore a new outfit that reflected the character of the wearer – Ned was the peacock of the gang in his blue sack coat, brown tweed trousers and waistcoat, a grey striped shirt and a lavender necktie; Joe was dressed much the same save for a crisp, white Rob Roy shirt and grey coat giving him the appearance of a romantic poet; Dan was more sombre in black and grey, but a brown and black tie added a hint of colour like a stubble quail; Steve meanwhile had the appearance of a young dandy squatter dressed in light grey tweed with a handsome navy blue coat made of wool with silk trim and a black silk necktie. They all wore shiny new Chelsea boots with high heels and smoked aromatic cigars pilfered from the hawker's stash.

Finally, they had begun to shed the snakeskin of ignominy and villainy. They had become dashing bushrangers, robbing the banks to re-distribute the wealth to those in need. It so happened that those in need also happened to be friends and family who would be instrumental in keeping the gang hidden and supplied with provisions and fresh horses.

"I make it 1500 in notes, what have you got there, Dan?"

"Could be about £500, I reckon. I lost count," replied the younger Kelly.

Joe looked in the sack and saw documents in the bottom.

"What's all this?"

"Those are the documents of the debts owed to the bank," answered Ned.

"What do you want with those?"

"I'm going to burn them. One less yoke around the neck of the poor man."

Joe was sceptical, "I don't think that's how it works, mate."

Whether or not destroying bills and mortgages removed debts was irrelevant in Ned's mind. It was all about the symbolism of what he was doing. Not a drop of blood had been spilled during the whole affair in Euroa and at Younghusband's station, even though there were ample opportunities for a bloodthirsty madman, as Ned was reckoned, to have done so if he desired. He was determined to reshape the public perception of him and send the police up at the same time.

There would be no more sleepless nights with empty bellies, huddled under sheets of bark against the rain. Now the Kelly Gang would live like kings in the mountains.

In fact, when Ned had been asked by Scott, the bank manager, where the gang was headed, he had simply replied, "The country belongs to us; we go where we please."

***

Following the Euroa excursion, Captain Standish, the chief commissioner of the police force, had decided to follow through on a ruthless and ultimately morally dubious plan of attack. In order to starve the gang of their support network he authorised the arrest of men suspected of being sympathisers. Almost two dozen men were arrested and thrown into gaol on remand upon the merest suspicion they may be sympathetic to the outlaws, their farms left to go untended; their wives and children having to fend for themselves.

The really nefarious aspect of this scenario was that none of these men needed to have a charge levelled against them, and many were dragged before the court simply to have the remand extended so that the police had time to find something to pin on them. It was manifestly unjust and a complete subversion of what the outlawry act was intended to do.

Needless to say, the community did not respond well to this and word reached Ned Kelly about what had happened. It took him no time to decide on a response. In order to compensate the families that had been mistreated the gang were to go on another "fundraiser". This time they would traipse over the border and make an example of the police in New South Wales in the process.

✱✱✱

In the Benalla police station, Superintendent Francis Augustus Hare sat at the front desk, sipping his tea. Hare was a huge, husky South African with a voluminous silvery beard and a regal profile. He had been left in charge of the station, having assumed leadership of the pursuit for the Kelly Gang.

Suddenly the front door opened and Aaron Sherritt sauntered in confidently.

"Can I help you?" asked Hare.

"I've come to talk to Captain Standish. I've information," Sherritt replied.

"I'm sorry but Captain Standish is out of town for the evening. Is there something I can assist with?"

Aaron lazily slumped against the desk and stroked his chin, "I don't think so. I had a sort of arrangement with Standish. Who are you?"

"I am Superintendent Hare. If you tell me, I'll make sure Captain Standish gets the message."

"I need to speak to him privately," said Aaron as he leaned over the counter, "This information - it's important."

Hare became curious about this larrikin with his confident swagger and cryptic comments. He feigned disinterest to try and trick him into revealing more.

"Well, you'll just have to come back tomorrow when he's here."

"That's a real pity. He'd be very keen to hear about it. It's about the Kellys."

Hare's interest was piqued, but he hid it with a veneer of indifference.

"I'll be sure to let Captain Standish know you came, Mr...?"

"Aaron Sherritt. He knows me. We spoke at Sebastopol a little while back and came to a certain agreement."

"Sherritt," Hare mumbled as he took up a pencil, "Is that with one T or two?"

"Two."

"I shall tell to him first thing."

Aaron fidgeted as if he were about to burst.

"Alright, I think I can trust you with my information," Aaron blurted, "You see, Joe Byrne and Dan Kelly came to see me at my place yesterday about two o'clock. I was working the selection, you see, and Joe Byrne rides up - we're good friends he and I, went to school together and all - anyway, he hops off his horse and sits down beside me. Dan Kelly stayed on his horse, looked very suspicious, he did. Anyway, we talk for a long time and he, Joe Byrne that is, asks me to come away with them. "Come away with you?" I say. "Yes," he says. He tells me the Kelly Gang are heading over the Murray. They want to knock the flashness out of them Welshie police and Joe wanted me to be a part of it. We're old friends, Joe and I, as I said."

Hare took a moment to process the verbal onslaught, captivated and intrigued by Aaron.

"Where did he say they were going?"

"They're going to Goulburn. Says the Kellys have cousins there," Aaron replied, "They wanted me to scout for them. For a long time, he tries to convince me to go but I say "No, Joe, I have this selection to look after and you know my folks are always needing help, so I can't possibly join you in New South Wales." Joe understood, he did, he said "Well, Aaron, you are perfectly right; why should you get yourself into this trouble and mix yourself up with us?" Half an hour he was there and trying to convince me to go, looking all around in case anyone overheard."

"Do you know when they will be heading up?" Hare asked.

"They're already on their way. I can draw the brands from their horses, if you think it would help," said Aaron.
Hare passed Aaron a pencil and foolscap paper. He crudely drew a B in a circle and an E attached to a reversed K. He slammed the pencil down and pushed the sheet across to Hare.

"Well, it certainly sounds as if you have some very crucial information Mr. Sherritt. Be careful, now you are in Benalla, that you are not seen here; do not go into the town, but get some hotel near the railway station," instructed Hare.
"The advice is kind Superintendent, but I'm sure I'll be fine."

Hare opened a cashbox under the counter and withdrew two pounds and handed them to Aaron who accepted them cheerfully.

"...For the information."

"If there's any help I can offer, I will. Thank you, sir," said Aaron as he gave Hare a wink and turned to leave.

Hare examined the drawings and smiled to himself.

THE KELLY GANG IN NEW SOUTH WALES.

The following message, received by the Superintendent of Telegraphs from the stationmaster at Jerilderie, was forwarded to us last night:

JERILDERIE, MONDAY.

"The Kelly gang stuck up the office here to-day at 2 o'clock, cut the office connections, and cut down seven poles. My assistant and I were covered by revolvers, and were marched to the lock-up, which the gang had stuck-up. We were there locked up together with two constables. We were released at 7 p.m., and told not to touch the wire till morning, but I have done so and fixed a wire along the fence. They stuck up the Bank of New South Wales. Have just heard (9-p-m.) that they are in the township, again."

Our own correspondent at Deniliquin has sent us the following messages:

DENILIQUIN, MONDAY, 10 p.m.

"Information has been received here that the Kelly's made their appearance at Jerilderie to-day. They confined the police in the lock-up, and stuck up the Bank of New South Wales. It is reported they took about £2,000. They tore down the telegraph line, and threatened the operator if he should attempt to restore communication. The line has been temporarily repaired, and the above intelligence has just been received here."

TUESDAY, 12.47 A.M.

"A messenger has arrived here from Jerilderie, and a telegram has been received from Senior-Constable Devine confirming the intelligence of the Kelly gang being at Jerilderie. They surrounded the police camp there on Saturday night at 12 o'clock, and kept constable Devine, confined in the cell until 7 this evening. The other constable was allowed to show himself under surveillance, to avert suspicion: At 2 o'clock to-day they stuck up the bank and the telegraph operator, confining the latter in the lock-up and threatening to shoot him if he wired before to-morrow. Besides the money taken from the bank, as previously reported, it is said the gang has destroyed the books and deeds. It is reported that they were last seen in Jerilderie at 9 p.m. to-night, and are supposed to have gone in the direction of Tocumwal police station. There is no communication between Jerilderie and Tocumwal. They took arms, ammunition, saddles and horses from the Jerilderie police station. The superintendent at Deniliquin was absent at Hay, and the police sergeant at Tocumwal when the news reached here. Two mounted constables left here to-night for Tocumwal with information for the police there."

THE SYDNEY MORNING HERALD, 11 FEBRUARY 1879

The New South Wales Riverina rippled in the summer heat as the outlaws rested their horses by the Murrumbidgee River and discussed their plans.

"We shall divide and reconvene," stated Ned, "in two days we will meet up again at the Byrne selection at noon. Until then we make our own ways back over the border with a share each of the booty. That way, in the unlikely event any of us crosses paths with any mud-crushers and is nabbed – or worse - there will still be three quarters of the haul to distribute to our sympathisers."

The others agreed to the plan and set about preparing their horses.

Much had changed in the months that had elapsed since Constable Fitzpatrick's ill-fated attempt to arrest Dan. Although the Victorian government had increased the reward to £4000 for the gang, dead or alive, nobody had turned them over to the police.

In fact, Aaron Sherritt's false lead had been key to keeping the police distracted so the gang could execute their plans in Jerilderie. The police had raced to the border to catch the gang in Goulburn while the outlaws quietly crossed the border over 200 miles further west. Sherritt was laughing all the way to the bank at the same time his mates were laughing all the way back from one.

If Ned felt that his days were numbered, he certainly didn't show it. With the successful and bloodless execution of the heists in Euroa and Jerilderie he had finally transcended the popular perception of him as merely a cop killer and was becoming something altogether more symbolic and unusual. He mounted his horse and spurred towards Victoria with his saddlebags full of cash and a smile on his lips.

ACT ONE

I

Loyalty

The rhythmic thumping of hooves could be heard on the outskirts of the Byrne selection in the Woolshed Valley. The modest dwelling was surrounded by buildings that housed chickens and dairy cows. A goat wandered the yard, nibbling at clumps of grass that sprang out of the compacted dirt beneath the clothesline. The sound of the arrival had roused Kate Byrne, a thin woman of twenty-one, with barely tamed auburn hair that fluttered in the breeze as she walked out of the cow-shed into the February heat and peered around for the visitor. Her gaze swung around just in time to see a bay gelding vault over the perimeter fence and charge towards her. The horse pulled up right in front of Kate and gave her a good look at the rider.

"That was quite an entrance, Dan Kelly!"

Dan sat erect in the saddle, dressed in a black billycock hat, blue coat, skin-tight white riding breeches and police boots taken from the police in Jerilderie. He smiled.

"It doesn't take much to impress you, does it?"

Dan dismounted and pulled off his hat. He shook his head to loosen up his hair, which was heavy with sweat. His usually smooth face now bore a thick moustache and mutton chop sideburns. He gave Kate a hug and a kiss.

"I don't suppose there's room in the stable is there?"

Kate looked confused, "Why ever not?"

"Because of the other fellas."

"Nobody else is here apart from Ma and the girls. Paddy and Denny are off in town."

"Ned, Joe and Steve aren't here?"

Kate shook her head. A breeze dislodged an auburn curl from behind her ear as Dan ran his gaze around the property. He pulled out a cheap looking fob watch from his waistcoat pocket and checked the time. He frowned.

"Well," he said, "I'd best get this fella out of the sun before he dries up."

"Good, he can keep Charlie some company."

As Dan began to walk towards the stockyard, he shot his hand out and smacked Kate's posterior through her skirts. Kate jumped with a quiet exclamation. Dan merely shot her a wink.

***

Inside the Byrne homestead an hour later, Dan mopped up the juices from his dinner with a lump of bread. Margret Byrne, matriarch of the family, sat by the hearth in her rocking chair with a paper fan to cool her down. She was a tiny woman with bony features that bore a stern expression most of the time, but despite her general disdain for the larrikin youths her sons mingled with she had taken a shine to Dan, who always treated her daughters kindly and was polite to her. He was also easy on the eyes, though she was far too old for that kind of nonsense. Her eyes were blue as glaciers and could burn holes through you when she was in a foul mood, which was most of the time. Her hair, ginger in her youth, had aged to a dirty blonde colour. The meal finished; Kate cleared away Dan's plate.

"Thank you, Mrs. Byrne. That stew filled the hole splendidly."

"You're always welcome, Daniel," Margret replied. Her County Clare accent gave her words a sing-song quality. Dan looked at his watch again.

"You haven't heard from Joe or any of the others?"

"No, not a peep. Should we have?" Margret replied.

"We were supposed to meet here at noon. Joe's got money for you from Jerilderie."

Margret pursed her lips and fanned herself.

"We won't get into any trouble over that, I hope."

"No fear, Mrs. Byrne. The banknotes are unmarked so there's no way they can trace them. You can spend it where you like and nobody will be able to tell where they were knocked off from," Dan said brightly. Margret gave a gentle half-smile.

"That will be a relief. Not making much money from the milk at the moment but the debts keep gathering."

"Well, if Joe's not here, there's really only one other place he'd be right now," Dan replied. Kate and Margaret hummed knowingly in unison.

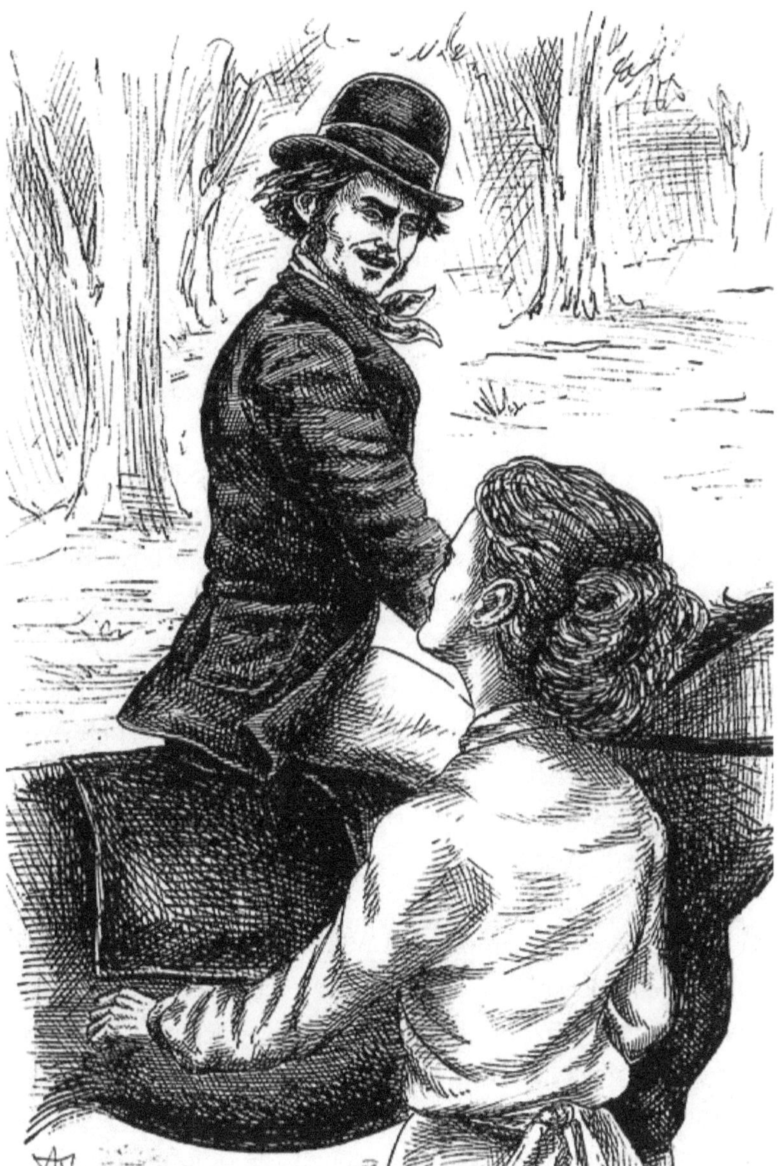

"That was quite an entrance, Dan Kelly!"

***

In Aaron Sherritt's dingy hut, he lay with Joe Byrne on the floor staring up at the ceiling. Between them a small lamp burned brightly, and they took it in turns to hold opium pipes over the heat. The vaporised tar wafted from the pipes in thin, oily strands. Joe inhaled deeply. Aaron flopped to the ground with a blissed-out expression.

"£290," Aaron mumbled.

"Yup, you can pay off this selection and get it fixed up a bit," Joe said.

"Fixed up?"

"Without me here to keep the place up, it's looking rougher than where I've been sleeping," Joe smirked.

"Well, I have been busy, haven't I? Unlike some bush telegraphs I actually keep an ear to the ground for you."

"I bet the traps were furious when they found the information you gave them was wrong," said Joe. Aaron sucked on his pipe while Joe hummed to himself. After a pause Joe leaned over to his mate, "Here, I was thinking; if it's so easy to fool the traps, do you reckon you'd be able to keep them distracted for us?"

"Well," said Aaron, "I suppose so. What did you have in mind?"

"You know the caves near Ma's place? I reckon if you kept them up there, we'd be free to come and go as we please seeing as they can't see the back of the place from up there. And the longer they stay still the easier it is to move around them."

Aaron considered the proposal through the opium haze, "It's worth a shot."

***

That evening Ned and Dan Kelly sat at the dining table in the Kelly selection relaxing. Ned smoked a pipe, puffing merrily as Maggie Skillion, Kate and Grace showed off their new outfits, bought with money pilfered from the Bank of New South Wales in Jerilderie.

Dan signalled for Kate to do a twirl, which she did excitedly. She was dressed in an elegant navy-blue riding habit with black frills, and a tall hat decorated with crepe and a fly veil. Grace smoothed out a yellow dress covered in lace, the first new dress she had ever owned, and she was overwhelmed by how crisp the fabric felt.

"Kids, come and show your big brothers your new rig outs," Maggie called to her half-siblings.

Maggie herself was decked out in a black silk dress with white lace frills and scarlet underskirt. Despite her more masculine behaviours, Maggie couldn't help but take pleasure in the odd, typically feminine interest; pretty dresses being a particular vice.

Nellie entered from the sleeping quarters, veritably bouncing with glee. Jack followed, waddling uncomfortably and fidgeting in his handsome new clothes and boots. Jim and Ellen Skillion also toddled along looking adorable in new outfits.

"These boots is too big, Maggie," said Jack.

"That's so you can grow into them. Shoes should last you a long time," Maggie replied.

Nellie padded across the room to Dan and tugged on his coat, "I feel like a princess. Do I look like a princess, Danny?"

Dan smiled, "Oh, you don't just look like a princess - you look like a queen!"

"No, I don't. Queens are old and fat!"

"She's got you there, Danny," Ned chuckled.

***

Later, with the younger children put to bed, the older siblings began to discuss important matters.

"Any word on an appeal for Ma?" asked Dan.

"We asked Mr. Zincke about it, and he said that he would feel bad taking our money because it was a lost cause," replied Maggie. Ned began to fume.

"Lost cause? *Lost cause?* That bastard!"

"He's right though, Ned. We tried to get a fair go and the jury sided with Fitzpatrick. Another appeal won't change anything. They'll always back a copper over one of us," said Maggie.

"It's not right!"

"Nobody said it was, Ned, but it's the hand we were dealt."

"Then we need to change that," Ned grumbled.

"It's all well and good to say, but how do you propose we do that?" interjected Dan.

"We need to do something that will make them sit up and take notice. To let them know we aren't to be trifled with."

Kate reached across and grasped her big brother's hand, "Ned, can't we just let the dust settle a little?"

"The moment we stop, they catch up to us. We have to keep upping the ante," said Ned.

"Where does that end?" asked Kate. Ned had no response.

***

The following Saturday night Superintendent Hare met with Aaron

Sherritt in Beechworth at the police station. Hare anticipated receiving some important new information from the young man who had showed promise as an informant.

Joining Hare was Detective Michael Edward Ward. He was an athletically built Irishman with a moustache waxed into neat curls, and tapering beard. Ward was in charge of the station at Beechworth and knew Aaron well from the larrikin's trouble-laden past. After a discussion about where the gang had been seen, Aaron leaned forward in his chair and gestured for the others to come near.

"Now, you had better come tomorrow night. I have good reason to believe they will be at Mrs. Byrne's house. You better come and watch the place."

Hare was sceptical but willing to follow along with the suggestion. Other information Aaron had given that night correlated with information already known to the police, so there was little doubt in Hare's mind that the belief that the Kellys would be visiting the Byrne selection must be well founded.

"Very well," said Hare, "We shall rendezvous in Eldorado, then you can guide us."

Aaron shook hands with the men. He smiled reassuringly; so far, the plan was going ahead without a hitch.

***

The following evening came, and with it Hare and Ward headed for Eldorado where they met Sherritt.

Hare had requested a party of police from the local station under Senior-Constable Strahan to meet them. When they arrived at the meeting place the police were nowhere to be seen. An hour passed but the police still did not appear. Sherritt became anxious. If he was spotted with the police on the road there would be trouble.

"Mr. Hare, if we do not go at once, you will lose the chance of getting the gang."

Hare turned to Ward, "Will you stick to me if we go by ourselves?"

"I will, Mr. Hare," replied Ward.

Hare turned back to Sherritt, "All right, lead the way."

The road to the Byrne selection saw the trio ride their horses through the scrub. The way was rocky and dotted with shabby trees. Suddenly Aaron drew to a halt and raised his hand for the officers to do the same.

"Mr. Hare, do you see anything?"

Hare strained his eyes in the gloom, "No, I do not see anything."

Aaron was almost surprised that Hare, who famously tracked the bushranger Harry Power down, was not well attuned to looking for signs in the bush.

"Do you not see a fire ahead there?" Aaron asked gesturing to a light in the distance, "Those are the bushrangers; they have made a fire tonight, and they're camping there. It is a thing I never knew them to do before; they must have some drink in them, otherwise they would not make the fire so foolishly."

Ward and Hare both focused on the firelight but remained sceptical. Only Aaron knew that the fire had no connection to the outlaws at all and he was merely stalling for time.

"How can you be so sure it is the outlaws?" Ward asked.

"This is the bushranger's country, and no one but them would be out in this country."

Hare dismounted and signalled for the others to do the same. They kept low as to avoid being spotted.

"Mr. Hare, what do you want me to do?" asked Aaron.

"I think the best plan is to make certain the outlaws are at the fire," replied Hare, "You crawl up to it, take your boots off, and get as close as you can, and ascertain if you can hear voices or anything else."

Aaron nodded and shed his well-worn boots, which he tucked under his arm as he ventured into the bush. Hare and Ward tied the horses up and ten minutes later Aaron returned, sauntering without a care in the world, his feet still bare.

"What is the matter, Aaron?" Hare asked.

"Mr. Hare, how far do you think the fire is from us?"

"About 150 yards, I thought."

Aaron chuckled and said, "It is nothing of the kind, it's three miles away."

"Nonsense, Aaron, you have sold me; you have gone and warned those fellows to be off," Hare snapped indignantly.

"No, come, get on your horses and we'll ride up to it."

Aaron guided the two police through the rough terrain, kicking up clouds of dust as they went until they reached a precipice overlooking a gully and dismounted for a closer look. Aaron extended his arm and pointed to the fire on the hill above them. He said nothing as he waited for a reply. Hare looked deflated.

"You are right. What's to be done?"

"Hurry along, quick as you can, and come on towards Byrne's house," said Aaron.

With renewed resolve, the trio galloped until they were half a mile from the Byrne selection. They hitched their horses and proceeded on foot. Standing on the edge of the clearing around the selection, they monitored the house briefly before Aaron gestured for the police to stay put. He stayed low to the ground and darted to the homestead, where a light was visible in the window.

From their spot, concealed in the bush, Ward and Hare watched Aaron who appeared to be listening for any voices from inside the building. After a few minutes he returned.

"That is where they tie up their horses when they come here," Aaron said, pointing to a spot on the opposite side of the house, "After they have their meals they lay down beside their horses at that spot."

"Ah, yes, I have seen that spot pointed out to me before," said Hare, "Let us go and see what's there."

They moved stealthily along the outskirts of the property to the spot but saw nothing save a few rough looking trees that had been chewed on by horses. Aaron sought to allay the doubts of the two officers.

"Now, Mr. Hare, if the outlaws come at all, they must come this way, through the stockyard, and towards the scrub I have shown you. We will wait here now till the morning for them."

All through the night the trio sat in the bush waiting and watching but no arrivals ever came. Ward was livid, but Hare still believed Aaron was earnest in his desire to help; after all he had stayed by their side in the cold all night, rather than ditch them for a warm bed and a belly laugh at their expense.

Aaron extended his arm and pointed to the fire on the hill above them.
He said nothing as he waited for a reply.

Aaron extended his arm and pointed to the fire on the hill above them. He said nothing as he waited for a reply.

When they parted ways, Hare agreed to assemble a watch party to keep an eye on the homestead. Ward remained suspicious of Sherritt, unwilling to believe for a moment that he would turn on his friends. For Aaron's part, he was not even sure if the gang had taken the opportunity to visit the Byrne selection while the police were distracted, but so long as Hare believed him, he was satisfied.

***

Paper lanterns punctuated the darkness outside of the shops and tents in the bustling, grimy Chinese quarter of the mining town of Sebastopol. Joe Byrne and Dan Kelly rode quietly down the main strip where strange sickly, oily smells wafted from shops and eateries. The muffled sound of men revelling in Cantonese could be heard from a shop where Joe would frequent for a spot of gambling and mijiu in easier circumstances.

They kept their hat brims low over their faces as if a pair of white men simply being there among the Chinese was not already suspicious.

They arrived at a small wood-panelled store; a large banner out the front stated in Cantonese that this was the business of the merchant Ye Fang. Unlike the whites in Beechworth, the Chinese had no qualms in keeping their businesses open late; money is money no matter what time of day it is.

Joe entered the store, ducking low to compensate for the smaller doorframe. As the outlaws stepped down into the store, Ye Fang, a wizened man dressed in silk and smoking from a long, thin pipe, bowed to his customers. Joe returned the gesture. He approached the counter and greeted the merchant in Cantonese.

Dan understood none of it and kept his distance, occupying himself with examining jars of strange smelling powders, labelled with symbols he could not comprehend. In a corner he saw a collection of skyrockets. He had seen fireworks when he was lucky enough to have been in Beechworth for the Chinese New Year, but that was a rare occurrence even before he was outlawed.

At the counter, Joe looked around himself before running his index finger along the brim of his hat. Ye Fang understood the signal and withdrew a small paper parcel from under the counter. Opening it, he revealed a lump of opium tar. Joe grinned and passed the merchant a few bank notes and tucked the parcel into a saddlebag he had slung over his shoulder.

***

Sometime later in a quiet, secluded spot on the banks of Reedy Creek, Joe and Dan lounged, smoking the opium from small metal pipes. Dan flopped on the ground and looked up at the stars. Joe did the same.

"What do you reckon, Danny?" asked Joe.

"I feel like a feather. All the stars look very pretty," replied Dan, sounding sleepy. His eyelids drooped heavily but he maintained a placid expression. He reclined and let the effects from the drug wash over him.

"Ned doesn't know what he's missing," Joe sighed.

Dan lay silent for a moment in contemplation, before turning to Joe.

"Do you reckon the traps will ever catch us?"

"They couldn't catch a cold."

"Okay," said Dan before he passed out as the opium hit him full force. Joe chuckled. There were few comforts left for the gang, but at least for now there was still enough money for Joe to get his fix and forget his troubles for a while.

****

In the waning afternoon light, Aaron reclined in his bed. His broad, smooth chest was dewy with sweat. He tucked his arms behind his head and gazed, unfocused, at the moth-eaten canvas ceiling of his hut where light twinkled through the holes. Kate Byrne snuggled into him; her soft skin felt warm against his. Her cheeks were flushed and her hair wild. She gazed up at Aaron's face.

"I've missed you Aaron," she said softly. Kate had become almost a recluse, rarely leaving the family farm except to go to her job as a maid. Everywhere she went, she felt there were eyes on her, judging and waiting for her to slip up and reveal her brother's location. This secret rendezvous with Aaron allowed her to relax for the first time in weeks.

Aaron said nothing. He merely lay thinking to himself. Kate looked at her lover's squalid den, devoid of creature comforts like decoration and furniture save for a rickety card table with tree stumps for seats.

"Do you know when Joe is likely to pay a visit to your Ma's place again?"

"I don't know. You know how things are with him and Ma. I think he worries she'll turn him in for the £2000 herself," Kate sighed. She traced Aaron's nipple with her index finger.

He stood up and walked to the door of the hut. He opened it and allowed the dimming light to bounce off his nakedness, a soft breeze tickled his skin as he stared out at his selection. The block was scrubby and blackberry bushes choked a fence near a pair of disinterested goats.

"I wish I could just whisk you away from her and keep you here with me," Aaron said.

"And how would you support us? You can't just live on handouts from bank robberies."

"I do alright. I make enough to get by and then I can make a bit more on the side playing cards or duffing."

"A plan with your usual amount of forethought, of course. And what exactly is it you do these days to make all of your money, Aaron?" Kate asked pointedly.

Aaron's voice took on a hard edge, "What's that supposed to mean?"

Kate sat up and glared at Aaron.

"You're making money off the police, aren't you? Don't get uppity with me!"

"Is that what your ma has been saying about me? You think I'm selling Joe out?"

"Are you?" Kate snapped back.

"He's like my brother. I'd have to be a certain kind of dingo to sell him out, wouldn't I?"

"It wouldn't be the first time," Kate huffed as she sat up and folded her arms in front of her naked breasts. Aaron turned to Kate with a vexed look on his face.

"I'm not selling Joe out. I'm trying to save the fool from the gallows, but I don't know if I can keep the traps fooled. I'm trying to get them to trust me so that the boys can move without the risk of getting caught. I even have an arrangement with the Chief Commissioner himself to keep

Joe's head out of the noose! You have to believe me; I'm trying to do the right thing."

Kate got up and crossed the floor to Aaron. She held herself against him and rested her head on his shoulder.

"I hope you're telling the truth, Aaron, because if you ever lied to me," Kate said as she placed her hand on Aaron's privates, "I'll cut this off and nail it to the wall."

"You think I'd be stupid enough to lie to a Byrne?"

"You're not as clever as you think you are, Aaron."

"Oh, hush. Get your gear on so I can get you back home before your ma starts looking for you."

***

Cape Bedford, Queensland, was idyllic. A glorious sun-drenched conglomeration of soft, golden-brown sand; majestic mountains; vibrant, verdant trees; and turquoise water. The gentle rush of the waves lapping at the shoreline was suddenly mingled with screaming and the blast of rifles.

Emerging from the bush, scores of Indigenous people - men, women and children - burst forth in panic. Hot on their heels was a party of native police dressed in blue and red uniforms, firing with chilling accuracy at all and sundry. Women shrieked and wailed as their husbands were exterminated beside them. Children ran as fast as their feet would take them, confused and overwhelmed with abject terror, before being snuffed out. The beach was soaked in blood as the native police fanned out, chasing the survivors into the water.

Emerging coolly behind them was a thin man in hunting tweeds and a white helmet with a cloth puggaree. Little of his face was visible in the visor's shade beyond a straight nose and handlebar moustache. This was Sub-Inspector Stanhope O'Connor of the Queensland police. As he walked onto the beach, he observed his native troopers, "boys" as he called them, watching survivors swimming out to sea. He whistled at Corporal Sambo to come to him.

"Why aren't they firing?" O'Connor asked.

"No point wasting bullets, boss. They swim till they drown," Sambo replied. O'Connor nodded.

"How many do you make it, boy?"

Sambo looked around the beach at the carnage. He tried to hide his revulsion.

"Could be 'round thirty, boss. What do we do with all the dead blackfullas?"

"No need to concern ourselves with that now," said O'Connor, "Just keep an eye on the others."

Sambo joined his colleagues as O'Connor sat on a rock next to a dead Aboriginal woman. Her ebony skin glistened with sweat and blood. Near to her lay her dead infant. O'Connor filled the bowl of his pipe with tobacco and struck a Lucifer match on the rock. As he lit his pipe he looked out to sea and felt the warmth of the sun on him.

When O'Connor returned to his office, he found an envelope for him. Inside was a missive informing him that he and his native police were to head to Victoria to assist the police effort to capture the Kelly Gang. Naturally, the potential for glory was irresistible. Especially with £8000 at stake. Within hours O'Connor and his native police Sambo, Hero, Barney, Jacky, Jimmy, Johnny and Moses were packing and preparing for

"No point wasting bullets, boss. They swim till they drown."

their trip south. By the time the press would catch wind of their actions in Cape Bedford they would be well away from the firing line.

***

On a mild afternoon the gang descended from the ranges to attend to their hygiene. The four converged upon a spot along the Ovens River and disrobed, wading into the water with bricks of soap that Maggie Skillion had provided them in one of her various care packages. The outlaws scrubbed the filth from their skin and watched it float away on the current.

They became aware of the sound of hooves. Ned emerged from the water and grabbed a rifle. He peered through the trees and saw the source of the sound. Riding towards him was Ettie Hart, dressed in a pale blue dress and straw hat.

She pulled up little more than arm's length away from Ned and dismounted. Ned's grip on his rifle relaxed.

"What are you up to?" Ettie asked with a giggle, noting Ned's nakedness. She kissed Ned tenderly but tried not to get her dress wet.

"I wasn't expecting you yet," said Ned. As he headed back to the camp, his wet skin glistened in the afternoon light.

"I thought I'd give you a little surprise, but it looks like I was the one who got the surprise," Ettie replied, leading her horse along as she followed Ned to the camp by the creek, noting the way his wet back and buttocks, muscular and taut, twitched and gleamed in the afternoon light.

Ned rested the rifle against a tree and looked for a cloth with which to dry himself.

"Did you find out what it was?" asked Joe.

As if on cue, Ettie appeared from the bush.

"Don't mind me," said Ettie as she hitched the horse to a tree.

She couldn't help but take a look at the men as they clambered out of the river with their anatomy on show for all the world. Though they were young men in their prime, the strain of being fugitives had taken its toll on them. Once firm, well-defined muscles rounded their shoulders and broadened their chests, but they now appeared thinner and more wasted like underfed horses, all skin and bones. Even still, they were impressive specimens and Ettie found her gaze wandering over the sinewy limbs and dangling manhood that bounced around amusingly as the outlaws stepped up onto land and dripped dry.

While Dan and Steve were quick to get dressed, Joe decided to roll his swag out and let Mother Nature dry him off before making himself decent, just the way he used to when he and Aaron would cool off at the falls in the Woolshed.

"Put that thing away, Joe," Ned grumbled.

Joe arched his eyebrow and deliberately rolled over onto his side to give Ettie an even better view, waving his hand over his crotch to draw attention to his pendulous parts. Ettie giggled as Ned threw a block of soap at Joe, who ignored it and continued to soak up the sun, flopping his genitals into a more comfortable position as he rolled onto his back.

Ned handed Ettie a pannikin of tea, fresh from the boiled billy over their campfire. She held the cup in both of her tiny, slender hands and let the steam waft into her face.

"Have you got any information on the banks?" Ned asked.

"I have, but you won't like it," said Ettie.

"Out with it, girl," said Ned impatiently.

"You know as well as I do that there's soldiers from the garrison artillery guarding the banks in all the towns worth looking at. The only thing that's changed since Jerilderie is that there seems to be more of them. If you try to rob another bank, they'll gun you down."

Ned leaned back against a tree and thought to himself. They were getting desperate for money after giving out so much of their booty from Jerilderie to the sympathisers, but they needed a source to target. Robbing a guarded bank was off the cards – the sympathisers may have considered Ned invulnerable, but he was not bulletproof. Surely there was another way.

***

Riding down from Albury by train, Stanhope O'Connor was dressed in his officer's uniform and reading a newspaper. In a neighbouring booth rode Captain Standish who was expected to be in Benalla to personally oversee the Kelly pursuit in his capacity as chief commissioner of police.

Around O'Connor were his native police, men from Fraser Island that had left their jobs to enlist in the police force, and each one more formidable a tracker than any in Victoria or New South Wales. They had only ever known tropical climates and were rugged up against the cooler temperatures with heavy coats over their uniforms.

"Getting cold, Boss," said Moses, who was short and portly.

"I know," O'Connor replied.

"Jacky getting plenty sick too," Moses continued.

O'Connor looked across to the trooper, "Seems alright to me. You alright, boy?"

Jacky was shivering uncontrollably but was full of pluck as ever, "Gonna catch them Kellys, Boss," he said weakly.

The native police disembarked at Wodonga where they had lodgings and O'Connor continued on to Benalla with Standish. The trip was uneventful, which gave O'Connor an opportunity to catch up on the situation with the Kellys. Hunting whites in the bush was a far cry from the sanctioned slaughter of Aboriginals on the golden shores of Cape Bedford and would require some strategy in order to use the trackers to the best of their abilities in unfamiliar terrain.

***

In the Woolshed Valley, a police party sat nestled among rocks by a cave on the edge of the Byrne selection. The cave allowed space enough for a sole occupant at any given time, any others forced to lay swags out in the open. The camp was littered with empty tins from bully beef and sardines, with the odd bottle thrown into the mix.

As the men sat shivering under possum-skin blankets they eyed their special agent approaching from downhill. Aaron Sherritt's dark brown hair was slicked back under a felt hat worn on a jaunty angle. He wore a white shirt, corduroy vest and white moleskins, which made him stick out in the moonlight. He curled his shirt sleeves up over his elbows and prepared a corncob pipe.

Over the past few weeks with the watch party, Aaron had found himself in the difficult position of genuinely liking Superintendent Hare - or the "kaffir" as many of the lower ranked police mockingly referred to him behind his back. In kind, Hare's admiration of Sherritt had been quick to form and Aaron had no qualms in accepting gifts of clothing and other useful items on top of his pay for his role in the hunt, though the thought of betraying someone he was beginning to consider a friend made him feel guiltier than he had anticipated. Worried that Aaron's uncommon name might betray him, Hare had begun referring to him as "Tommy". Aaron in return had begun to refer to the superintendent as "Frank".

"Tommy," Hare began, "I can't comprehend how you endure this blasted cold in shirtsleeves!"

"Oh, it's no concern, I don't care about coats," said Aaron, surreptitiously running his hand over the hip flask concealed in his trousers.

"Can the outlaws endure as you are doing?" asked Hare.

"I can beat all the others. I am a better man than Joe Byrne, and I am a better man than Dan Kelly, and I am a better man than Steve Hart. I can lick those two youngsters to fits; I have always beaten Joe, but I look upon Ned Kelly as an extraordinary man. There is no man in the world like him, he is superhuman."

Ward, who had accompanied the party on this occasion, gave Sherritt a greasy stare. Aaron's bragging grated on him, whether it be about the bushrangers or his own lawless activities. Aaron took no notice of Ward and continued lighting his pipe, striking a match and sucking the flame into the pipe bowl, toasting the tobacco until it glowed orange in the cold darkness.

"You have your work cut out for you trying to catch him. You'd have better luck putting darbies on the wind. He can read the land like a book," Aaron said, puffing tobacco smoke.

"We shall see, Tommy," Hare replied with a soft smile.

***

The next morning, the sun rose into a clear sky. Margret Byrne walked into the courtyard and rested her hands on her hips as she paced along the perimeter of the selection. She referred to these laps of her property as her "exercises" and believed very strongly in the health benefits of perambulation and lungfuls of clean air, but more importantly she used them as a way of checking for signs of police having been on her property. She checked the waterhole for signs of footprints then began walking out beyond the farm into the bush where she would allow the cows to go and graze before calling them in for the evening.

As she walked, she noticed something gleaming just beyond a ridge in the grass. As she got closer, she saw the sun was reflecting off a sardine tin. She furrowed her brow and walked closer still. Sensing that there was a chance that something dangerous lay in wait, she got down low, crawling a short distance to peek over a boulder.

In doing so, she spotted several men curled up, asleep, under possum skin blankets. These men were strangers to her, but as she scanned the scene her eyes fixed on a figure in white shirt and moleskins. She scowled when she recognised it as Aaron Sherritt, dozing with his hat over his face. Margret climbed down and spun on her heels back to the homestead.

The movement roused Superintendent Hare who immediately recognised that their cover had been blown. He quickly woke Aaron.

"Tommy, wake up!"

"What is it?" Sherritt said groggily.

"Mother Byrne was just here; she may have spotted you. Take my coat and helmet as a disguise and head into town. Get an alibi," Hare insisted. Aaron sat, shaken. The colour had drained from his face.

"No, no, the damage is done. I'm a dead man now, for sure."

***

It had been barely a matter of weeks when O'Connor's party was struck by misfortune. After an unsuccessful trek into the bush after the outlaws they had been forced to turn back due to insufficient supplies. Jacky's cold had begun to settle, but suddenly Corporal Sambo had taken ill with a fever. His breathing had become laboured, and he began hallucinating so was sent back to their lodgings in Wodonga. O'Connor soon received word that Sambo had died. The news hit him hard, and he dropped everything to join his "boys" who were all in an advanced state of mourning.

It would soon emerge that pneumonia was what had claimed the life of O'Connor's most trusted trooper, and after some heated debate between Captain Standish and Assistant Commissioner Nicolson, Corporal Sambo was buried in a pauper's grave in Benalla. This tragedy seemed to rally the men to throw themselves at the pursuit even harder to ensure that Sambo's life had not been lost in vain.

***

Despite the strife that the Queensland native police were enduring, the rumours continued to filter to the gang that these men were extremely dangerous. One of the gang's most notorious sympathisers, a man named Wild Wright, was one of the most vocal when it came to imparting rumours.

Wright was a huge lump of a man covered in scars, and he had a reputation as a pugilist and a troublemaker. It had taken a thorough belting from Ned Kelly to get him to align himself with the rebellious young man. Ned had served a torturous sentence in gaol over a horse that Wright had "borrowed" and was desperate to settle the score once he got out. From that day on, Ned was seen by many of his associates as indomitable

Despite his toughness, the rumours about the trackers being cannibals and able to track through even the toughest of terrains had shaken Ned. He had begun to have nightmares about the trackers sneaking up on him in his sleep and ripping him apart to feast on his flesh. He never spoke to anyone else about his fears, but the rest of the gang had noticed a considerable change in Ned's demeanour.

The droning wheeze of a concertina reverberated around a rocky outcrop in the Strathbogie Ranges. It soon took shape as the tune *The Wearing of the Green*. Though the jaunty tune was one of Irish persuasion, Joe Byrne sang it with words of his own creation to give it a more local flavour.

Oh, sure Paddy dear and did ye hear the news that's goin' 'round –
on the head of bold Ned Kelly, sure, they've place two thousand pounds;
and for Joe Byrne, Steve Hart and Dan two thousand each they'll give,
but if the price was doubled then the Kelly Gang would live!

Ned approached the camp dressed in the clothes stolen from Gloster's wagon. The handsome outfit no longer had the fresh, clean look it had when the gang returned from robbing the Euroa bank. Having been lived in for so long among the mountains, they looked much scruffier and worn down. Scanlan's Spencer repeating rifle was slung over his shoulder and several revolvers were tucked into his belt. Joe continued to sing.

Twas in December '78 when the Kelly Gang came down,
just after shootin' Kennedy, to sweet Euroa town.

To rob the bank of all its gold was their idea that day.
Blood horses they were mounted on to make their get-away.

"Cut it out, Joe. You'll give us away," Ned grumbled.

Joe disregarded him, "Oi, Ned, remember this one?"

Joe began to play *The Eumerella Shore*, a song about stock thieving, which was something Joe and Ned both had extensive experience with. Ned ignored him and moved to Dan and Steve who slept under grey woollen blankets.

He unslung the Spencer and jabbed Dan with it to wake him. Dan sat up, groggy. His normally clean-shaven jaw was covered in thick stubble, his moustache was long and droopy. Ned handed him the weapon.

"Your watch."

Dan stood and straightened himself out while Ned walked to a precipice and looked out over the vista. It was beautiful in the dying light.

Ned was tired in every fibre of his being. They were forced to hide in more and more difficult to reach locations and primarily travelled on foot so as not to leave horse tracks to be found. This was what being an outlaw meant - forced to live like wild animals, ever hiding from a poacher's bullets.

Since returning from New South Wales, Ned had been afflicted by Sandy Blight resulting in painful eyes and poor vision. The irritation had made Ned want to rip out his eyelashes – anything for relief from the scratchy, unstoppable discomfort. On top of this he had developed sciatica, a painful condition in his lower back that made it difficult for him to ride, or indeed do anything that didn't require him to be prone. He slumped down onto his swag and rolled himself up in it. He quickly fell into a deep sleep; his body was too exhausted to resist.

***

The Benalla police station was the hub for police activities pertaining to the hunt for the Kellys, as it was the seat from which all decisions related to police in the district were made. The man in charge was Superintendent John Sadleir, a man of middle age who had been involved with the police force almost as long as it had existed. He was a tall, severe man prone to appear sullen or morose. His previous posting had been at Mansfield prior to the murders in the Wombat Ranges. In fact, it was him that had sent Kennedy's party out as one of his last acts at the station before taking up his new position.

The hunt for the Kelly Gang, directed by Standish and Superintendent Hare, had put severe strain on the police force and Sadleir felt powerless to do anything about it, as most decisions on such matters were made by people above him in rank. Sadleir, Sub-Inspector O'Connor and Detective Ward, were subordinates, though each one of them felt they were more capable, and better suited, to leading the pursuit themselves.

Despite his belief that the hunt was being handled incompetently by both Standish and Superintendent Hare, Sadleir had decided to hold his tongue rather than invoke the ire of the chief commissioner. He considered Standish to be no more than a vain, effeminate, gambler with friends in high places keeping him insulated from due scrutiny. He believed Standish to be completely out of touch with the reality of police work and prone to bad decisions because he was more interested in horse races than law and order.

Standish, meanwhile, was under pressure to be seen to be taking the Kelly issue seriously, which involved being in the district where the pursuit was occurring as much as possible. Much to his chagrin Standish had to return to Benalla by train on a frequent basis, though it frequently impacted on his other duties; many of which were left to Superintendent Nicolson in his absence.

On one such occasion, Hare waited at the train station to escort Standish back to the office. As plumes of steam curled back over the platform from the new arrival, Standish swung open the wooden door of the carriage and descended to the platform dressed in a grey Homburg hat, shiny bluchers and a tawny fur coat. The outfit combined with his silver beard made him look like some kind of gentrified marsupial.

He planted the brass tip of his cane on the platform declaratively and tilted his head back to look up at the approaching Hare, who was nearly a foot taller.

"My dear fellow, I am so terribly overjoyed to see you," Standish declared with the drawling, over-pronounced Englishness that so many of the college-educated possessed.

"How was the trip, Captain?" Hare replied as Standish opened his arms to embrace him.

"Oh, dreadful, my dear. I certainly hope there's something decent to drink."

"I can't guarantee we have anything comparable to what you're used to at the Melbourne Club, but I will do my best."

* * *

At the same time as Hare was gallivanting around the country with his men, O'Connor and his native police were following other leads accompanied by Sadleir and a number of Victorian constables, despite O'Connor's dispute with Standish over the matter, bringing the party to sixteen in total.

Hare had two trackers with his party: Moses of O'Connor's men, and Spider, a tracker from the Aboriginal reserve at Coranderrk. The South African had expressed misgivings about having a large number of Aboriginal trackers in the party, stating that his experience with the Africans in Cape Town proved the effectiveness of using them sparingly. It seemed that Standish presented no opposition to this.

O'Connor's party had elected to follow up leads along the Broken River, eventually reaching a station where the gang had left horses from their Jerilderie excursion. As O'Connor monitored his native police, a messenger arrived and handed a letter to Sadlier. The letter was from Standish, asking the party to return unless they had a good lead.

"Mr. O'Connor," said Sadleir, "what do you think? Is it worth following this one up?"

"The boys seem to think so," said O'Connor.

"Alright, let's keep at it then."

Sadleir hastily wrote a letter back to Standish stating that the lead on the horses was looking promising and they would not yet be returning and sent it off with the messenger.

The going had been slow with so many riders and packhorses in tow. They set up a camp and spent the night under the stars, ready to push ahead with the investigation at first light.

As the party packed up the following morning the rumble of hooves was heard approaching and the messenger was spotted riding to them at top speed. He pulled up, his horse panting and foaming, and addressed the heads of the party. He handed Sadleir a letter and quickly returned from whence he came. It seemed Standish had given instructions not to receive any follow up messages. Sadleir read the letter and conveyed the message to O'Connor.

"It's Standish. He wants us to drop the lead and return to Benalla."

"I really don't understand how your police force functions under that man," replied O'Connor with venom.

"Nor do I, yet somehow we manage," Sadleir replied.

***

Though O'Connor and Sadleir had elected to go through the lowlands, Hare was determined to seek the outlaws in the high country, taking his party up into the mountains. Hare directed that the party ride in formation, spaced well apart so that in the event of an ambush not everyone would be taken down. Though most days were unsuccessful, some days they would pick up a strong lead and follow it.

On one such day, Hare had felt like he was being watched. Hare, uneasy, unbuttoned the flap on his holster. He slowly withdrew his service revolver. His fingers tensed around the grip and diffused sunlight reflected off the blue-steel shaft of the muzzle. His heartbeat began to intensify.

Unseen by him, on an incline above, Ned Kelly watched the party from the cover of a cluster of trees. He had spent the morning scouting through the bush and had found the tracks from the party, so followed them. He was pale and his eyes were ringed with purple. His lower back and hips burned with pain, but he distracted himself from the agony by clenching his fist until his nails dug into his palm. He knew even the slightest noise could give him away.

Ahead of the party, Moses and Spider spread out and examined the terrain. Suddenly Spider paused and scrutinized a slight indentation in the dirt. He was slightly built but sturdy. His dark, intelligent eyes peered out from the shade of his hat. His moustache twitched.

"Hey, boss," Spider said, "he gone up this way. Ned Kelly fulla on foot."
"Good boy. Lead on," Hare called back.

Moses and Spider began moving up a slope through the trees. They followed signs only they could read. Ned had done a respectable job of covering his tracks, but it was his cleverness that gave him away. The trackers smirked every now and then as they noted a branch torn off a tree to cover a footprint or a scrape in the dirt that indicated a slipped foot. The police hung back, struggling to manoeuvre their horses through the dense bush. The trackers halted at a ridge.

"You gonna climb?" Moses asked Spider.
"They don't pay me to climb," Spider replied.

The pair returned to Hare, who waited impatiently for them.
"Hey, boss, Ned Kelly gone up the rock. Horses can't get up. What we gonna do?" said Moses.
"Is there a way around?"
"Nup. Gone up here cos he knew you was on horses, I reckon. Clever for a whitefulla," Moses answered.
"Indeed," Hare grumbled.

As the police and trackers turned around to regroup, a wind kicked up.
Close by, Ned Kelly frowned to himself and headed back to where he had hobbled Mirth, who chewed on a sapling. Struggling with the pain from his back he stumbled and was forced to propel himself through

the bush by pushing himself off the trees. With considerable effort he removed the hobbles and mounted. He sat in the saddle and panted like a marathon runner.

He rode through the ranges until he came to a cave where a small camp was set up; one of many dotted around the area he could stop at any time. He dismounted and allowed Mirth to graze freely nearby. He entered the cave and made his way to where he had a swag set up, his hands clutching at his lower back, his face contorted in a grimace. He sank to the ground painfully.

"Ugh! I understand why Power was such a grumpy bastard all the time," he said to nobody in particular. As he lay on the swag, Ned's head was filled with all sorts of curses and oaths. He felt like he was losing his grip on his mind from the pressure of the search parties coming so close to him. He yearned for even just one night where he could live like a normal young man paying court to his sweetheart without a care. Tears welled in his eyes as he accepted the fact that he had now forfeited his humanity in the eyes of the law.

***

There was good news for the sympathisers emerging from the courts. After all of Standish's attempts to pervert the provisions of the Felons Apprehension Act to keep anyone suspected of providing shelter or sustenance to the outlaws under lock and key, the magistrate was finally fed up to the back teeth and was setting the men free. Months in custody with not a single solid charge against any of them had caused a lot of bad blood to brew.

The only thing the circus had succeeded in doing was to fortify the sympathisers against the authorities. Any time that a self-proclaimed Kelly sympathiser crossed paths with a policeman they didn't like or were taken to task over some minor misdemeanour they would look the officer in the eye and say boldly, "I will tell Ned about you."

Despite such sentiments, many of these people had no intention of ever encountering the outlaws except if there was cash from a bank robbery to be had. Of those who were actively harbouring the gang, most only ever really provided a paddock for their knocked-up horses, if anything.

It was the inner circle that were doing the hard yards. Maggie Skillion in particular was constantly under surveillance by police, who knew that somehow, she was getting supplies to the gang but could not figure out how.

Maggie had a mischievous streak and decided to amuse herself one day by tricking the police into revealing themselves.

She collected her undergarments up in a sheet of cotton and carried the bundle conspicuously on the front of her saddle as she rode out of the selection.

Sure enough, she was promptly followed by two men in plain clothes who pursued her up into the hills. Scrambling over the boulders and dodging tiger snakes, the undercover troopers found Maggie seated and waiting patiently for their arrival. Upon spotting the men she thumbed her nose at them.

They tore the bundle away from her and opened it up only to be greeted by drawers and slips.

Meanwhile, Tom Lloyd and Ettie Hart continued to get supplies and information to the gang at great personal risk. The outlaws never remained in one place for long and were constantly on the move, usually in pairs or split four ways to avoid the whole gang being caught.

Joe in particular was frequently spotted around the Woolshed, sometimes visiting his family or just galloping from point A to point B on his grey mare. In fact, so well-known was it that the gang rode three bays and a grey, that some of the cousins of the Kellys had begun riding in the same formation to confuse police.

Moreover, the gang had taken to wearing more inconspicuous outfits so that they would not arouse suspicion when travelling during the day. This wasn't always a success.

Indeed, on one occasion Steve, Ned and Dan had been spotted by a travelling photographer, of all people. The enterprising gentleman recognised Ned and Dan from photographs he had seen.

He boldly asked the gang to halt for a photograph, which they did with no small amount of amusement. The gang left the impromptu photo shoot telling the photographer to make as many copies as he liked to show that a photographer could capture three of the Kelly gang when the police couldn't even catch one of them.

While this had been transpiring Joe was otherwise engaged in Eldorado, paying a visit to Aaron and his sister Anne. He later regretted that he had not been there to join the fun.

***

Ettie was sleeping peacefully when she was rudely awoken by the sound of rapping on her window. Groggily, she got out of bed and looked through the window to see Ned waiting for her outside. With a grin she ran outside as swiftly as she could. Ettie rushed up to Ned, barefoot and in her shift. She hugged him tightly and they kissed.

"Come on," said Ned.

"Come on?"

"Yeah, come with me," Ned replied. He mounted his mare Mirth, who was happily munching on the grass behind the homestead.

"I don't know if you've noticed," Ettie said, "but I'm not exactly dressed to be riding."

"Stop griping and get up here."

Ettie pouted, "If you were anyone else, I'd be giving you the biggest slap right now."

"Ain't you glad I ain't anyone else though?" Ned grinned.

Ned plunged into the bush with Ettie seated astride the horse behind him, her arms wrapped around his girth. She could not see him wince from the movement of the horse. They emerged at a clearing where the moonlight bathed the ground in a dreamy, milky glow. Ned dismounted and gestured for Ettie to hop down. As she swivelled, her shift rode up, showing off her legs. Ettie straightened herself up, embarrassed. Ned smirked. He lifted her off Mirth with a groan and hobbled the horse as Ettie examined the surrounds.

"Why have you brought me here?"

"Do I need a reason?"

Ettie folded her arms petulantly, "It's the middle of the night, we're in the bush and I'm undressed. Yes, you need a bloody reason!"

Ned laughed, "You kiss your mother with that mouth?"

"Sometimes," said Ettie, "But I would rather be kissing you with it."

Ned took his cue and kissed Ettie passionately. While embracing her, Ned slid a hand down Ettie's back and smacked her buttocks playfully. She jumped, shocked.

"Excuse me!"

"I have something for you," Ned said.

He removed a bunched-up handkerchief from his jacket and opened it. Inside was a delicate silver ring. He took Ettie's left hand and slid the ring delicately onto her finger.

"It's beautiful," said Ettie, admiring the ring.

"I'm sure it was some wealthy squatter's wife's, but it suits you better. Wait here."

Ned went back to Mirth and searched through a saddlebag. He withdrew a bar of chocolate and gave it to Ettie.

"Chocolate!" Ettie squealed in delight.

"I thought I should spoil you for putting up with me," Ned replied.

"Or you want me to do something for you," Ettie said, suspicious.

"What do you take me for?"

"I know you a damn sight better than you think I do, Edward Kelly."

"I swear I have no ulterior motive," said Ned, raising his hands as if in submission.

Ettie hummed, unconvinced. She took a bite of the sweet treat.

"I don't even want to know how you got this stuff," she said as the sweet flavour of the confection coated her mouth. "By the way, you do realise that this shift is not exactly warm, don't you?"

"I suppose I'd better warm you up," Ned said as he took off his coat and went in for another kiss, clutching the chocolate away.

A possum clung to a nearby gum tree and watched the pair in the chill of night, their hands wandering over each other. Ned planted his lips on Ettie's and kissed the flavour of chocolate from them. As much as he ached to have her, he knew that he should not. He pulled away.

"What's wrong?" Ettie asked.

Ned plunged into the bush with Ettie seated astride the horse behind
him, her arms wrapped around his girth.

"I don't want to get carried away."

"We're alone in the middle of the bush. What's the worst that could happen?"

Ned averted his gaze, but Ettie pulled his eyes back to hers. She placed her hand on his chest and could feel his heart rampaging within.

She spoke softly, "What do you want?"

"I want you, but I can't have you. It's too dangerous."

"Then why did you do all this?" Ettie asked, brandishing her ring.

"Because I'm afraid I will never get another chance. The traps and their blacks are nipping at my heels and I'm only getting slower. It terrifies me, more than anything else."

Ettie ran her hand over Ned's cheek gently. Her brow furrowed as she scrutinised his face. She felt how chapped and dry his skin was from the abrasive winds up in the mountains. She traced his lips with her finger, they at least were still soft. His eyes seemed watery. Her skin prickled, she felt flushed. She moved her hand around under his coat, feeling the rippling of muscles underneath the fabric.

"Ned..."

Ettie took a step back and slid her shift over her shoulders and it tumbled to the ground in a neat bunch at her naked feet. Ned tried to look away from her and shifted uncomfortably. Ettie reached out and grabbed Ned's hand.

"Your hands are hard," said Ettie, "be gentle."

She put his hand against her breast, and he moved it around, feeling her nipple poking into his palm as he pressed his fingers into the yielding flesh. He slid his hands over her delicate curves, her soft belly, and tickled his fingertips with the hair between her legs, such sensations a man of his ilk should be denied. His breathing became more laboured as he was overcome with a passion that heated his blood. Ettie closed her eyes and focused on the sensation of his hands exploring her, the tickle of his breath on her neck and the scent of the lavender perfume he wore to cover the smell of smoke and horses. He suddenly paused and Ettie could feel him trembling and opened her eyes. Looking up into Ned's face she saw tears in his eyes.

"What on earth is wrong?" Ettie asked, clasping his face with both hands.

"I can't do this," Ned said, "I shouldn't. We're not married. It's not the right thing to do."

"What does marriage matter? You have my heart and I have yours. Isn't that enough?"

Ned shut his eyes. He felt confused and overwhelmed. He was torn between what he desperately wanted and what he thought was the right thing to do. He had killed men, but he was terrified at the prospect of spoiling the honour of the woman he loved; it made no sense, but then this was a new and alien situation that he found himself in. He felt light-headed and buried his face in his hands. Ettie ran her fingers through the tangles of his hair.

"You're a man. You're *my* man. Make a woman of me."

Ned gave in to his desire and held Ettie close to him, his arms tight around her as he kissed her forcefully. Ettie fiddled with the buckle of his belt as Ned kissed her neck and squeezed her backside. By the time she had freed his manhood and taken it in hand she was almost breath-less herself.

Ned's coat was laid over the grass and Ettie reclined upon it, opening herself to Ned. He went on all fours above her, nibbling at her throat as they merged. She winced at first, but quickly relaxed as Ned stroked her hair and kissed her tenderly. He squeezed his eyes shut, overawed by the intense, new sensations he was experiencing. He bucked with a primal lust, such that Ettie worried he might lose control. She wrapped her legs around him and studied his face as he moved, mouth agape and head thrown back as if at any moment he might howl at the moon like some wild thing. Their cries of ecstasy and gratification filled the night, and as Ned climaxed his face was contorted with a potent blend of bliss and agony, the jarring pain from his ailing back finally breaking through, and his muscles cramping in protest at his sudden outburst of activity. With a whimper he collapsed beside Ettie who curled into him.

"I need your arms around me," Ettie whispered.

Ned pulled his coat over her body and held onto her as if he was frightened that she would blow away in the breeze. He gazed into the heavens and was overcome with a sense of guilt, though he could not pinpoint what he was ashamed of.

"Is that what you wanted?" Ettie asked.

"It was. But it will never be enough. I need you to be with me always, but it's not a life we can share. I don't know what to do," Ned said, kissing Ettie's crown.

"Then don't think about that. Just be here with me now."

Ettie shut her eyes and rested her head against Ned's chest.

"I will make an honest woman of you, Ettie. As soon as I can."

"An honest woman needs an honest man," Ettie replied without looking up.

"Am I not an honest man?"

Ettie smirked. "When it suits you, I suppose so."

* * *

As Maggie stood over the dining table kneading dough for the bread, the front door opened and Tom Lloyd entered, sleeves rolled up, brow slick with sweat.

"Got that fence fixed for you. Shouldn't be a problem keeping the horses in now."

Maggie stopped kneading and wiped her hands on her apron.

"Thank you, Tom. You're a Godsend. You look bushed. Sit down, I'll get you a drink."

Tom sat at the dining table as Maggie scooped water into a cup from a bucket on the bench. She took it to Tom who accepted it gladly and gulped the water down in seconds. Maggie took a cloth from the pocket of her apron and wiped the sweat from Tom's face gently.

"Have you heard from Bill?" asked Tom.

"No. I'll see him when I can," Maggie replied as she sat next to Tom, exhausted. "Five more years without a husband; how am I to do it all on my own?"

Tom took her flour encrusted hands in his and squeezed them tenderly.

"You're not on your own. I'm not going anywhere, Maggie."

She smiled warmly and stroked his face tenderly. "Stay with me tonight."

"I don't have my swag," Tom replied.

"You know you don't need it," said Maggie.

They moved close each other and tenderly kissed. Maggie giggled.

"What?" Tom asked.

"Your beard is tickling me," Maggie said, gazing into Tom's eyes.

***

In Melbourne Gaol life was hardly wild or romantic. The drudgery of day-to-day life was interminable for Ellen Kelly. Separated from her children and so far from home, Ellen had struggled to be on her own for the first time in her life, but eventually settled into a routine out of necessity. She still yearned to hold her little ones close but buried the longing in order to continue to function from day to day

Each night in her cold, cramped cell embittered her deeper against the police. In her darker moments she fantasised about doing unspeakable things to Constable Fitzpatrick for what he had inflicted upon her and her family.

She often wondered what was happening to her sons and whether they were keeping out of the reach of the law. Though her boys were the most wanted men in Australia, Ellen had no inkling of the extent of their notoriety. News travelled slowly through bluestone walls. All she knew was that when the police finally caught up with Ned and Dan the results would be devastating.

She was unaware of the attempts they had made to negotiate her freedom in exchange for theirs. Though Ned had sent word to the police through his sympathisers, the proposal was outright rejected, even ridiculed, as no more than an audacious joke. The resounding silence in response to his offer was an indignity that Ned continued to carry with him and ruminate on.

***

Kate Byrne was reading behind the cowshed when she heard the shrill, reedy sound of a tin whistle close by. She looked up to discover Aaron by the chopping block playing a tune poorly. Kate scowled as he gestured for her to join him.

Kate stormed over to Aaron, who opened his arms to embrace her. She refused the hug and pushed him away violently.

"You have got some bloody nerve showing your face here," Kate snapped.

"Whatever are you talking about?"

"Ma saw you with those policemen watching the house."

"Listen! I can explain," Aaron said weakly.

"There's nothing to explain. How dare you do such a thing; I can't believe I fell for your lies about looking out for Joe and keeping the traps away. Get out of here. I don't ever want to see you again!"

"But Kate... Please," Aaron begged.

Kate shoved him with as much force as she could manage, "Get out of here, I said!"

"But I love you, Kate. Doesn't that mean anything?"

Kate's eyes were awash with furious tears. She clasped the handle of an old axe from the wood pile and yanked it out, brandishing it menacingly.

"Get going or, so help me God, I will use this!"

Aaron didn't believe her. To prove she meant business, Kate swung the axe threateningly inches from Aaron's face. He stepped back and raised his hands in submission. He reached into his pocket and pulled out a silver Claddagh ring and placed it on top of the woodpile. Without uttering another word, he left.

Kate picked up the ring - a band joined in the middle with two outstretched hands clasping a heart: an engagement ring. She placed it on the chopping block and brought the axe down on top of it. She sobbed bitterly.

***

High among the Strathbogie Ranges Ned Kelly gazed out over his domain. The rocks and trees did not care that they were in the presence of Australia's most infamous son. The cockatoos that screeched as they flew past had no interest in reward money; the wind that whipped his hair and beard found no entertainment in the tales of his raids in Euroa and Jerilderie. Up here, Ned was as free a man as he could hope to be, far away from where policemen dared to tread; but it was a false kind of freedom.

More than anything Ned craved to be sitting at a dining table with Ettie Hart and a home-cooked meal of something more nourishing than damper and preserved offal. The thought of a soft bed to relieve his back filled him with yearning. The time that had passed since his night of passion felt like forever and he became frustrated as he thought about how it had felt and how much he wanted to do it again.

This combined with the mental strain of knowing that any day could be the one where he slipped up and he let his pursuers catch up to him had made Ned sullen and irascible.

Behind him, sheltering from the biting cold of the wind were his gang. Dan dozed, wrapped in a black poncho. A mop of uncut raven-black hair hid his brow. Steve's pouty lips pursed as he poured molten lead into a bullet mould by a small fire and Joe Byrne sat in the shade of a withered looking gum tree reading *For the Term of His Natural Life*. His complexion was florid; reddened by the abrasive mountain winds, his reliance on whiskey and the harshness of the sun on his sensitive Irish skin. He was a far cry from the well-groomed young buck that joined Ned and Dan at Stringybark Creek.

Ned climbed down from his perch and joined the group, his tall-heeled concertina boots slipping slightly on the gritty surface as he walked. He warmed his hands by the fire and inspected the ammunition Steve had made.

"You're finally getting better at casting," Ned commented.

Steve gave Ned a sidelong glance. Ned cleared his throat.

"Joe, do you know how much money we've left from Jerilderie?"

Joe nodded, not looking up from his book.

Ned stood expectantly but nothing came. He strode across and snatched the book out of Joe's hands.

"Oi! What's biting you?" Joe grumbled.

"How much do we have left?" Ned repeated.

"Nothing; it's all gone!"

"What do you mean, 'all gone'?"

"There's nothing left. After you gave money to the sympathisers, we had just enough left to buy supplies for about a couple of months at most. I gave most of my cut to Aaron to help him pay off his selection and the rest went to Ma. Unless you and Danny hid some away, there's none left," Joe said.

"Jerilderie was a long time ago, Ned," Steve chimed in as he began to pack away his equipment.

"Shut up, Steve," Ned snapped. He gave Joe his book back and began to pace. The movement usually helped him think when he was stressed.

"We need more money. We need to hit another bank," Ned said as he thrust his hands into the pockets of his oilskin coat and turned to Steve.

"Steve, I want you to scout around Benalla and find a good target."

Steve threw down his kit, "You want me to get shot? The only reason I managed to find the bank to rob in Euroa was because nobody knew I was part of the gang. Now there's people buying copies of my photograph. I'd be spotted in an instant. I'm not bloody scouting."

"You need to pull your weight around here, boy. I'm carrying it all on my shoulders right now. The least you can do is the one thing you're good at," Ned growled. Steve rose to his feet and approached him.

"On your shoulders? Are you forgetting that we all have a price on our heads too? All it would take is some cove with one bullet and a decent aim to send me to meet my maker and earn £2000. This isn't just about you anymore."

"Watch your tongue. You'd be nowhere without me!"
"Without *me* you'd have drowned in the Murray months ago trying to cross those bloody flood waters. I bet your ma's proud as punch with what you've become," Steve sneered.

Ned's face twisted with fury, and he swung a fist straight at Steve's head. The younger man dodged the blow with a chuckle.
"Get over here, I'll throw you in that damned fire," Ned roared as he grabbed Steve by the throat.
Steve gasped for air and managed a well-placed strike to the side of Ned's head. Ned released his grip and clutched his head in pain. Steve struck again; a golden signet ring proudly placed on his finger slamming straight into Ned's cheek. The older man howled in pain and rage. Joe put his book down to watch.

Steve grew overconfident and went in for another blow only to be blocked by Ned and repaid with a head-butt to the face. Blood gushed from Steve's nose. Ned grabbed Steve by the hair and threw him to the ground, pinning him down with his foot.

Dan snapped to attention and rushed to his friend's aide, shoving Ned aside. "That's enough!"

Steve stood and brushed himself off.

"Aye, it is. I'm taking my chances and going home. Anywhere is better than stuck up a bloody mountain with this gorilla," Steve grumbled. He spat blood into the dirt as he stomped towards the horses. He had a split lip, a broken nose and his face was numb where he thought Ned had knocked out some of his front teeth, "Come with me, Dan."

"Yes Dan, go off with your lover boy," said Ned sarcastically.

"Shut your bloody mouth, Ned. Steve's right," Dan said, gathering his things. "We've been up here for months freezing our arses off waiting for you to come up with your grand plan. How is that coming by the way?"

"I don't see you offering any bright ideas," replied Ned.

"I told you we should be heading for South Australia and starting fresh under new names. Then we could send money back for the girls. It's the smart thing to do but you don't go in for the smart thing, do you?"

Dan scooped up his things and mounted.

"If you're going past the Woolshed, could you check in on Ma and everyone for me, Danny?" said Joe.

"You could always do it yourself," said Dan.

With that, Steve and Dan rode off. Ned sat by the fire across from Joe and stared into the flames.

"The whippet got you good there, Neddy," Joe smirked pointing to his cheek.

"Bloody Hart. And what good are you? You just sat and watched!"

"Not my fight," Joe said returning to his book.

"Is that how it is? I thought I could depend on you."

"What are you on about?" asked Joe.

"You're losing your faith in me too," Ned said.

"Ned, you've been up in these mountains too bloody long," Joe closed his book and paused. "I reckon the boys had the right idea in leaving. I'm going to meet Maggie. It's that time of the week anyway." Joe put his book away in his saddlebag and rose, slinging the bag over his shoulder. His grey mare, Music, was hobbled behind the camp and Joe moved towards her. Ned continued to sulk as Joe mounted.

"Get out of the bush, Ned. Go see someone. You could use a good fuck, so maybe you ought to pay Ettie a visit. You can move as free as you like if you're careful."

Joe turned his mare in the direction the others had gone, leaving Ned alone by the fire to stew.

***

At the Hart selection at the foot of the Warby Ranges, Ettie dabbed at Steve's nose with a wet cloth. He sat on the edge of a bed with his face badly bruised and his nose swollen.

"Is it bad?" Steve asked, his voice nasal.

"Let's just say you won't be getting any prizes for your good looks for a while," Ettie replied.

"Nothing much has changed then," said Dan with a chuckle.

Ettie rinsed out the cloth and shook her head.

"I don't understand what it is between you. Why are you always getting into fights with Ned?"

"Because he's an imbecile and a hothead," Steve said.

"Well, I hope you plan to stay here a while. We never seem to really get police here, thank goodness. They always seem to be more interested in Byrne's place. Will you be staying too Dan?"

Dan stood and collected his coat. He planted his hat on his head and turned to look at the Harts.

"No, just wanted to see Stevey right. I need to go check on Kate and the kids. I'll be back later."

With that Dan left to mount his mare. Ettie turned to Steve.

"You can't afford to be getting into these scrapes, Steve. You all need to work together and look after each other until we can figure out a way past all this," she said.

"We try, but Ned seems to think it's all about him and we're just there to do what he says. I don't think I could trust him to stick by us if things got out of hand again like they did at Stringybark."

"With any luck you won't have to worry about that. You'd best get some rest. I'll bring you some supper directly," said Ettie. Steve wrapped himself up in a poncho and eased back into his bed.

***

At the Vine Hotel in Beechworth, the general maid, Maggie, bade her employer Mrs. Vandenberg goodnight and closed up for the night. She walked around the side of the hotel to a small outbuilding, little more than a shed, where she had lodgings.

As she reached the door a hand touched her arm. Maggie jolted with fright but within a second saw that the arm belonged to Joe Byrne.

"Joe!" Maggie chided, slapping the outlaw's hand.

"Quick, let's get inside."

As the pair slipped into Maggie's sleeping quarters, she lit a hurricane lamp on a small side table. The room was sparsely decorated with the bare essentials for living. Joe pulled Maggie toward him and kissed her passionately. Maggie pulled away to catch her breath.

"Joe, what's gotten into you?"

"I have been aching to see you," said Joe breathily, "I'm tired of being up in the mountains with the boys. They don't like to cuddle, and they don't smell anywhere near as nice as you."

"Giss on! Well, I'm not complaining, mind," Maggie responded, "I assume you had a wash before visiting this time, though."

"Anything for you, petal."

Maggie removed her apron and began to unbutton her dress.

"'Ere don't just stand there, help me out of this, like. Many hands make light work, as they say."

Joe needed no further motivation to help Maggie undress and worked his thick fingers around the buttons.

"So, have you heard anything about the police up this way?" Joe asked.

"Detective Ward is always poking about, like," said Maggie.

"I thought I was the only one that could poke about here," said Joe with a grin as he pulled the dress off Maggie's tiny frame. Maggie rolled her eyes and removed her shirt and loosened her corset. She breathed a sigh of relief as she unhooked and discarded the garment.

"You know what I mean. He and bloody Senior-Constable Mullane are always looking for information. Luckily nobody seems to have noticed your visits here right under their noses."

Joe ran his hand over Maggie's breast to feel its fullness beneath her slip as she let her hair down. He held the tiny maid close, and she stood on tiptoe to nuzzle under his beard.

"Let's make the most of your visit, shall we, me 'ansome," said Maggie, squeezing Joe's backside.

***

Kate Lloyd was sixteen years old but far more mature than her age would suggest. When her father had been arrested for being a Kelly sympathiser, her responsibilities had increased around the farm, and she had stepped up admirably.

Lately she had taken to sneaking outside after tea to knit under the veranda as a way of unwinding and maintained the habit even after his return. As she sat knitting a green scarf, she became aware of the approaching sound of hooves.

She stood and looked into the dark where she faintly saw a horseman vault over the post and rail fence that bordered the selection. As the mounted figure drew nearer, she recognised her beloved cousin, Ned. She looked back into the house through the window to make sure everyone was still in bed then ran over to join him.

Ned hitched his mare to a rail near the house and dismounted. He saw Kate running towards him, her black hair cascaded over her shoulders and bounced with each stride. She was dressed in the minimum possible layers to stay comfortable while remaining decent. The pair hugged tightly; Ned's muscular arms strained against his sleeves as he lifted the girl off her feet.

"How you doing, Kate?"

"I'm so happy to see you, Neddy. Come, come, have you eaten?"

"Nothing I'd recommend you try," Ned chuckled. Kate took his hand and guided him inside.

"I think there's some bread and marmalade but my sisters eat like horses so I can't make any promises," Kate whispered, trying not to wake anyone. Her father, recently home from gaol, could be heard snoring loudly in another room. Ned noticed Kate's feet were bare and dirty from walking in the dust.

"May I take these boots off?" Ned whispered back. Kate looked at the boots; handsome, calf-high concertina boots with tall heels and a narrow cut. His feet were larger than the boots were intended for, causing the leather to bulge at the sides. Kate nodded.

Ned sat on a wooden chair, unbuckled his spurs and tugged at the boots until they slid off. He planted his naked feet on the dirt floor and wiggled his toes with a sigh.

Kate rushed around gathering food and utensils and poured a bowl of warm water from the kettle by the fireplace. She placed the bowl on the floor and guided Ned's feet into the water. Ned rested a plate of sliced bread on his knees and smeared marmalade on the slices while Kate bathed and rubbed his feet.

"That feels lovely," said Ned with a mouthful of food. Kate smiled up at him.

His beard was full of crumbs and his face was smeared with grime and his clothes stank of smoke, sweat and filth. Kate did her best not to be offended by the smell.

"I think you need a proper wash, and fresh clothes," Kate said. Ned nodded.

"Been a while since I was able."

"Finish your dinner and I'll grab you some."

After Ned had eaten, Kate took him into a small building next to the house where her mother would wash the clothes in a big copper tub. Kate hung a lantern on a nail in the wall, bathing the room in a dull amber glow. Ned placed a ceramic hand basin full of water down on a bench and began to undress.

Draping his discarded jacket, waistcoat, shirt and undershirt over the edge of the copper tub he turned to see Kate watching him. He gave her a confused look and she blushed.

"I'm sorry," Kate said, turning away.

"No, it's alright," Ned mumbled awkwardly. He hesitated and removed his neckerchief.

Kate walked over and grabbed a washcloth from the basin and squeezed the excess water out of it. She moved to Ned and wiped his face tenderly.

"Why aren't you with your donah tonight?" Kate asked.

"Well, I don't think I shall be visiting the Harts for a little while. There was some unpleasantness."

Kate tutted as she ran the cloth over Ned's neck. She watched as tiny rivulets dribbled down over his chest, mingling with the hair around his nipple.

"You're trembling like a leaf," Ned said quietly. Kate allowed an awkward smile to creep across her face and she wrung out the cloth in the basin. She grabbed a bundle that she had placed on a chair near the door.

"I found you some clothes. I'm not sure if they'll fit you well but they were Jack's and he was pretty big for a nineteen-year-old," Kate's turquoise eyes took on a sad aspect.

"I was sorry to hear about what happened," Ned said, holding Kate's hand gently.

"That's alright. Jack was a silly boy, and he was always playing stupid games, but nothing ever prepares you for losing someone I suppose. Not like that."

A month earlier Tom and Jack Lloyd had been mucking around at the pub after a few drinks when Jack told Tom to hit him as hard as he could to test his strength. Tom had done so and sent his cousin toppling. He struck his head and died within minutes. The aftermath had put significant strain on the families and would take a long time to heal.

Kate paused for a moment to compose herself. Ned pulled the girl in to his chest and held her, "It doesn't rain but it pours, eh, Kate?"

Kate closed her eyes and felt the warmth of Ned's skin against her cheek. It was comforting to feel him hold her so tightly. She felt like she could easily fall asleep to the rise and fall of his chest. Suddenly she became self-conscious and pulled back.

"What's wrong?" Ned asked.

"I should let you get on. I'll be outside if you need me."

Kate went out and shut the door behind her.

Inside Ned stripped off and ground the cloth into every crevice to get at the ingrained filth. Outside, Kate waited patiently and noticed a crack in the wall that gave out just a hint of the golden light from inside. She silently put her eye to the crack and looked through. She saw Ned in all his glory - sinewy limbs and broad shoulders. As he shifted around, she fancied she caught a glimpse of his member caught in the light as it was bounced about by the shifting of muscular thighs, and she felt her heart race.

Ned heard a gasp and looked around. He saw movement through a conspicuous crack in the wall and smirked. He took his time drying off.

After Ned had washed and changed, Kate gathered up his dirty clothes. As she did so a gold watch fell out of the waistcoat pocket - Sergeant Kennedy's watch. Ned snatched it up and held it tenderly.

"I'm sorry," said Kate.

"It's alright. It's just... I'm looking after this," Ned replied.

"Who for?"

"The widow Kennedy. By rights it belongs to her, but I just haven't been able to get it to her. I don't know if I ever will. For now, I keep it as a reminder."

"Reminder of what?"

"Of what I've done; of the fact that this time I'm living on is not mine, and the traps can take it away at any moment. It keeps me straight, I suppose."

Kate frowned as she watched Ned stroke the golden face of the watch.

"Wait here," she said as she ran inside the house.

She returned in a moment with the green scarf she had been knitting and a silver watch. She gave them to Ned.

"What are these?" Ned asked.

"Well, the scarf is to keep you warm, but the watch is mine. I'm giving it to you," Kate replied.

"What for?"

"Because I want you to remember that any time you feel lonely or like things are too much to bear alone you should come see me. I'll do anything for you Ned; you just ask." Kate's eyes began to well with tears.

"You're sweet. Thank you," said Ned. He held her head and kissed her crown softly.

"I don't like thinking of you staring at that trooper's watch and being sad or worried. Look at mine instead. It keeps good time too. It's from Geh-neh-vah. Da says that means it must be good."

Ned looked at the watch. It was ornate but did not appear especially fancy. He examined the face and saw the word Geneva stamped behind the hands.

"Well, if Uncle Tom says so, it must be."

***

As dusk began to set in over Benalla, Captain Standish stood by the railing outside the police station waiting anxiously for Superintendent Hare's return. He checked his watch with an expression of deep distress. Superintendent Sadleir watched the pathetic display through the window of his office. Sergeant Whelan, gaunt and grey, entered the office bearing papers for Sadleir.

"It's pathetic. He's a grown man but he's been out there all afternoon waiting for Hare like an anxious child waiting for its mother to return from town," Sadleir grumbled.

"I'm sure you've heard what the constables think about the pair of them," said Whelan.

"I have, but I'd rather not buy into that kind of gutter talk, thank you very much."

Sadleir flicked through the papers absent-mindedly.

"Well, you know what they say about smoke and fire," Whelan continued as he left the room with a smirk.

For months Hare had been throwing everything he had at the hunt, but it had taken its toll on him, and this day was to be the straw that broke the camel's back.

Returning from the day's hunt, the police party found a set of closed railway gates that Hare had specifically requested to be left open. It had been a drizzly July day and not feeling bothered to find the stationmaster, the police jumped their horses over the gates. Hare, being hefty in weight and lofty in height, proved to be ill-suited to such a feat and as his horse landed on the dewy ground, the excess weight caused Hare to land heavily and the poor animal slipped. The result was excruciating pain in Hare's lower back.

When he made it back to the police station his constables had to help him inside. Standish was beside himself to see Hare being held up by his subordinates and groaning in pain.

"What happened? Are you shot?"

"No, no, I'm not shot. I've done something to my back," Hare said with a struggle.

Hare was seated by the fire and a doctor was sent for post haste, and just like that Hare was out of the race.

****

As Aaron Sherritt took lunch in his hut with his brother Jack there was a rapping at the door. The brothers looked at each other and Aaron stood up.

"Who is it?"

The voice on the other side of the door was shrill, "Open up, Sherritt!"

Aaron frowned and complied. Yanking the door open he looked down to see Margret Byrne, sour-faced and pulling a shawl around her shoulders.

"Yes, Mrs. Byrne?"

"You had horses in your paddock yesterday."

"Did I?"

"Aye, you did. Police horses."

"I don't recall any horses. Jack, do you know anything about some horses in my paddock yesterday?"

The younger Sherritt replied from his seat at the table, "Oh, yeah,

Scotty was grazing his horses on his way back to Sebastopol. Couldn't have been more than an hour."

Aaron looked at Margret with a wry expression.

"There you have it, Missus. Nothing sinister."

Margret scowled, her already severe face taking on a menacing aspect.

"Well, count yourself lucky, boy, because if I thought you knew those were police horses, I'd burn your fecking house down."

As Margret turned to leave, Aaron called out, "Mrs. Byrne, I don't suppose you've got the money from selling that filly I gave Kate?"

"I don't have anything for the likes of you."

With that Margret stomped back towards her own home. Aaron closed the door and shook his head.

"I've had it with that woman. As if she could tell a police horse from a donkey. Some bastard's been in her ear. Y'know, I had an agreement that if Kate didn't want the bloody horse I gave her I'd take it back, but the old cow went and sold it just to spite me," he snarled.

"Reckon you ought to teach her a lesson," Jack said.

"I reckon you're right, Jacky boy."

***

As darkness fell over the Byrne farm, Aaron Sherritt crept past the fence and headed to the stables. Inside he found a bay gelding belonging to Joe's seventeen-year-old brother Paddy. This was Charlie, a horse Aaron had borrowed on several occasions and was familiar with. Charlie recognised Aaron and stirred.

Aaron opened the box and lured the horse out, looping a rope around his neck. With extreme caution he guided the horse off the property to a patch of scrub where Jack waited on horseback.

"Nice work. Nobody saw you?"

"Not a soul," Aaron replied, "Patsy is up north for work and the old biddy is probably asleep by the fire with a belly full of sherry. Besides, I'm an old hand at this caper. Let's get going."

***

"No, Aaron, I don't want the bloody horse," complained Maggie Skillion. Her expression was a twitch away from an accommodating smile becoming a fierce rebuke. Her patience with Sherritt was wearing thin.

"Come on, he's a good horse. Gelded. He'll be no trouble," said Aaron.

For two weeks Aaron had been trying to get rid of Charlie the stolen horse in an effort to get back the money he had spent on Kate Byrne's filly with no luck. With no other options he had decided to try Maggie again.

"Aaron, what do I need to do to stop you bothering me?"

"I need to sell this horse."

"So, if I buy the bloody horse, you'll leave me alone?"

"Buy the horse and you won't hear another thing about it. Hell, you'll be thanking me for it."

Maggie sighed to herself, "Oh, Margaret, Lord help you..."

***

Of course, it was not the last to be heard about it. In fact, Margret Byrne had gone to the police straight away, and as soon as Maggie had caught wind of the trouble, she had turned Charlie the horse over to the police.

Aaron was arrested and taken to Beechworth for trial, held in the granite cell outside the courthouse. For the first time in years, he had to endure the biting cold without the benefit of booze to warm him, all the while jostling for floor space away from the bucket in the far corner that was to be used as a chamber pot by the mix of drunks, vagrants and thieves. As he curled up on the gritty floorboards with the jagged granite wall against his back, he tried to grab what sleep he could.

The ensuing trial was a farce. Each witness gave an account of the situation that was in some way contradictory to everyone else's. The whole time Aaron stood in the creaky dock; Margret Byrne scowled at him.

When she took to the witness stand, she was determined to publicly distance him from her family when asked about the rumoured engagement to her daughter.

"He's no relation of mine and was not in a fair way to become my son-in-law," Margret had said as venomously as she could muster. When she was questioned about whether she had seen the horse in question in Aaron's paddock she narrowed her eyes and stared straight at the defendant.

"I would not have been surprised to see anything in *his* paddock."

Even though Aaron thought he was licked, the case was dismissed, and Aaron went free. Margret cursed as she was escorted out by Paddy Byrne. Paddy was closer to his mother in his features than Joe was; a wide, tight-lipped mouth, sparse eyebrows and severe cheekbones affecting an overall more hardened appearance, though the brothers were similar enough to be confused with each other. Aaron watched the Byrnes leave knowing that this was far from the end of the unpleasantness. He wondered how Joe would take the news.

***

Several days after the trial Aaron awakened to a pounding at the door of his hut. He got up, pulled on some breeches, and answered to find Paddy Byrne fuming, a faint smell of brandy was on him.

"You bastard," Paddy growled, "Come near my family again and I'll shoot you dead, you hear?"

"Steady on Patsy --" said Aaron, using the nickname that Joe used almost exclusively.

"It's Patrick to you. Stay away!"

With that he stormed off and mounted his horse. Aaron closed the door and listened to him ride away. As much as he tried to shake it off, the confrontation had hurt him. He sat at his table and prepared his pipe for a smoke to steady his nerves. The sun was high, and he knew he'd need to get more sleep before taking the police to watch the Byrne selection again. He was exhausted.

Suddenly he clenched his jaw and hurled the table across the room with a scream. He burst outside and stomped to the woodpile. He picked up his axe and began chopping firewood to get the anger out of his system.

***

Though Aaron Sherritt found himself once more a bachelor, he had grown tired of canoodling with barmaids and certainly couldn't afford the services of the ladies in red at Little Bourke Street whenever he needed to satiate his urges. Rather, he had decided to make a move on Kate Kelly, though since the incident with Charlie the horse she had been wary of his advances. One evening Aaron visited the Kelly selection in an attempt to remedy Kate's coolness to him.

"Good evening, Miss Kelly," Aaron said, leaning against the door jamb. Kate busied herself fussing over the plates in the pantry and barely acknowledged the presence of the Woolshed larrikin.

"What do you want, Aaron?"

"I was wondering if you'd like to come for a stroll with me. It's nice out and I figure you work pretty hard running around after the kiddies, so why not take a break?" Aaron grinned his most charming, dimply grin. Kate knew about Aaron's reputation in Beechworth and part of her was curious about what kind of lover Aaron would make, but she also knew that having a man around the house was meant to be about having a provider and protection in the absence of her brothers, and Sherritt was not an apt candidate.

"I don't think it's a good idea, Aaron," said Kate.

"Come now, it won't take long. Just a little stroll down the creek to cool off."

Kate paused and looked at Aaron, standing in the doorway with his hand in his pocket and his handsome face clean-shaven and beaming. She was only human, and against her better judgement she gave in to her desire.

"Alright, but I can't stray too far as I'm to be back before dark. Maggie is due for supper," Kate said.

"No worries, Miss Kelly," Aaron replied with a wink.

The pair walked side by side along the creek, cicadas creating an awful din and birds singing their evening tunes as they took their places in the trees.

"Kitty, you've been awful cool towards me lately, what's wrong with making a go of things?" Aaron asked, unbuttoning the collar of his shirt.

"You've got a reputation and I have responsibilities. If you're going to be courting, you need to know I can't be whisked away to the Woolshed on a whim. The little ones need me here."

"I know that, but Grace has it under control and Maggie is just a couple of blocks away. I'm not going to steal you away from them. Come on, you're only young once!"

"You don't understand, I can't afford to be irresponsible, Aaron!" Kate snapped.

"Who's irresponsible? Nothing wrong with ducking off to dip your toes in the stream once in a while. Look..." Aaron tugged his boots off and slid his feet out of his socks. For good measure he removed his trousers.

"What are you doing?" Kate gasped.

"You like my Long Johns? Red is my favourite colour," Aaron said with a grin as he walked off the bank into the creek. "Come in!"

Kate watched Aaron splashing about and dancing a little jig in the water.

After some hesitation and glancing around Kate untied her boots and slid them off before hitching up her skirts, unfastening her suspenders and rolling her stockings off. The grass by the water felt pleasant against her naked feet, far more pleasant than the hard dirt and gravel of the selection. She waded into the creek, her porcelain pale skin almost glowing in the fading light of dusk.

"You've lovely legs, Kitty. If only I could see them for the glare," joked Aaron shielding his eyes mockingly.

***

When Kate returned to the selection, Maggie was already inside waiting. She had arrived in Kate's absence and prepared the supper on her own for the children.

Unlike the bulk of women in the region, Maggie enjoyed smoking and had a wooden churchwarden's pipe with a long mouthpiece that she called her 'witch pipe'. As Kate walked in the door, she was greeted by Maggie puffing away with a look of disapproval.

"Where have you been?" Maggie asked.

Grace had already told her what Kate was up to, but Maggie was always one for coaxing confessions out of her siblings.

"I went for a walk with Aaron Sherritt, but I shan't go with him again," said Kate cryptically as she fiddled with her skirts.

"I should hope not, the kiddies were very hungry until I made the supper. That was very irresponsible of you."

"I know, I'm sorry. It won't happen again."

"You be careful around that Sherritt. He's trouble."

***

"You mark my words, son, Aaron is working against you," Margret Byrne said as Joe sat by the fireplace with a bowl of oxtail stew.

"I've spoken with him. He says he made a deal with the chief commissioner to keep me safe. Why would he lie about that?" said Joe.

"Don't be such a fecking idjit, boy! Think! He's out for the reward," Margret bellowed.

Joe remained silent and poked his stew with a fork. His sister Kate planted a hand on his shoulder.

"Joe, are you really willing to risk it? How many times has he gotten you in trouble?"

"What are you trying to say, Kate?" asked Joe.

"I'm trying to say that maybe Aaron isn't as loyal to you as you are to him."

"What do you want me to do about it then?" Joe snapped.

"I know right well what I'd do, Joseph, and it involves Da's old hunting rifle and a steady hand," said Margret.

"Paddy reckons that Jack Sherritt is in with the traps too. I suppose he's made a deal with the chief commissioner too, has he?" said Kate sarcastically.

"If I can't trust Aaron, then who can I trust?" asked Joe. His throat felt like it was squeezing shut.

"Blood. Blood is the only thing that matters, Joseph. Not that it has ever mattered much to you," replied Margret. She stared at her son with fury in her ice-blue eyes. Joe stood up and handed his bowl to Margret with a look of contempt.

"Sorry. I'll be off," said Joe in a monotone. Without looking back, he stormed out and headed to the paddock where Music was chasing the other horses. Joe whistled to catch her attention. As he mounted, he saw Kate staring at him from the door of the house. He shot her a withering stare and spurred off into the evening.

***

Dan and Joe had been camping around the Sebastopol flats and took to sneaking into the Chinese settlement to gamble and smoke opium with some of Joe's associates. Dan was not very fond of the opium smoke, but Joe was hopelessly addicted and had become increasingly dependent upon the drug to cope with his melancholy. When their money ran out so too did the hospitality of their companions and Joe found himself deprived of his opium supply.

Dan and Joe took refuge in an abandoned hut on Mount Buffalo. Joe lay on a striped blanket, barely conscious with cold sweats, unstoppable shivering, stomach cramps and mood swings that plagued him as his body screamed for drugs.

Groggily he raised himself up onto his elbows and searched through a saddlebag next to him on the ground. Dan watched with concern.

"Danny," said Joe.

"Yeah?"

"Did I misplace my opium?"

"No. You used it all up. We have already had this conversation."

Joe sighed and buried his face in his hands. "I forgot. I can't think straight."

"You're sick as a dog, Joe. You need a doctor," said Dan. Joe looked up with bloodshot eyes and a murderous expression.

"Fuck doctors. I need opium!"

With that Joe doubled over and vomited. As he heaved half-digested bully beef and biscuits onto the ground, he began to feel a coldness wash over him. Without warning he blacked out and collapsed. Panicking, Dan rolled Joe over and smacked his face to rouse him. As Joe came to, Dan helped him up and guided him to the horses. With considerable effort Joe climbed into the saddle. Music was uneasy. They rode to the Byrne selection as fast as their mounts could carry them.

He dismounted and rushed to the homestead door. There, Paddy met Dan and informed him that Joe was not permitted into the main house, so he had set up a swag in the stable. The pair lifted Joe down off Music and guided him to the stable where Joe laid down.

"What in heaven's name is wrong with him?" Paddy asked Dan.

"I reckon the celestials poisoned him with that opium."

"You reckon there's anything we can do?"

"Reckon you can find something for his pain?" Dan suggested.

"I reckon I might," replied Paddy.

He rushed inside and found a supply of laudanum, which his sister kept aside for combating the pain of menstruation. The combination of opium and morphine had seen many women become hooked on the blissful wooziness it created while blocking out pain, and subsequently was extremely dangerous and addictive but it was the only option Paddy could think of.

He ran back to the stable and gave the tincture to Joe.

"Whazzis?" Joe slurred.

"Drink a little, it's for the pain. Just a little should do it," Paddy instructed.

Joe pulled the cork on the bottle and took a small amount. The bottle was adorned with a label that bore skull and crossbones. Joe examined the illustration with bleary eyes as he waited for the tincture to kick in. Within minutes he felt his pain dissipate and he relaxed, dozing off into a welcome slumber.

***

Having entrusted Joe to the care of his family, Dan Kelly headed out to find Ned. He knew there were only a few places he was likely to be and headed into the Strathbogie Ranges. After hitting the gang's usual haunts, Dan set course for Ned's favourite cave overlooking the tablelands.

Reaching the cave at dusk, Dan hobbled his horse and ventured into the cave. He had barely stepped foot in the hideout when he heard the click of a rifle hammer.

"It's me, you fool," said Dan.

"What do you want?" Ned replied.

"We need to talk."

By the light of a lamp, Ned and Dan began to reconcile.

"We need to bring everyone back together. There's strength in numbers and we're straining right now. Joe is suffering greatly between the opium and the stories about Aaron. He's been out of sorts since everyone has been in his ear about Aaron helping the traps," Dan said, "All of the Sherritts are in with the traps. Figures given the old man used to be one. But you know how dangerous Joe can be when he's upset."

"I don't believe Aaron would willingly turn against us. It must be a ruse," said Ned, "he knows what I'd do to him if I ever believed he was working for the police."

"If we don't figure out a way to get more money, then more and more sympathisers will do the same. Good will has a price."

"I bloody well know that. How do you propose we rob a guarded bank without getting shot then?" Ned snapped.

"I know we're not bulletproof, Ned," said Dan.

Ned went quiet. He had been struck with an epiphany. He turned to Dan and grinned.

***

Returning to the Kelly selection was always sweet relief for Ned and Dan. As the brothers put their horses in the paddock, the sun had already dipped below the horizon. When they entered the household, they were greeted with open arms by their younger half-siblings Nellie, Jack and Alice. Ned whisked little Alice up in one arm while Dan lifted Nellie and Jack up, one in each arm like giggling sacks of flour. It was almost impossible to see these two as desperadoes who had spent the past few months suffering in the elements. Kate Kelly went to Ned and gave him a peck on the cheek.

"Welcome back, Neddy. The tea is almost ready," Kate said, bustling about the stove.

Ned sat at the dining table and perched Alice on his knee. Dan waddled to Kate with his wriggling siblings and gave her a kiss on the lips, his moustache tickling her. They were presently joined by Grace, the impish thirteen-year-old, in an old-fashioned dress with a ragged hem that reached just above her bare ankles.

She remained quiet. The life she had led since the family had moved to the district had been particularly hard as she had not known a single year of peace in her living memory. Every time she heard hooves it would put her on edge, never knowing if the police were back to push the girls around, tear the place up and wave pistols in their faces, until she walked into the house and saw friendly countenances. Dan immediately responded to his little sister's arrival by putting the children down and offering up a bear hug that she accepted eagerly.

After the repast the children were sent to bed and Kate stayed up to talk with her brothers.

"Joe Ryan was here a few days ago," Kate began, "He left some plough parts for you. Said you'd asked for them."

"That's right," Ned replied.

"What do you want with plough parts?"

"We're going to make bulletproof jackets," Ned replied, "That way, we can strike at the banks and the guards can't just shoot us. I've got Tom Lloyd arranging a blacksmith to help us create one to test. If this works, it will completely change everything."

Kate shot Dan a worried look. He replied with a dismissive shrug. As outlandish as the idea was, there was some merit to it. It remained to be seen if it could work.

***

The heaving breath of bellows could be heard through the trees, accompanied by the crunching rattle of coals. Here, in a secluded spot within the Bald Hills where sunlight dappled the trees and tiny birds flitted about, George Culph demonstrated the process of heating iron in a forge to the Kelly brothers and Tom Lloyd. The preceding months had been difficult for Tom having spent time in gaol for striking a policeman and then enduring the tragedy with his cousin, but he was once again at liberty to assist his infamous cousins.

They watched intently as Culph jostled a plough mouldboard in the coals and brought it out with tongs, glowing red as he placed the steel on a makeshift anvil, bashed it with a hammer, and curved it around. Ned scrutinised every stroke.

Within a few hours Culph had taken two thick iron mouldboards and cut them and shaped them, riveting them together like a buttoned shirt. The crude object was rested against a tree. Ned took aim with a Martini Henry rifle – a police weapon dropped by a careless trooper spying on the family. A crack and a blast were met with the ringing of lead on iron. He pushed the lever out and ejected the spent cartridge, which fell, still smoking, to the ground. Ned went up and examined the deep indentation he had made in the underside of the plate. The dent was deep and smooth where the plate had been struck but not broken at all. He grinned.

***

Galloping rumbled as a grey mare blazed through Glenrowan in the night, carrying a well-dressed rider with his face obscured by a paisley scarf. He approached the train line and drew a revolver, before moving to the door of the gatehouse. He rapped upon the door violently.

"Open up! Open up!"

There was movement inside the gatehouse and the door opened to reveal John Stanistreet, a middle-aged stationmaster, in a state of undress. He was used to the Kelly sympathisers rousing him at all hours to open the railway gates.

"What is it?"

"Open the bloody gate or I'll blow your face inside out," came the reply.

"Who do you think you are?" Stanistreet growled.

"I'm Byrne the Bushranger. Do as I bloody say, you bastard," came the reply.

Stanistreet went to speak but was cut off by the cocking of a revolver. He stood agape.

"Gate! Now!"

Stanistreet's face took on a determined expression and he ducked inside his office to fetch a pistol of his own.

"I don't care who you are," Stanistreet declared as he re-emerged, "I'm prepared to use this. Are you prepared to cop it?"

The ill-tempered visitor reconsidered his position. To prove he was not bluffing, Stanistreet fired a shot in the air past the intruder's head, spooking his horse. The antagonist took off. As Stanistreet watched him leave he lowered his weapon and sighed with relief. His heart was racing so fast he could hear the sloshing of his pulse in his ears.

Down the road, "Byrne the Bushranger" removed his scarf to reveal the smooth, high-cheeked countenance of Jack Sherritt. In the morning he intended to get word to the police that Joe Byrne had been spotted in Glenrowan, hoping for some quick pocket money from Detective Ward.

****

By the light of a lamp, Ned, Dan, Joe, Tom Lloyd and Maggie Skillion sat around the dining table in Maggie's hut. The mood was solemn. As news had been going around the bush telegraph that the Sherritts were in cahoots with the police, Tom, as the gang's unofficial spymaster, had taken it upon himself to discuss the news with the outlaws. Joe had not taken it well and sat in sullen silence.

"I know what you're thinking, Joe, but I'm just telling you what I've been hearing."

"I would trust him if my neck was on the block and the axe was in his hand," Joe said finally, his voice catching in his throat.

Tom removed an object the size and shape of a playing card from his coat pocket and slid it across the table. On the side facing up the word BEWARE had been written.

"I was given this by the Quinns," said Tom. Joe flipped the object over to reveal a *carte de visite* of Aaron Sherritt as a younger man, dressed clownishly in baggy moleskins, a spotted shirt and a floppy felt hat with the chinstrap under his lip. Joe scowled, his eyes taking on a dangerous edge.

"What evidence do they have?" asked Ned.

"He's been spotted going into the police offices in Beechworth and Benalla. He's also been wearing lots of new clothes that appear to have belonged to Detective Ward, and there's whispers that it was the police pulling strings that got him off on that horse stealing charge your ma took him to court over, Joe."

Joe shook his head indignantly.

"Aaron has been posing as an informant to throw the traps off our scent. If they are paying him for it, why shouldn't he thumb his nose at the traps by flaunting it?"

"Joe, the sympathisers are trying to warn you. Listen. They want Aaron dead," said Tom, straining to bring Joe to reason.

"I'm not listening to this shit," Joe growled as he stood abruptly.

"Sit down, Joe," said Ned.

"No! This is absurd! Aaron has been nothing but a pillar of strength to us, just as much as you have, Tom. I can't believe you have the gall to even entertain this."

Ned stared his mate in the eyes and gestured for him to sit.

"Joe, if they're saying this then there must be something to it. You and Danny should check it out. See if he really is on the up and up still."

"It's alright, Joe," said Dan, "I'm sure we can prove these to be nothing more than rumours if that is the case."

Maggie remained quiet but held Tom's hand tightly. Joe's lip trembled.

"Alright," said Joe, "Alright; I'll arrange a meeting. He is true to us, Ned, you know that as well as I do."

"We can't be too careful. My own uncles let me take the rap for Harry Power being turned in while they pocketed the reward money and didn't dole out a single shilling to help us out. I know what money does to people," replied Ned.

"I need air," Joe mumbled, glaring at Ned before storming off, slamming the door behind him. Ned sighed dejectedly.

"What do you think, Dan?"

"If we can't trust our own sympathisers, who do we have left?"

****

Aaron waited in the Puzzle Ranges for Joe Byrne. In his hand he held a letter from Joe dated the twenty-sixth of June, which had been delivered to him that morning. The letter had requested Aaron bring his brother Jack as well, but Jack was being put to work by their father on the family selection, or so he said. Aaron felt he must have been waiting upwards of a half hour at least. Sunset was beginning to settle in when Joe appeared on the path before Aaron.

"Joe," Aaron said opening his arms and encouraging an embrace. Joe hugged his mate unenthusiastically. Aaron couldn't help noticing the lingering smell of alcohol. Joe's appearance was haggard and pale.

"How are you keeping?" Joe asked.

"Aye, alright. A damn sight better than you by the looks," said Aaron, "Now, what's this about Neddy wanting me to join you lads?"

"After all the fighting between Ned and Steve we reckon we need some fresh blood. We reckon you'd be the best fit to replace him."

Aaron raised an eyebrow quizzically as Joe continued.

"We're planning another bank robbery. Ned reckons Benalla this time. We're going to need some proper muscle. The troopers they've got guarding the banks are a real problem."

"Aw, now, you know I'd love to help you there, but I can't do it. I've worked too hard to keep the traps on side so you lot can go unmolested. If I'm up in the ranges with you, who's keeping them under control?" Aaron replied.

"I thought you might say something like that," Joe sighed, "You can't even scout for us?"

Aaron hummed, "Well, alright I'll see what I can manage, but only for you. Ned and the others are not my concern. But you, you're my brother."

Joe hesitated to respond.

"People have been saying some concerning things about you lately. I'd hate to think you'd sell us out for a bag of silver."

"Don't trust the rumours, Joe. There's a lot of people jealous of you and me," Aaron replied. Joe began walking back to his horse, paused then looked back over his shoulder. His gaze drifted down to a pair of polished brown boots Aaron wore proudly.

"Those are some nice boots, Aaron. I might have to get myself a pair. Where did you get them from?"

"Oh, I got them from Paddy Allen, but I can't picture you in anything but those elastic sided things."

Joe smiled. Aaron smiled back.

"Goodbye, Aaron," Joe said weakly.

"Stay safe," said Aaron.

***

At the Woolshed Falls that evening, Aaron waited in the bush for Detective Ward. Behind him water gushed noisily down the falls, cascading over granite boulders and crashing into the creek. It was here in happier times that Aaron and Joe would come to relax and slough off the sweat from relentless summer heat in the cool waters. Those days were distant memories now and this spot had taken on a very different purpose.

Movement in the bush alerted Aaron to the detective's presence and he moved to greet him.

"Detective," said Aaron, extending his hand. Ward shook it gingerly.

"What news of the bushrangers?" Ward asked.

"I reckon they're looking to come back into the open. They've told me they wanted to rob another bank, but the guards are making it too hard for them. They want me to scout."

"And what did you tell them?" Ward's dark eyes flashed brightly for a moment.

"I told them I'd need to think about it. I thought I should tell you, Mr. Ward. We've had our differences, but I can tell you're a good man. Can you promise me that the police commissioner will keep his word to save Joe Byrne from the gallows if we hand you the others?"

Ward thought to himself, his leather gloves creaked as he tightened his fingers.

"You deliver the outlaws to us, and I'll do what I can to make sure he keeps his promise," Ward replied.

"Alright, Detective. I feel I can trust you," said Aaron extending his hand.

"Trust is everything, is it not?" Ward said, concealing a smirk as he shook hands with Aaron.

"Aye, a man needs to know where he stands."

With a nod the men went their separate ways.

2

Ned Kelly's Masterplan

Following Hare's removal from the hunt for the Kellys, he was replaced by the assistant commissioner, Superintendent Charles Hope Nicolson. Nicolson was a Scotsman of middle-age who had risen through the ranks very quickly, distinguishing himself as a mounted cadet before becoming superintendent of detectives. Nicolson was a strictly by-the-book kind of policeman, a staunch believer in the rule of law. His perspective on the Kelly outbreak was that it was unfortunate but inevitable, given the criminal proclivities of that family and class. He knew only too well the lawlessness that ran rampant in that part of the colony in the years leading up to the Fitzpatrick incident, and had tried to suffocate it before it spread by encouraging the police to pull the Kellys and their associates up on even the most minor of offences at every opportunity to take the "flashness" out of them. It had backfired horrendously.

Nicolson had been on the initial Kelly hunt following the killings at Stringybark Creek, but the gang's excursion to Euroa had seen him swiftly taken off the case. Standish had no affection for Nicolson and had been looking for an excuse to supplant him. Now he had no choice but to reinstate Nicolson as head of the hunt and had done so under considerable sufferance.

Upon his return to Benalla, Nicolson spent considerable time attempting to get up to speed with what Hare had been doing and made appointments with the informants that Hare had been reliant on, including the Sherritts. All of the family seemed to be on board in telling the police as much information as they could muster. In fact, the Sherritts' assertion that the gang had been frequently spotted around the Byrne selection prompted Nicolson to install a permanent watch party in the cave overlooking it, of which Aaron was naturally a part. Nicolson held no truck with Hare's reckless approach of chasing the gang around the mountains, but rather believed strongly in the value of a web of spies that he could utilise to slowly close in around the outlaws. Time would tell if it worked.

****

Towards the end of 1879 public attention was briefly diverted from the Kelly Gang by a dramatic siege in New South Wales. A bushranger named Andrew Scott, better known as Captain Moonlite, had stuck up a station in Wantabadgery and held the staff prisoner with his gang. A party of police had engaged them in battle and been sent running, but the following day a second party ambushed the bushrangers as they travelled, trapping them in a tiny farmhouse. The siege saw a policeman mortally wounded and two of the bushrangers killed; the rest were arrested. It was a turn of events that Ned and Joe had read about with great interest.

"You know, I was in Pentridge with him," Ned said.

"Is that so, Ned?" replied Joe.

"Aye. Nothing but trouble that one. The turnkeys had a real down on him. Still, if you ever needed something smuggled in, he was your man. Queer fellow. Never met him myself, but we all knew who he was."

"Well, I hope we don't end up the same way," said Joe.

"We won't."

Ned leaned in conspiratorially, "I've been thinking about our next move. We need to demonstrate the armour. I was thinking of hitting the bank in Yackandandah."

"What would that entail?" Joe asked.

"With the armour on we can just push our way in and clean the place out. If the police or any guards shoot at us, the armour will protect us. We don't need any more elaborate plans, we just ride in, strike the banks, then we get out."

"You make it sound so simple," Joe replied.

"Sometimes simple works."

***

A balmy night in the Woolshed Valley saw Jack Sherritt emerge from his parents' home to take in the night air. Insects chirruped to each other, and the dogs barked. As he stood in the shadows behind the homestead, he heard movement. He turned to see what the source was and discerned a figure in a long overcoat with a wide-brimmed hat coming towards him.

"Who's that?" said Jack.

"You know very well who I am, Jacky boy," replied Joe Byrne. In the gloom Jack began to note the familiar features.

"What brings you here?" Jack said.

"I have something I want you to pass on to Detective Ward for me," Joe answered. He reached into his coat and withdrew an envelope. He passed it to Jack gingerly. "I need you to make sure it gets to where it's going without raising any alarms. Anyone asks where you got it, you tell them it was a stranger. Make up a description if you must, but they mustn't know I saw you directly."

"Of course."

"Mind you stick to my instructions. I will see you again soon."

With that, Joe retreated into the shadows.

The following day Jack forwarded the envelope to Ward. When he received it, the detective opened it without hesitation. Inside was a string of handwritten ramblings threatening the detective, accompanied by cartoons depicting Ward stuck in a log, a death's head and coffin. Ward was naturally greatly perturbed by the message, but it didn't take much detective work to discern who had penned it. Though the outlaws were on the run, it seemed they still had the time and wherewithal to taunt the police and plenty of ink to do it with.

****

A month passed and Joe continued to monitor the Sherritts. He and Dan considered that the real test of their faithfulness had to come from giving the brothers big news. After meeting Jack early in November, Joe organised a meeting at Evans' Gap with the Sherritts to occur a week later. Joe and Dan made a point of keeping these plans hidden from Ned.

On a balmy night, Aaron was suddenly roused by a knock at the door of his hut.

"Who is it?" he called out.

"Messenger," came the reply from outside.

Aaron opened the door where Dan was waiting for him, holding his horse by the reins.

"I have a message for you from Joe. He says the plan has changed. You're to meet him at your folks' place instead of the gap."

"Alright then," said Aaron "Why the change?"

"He has his reasons. Just head to Sheepstation Creek. That is all."

Dan mounted and galloped away into the evening. Aaron had not noticed the revolver in Dan's hand, obscured by his coat.

At the Sherritt selection at the appointed time, a rapping at the door was answered by Jack. Aaron stood at the threshold dressed in his town clothes with a bottle of whiskey in his hand.

"Evening, brother," said Jack, "Keeping well, I see."

"I came upon this rough looking beggar along the track," Aaron replied. He stood aside and Joe walked into the light. He looked sickly and tired but shook Jack's hand firmly.

"Evening, Jacky; thanks for all the running about you've been doing for me."

The arrivals entered the house with Dan Kelly a short distance away unseen in the bush guarding the perimeter. The Sherritt brothers were joined by their sister Anne who greeted Joe with a kiss. Anne resembled her brothers closely, her features heavy and broad. Anne was also very much a larrikin like her brothers and her crush on Ned Kelly was common knowledge.

"How's my Neddy?" Anne asked Joe.

"You know Ned. Always got something on the boil," Joe replied.

Everyone took a seat around the dining table and all eyes were on Joe, who sat at the head. He pulled his leather riding gloves off and planted them next to his hat on the table in front of him.

'Now Joe, what was it you wanted to meet us for?' asked Aaron.

'We're getting ready to come back into the open. Ned's got his sights set on robbing a bank in Yackandandah."

"Alright, so do you want us to keep the traps off your tails?" asked Aaron.

"No, that's not why I wanted to meet. You see, he's got this idea about wearing armour so we can just burst in and raid the place. It's foolish. But I have my own ideas."

Aaron and Jack sat forward and gave Joe their undivided attention.

"Firstly, Yackandandah is too dangerous. I reckon we stick up one of the banks in Beechworth so we can head into the Woolshed when we're done. I don't think hitting the bank in the daytime is wise either. There were too many errors at Euroa and Jerilderie. Ned was sloppy and let the people at the business end of his pistol dictate how things played out."

Joe lit his pipe and tobacco smoke coiled in front of his face.

"You remember when the bank at Mount Egerton was stuck up a few years ago?"

The others nodded in the affirmative.

"That's the kind of job I reckon we need to do. Quiet; at night; as few witnesses as possible. We get the manager out of bed and clean out the safe. If he doesn't have the keys, I'll need someone to come with me to find the cove that does. We keep the bankers covered and I take the booty with me. We split up and reconvene at the falls. What do you think?"

Aaron and Jack took a moment to process the information.

"Where do we fit into this?" asked Jack.

"I want you to help me and Dan stick up the bank. I need fellas I can count on."

There was an awkward silence over the room before Aaron spoke out. "It's certainly a tempting offer but I don't know how wise it is for us to start getting in on the bank robbing caper at this stage."

"Can I say something?" said Anne, "Joe, you know that there's a chance that if you turned the others in that you could get a pardon. Wouldn't that make more sense than causing more problems for yourself by robbing more banks?"

"I don't think so. This way we rob the bank like Ned wants, we'll just do it more efficiently than he will. When he sees the result, I have no doubt he'll come around to my way of thinking," replied Joe, "Besides, it would take a real mangy dog to give his mates away when they're wanted for a hanging offence. Wouldn't it?"

When the meeting concluded the Sherritt brothers stated they would consider the plan. Joe left carrying a letter for Ned from Anne and the bottle of whiskey Aaron had brought then headed into the bush where Dan Kelly awaited on horseback.

"How did you go?" asked Dan.

"Just as I expected. I think they understand that we're aware of their indiscretions. We will have to see if they do the right thing," said Joe.

"Do you honestly believe they will?"

"I wouldn't trust Jack with a jar of jam. The lad is a fizgig; no doubt about it. I still have faith in Aaron. After all we've been through together, I just can't bring myself to believe that he would willingly turn on us. Not even for £8000."

They waited in the bush, watching the Sherritt selection. Barely half an hour had passed when they saw Jack Sherritt leave and gallop at breakneck speed towards Beechworth. Shortly after Aaron sauntered out and mounted, riding casually towards his own selection.

"I wouldn't trust Jack with a jar of jam..."

"What do you think of it?" Dan asked.

"I don't care to think of it at all," Joe replied angrily, turning tail and riding deeper into the bush.

The pair rode together to a small clearing where they indulged in the whiskey while Joe read Anne's letter aloud to Dan by the light of a small campfire. It caused much amusement to the pair to discover the lascivious and lustful things that the larrikin Sherritt sister wished to do to Ned. The merriment was no doubt enhanced by draining the whiskey bottle of its contents. Eventually Joe fell asleep, leaving Dan on watch as the sun came up.

***

Aaron, not one to stand idly by when he had an itch to scratch, had once again found romance. This time it was in the form of Ellen Barry, otherwise known as Belle. Belle was a frail fifteen-year-old, thin with equine features and hair the colour of autumn leaves. Though young, she was at a perfectly respectable age for courting and wedding, which was good enough for Aaron, though she had lied and told him she was seventeen. He had never come across someone so smitten with him, and their whirlwind love affair had produced an engagement in only two months.

After a day of doing chores around his selection, Aaron ventured inside his run-down hut where Belle was jabbing a pot of stew that bubbled sloppily in a crock pot. Aaron strode up behind and grabbed her in a big bear hug, lifting her off the ground. Belle squealed in protest and Aaron set her down. On her shirt were two large brown handprints where Aaron had clutched her with dirty hands.

"Aaron," Belle whined, "look what you've done!"

"Oh dear, you'll have you take it off."

Aaron reached out and began unbuttoning her shirt.

"You'd better wash those hands."

Aaron brushed open the shirt and rubbed dirt on Belle's slip.

"Looks like that needs to come off too."

Belle repeated herself with a little giggle, "Aaron, don't! Go wash your hands!"

Aaron smirked and walked to a ceramic basin with cerise blooms painted on it. He dunked his hands in the water and the dirt floated away to join the rest of the muck floating there. He looked over his shoulder at Belle as she disrobed. His eyes lingered on her lily-white skin. Her legs, which stuck out from under a cream-coloured petticoat, were covered in barely perceptible downy blonde hairs. He observed the way her toes twitched on her naked feet when she pulled the slip off over her head. He whipped off his shirt and tugged at his boots. They fell to the ground with a thud. Belle sat down on the bed, the frame creaking even under her slight frame. Her strawberry blonde locks twisted down over her shoulders to her breasts, covering them up. She looked up at Aaron as he approached, naked as the day he was born and impressive to her by every measure – strong and well-proportioned. She wanted to share Aaron's desire, but he was rough and crude in his lovemaking.

Aaron hesitated. He could read Belle's trepidation as if written in bold over her face. He frowned.

"What's wrong?"

"Nothing, it's fine. Come."

"No, something is wrong."

Aaron sat next to Belle; she averted her eyes.

"Why won't you look at me? Is it because of your clothes? I was just larking about, I'm sorry about the mud."

"It's not the mud, it's just..." Belle sighed, "Instead of doing that, I just want you to hold me."

"Hold you?"

"Yes, a cuddle."

Belle touched Aaron's knee. Aaron curled his arms around his wife-to-be. The strength in his arms was reassuring to her. The couple laid down and Belle rested her head on Aaron's chest while he played with her hair. Her mind was abuzz with questions. She knew that he made his money from the police, and she had always avoided the topic of police and bushrangers, but in the moment, feeling comforted as spring rain tickled the roof, she was now game.

"Aaron, I was wondering, if you care so much for Joe Byrne, why do you help the police who are trying to catch him?"

"I don't want him caught. Not really," he stated, "but I made a deal with the traps to save him from the noose, and the longer the gang go without getting caught the harder it will be for me to get the police to hold up their end of the bargain. They already suspect I'm not with them at heart. I guess I'm just delaying the inevitable." Aaron went silent for a moment.

"I miss the old days before the Kellys when it was just the pair of us. Ned Kelly stole Joe away from me. When I saw him the last time, the Joe I grew up with was gone. Ned Kelly has turned him into someone I can't even recognise. The man the police are chasing is not Joe Byrne. Not the real Joe Byrne, at least. I guess I really don't know why I'm still helping the traps anymore. I'll never get Joe back."

Belle looked up into Aaron's face, his jaw was rough with stubble that he was cultivating into a short beard, his eyes were red from lack of sleep. She had never seen such sadness in him as now.

"How do you think your ma will take you marrying a Catholic?" asked Belle, changing the subject.

"Well, I haven't been game to say anything yet, but if her opinion of the Byrnes is anything to go by, I don't expect she'll take it well," said Aaron, "But I'm willing to make that leap for you. Besides, any church that gives out free wine is alright in my book."

"I'm a very lucky girl," Belle smiled.

"Aye, you are," replied Aaron with a smirk. Without warning he rolled on top of Belle, positioning himself between her legs. "I reckon I ought to make you practice your wifely duties."

"Oh, Aaron!" Belle moaned with disappointment, "We were having such a nice moment."

***

The gang continued to maintain a low profile throughout the New Year, though the dynamic was quite changed without Steve Hart in the mix. The reduction in search parties meant that the gang were more able to take their time going from place to place. Joe's brother Paddy also came up with the idea of disguising himself as Joe, even going so far as to get a grey mare of his own to ride as a distraction, enabling Joe to visit Maggie regularly.

Of a Saturday night, Joe descended upon Beechworth from the Woolshed Valley. At the same time Paddy rode in the opposite direction from the Byrne selection. Joe, upon reaching the Vine, sneaked up to Maggie's door and gained admission for a night of passionate fornication before he emerged in the wee hours and took a nap in a haystack on the farm of one of the gang's nearby sympathisers. It was audacious, but it worked.

The general public had become so baffled by the apparent vanishing of the outlaws that rumours started gaining traction that they had left

Australia entirely to settle on a farm in California with Frank Gardiner, the infamous highwayman. Though patently absurd, most people were of the opinion that it made more sense than the police simply being incapable of capturing them, given the amount of money and resources being expended on the pursuit. Yet, despite the fact that Joe demonstrated how easily he could go unmolested by the police for the purposes of carnal adventures, Ned refused to emerge from hiding. Instead, he spent more and more time as a recluse in his cave in the Strathbogie Ranges, plotting his next move, increasingly obsessed with revenge against the police. He still felt a profound anger over his mother's imprisonment, now into its second year, and vowed to release her, though he knew not how. Dan, desperate to help his brother, sought out Tom Lloyd to go and speak sense into him.

Tom arrived at the cave and wandered inside. The smell of burning kerosene from a lamp wafted through the space and there at the end of it was Ned wrapped in a threadbare quilt, dishevelled and writing furiously on a page of foolscap paper.

"Ned," said Tom, "what are you doing there?"

Ned said nothing, merely raising a hand to signify a need for silence as he finished writing his thought. When he was ready, he put his pen down and looked up at his visitor.

"What brings you here, Tom? Is there news?"

"No. I'm here for you. Everyone is worried about you. Why have you been hiding away in here?"

"It's not safe for me out there," said Ned, "Those black devils are out there."

"What black devils?" Tom asked.

"You know the ones, the man-eaters from Queensland. They can

"I'm not a king anymore, Tom. I'm an animal. Wild and hunted."

track me in the dark, don't you know," said Ned. In the dim lamplight he looked half-crazed with his greasy hair a mess, and his eyes purple-ringed. Beneath the quilt Tom could see Ned was dressed only in his underwear, which was starting to yellow with sweat stains, and his elegant concertina boots.

"But they haven't found you, have they?" said Tom, "You're still here; still alive."

"I've been writing," said Ned.

"I can see that."

"Joe won't write my letters anymore so I will do it myself. I just need practice."

Ned handed a foolscap page to Tom. His hands were filthy and covered in ink. Tom held the page to the light, but the handwriting was almost illegible.

"What's it for?" Tom asked.

"That bastard Gill in Jerilderie didn't publish my letter so I'm writing a new one. I'll find a printer and if he doesn't print it as I say I'll put a hole through him and do it myself. Why shouldn't my voice be heard?" Ned rambled.

Tom shot his cousin a worried look. "Come out of the cave with me. Let's get you in the light," he said. Ned viewed his cousin suspiciously but relented. He stood up and ventured out into the sunlight, blinking and straining his eyes against the glare. The pair looked out over the table-lands. Ned, looked like a mad swaggie as he staggered towards the edge. Tom grabbed his shoulder and pulled him back.

"Look at the view, Ned. This is where you should be, King of the Mountain, not hiding in a crack in the rocks like a spider. Where's my cousin gone?"

Ned looked embarrassed as he turned to Tom.

"I'm not a king anymore, Tom. I'm an animal. Wild and hunted."

"Only if you allow yourself to be," said Tom, "only if you let them hunt you."

⁂

It was a blistering hot Boxing Day morning when Aaron Sherritt visited Paddy Allen in Beechworth; clean-shaven and dressed in his Sunday best, including a pair of handsome Wellington boots and a brown velvet jacket. Allen was surprised to see Aaron presenting himself with such grooming but noted the twitchy demeanour and frazzled expression on his face.

"What's the matter Aaron?"

"I need your help Paddy, I'm getting married in a few hours and Belle thinks I'm flush," Aaron said breathlessly.

"Well, aren't you?"

"No, I've got nothing!"

Allen was a kind-hearted enough man, but the pay arrangements he had with the police to cover Aaron's expenses meant that loaning the poor beggar a few quid would not leave him out of pocket. He opened the till and withdrew twenty pounds that Sherritt quickly stuffed into his pocket with thanks.

"I hope this isn't because of gambling. It's a bad business," Allen said with disapproval. Aaron looked weary.

"Every day is a gamble for me."

For the next few hours Aaron walked the streets of Beechworth trying to find shade. For a moment he lingered outside the Burke Museum, named after the ill-fated explorer who once was a local policeman. He remembered how he and Joe would visit here so Joe could devour books and newspapers. Aaron, however, was more interested in the taxidermy display. Something struck a nerve with him while he stared at the scruffy looking animals with their dusty pelts, mangy feathers and black glass eyes, positioned in a crude approximation of life. Joe always told Aaron that something irked him about looking at animals cut down in the prime of life to become some grim display piece. As he stood outside the white building, gleaming in the summer sun, Aaron wished he had Joe with him.

Aaron soon made his way to the presbytery of Father Tierney at St Joseph's. He breathed a sigh of relief as he saw Belle arrive in her best dress. As they made their vows Belle glowed and Aaron thought she was the most beautiful thing he had ever seen. The event was witnessed by a handful of Belle's family members but there were no Sherritts and no friends in attendance. On what should have been his happiest day, Aaron could not stop thinking about what he was missing.

Once the ceremony was completed the paperwork had to be signed. Aaron scrawled his name in his typically laboured handwriting. The priest was paid, and the newlyweds headed to the Hibernian Hotel where the marriage was promptly consummated. Aaron took his time with Belle, treating her with uncharacteristic tenderness. He studied the contours of her tiny body in the amber hue of afternoon light filtering through the curtains. Belle smiled as she watched her husband's muscular body heaving above her, glistening with sweat, and stared into his smiling Irish eyes. The pair were completely in the moment and their worries were far behind. But it was all too brief. When the throes of passion reached their climax, Aaron finished with a groan and collapsed onto the bed, sprawled on his back, and napped until dusk with Belle curled into him stroking his chest.

***

Aaron awoke in the evening, Belle still curled up next to him, snoring gently. He rolled around to admire her and kissed her crown. As he got up cautiously, trying not to wake his bride, his mind wandered to his mother's disapproval of his marriage.

"I can't believe you would desert this family for that papist whore!" she had screamed and ranted. His father had uttered no word to him at all, rather choosing to avoid him altogether as if he were some vexing aberration to be dismissed. At times it felt as if he couldn't tell who hated him more: the Byrnes, the sympathisers, the police or his own family. Aaron was aware that his brother Jack was nearby winning prizes on the racetrack but knew better than to show his face there and risk making a scene.

Aaron found himself in a dark state of mind and with no healthy outlet for it. His thoughts fixated on his dire financial situation. He had recently sold off his old selection after months of Belle nagging him about being closer to her family. He missed the place, though it was full of painful memories. After the honeymoon the couple were to move in with Belle's mother and siblings, but Aaron had eyed off an abandoned miner's hut in Eldorado at a bend in the road known as The Devil's Elbow. It wasn't much but it was a fresh start. Aaron had a new life to look forward to, if not for the fact that his funds were fleeting like the last rains before a drought. Aaron's desperation led him to gamble the little cash he could muster after his expenses were seen to in the hopes of striking it big, but so far, his luck had all but vanished along with his cash. Unfortunately for Belle, these were burdens that she now also had to bear, and it would only get worse.

***

In early January a "hurdy gurdy" had been brought to Beechworth and was attracting large crowds. Children giggled with delight as they rode around and around the carousel. Young lovers and old couples held hands and sat on their wooden steeds, spinning to the reedy tunes played by the accordionist.

It was here that Aaron and Belle ventured in the afternoon with her family. In the crowd, Aaron could see his brother Jack, unmistakable with his floppy hat and chequered tweed outfit. Nearby he spied Paddy Byrne, much taller than Jack and more solidly built, dressed in the same dandy clothing favoured by Joe.

Aaron kept his distance and stood up onto the carousel with Belle. They headed for a pair of black wooden horses. The ride began, slowly and creaking at first then off and running. As he circled around, Aaron tried to keep track of his brother and Paddy in the crowd. After the second circuit he could see Paddy, but Jack had disappeared. Aaron pursed his lips and tried to put it out of his mind.

As everyone arrived at the Barry homestead that night, Aaron saw the back door had been forced open. He told Belle to be quiet and stay outside with her mother and the children while he checked it out. Grabbing the axe from the woodpile, Aaron stepped into the house quietly and saw the place in disarray. There was nobody in the house, but Aaron did notice a number of items missing, specifically the new side saddle he had gifted Belle mere days earlier. He had taken out a loan for the thing and the saddler had been breathing down his neck about the debt, could he have been the one? As he moved through the building, he noticed a blue silk necktie on the floor. He picked it up and noticed the initials MW embroidered on it. Aaron knew at once who was responsible.

***

The following day Aaron took off on horseback to the Sherritt selection on Sheepstation Creek.

The sound of hooves roused Jack Sherritt who was in the stockyard. He peered down the road and recognised his brother. He ran to the paddock where he mounted his horse and bolted, riding bareback. Aaron gave chase, riding like a madman into the bush after Jack.

"Come here you little bastard!" Aaron screamed as he gained on Jack. As he came up alongside, he grabbed his brother and yanked him off the horse, causing him to land heavily in the dirt. Aaron dismounted and allowed his own horse to gallop off. He stalked back to where Jack was trying to get up.

"What are you doing, you lunatic?" Jack barked.

"I know it was you who robbed us, you maggot!"

"What?"

"You left your tie on the way out," Aaron presented the monogrammed tie in a clenched fist. It had been gifted to Jack by Detective Ward.

"You turned your back on us for that Catholic whore. You deserve to rot as far as I'm concerned," Jack growled, spitting at Aaron's feet.

Aaron swung his arm at Jack and knocked him off balance. The pair exchanged blows viciously until Aaron got his hands on the shaft of a dead sapling and yanked it out of the ground. He swung the plant like a quarterstaff and shattered it on Jack's head, knocking him to the ground.

Jack was unresponsive and bleeding heavily from the head. Aaron went white. He ran to where his horse was wandering around the scrub and vaulted into the saddle. With a haunted expression he spurred on to Beechworth.

Aaron's first stop was Paddy Allen's store. He needed to see a friendly face and the bottom of a glass of whiskey before making his next move.

"What's the matter with you?" Paddy asked.

"I'm after murdering Jack," Aaron replied, "I've come to see Ward and give myself up."

Paddy Allen wore a look of confused concern, "You fool, you should be clearing out over the border," he said. Aaron simply stood, shaking. Allen poured a tumbler of whiskey and placed it in Aaron's hand, which was covered in blood from where the splintered wood had cut him. He drained the booze in one motion. Allen guided Aaron to a seat and got him another drink.

At that moment the door swung open and, in the doorway, stood Jack Sherritt, white as death and covered in blood. He stumbled to Aaron and grabbed his shoulder.

"You bloody wretch; you thought you'd murdered me!"

"Well," Paddy Allen said with a stunned chuckle, "looks like you both could use a drink."

That afternoon the liquor flowed until the brothers had become amicable. Jack's head was stitched up and by the time the shop closed they were both staggering out arm in arm. The peace lasted until the booze wore off.

***

By moonlight two thirds of the Kelly Gang resumed their travels together. Ned rode up front with Tom Lloyd, Dan behind with Joe Byrne, headed for the Warby Ranges. Ned winced and sat awkwardly in the saddle, his lower back was still afflicted with searing pain with every bump from the ride and he had lost a lot of weight. The outlaws looked far more bedraggled than usual; hair long and lank, clothes filthy, facial hair ungroomed. As they reached the foothills Ned turned wearily to Tom.

"I think this is going to be the last time we head into these ranges. My body isn't keeping up like it was."

Tom nodded, "I'll organise some tents for you so that you can camp in the lowlands from now on," he said.

"Can't say I'll miss sleeping in a crack in the side of a rock," Joe quipped.

As the gang rode up through the scrub, their escort waited behind to see them off. Nearby a territorial possum began to hiss and growl. As soon as the outlaws were out of sight Tom turned and rode back to Maggie Skillion.

The gang continued on through the gully towards the Warby Falls. Huge lumps of granite dotted the landscape where spindly cypress-pines jutted out of the ground like the shafts of great spears and smooth ghost gums forked like lightning. High above them Halley's Comet streaked across the sky, its white tail streaming away into the eternal blackness of space. The horses began to tire as they continued the climb to the falls, but soon enough the gang heard the gushing of water and found a rock face with water cascading down it into a small pool and out into a creek. They allowed their horses to drink while they rested nearby. Joe dug into his saddlebags and withdrew a bottle of whiskey, which he offered around. Ned refused while Dan drank eagerly.

"Is your back still giving you grief?" Joe asked Ned.

"Aye, I'll be fine."

"Here, take some of my medicine. It'll perform marvels," said Joe producing a bottle of laudanum tincture from his coat pocket. In the moonlight the label was impossible to read.

"How am I supposed to know how much to take?" Ned grumbled.

"I don't know, I just drink enough from the bottle to coat my tongue. Five minutes, and the pain just fades away like a summer cloud."

In too much discomfort to turn down the potential for relief, Ned pulled the cork from the tincture bottle and allowed the liquid to coat his tongue. It was bitter and burned as he swallowed it. He cringed, but as Joe had said it was barely five minutes before Ned found himself completely relaxed and pain free. He sat against a sapling and within a few moments he was out cold.

In his head, Ned drifted through wild imaginings of trains flying off their tracks in a shower of sparks and hundreds of bursts of gunfire. Halley's Comet tore across his vision with a roar like the crash of ocean waves. He saw Superintendent Hare on the ground with a hole in his eye just like Lonigan at Stringybark Creek. In his hands were a key and an open lock. Ned felt incredible weight on his shoulders and a crackling of energy in his limbs. The voice of his mother singing hymns and the mewling of infants echoed through a purple mist. Then Ned felt himself sucked through a hole in the ground and out into space, whereupon he snapped wide awake, soaking wet. He looked up at Dan holding his billycock hat, which was soaked through and dripping. The teen's eyes were wide with panic.

"What..." was all Ned could manage.

"Thought we'd lost you there," Joe called out from where the horses were hobbled by the water.

Ned staggered to his feet; Dan supported him. He stumbled across to Joe and grabbed his shoulder.

"What is that stuff?" he growled.

"Gone is what it is; you cleaned me out last night!"

Ned's face softened and he noticed it was dawn. His face then screwed up as he suddenly lurched and emptied the contents of his stomach onto the ground. As he stood, doubled over, the images from his dreaming lingered in his mind and he began to fixate on them not as mere figments of his mind, but visions of a future he was destined to make manifest.

***

Dan and Joe set off on horseback to keep tabs on the sympathisers, leaving Ned to make amends with Steve Hart. Under cover of darkness, he rode Mirth to Wangaratta and on to the Hart house. It was a respectable looking farm with a humble, yet handsome, homestead, barn and stables. The space between the buildings was littered with vehicles and tools and a big fig tree grew behind the homestead.

As Ned entered the selection, he was greeted by Ettie who had gone outside to empty a teapot that had gone cold. She met Ned with a warm embrace.

"What brings you here tonight? I had no idea you were coming. Where have you been?"

"I have some business to take care of with your brother," Ned replied.

"How foolish of me to assume you were here to see me," Ettie pouted.

"Don't be like that."

"Oh," Ettie said, "and how am I supposed to be? I haven't seen you in months and nobody would tell me anything. Do you have any idea how that makes me feel?"

"I'm an outlaw, Esther. I can't just visit you like I'm courting anymore. Me even being here puts you in danger," said Ned. He patted Mirth's neck and gazed at the ground.

"Seems to me that you were perfectly able to visit when you liked until you got what you wanted from me. Being an outlaw is no excuse for keeping me in the dark. Why couldn't you have at least sent one of your sisters or Tom Lloyd to see me and let me know what was happening? I know you had a falling out with Steve but that's not fair on me. I thought you loved me," said Ettie.

"You know I'm not like that. I do love you," Ned replied, "I'm sorry I upset you."

Ettie gently placed a hand on Ned's arm. He turned and she wrapped her arms tightly around his neck. Her tears rubbed into Ned's beard as she kissed him passionately. Slowly she came up for air. For the first time she could see the weathering and tiredness on Ned's face. It was as if he had aged ten years in a matter of months.

"I will always do what I can to make sure it's safe for you to see me, Ned. You know that. Please don't leave me in the dark again. I couldn't bear it."

Later, Ned and Steve walked through the selection smoking pipes. Steve had by now attempted to disguise himself by growing his beard out as much as possible and exchanging his dandy clothing for earthy-coloured labourer's garb, the sole exception being his blood red necker-chief. Despite the length of his beard, it was still wispy and patchy, but it created enough confusion about his identity for Steve to ride unrecog-nised once again. Even those who knew the family had mistaken him for his brother Dick. Unlike Ned, who strode confidently, Steve was plagued with a limp, the result of a horse-riding accident years earlier. The leg often ached, but otherwise he was in much better health than when he had been camping out with the rest of the gang in the mountains. He refused to look at Ned and hobbled ahead of him.

"What is it you want from me now? Breaking my bloody nose not enough?"

"I came to apologise," Ned replied, "you didn't deserve that."

"You're damned right, I didn't."

Steve shoved his hands into his pockets and scowled into the darkness. Steve's refusal to look at Ned irritated him.

"Look, I'm sorry I hit you. But you know that if I really wanted to peg you out, I could have easily done it. You were out of line."

"I was not. You just can't handle it when someone points out when you're wrong," said Steve.

Ned's lips tightened.

"See here, I want you to come back to me and the boys. I've got something big cooking up and you were right, you're in it as much as we are, so you need to be there with us when it goes ahead."

Steve stayed quiet and pondered. The wind kicked up and caused his neckerchief to flutter wildly in his face.

"What have you got cooking?"

"We're going to give the traps and the toffs something to talk about. Not just a bank robbery. Trust me, it'll be one for the history books. The others are all in; will you join us?"

Steve turned to face Ned. "Alright," he said, "I'll come."

***

The gang returned once more to the safety of the ranges, but rather than climbing into the mountains they set up camp nestled in among great hunks of smooth granite and a smattering of mangy looking trees in the foothills. Once the camp was established, Dan and Steve went on sentry as Ned and Joe sat by the fire.

"I know what we have to do now, Joe," Ned said, "We need a train."

"A train?"

"Yes; in a train, in our armour, we'll be unstoppable rushing up and down the line robbing every bank from Beechworth to Melbourne."

Joe stared at Ned with utter confusion, "How do you expect to get a train?"

"We'll lure the mud-crushers out on a special train from Benalla," Ned began, "trap them on the tracks and steal the thing right from under them. Then we can take the barracks in Benalla to use as our own base of operations. From there we strike all the banks in the area to get the funds to distribute among the sympathisers. Standish won't know what hit him and he will have no choice but to withdraw the men from the district."

"The traps won't go without a fight and a bloody iron jacket won't be enough protection against a train full of police," said Joe.

"The armour will protect us, but we need to make some adjustments," Ned said. He stared into the fire and began to imagine a mighty armoured warrior emerging from the flames sending his enemies fleeing like mice. A tall cylindrical helmet, a flowing white cape and a voice like rolling thunder, just like a mediaeval crusader. He looked back up to Joe.

"Do you recall the comet we saw?" Ned asked.

"Halley's comet, yes. What of it?"

"Did you know that in days past people said that a comet was a sign from the heavens that war was imminent?"

"What are you talking about?" Joe scoffed.

"That comet was right over us when I had those visions. Don't you understand - It was a sign!"

Joe rolled his eyes and folded his arms. His patience with Ned was wearing thin.

"All this time the police have hunted us down like wolves; cut us off from our supporters; bullied our families and made it a crime to have known us. They locked up men for months without charge while their crops died in the field and their women and children starved, all in the hope of getting at us. These are not the acts of men protecting society, these are acts of war. They're pushing us to retaliate so now we'll show them how we fight a war. We're going to make them regret the day they ever crossed paths with the Kellys," Ned stood and paced around the fire, "The comet - the visions – they were telling me that this is the path I must go down. The police are my natural enemies. They chose to bully and persecute those I care for. Now they'll reap what they've sown."

Joe interlocked his fingers and sat forward, resting his elbows on his knees.

"Where will this all take place?"

"I have an idea," said Ned, "but I just need to be sure."

***

Between Benalla and Wangaratta on the train line, the tiny township of Glenrowan was little more than a small cluster of buildings built along the train tracks. It was the sort of place that one merely passed through en route to other places. The most successful things in Glenrowan were the two pubs: McDonnell's Railway Tavern on one side and The Glenrowan Inn on the other.

The Glenrowan Inn was owned and operated by Ann Jones, a resilient and cunning hotelier from Tipperary. She had procured the block upon which the inn stood in 1874, but had to wait until 1878, when the colony was abuzz with the news of the Kellys having robbed the bank in Euroa, to procure a licence to operate a hotel. Up to the time that she was able to move into the inn, she ran tea rooms in Wangaratta South.

Her husband Owen and eldest son Thomas were off in Gippsland constructing railroads and sent money regularly to supplement the modest takings from the inn. Ann lived with her daughter Jane and her boys Johnny, Owen, Jeremiah and Heddington. The children all worked in the pub and entertained guests, making it much more affordable for Ann who didn't have to spend money hiring staff.

On a mild day in early April of 1880, Ettie Hart rode into Glenrowan from the Hart selection on Deep Creek and headed to Ann Jones' inn. The Harts knew Glenrowan well and Ettie had suggested it could be the ideal place to attack a police train.

Riding along the railway line, the road punctuated with telegraph poles, she followed the curve of the track as it ran along a steep embankment and then sloped down to a fork in the rails and a crossing where the train station was situated. Ettie was on a mission to test the sympathies of Ann Jones. While the rival hoteliers, the McDonnells, were openly sympathetic to the gang, Jones was an unknown quantity as she was seen to serve police and sympathisers alike. To Ann Jones, money was the same colour regardless of who was paying with it. As she passed the train station, Ettie rode through the gates at the crossing and past the stationmaster's house towards Mount Morgan, which loomed over the town. On her immediate right she saw the inn with its whitewashed weatherboard exterior book-ended by chimneys.

Putting her mare in the paddock at the rear of the building where a detached stable stood, Ettie made mental notes about the facilities as she moved through the grounds - the stables; the skillion where the food was prepared; the inn itself.

Walking around to the front of the inn and entering the bar room, she was soon aware of the diminutive figure of Ann Jones behind the bar dressed in black. A wiry woman with pale complexion, frizzy auburn hair and a permanent look of tiredness from various ailments, she pushed through her discomfort and greeted the newcomer jovially with her Tipperary brogue.

"Oh, Miss Hart, it's been such a long time since I've seen ye!"

The Harts and Joneses had lived in the same district for years and the Harts had frequented Ann's tea rooms before the ailing business finally went belly-up thanks to Owen's gambling and wildly spiralling debts.

"Good afternoon, Mrs. Jones; how are you keeping?" Ettie chimed.

"Oh, ye know how it is, the neuralgia has been playing up again and all that, but I mustn't complain. How is it with yer folks?" said Ann as she polished the counter, her voice soft and musical. The conversation continued to hover around small talk for some time, each trying to get a read on the other, until Ann felt comfortable enough to raise the issue of the outlaws.

"And how is it with yer brother? I can't imagine yer ma is taking it too well."

"Ma took it pretty hard. The police don't seem too bothered to molest us the way they have the Kellys and Byrnes, thank goodness, though Sergeant Steele pokes his nose around from time to time. It's terribly hard on Ma and Da, but Steve's safe enough."

Ettie was careful not to give much away. She watched Ann's body language carefully. Suddenly the hotelier reached across the counter and clasped Ettie's hand.

"Steve was always such a good boy; I couldn't believe it when I heard. I'm so sorry about what ye've been through. I've had issues of my own with the bloody troopers, if you'll pardon my language, so I can only imagine what pushed Steve to take up bushranging with the Kelly boys."

"Thank you, Mrs. Jones. I was wondering if there was a chance that I might be able to stay in one of your rooms for a few days."

"Oh, of course! I'm sure Janie will love having ye around. She gets ever so lonely these days after our Annie passed," Ann sighed. Just after the inn had opened for business, her sixteen-year-old had been crushed under a falling tree. The incident had almost forced her to shut up shop but, as was typical of the frontier women of Australia, she grieved for a time and got on with life because there were mouths to feed.

By that afternoon Ettie had a detailed map in her mind of what she believed would be the perfect base of operations for Ned Kelly's masterplan.

***

In the Kelly homestead, there was a small gathering of the Kelly Gang and their inner circle of sympathisers. The assemblage sat around the dining table – the outlaws, Tom Lloyd, Wild Wright, Dick and Ettie Hart, Kate Lloyd, Paddy Byrne, Kate Kelly and Maggie Skillion. Unfurled on the table was a sheet of paper with a crude map drawn on it in charcoal showing the approximate layout of Glenrowan based on Ettie's descriptions. Ned held court while the others listened carefully as he explained his new plan, which he had continued to spice up as it simmered in his mind.

"If we can lure the traps from Benalla to Beechworth by train they have to pass through Glenrowan. If we make ourselves known on Saturday night, they'll head out on Sunday morning. No civilian trains run on a Sunday, so we won't run the risk of unintended victims, only police. When Hare attempts to pick up our trail, you can be damn sure O'Connor and those black devils of his will be with him."

Ned took a breath and continued, "They won't want to lose time, so they'll be going full speed with no stops. Just past the Glenrowan station the track goes up an embankment and curves. If we break the line there, they won't stand a chance. They must stop the train before the break if they want to survive, in which case we can take it from them by coercion or by force. If they keep going it makes no difference, the train will take the troopers straight to Hell - Hare, O'Connor, the whole bloody lot. If we can capture any of the leaders alive, we can use them as hostages. We offer their release in exchange for our mother and any other innocent people they've lagged on our account. If not, at the least we've crippled the police forces and we can proceed unmolested."

The room remained quiet. The ruthlessness of this bonkers plot surpassed anything Ned had ever planned in the past. While he was prone to hyperbole about torturing and slaughtering his enemies, everyone in that room had dismissed it as colourful, but hollow, rhetoric. But given the recent decline in his mental state, nobody was certain how far Ned was willing to go anymore. Ned took no notice of the worried expressions.

"I'm going to send Joe and Dan to make some noise in Beechworth to lure the train. I haven't decided on how yet. Meanwhile, Steve and I will arrive at Glenrowan and tear up the tracks."

Ned placed his hands on his hips and shifted his weight.

"Tom, you'll wait at McDonnell's with Wild and Dick. Once we're finished, you'll all come down and gather every gun you can find in the train. We can divvy them up among the sympathisers who will accompany us to Benalla, where we will rob the bank and take possession of the police barracks. We'll get skyrockets to signal that we've been victorious."

The room sat in astonished silence until Dick Hart spoke up, his face grim. He was a slightly taller, more robust looking version of his brother, with a neat beard and a thin moustache.

"We do this, Ned, and the whole empire will come after us with everything they have. Not just police, but redcoats too. What you're proposing is surely treason."

"No. It's war," Ned said. He rested the weight of his body on his knuckles as he leaned over the table, "We can't hide forever. Sooner or later, they will catch up to us, and they've come close a few times. When they do, there will be no mercy for us, so I say we strike first and strike hardest. We cripple their forces, and we take the land for the common people, away from English law."

"How will ye do it without getting shot to pieces?" asked Wild Wright.

"With this..." Ned said.

Ned and Tom strode to the end of the room and whipped back a canvas tarpaulin under which was a suit of crudely made iron armour.

The group crowded in to get a look at the bizarre collection of curved steel plates, strapped, bolted and riveted together. Ned proceeded to don the armour, assisted by Tom, with much grunting and effort.

He stood with arms outstretched and turned slowly giving everyone a chance to get a good look at the prototype suit: a breastplate; back plate; a curved plate on both biceps; a semicircular piece over the groin, suspended from the bottom edge of the breastplate by cords on the left and right corners; and a small, squared piece over the buttocks, attached to the bottom of the backplate with a single leather thong in the centre.

Ned gestured for Tom to hand him the helmet, a steel cylinder with a faceplate that formed a narrow slit to see out of. Around the top of the helmet a series of double holes had been punched with cords looped through them to create a cross shape. These cords rested on his scalp to stop the helmet from resting on his shoulders, which would make the eye slit improperly positioned. The faceplate extended over his collarbone, protecting his throat and keeping the helmet facing forward.

In his armour, Ned presented a strange vision indeed - a bushman's parody of a Templar knight.

"With this the traps can't hurt us; we can get close to them without fear of being killed," said Ned, his voice muffled and metallic inside the helmet. The crowd all looked at each other, as if to verify whether they were all seeing the same thing.

"I'm in," said Wild as he slammed his fist on the table.

Everyone in the room expressed their approval except for Joe who calmly tipped the ashes out of his pipe into his hand and threw them into the fireplace. He cleared his throat.

"This'll bring us to grief; but a short life and a jolly one, I suppose?"

*

That night, Joe Byrne made his way to the Vine Hotel. He stood outside Maggie's door and made a bird call. The door was opened, and Maggie dragged Joe inside. It didn't take long for the lovemaking to commence, as was usual, but this time there was some extra spark that invigorated them more than was typical.

The pair ravenously whipped each other's clothes off and Joe pressed Maggie backwards onto the bed. He took a moment to appreciate the view of her pale skin and round features. Her mousy hair was inclined to curl into wispy ringlets that sprawled over her pillow, and she glided her delicate, red-knuckled fingers gently over her soft belly to the tangle of brown hairs where Joe was teasing her with his manhood.

She was certainly not the sort of woman one would imagine working the land on a dusty acreage or having a brood of rowdy children stomping about the place. She was far too delicate to the untrained eye, but the scars she kept hidden on her flesh hinted at a resilience and a troubled past that made her the perfect partner for an outlaw.

"Come along my sweet birdie, I've been waiting all week," Maggie giggled.

"Now, now, when you only get a good meal once in a while you learn to savour it," Joe said with a sly grin as he moved his head down between Maggie's thighs, "You have to go slowly so you can really enjoy it all."

"Well, don't take too long. I'm hungry too," Maggie said, running her fingers through Joe's coppery hair and pressing his face into her mount.

Joe devoured her like a starving wolf, the sensation caused the maid to buck and gyrate wildly. Joe savoured the flavours and textures and his nostrils filled with the scent of her skin. In that moment he desired to have her be a part of him, to meld with him so that he would never have to be alone again. The more he ached to be one with her, the more passionately he indulged her flesh.

Outside her room she would have been heard moaning Joe's name as she climaxed, had anyone been there at the time to hear it.

Joe climbed up between Maggie's knees and slid himself into her with a deep moan, doubling over her. His skin ached deliciously as her warmth filled him with relief. He inhaled deeply and tried to force the anxieties of the past weeks and months out of his mind as he began to buck like a brumby trying to shake off a saddle, Maggie gripping on for dear life. Joe was wild with passion and bit Maggie's neck just hard enough to cause a conspicuous blemish. His chest hairs chafed against Maggie's breasts with each thrust. There was a desperation to his movements that Maggie had never experienced before that almost frightened her. The lovemaking was noisy and chaotic, and Joe came with a roar, his pelvis grinding into Maggie's as the explosion of pleasure overwhelmed him. It left both participants panting and glistening, and the tiny room smelling of sex and accomplishment. Joe lingered in place and buried his face in Maggie's shoulder.

The pair lay in the afterglow of their long-awaited release and Joe took Maggie's hand. He looked deep into her eyes, breathless.

"My sweetheart," Joe began softly, "I have something I have to tell you; I want to marry you."

Maggie's mouth dropped open in shock. "Joe," she gasped.

"I know it seems queer coming from me of all people, and I can't offer you much of anything right now, but we've got something big coming soon. After that, I reckon, we'll have a chance to really make a go of it - if you'll have me. I'm tired of this outlaw life and I need someone to start over with."

Maggie nodded wordlessly, a huge grin on her face, her eyes glossy. Joe got up, weak-kneed from his exercise, and rummaged through his topcoat until he found a small prayer book. He opened it, and on the title page was a short message in infantile lettering. It was the laboured handwriting of a determined but mostly illiterate person, preserved in pencil. It read:

To deer Joseph, GOD bless mar.

It was a rare display of affection towards Joe from his mother. Joe flipped the page, revealing that the actual pages had been torn out and replaced with scraps of paper and letterhead from his adventures, all scribbled upon by the bushranger himself. This was his journal, his secret history. He flicked through the pages, selecting a bunch and then handed them to Maggie.

"What's this?" Maggie asked.

"This is the history of you and me up until now. It's my gift to you."

"That's sweet. I'm sure it will be very lovely when I learn how to read!"

Maggie laughed a deep belly laugh. Joe smirked and hid the prayer book back in his coat.

"Oh, Joe, take this," Maggie pulled the ring from her finger; a silver band with a small diamond set in it; a relic from her tragic past. She placed it in Joe's palm. Joe kissed the token and attempted to slide it on his own finger, but the ring barely went past the first knuckle.

"I'm a bit big for it," Joe chuckled.

***

Outside the room, nocturnal creatures flapped, cawed and scurried about in the pre-dawn. Joe looked through a gap in the curtains of Maggie's window and knew he would soon have to leave.

Maggie lay asleep behind him as he sat at her dresser with an ink-well, a pen and several scraps of paper; one of which was an old flyer for Ashton's circus that he had picked up on a visit to McDonnell's Railway Tavern in Glenrowan. He began to write by candlelight:

Proposed to my sweetheart. I have promised her a future with me that I hope I can fullfil. I shall carry the ring she gave me always to remind me of the future that awaits me when Neddie's plan is successful. He has never shown such determination before. He assures me that if he is the general I am his leftenent in all this. I have never thought myself a military man before. I do not care for conquest but I think General Joe Byrne sounds much better than leftenent. If I could live a thousand summers with Maggie drinking her sweet necter I would be a happy man. She reminds me of what happyness is in these dark days.

Joe looked back over his shoulder at his betrothed. He felt complicated emotions that he had only ever experienced once before when he gazed upon her. He considered even one night's passionate embrace from this simple girl from Cornwall worth him risking his life for, though he began to question if it was love or some reckless drive to live life as much as he could before it was snuffed out that filled his thoughts with such sentiment. Though he was a lapsed Catholic, Joe prayed that Ned's plan worked so that he could pursue the life he desperately dreamed about with Maggie.

***

Throughout April and May of 1880, farmers around Northeast Victoria awakened to begin the day's toil only to discover their ploughs inoperable due to the absence of the big, curved plates that turned the furrow for planting seeds. Soon reports were flowing into the police from all over the region but the only clues as to the identity of the offenders were the presence of footprints from a man with peculiarly small feet. These were the prints left behind by a narrow boot with a "larrikin heel" as favoured by the Kellys.

George Culph, Pat Delaney and Tom Straughair, however, knew

exactly what was happening. As more iron went missing the more the blacksmiths went on mysterious trips to the bush. They were, in fact, employed forging the stolen steel into pieces of armour; each tailored to the design requests of the gang member who planned to wear them. Joe had proved to be a fly in the ointment, complaining about the level of protection the armour offered and the way the apron piece inhibited the wearer from mounting a horse.

While the blacksmiths toiled on parts for Dan and Joe in their workshops, the gang themselves were utilising techniques they had been shown and created armour for Steve from whatever steel remained after giving the best bits to the smithies. Rather than risk the loud clang that shaping the armour around an anvil would make, they half-submerged a green log in a creek, peeled the dry outer layers of bark and used this to shape parts of Hart's armour from a mix of mouldboards and sheet iron from Culph's shop. It was much harder work than if they were utilising the appropriate tools and facilities, but the gang were not immune to hard labour, as their prison records would attest. Ned maintained that the armour would make the gang invincible, bragging about how if Ben Hall had been so clever, he would still be menacing the roads.

After months of toil, the completed pieces of body armour were slid into large leather saddlebags and kept hidden in a special stable Patsy Byrne had recently completed at his mother's selection for storing his grey horse during the day. The helmets, being too bulky for the saddlebags, were kept in flour sacks and buried under the piles of hay that the horse grazed on. Here they would remain until they were needed by the gang.

***

Steve rode out of the Warby Ranges to his family selection and was in the stables when Dick joined him, clapping a hand firmly on Steve's shoulder.

"It's good to see you, brother," said Dick.

The siblings went inside and took a seat at the dining table where their younger sisters were practicing their stitching on scrap fabric.

"That's a mighty small quilt," said Steve to his sister Rachel. She looked up at him and giggled.

"Girls, can I have a moment with Stevey alone please?" said Dick. The girls scampered away leaving the brothers to talk. Dick turned to Steve with a grave expression.

"This plan of Ned's has me worried. If it goes wrong, it will go badly for all of us."

Steve nodded.

"I've organised two passes for a steamer to take you over the border. They're under an alias. If things go bad, you are to take Ettie and get her out of the colony. If they find out her involvement in this, I hate to think what they'll do," said Dick.

"Ned's plans have always worked before," said Steve.

"Not at Stringybark Creek it didn't. Euroa and Jerilderie worked because of the effort you, Dan and Joe put in to make them work. He's had Ettie running around like a chicken with its head cut off trying to curry favour with Mrs. Jones and he's had you lads up in the bush putting bloody armour together; but the plot is all his, isn't it?" said Dick.

"I don't think he trusts Danny and me to be involved," Steve replied with a sigh of frustration.

"It scares me," Dick confided, "The risks are immense and it's my responsibility to keep our mob safe. Promise me you'll follow my plan if things go bad."

"Alright, but we need to keep this quiet. I don't want another thrashing," said Steve.

"Nobody needs to know for now except the two of us," Dick replied.

***

At the end of May, Nicolson received word from Anne Sherritt that Joe Byrne had been spotted leaving his mother's place near Sebastopol. She went further and conveyed that Aaron desired to meet them at the Beechworth police station. The entire region was awash with heavy rains but once the rain had cleared somewhat, Nicolson, Sadleir, and O'Connor proceeded to Beechworth. Aaron stood under the cover of the police station's veranda as the men arrived. He was dressed in a borrowed hat and a greatcoat with the collar popped.

"Good day, Aaron," Nicolson said with his distinctive Scottish burr. Aaron offered a weak nod in reply. "I have it on good authority that you spotted Joe Byrne in the Woolshed. Will you take us there so we can pick up the trail?"

"Mr. Nicolson, if I take you there and I'm recognised I'm as good as worm food. The tracks go straight past the Byrne selection out in the open. The gang has eyes and ears everywhere around there and if they see you following those tracks, they will know it was me that told you, and the outlaws will murder me and my family in retribution."

"Well, what do you intend for us to do with your information if not follow the tracks?" snapped O'Connor.

"Look, I only wanted to let you know what I saw, but I also know you lot wouldn't know the meaning of discretion if it bit you on the arse. The sympathisers have a down on me and they will take any opportunity to set the outlaws upon me. I suggest you be careful how you go, but you do with the information what you will. Just know that if I or any of my connections are killed because of your blundering about in broad daylight it's on your head," said Aaron before he stormed off to find his horse.

The three heads of the hunt went inside. Nicolson was anxious to go out as he was due to be relieved of the case by Standish, and asked Sadleir, O'Connor, Senior-Constable Mullane, and Detective Ward if it could be justifiable to risk the lives of informers by following up on such a lead. The subsequent decision was made to wait until the rain had cleared then follow up on the tip. That afternoon Nicolson and O'Connor searched for the tracks but found that anything of use had long washed away in the deluge.

For the next few days Nicolson remained stationed in Beechworth to receive information from the network of spies he relied on so heavily, believing that if one outlaw had been spotted in the area then the rest of the gang must be nearby. On the last day of his stay in the town Jack Sherritt arrived, breathless from a hard ride, declaring that Joe Byrne was up in a gully a mile from his mother's selection. The police headed out straight away, meeting with Aaron who guided them surreptitiously through the area until they reached the exact place where Joe had allegedly been seen. The tracks were identified and followed from one side of the gully to the other, leading down to the Byrne selection. O'Connor and his trackers followed the tracks, noting that it appeared whoever had made them had been shifting cattle. As they came closer and closer to the selection, Aaron tipped his hat low over his face but saw the man in question herding cattle into the Byrne stockyard.

"That bugger, Jack, has done a mischief upon us. It's not Joe Byrne at all, but his brother Patsy," said Aaron.

Defeated, the party returned to headquarters, leaving Aaron to return home in his own time. Nicolson spent that evening in Benalla lamenting that despite his determination to show up Standish and Hare, he had failed to make substantial progress in the hunt.

***

The following day, Superintendent Hare resumed control of the hunt for the Kelly Gang. Captain Standish had tried everything in his power to get him back in the saddle as soon as possible, though Hare had initially refused to return. The investigation he inherited was a mess. It seemed as if Nicolson had tried to undo all the work that Hare had already done prior, and to sabotage the efforts of whoever superseded him. On top of this, there were scores of unpaid police spies all nipping at Hare's heels and refusing to cooperate until they were paid.

Hare had barely settled into his office when he was met by one of Nicolson's top spies, Daniel Kennedy. Kennedy was a former Greta school teacher with a huge grey beard, round cheeks and sparkling eyes. Kennedy had been operating under the moniker "The Diseased Stock Agent"; the so-called "diseased stock" was, of course, the outlaws. On this day Kennedy had intended to give Nicolson an update on the gang's activities, including the so-called "jackets" the gang had been building, but found Hare in his place.

"Jackets?"

"Yes, they are trying to make themselves bulletproof. I know the four outlaws each have one but there's stories doing the rounds that some of the sympathisers are making them too. They don't want to get shot by the guards when they try to rob a bank," Kennedy said. Hare sighed and wrote out a cheque for payment for Kennedy's services.

"I wish you all the best Mr. Kennedy, but I shan't be requiring your services any further," Hare said as he handed the cheque over and sniffled.

"Sir?"

"I'm sure Assistant Commissioner Nicolson was spellbound by your ridiculous tales of outlaws in shining armour, but I have a job to perform and that requires useful information. I've had my fill of false reports, Mr. Kennedy, and I do not desire to waste any more of my precious time chasing dragons or goblins or whatever other nonsense you dream up. Thank you very much."

Kennedy stood, mouth agape, stunned by the outburst, but tucked the cheque into his jacket and left the office. Hare rubbed his temples and gave an exasperated sigh as he reached for a brandy decanter to pour himself a drink. He turned to Sadleir.

"If this is the sort of poppycock Nicolson has been dealing with, it is no wonder you haven't made progress."

✳✳✳

The first of June was Dan Kelly's birthday, and he made his way down from the ranges to Greta to visit Kate who had made a cake for the occasion. As was usual, the younger children were in bed when Dan arrived due to the late hour, so it was just he and Kate sitting at the dining table eating. The cake was dry but sweet and a welcome change from the salted meats and charred lumps of damper that his diet usually consisted of.

After the food Dan was treated to a hot bath and a haircut by lamplight. Dan scrubbed dirt out of his skin as Kate set about trimming his black locks with shears.

"So, how does it feel?" Kate asked.

"Eh?"

"How does it feel to finally be nineteen?"

"Oh, well, so far it feels pretty much the same as eighteen, but with more cake," answered Dan.

Kate paused her trimming and rested her hand on Dan's shoulders. "How do you feel about Ned's plan?"

"The closer we get to it the more I worry. I keep thinking he'll change his mind, but he's obsessed with this idea of a war between him and the traps. It doesn't help that there's sympathisers telling him how much they love the idea. They seem to think he's going to destroy the British Empire for them. Ned can't see that as soon as things go awry those will be the same people standing around to watch the show as we get torn to shreds by troopers or strung up like Chinese lanterns."

Kate hugged Dan from behind and kissed him. There was a heaviness in her heart that had sat in place ever since Ned had revealed his scheme. The thought of losing Dan was a very real possibility if this went wrong and it terrified her. When Ned and Jim had been locked up in gaol for years it was Dan that she saw as her protector. He had been there when it mattered. She loved Ned but she barely knew who he was these days. She had only been seven when he started bushranging with Harry Power as a boy, and by the time he was back home from gaol as a man Kate was just starting to reach that delicate age between being a girl and being a woman. As soon as Ned was back, he was gone again. At first, he was making honest money then soon taking to exacting scores with those he saw as enemies. Though Dan frequently travelled to the Monaro for shearing work and traipsed about picking up odd jobs for extra money, Greta was still his home and he preferred to work on the farm with his sisters. Some considered him a spoiled brat, but his sisters saw nothing wrong with lavishing affection on their one brother who had not wasted away his youth in a gaol.

"I wish Ned would listen to us. He scares me with the way he talks these days," said Kate. Dan did not say anything back, he simply held Kate's hand and kissed it. The pair stayed silent for a considerable time, neither knowing what to say, just being comforted with each other's presence.

***

Detective Ward sat at Hare's desk, reclining in a wooden chair, and passed a nobbler of brandy to him. Hare took the alcohol and gave a brief toast, which Ward returned.

"Sir, it is certainly good to have you back in charge of the pursuit once again. Things were getting unstable. The feud between Nicolson and Standish threatened to make the investigation fall apart entirely," Ward said sipping his brandy.

"Yes, I must admit that as much as I have no time for Nicolson, Captain Standish's conduct has been unbecoming of late. I do wonder about his health. He seems not to be himself at the moment."

"Are you aware that some of the constables pitched in to buy a hut for Aaron Sherritt?" asked Ward.

"I had heard something about it. What happened?"

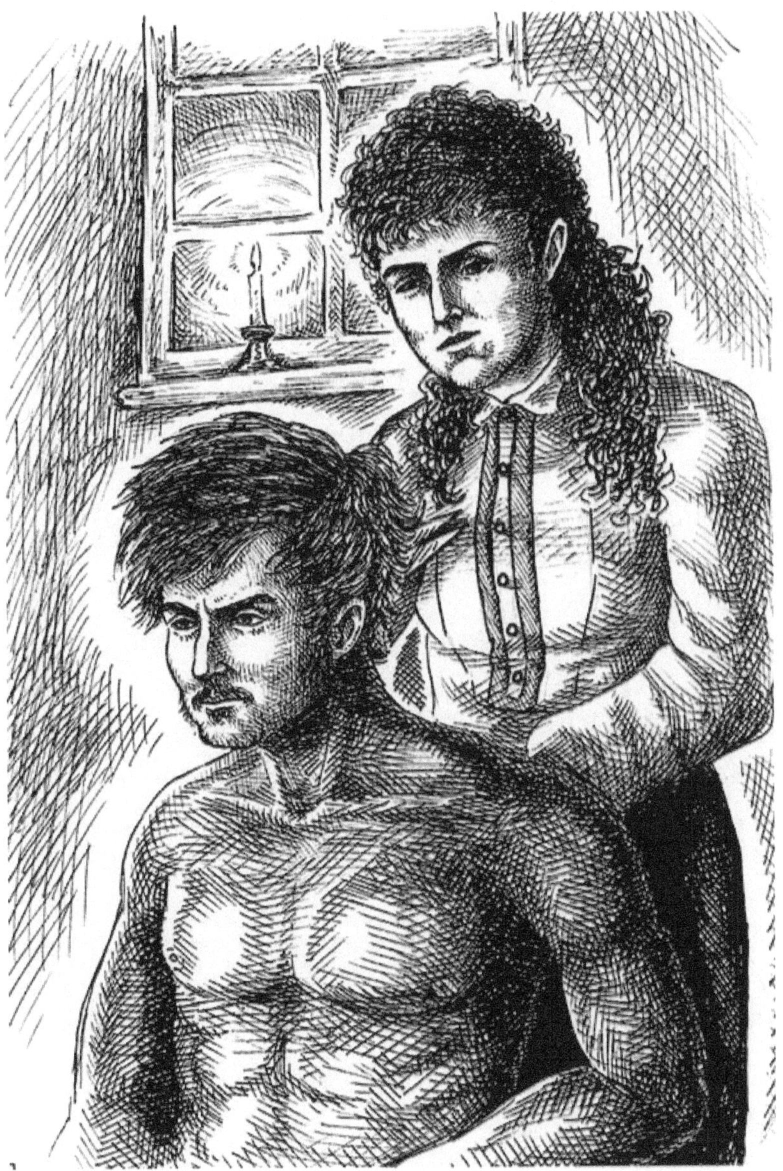

"I wish Ned would listen to us. He scares me with the way he talks these days," said Kate.

"The lad had begun squatting in an old miner's hut that had sat un-occupied for years. The moment the previous owner found out he started making things very hot for Sherritt, so the troopers from the cave party passed the hat around and bought the place outright to stop the miner from revealing their presence," Ward explained.

"What a dreadful mess," said Hare.

"So, it would seem; yet the hut will prove to be useful to us. It is positioned quite a good distance between here and the Byrne place. It's a perfect depot for the constables." Ward straightened up, "I must bring to your attention that the risk of the gang or their sympathisers attacking Aaron Sherritt is extraordinary, given the chain of events in your absence. He has very few friends these days."

"Go on," Hare said as he wiped brandy out of his moustache with the back of his hand.

"I propose we supply police for Sherritt's protection. Four constables with him night and day. Through the day, the troopers and Sherritt sleep like possums in the hut; then come the night-time they accompany him to the Byrne selection for their watch."

"That sounds rather impractical, leaving poor Tommy housebound all day."

"But that is the point. We don't want him leaving. If he's the target, we want the hunters to come to him where it is advantageous for us."

Ward stared into Hare's eyes with an intensity that unnerved the superintendent.

"He's bait?" Hare said.

"He's bait. If any of the bushrangers or their sympathisers dare go to his place to make mischief, the constables can capture them. There are only two doors in or out, and if the police keep the doors covered from the bedroom the outlaws will be gunned down easily if they try to get in.

Sherritt will be safe, the bushrangers done away with, and then we need only concern ourselves with collecting the reward."

Hare gave a thoughtful sigh. "It is certainly the best solution I have heard in some time, though I worry about the moral implications of using him as a lure."

"Desperate times require desperate measures, Mr. Hare."

***

Paddy Byrne rode his grey mare to meet Joe and Dan in the Woolshed Valley. He dismounted and hitched his horse to a tree, walking only a few steps before they appeared from the scrub. Paddy and Dan hugged and then Joe did the same, embracing his brother weakly.

"You look like death, Joe," said Paddy.

"Thanks for pointing that out, Patsy. I hadn't noticed," said Joe.

"Have you got the supplies there?" said Dan. Paddy took some small bundles out of his saddle bags and handed them over.

"There's provisions for the next few days, a couple of newspapers and a little something extra that our Kate put in for you, Danny," Paddy winked at the young bushranger. He withdrew a bottle from his jacket pocket and handed it to Joe.

"I could only procure one bottle of the laudanum, I'm sorry. But they did have these packets of powdered opium. You mix them with alcohol, and it does the same trick. It might be enough to tide you over until you're back in Yee Fang's good graces."

Joe took the bottle and the packets graciously, popping the cork on the bottle and pouring some of the tincture straight into his mouth. It tasted ghastly but Joe wasn't taking it for the flavour.

"I've got other news, though you're not going to like it," Paddy said quietly. The bushrangers looked concerned.

"What is it?" asked Dan, folding his arms.

"Well, it's Sherritt. He's got police living in his hut now."

"Fuck off," Joe spat with disbelief.

"It's true, I rode out with Denny to Eldorado to see for myself. I saw him taking some men into his house who I'd never seen before. Their horses had government brands on them. He doesn't go out much these days. Everyone reckons his folks have disowned him now for marrying the Barry girl. Can't say I blame them. Denny managed to get up close on his way home from the school and counted four plainclothes troopers in the hut."

"Do the traps still camp out in the cave by your place?" Dan asked.

"Every night sure as clockwork. It's like they aren't even trying to conceal it anymore," Paddy replied.

"It's like they want us to know they're there," said Joe sullenly.

"I'd better be heading off now. Stay safe, the pair of you," Paddy said before he mounted and rode away with fond farewells.

As the grey horse disappeared, Joe was lost in thought. Dan punched him in the shoulder as hard as he could.

"Snap out of it, we need to get moving!"

Joe shot Dan a withering stare. In his mind he wrestled with the realisation that his boyhood companion, his greatest friend and ally, had truly abandoned him for the enemy.

***

Aaron Sherritt and Constable Henry Armstrong, one of the policemen who had been assigned to keep him safe, sat in the bar room of the Hibernian Hotel imbibing spirits. Aaron had consumed far more whiskey than it was advisable for a man to have taken in the span of an hour and the effects were starting to show. Armstrong took this as an opportunity to grill him about what his real motivations were while his guard was down.

"What's in it for you Aaron? You lead us a merry dance, but the Kelly Gang do nothing for you either, so whose side are you on, really?"

Aaron looked at Armstrong with mild offence.

"They helped me keep my selection when I was behind; they've paid me very handsomely whenever they've liberated a bank of its coin. The Byrnes and Kellys have accused me of all sorts of things, but my own mother treats me like a leper. Ha! How Christian of her. I've not a friend left in the world, Constable Armstrong. I tell you; I never knew a man could feel so alone."

Armstrong grew tired of Aaron's self-pity and suggested a leisurely walk. Aaron recommended a stroll to the Vine Hotel. The pair strolled along the streets until the squat, stylish public house appeared before them. Inside was a warm and inviting place of drinking and socialising. The walls were decorated with a collection of hunting trophies and a lithograph of Albert and Victoria on their wedding day, hung above the fireplace.

When Aaron swaggered in through the windowed door into the bar room, he swept his gaze over his surrounds and locked eyes on his target - Maggie, Joe Byrne's sweetheart. She was dressed in the usual maid's attire of a black dress with a white apron and bonnet, and she collected glasses and mugs from the bar. Constable Armstrong entered behind Sherritt and wondered why he was standing still, barely more than a couple of feet in the door.

When Maggie came out, she stood behind the bar to take orders, Aaron stared at her, woozy with drink. He had long been jealous of her affection for Joe. Though he was a married man and prior to that had been more successful at bedding the targets of his affection than Joe, Maggie being the forbidden fruit stirred something green and nasty within him.

A drunk miner, short, stocky and endowed with a humongous yellow beard full of beer that had missed his mouth, slurred at Maggie. In order to hear what the patron was saying, Maggie leaned forward on the bar, coming close to his face. Innocent as it was, Aaron, in his addled, intoxicated state, saw this and was overcome. He stormed out into the street. Armstrong followed.

"Oi, what's wrong?" Armstrong shouted as Aaron stormed down the road.

Aaron turned and pointed at the hotel, shaking and red-faced. "That maid in there; she's Joe Byrne's girl. She sees him every Saturday night."

Constable Armstrong could not for the life of him figure out why this had made Sherritt so upset but left him to continue walking as he went straight back into the bar to ask questions. He gestured for Maggie to join him and took her aside.

"What's your name, miss?" he asked.

"They call me Maggie," came the reply. Maggie's Cornish voice was sweet as she assumed Armstrong was merely another patron, "Can I fetch you something to drink, sir?"

"I have it on good authority, Maggie, that you see Joe Byrne of a Saturday night," said Armstrong.

Maggie said nothing but wore a flustered expression.

"If we find out that you have been harbouring an outlaw, you'll be locked away for fifteen years," said Armstrong threateningly. "If you help us, not only will we not press any charges, you'll most likely get a portion of the reward. So, tell me, do you see Joe Byrne or not?"

"The devil a man could have told you that but Sherritt, and somebody else will soon know too," replied Maggie venomously.

She took her leave and as Maggie returned to her duties Armstrong fumed. He knew that Detective Ward would be furious at the failed interrogation. He decided to take his leave and find out where Sherritt had gone to. As he left, Maggie watched him from the bar. Her heart was racing like a greyhound chasing a rabbit.

***

Joe Byrne lay on the floor of Maggie's bedroom shirtless and in a stupor. Thin, oily wisps of opium smoke coiled above his face, dancing on the breeze pushing through the crack under the door. Maggie had visited the Chinese village and had procured some of Joe's favourite drug, which they shared from his pipe. He stared up into the darkness as a moth whizzed past, flocking to the oil lamp. The world seemed so far away, like his problems were flotsam drifting downstream.

"I heard that you'd seen Aaron about the place," Joe ventured.

"Aye. I don't trust him, Joe. He came in with another chap as I was serving and stormed out. Then the little bloke he was with stayed behind to ask me questions about you."

"Reckon he was a trap?"

"No doubt in my mind. The police have made a real scene here ever since. Mrs. Vandenberg has threatened to throw me out over it. Aaron is big trouble, Joe."

"Wasn't he always?" Joe muttered.

As the pair lay entwined in a haze of opium infused bliss, Joe kissed Maggie tenderly.

"I see you still have the ring I gave you," Maggie said, touching the token of her affection that Joe now wore on a leather thong around his neck.

"I like to keep it close," Joe said. He drew opium smoke into his lungs and closed his eyes. He felt a tugging at his trousers and looked down to see Maggie unbuttoning them.

"You're incorrigible," Joe said softly. Maggie merely grinned and continued.

"I get to see you so rarely now; I must make the most of it when I can. Not every man can make love to me the way you do; so few have the right tools."

Maggie pulled Joe's trousers down to his knees, then took a long suck on his opium pipe, filling her lungs and exhaling slowly. She ran her hands over his long features, smoothed out his wide brow and stroked his prominent lower lip. She straddled him and as she kissed his throat, she dragged her hands down Joe's taut, narrow body, every sensation heightened as the drug began to take effect. Joe gazed up at her; every delicate curve, every freckle enhanced by the opioid haze. Joe pulled Maggie to his chest and held her tightly.

"I promise you; the trouble will be over soon and then we can spend the rest of our days together. I wish I could hold you like this forever," Joe said, his voice choked with emotion as a single tear squeezed out of his eye and rolled down his cheek.

***

For weeks the provisions for the Glenrowan campaign had been gathered. Tom Lloyd and Maggie Skillion made trips to Melbourne to procure guns, ammunition and blasting powder. Paddy Byrne procured two Chinese skyrockets to act as signals to the sympathisers. The armour was brought together, and the pieces stored in saddlebags. Horses were gathered and kept in the paddock at Maggie Skillion's selection. When everything was ready, it was taken to the stables at the Hart selection at the foot of the Warby Ranges. Everyone waited for Ned to announce the date.

Mrs. Byrne, excited by the talk doing the rounds of what was being planned, boasted to anyone that would listen that the Kelly Gang was about to do something that would make the ears of the entire nation tingle. The word reached the police through their spies, but Hare treated the claims with caution as they had heard so much talk like this before that came to nothing.

Ned summoned the gang to discuss his latest changes to the plans. All four sat close to the campfire as rain began to fall on the camp.

"If what we're told is true, and Aaron does have police hiding in his place, I think we ought to shoot the traps and make Aaron raise the alarm," Ned said.

"What do we do about Sherritt, then?" Steve asked.

"I don't believe Aaron is stupid enough to turn on us on his own accord. Those traps must be coercing him somehow."

"They're paying him, Ned, that's coercion enough. All the Sherritts are on the traps' books," Dan grumbled.

"Aaron is one of them now. Do you think I would be saying this if I weren't convinced of the truth of it, Ned? I have more reason than anyone else to refuse to believe. If I say he's turned, then he's fucking turned!" Joe shouted.

"This is Aaron's last chance to set things right, then. If he cooperates, we let him leave the colony alive. If not, he suffers the same fate as the traps. But there needs to be at least one soul remaining to raise the alarm or this won't work," said Ned.

"So, you want Dan and me to shoot a bunch of traps on our own now?" Joe asked, exasperated.

"Joe, if you can shoot a penny out of the air, you can hit a handful of fat-necked unicorns in a tiny hut. Besides, you'll have the armour to protect you if they're game to fight."

"Denny gave us the layout of the hut. If there's one of us at either door the police will be trapped inside. It's almost unfair how easy it would be to take them out," said Dan.

Joe sighed and held his head in his hands. "When do we strike?"

"I say we move in the next day or so, so best you get some rest now. We are going to be very busy."

***

On June twenty-fourth, word spread through the bush telegraph that Joe and Dan would be attacking the police in Sherritt's hut that Saturday night. The sympathisers were told to look for the signal - one rocket for success, two for danger - before attempting to join the gang in Glenrowan for the march on Benalla. Maggie Skillion bought new outfits for her brothers using her savings from the Jerilderie cash: for Ned it was a polka dotted shirt, grey tweed jacket, yellow corduroy vest and strapped trousers to match; for Dan it was a black velvet coat, grey strapped trousers, a tweed waistcoat and a blue cotton shirt. She and Kate had also crafted quilted caps for their brothers to wear inside their helmets as padding. There was to be a great celebration of the end of the old tyranny and the beginnings of a new order in Kelly country.

3

The Devil's Elbow

Sunset over the smooth, undulating hills of Greta was always spectacular. The night of June twenty-sixth seemed even more so, with a canopy of clouds slowly rolling in from the south.

At the Kelly selection, there was no sign of activity to the outside observer. Kate had taken her siblings to Maggie's hut where they intended to wait for the victory signal from Glenrowan.

Knowing that the Kelly selection would be empty for the night, Ned took the opportunity to have time alone in the house with Ettie.

"I'm happy that you chose to spend the night before your grand victory with me," Ettie said.

Ned frowned, "I wish the future was more certain for us, but all I can promise is tonight."

"Ned," said Ettie, her voice tinged with frustration, "for once, just be here with me. Don't think about anything else, just think about us here together. We're safe; we're alone."

Ned held her hand tightly in his, her spindly fingers soft against his callused skin. He felt his heart raging in his breast as he gave in to his emotions and pulled Ettie toward him, kissing her with ferocity. Ned's lips were soft behind his bristly moustache, and he trembled as Ettie's perfume filled his nostrils. Ettie ran her hands through Ned's hair and beard, her face felt hot. She looked into Ned's eyes.

"I want you," Ned whispered with the pain of longing strangling his words.

Ettie began to disrobe, and Ned did the same. He nervously fumbled with his buttons. Ettie stood naked before Ned, her ebony hair cascading down her back past her shoulders, and she gazed upon him as he shook off his clothing. She ran her fingers lightly over Ned's body. His muscles twitched at her touch, like a stallion about to bolt, his chest heaved from nervous breathing and Ettie brushed the cluster of scars on his crown.

"Tell me what these are from," Ettie said.

"That's where Senior-Constable Hall struck me with his revolver."

She ran her hands over his shoulders, following the contours of his muscular arms and down over his chest. Her touch lingered on a raised lump of scar tissue on his ribs.

"What happened here?" she asked.

"That's where a bullet cut across me from Sergeant Kennedy at Stringybark Creek."

Ettie frowned.

"Promise me you'll be careful at Glenrowan."

"I promise."

Ettie pushed Ned onto the bed, but as he tried to sit up, she pressed her hand into his chest.

"Let me be in charge for a while," Ettie said calmly. Ned laid back and allowed himself to relax as Ettie explored his skin with her lips. As she moved her face to his most sensitive regions he panicked, but a chiding glance from his lover told him to stay put. Soon Ned allowed the pleasurable sensation of Ettie's gentle kisses to overcome his apprehensions. He was not accustomed to being submissive, but he could not help but appreciate the relief, however slight, that he felt at not having to be in control while it was safe to do so.

Thoughts of the impending mission remained at the back of his mind, but it was difficult for him to focus on them as Ettie sat astride him and began to ride him like a thoroughbred. She threw her head back with a confident smirk and sighed. As her riding caused her breasts to jiggle, she grabbed Ned's hands and pressed them against her breasts to tame them; now she was the wild thing. Her body tingled.

Ned had finally had enough of being the submissive one and rolled Ettie onto the other side of the bed. As he positioned himself between her legs the lovers gazed into each other's eyes, and he fulfilled his desire. His own confidence had improved dramatically since that first stolen night the many months before and he took his time to enjoy the intimacy and the sensations of their flesh merging.

Suddenly he paused. Ettie looked up, confused.

"What's wrong?"

"I just wanted to get a good look at you, so I can remember how beautiful you are in this moment."

Ettie smiled and stroked Ned's face.

"That's so sweet, but I'd really like you to keep going please. I was enjoying that."

***

As Ned spent the night in Greta with his sweetheart, the rest of the gang were at Maggie Skillion's hut. Joe had remained quiet unless spoken to, Dan also found it hard to converse with the knowledge of the task that awaited him. Maggie placed her hands reassuringly on Dan's shoulders.

"I know it's a frightful thing that's ahead," she said, "but you know, as do we all, that it is necessary."

"Would you feel so confident if it were you that was pulling the trigger?" Dan asked. Maggie had no reply.

Dan excused himself and headed outside where he was joined by Kate.

"Are you alright, Danny?" Kate asked.

"No," Dan replied, "How could I be?"

Kate said no further words, instead hugged her brother tightly. There was no other consolation that she could offer to dull the pain of such a terrible mission as Dan had before him.

With the arrival of twilight, the three outlaws gave a toast to the Kelly sisters and mounted. With a packhorse in tow, they made tracks from Greta towards Eldorado. Joe rode ahead on a large chestnut horse with a white face and hind legs that they had taken from Michael Ryan of Cashel. It was an impressive beast, renowned for its endurance in cross-country riding, which was precisely why the gang had procured it. Behind, Steve rode neck and neck with Dan on their respective bays. The saddlebags were heavy on the back of the packhorse that Dan guided. Inside was the body armour that was to protect Joe and Dan on their mission. As they reached the outskirts of Greta, the trio came to a halt.

Steve sat erect in the saddle and turned his gaze towards Wangaratta.

"This is me, lads. I'll be with Tom, Dick and Wild until Ned is finished. Then we're off to Glenrowan. Good luck."
Joe barely managed a nod as Steve and Dan clasped hands. With a solemn nod to Joe, Steve squeezed his horse's flanks, galloping off into the night.

"Let's be off," Joe mumbled. He and Dan headed towards Beechworth at a leisurely pace, neither feeling eager to undertake the task ahead. Joe drank whiskey from a flask he had kept in his coat pocket, sucking it dry. Dan was on tenterhooks as they rode, and he kept a close eye on Joe. He had trepidation about the mission but was more concerned about his partner.

The ride to Eldorado was silent and the cold air nipped at their exposed faces. Winter drizzle snagged on them as they rode, and as Joe shook off the dew, he began to get cold feet. As they plunged deeper into the bush, Joe pulled up short and slumped forward slightly. Dan came to a halt beside him.

"We should have got out of the colony when we had the chance," said Joe, "We could have headed up to Queensland. Nobody knows us from a broomstick there. We could say we're anybody and they'd go with it as long as our yarns were entertaining."
"And who would you be then?" Dan asked.
"Well, maybe I could bring Billy King back out of hiding?"
"The name you used when you were duffing with Ned?"
"Yeah; Billy King - rambling gambler, and lover of wine, women and song. Would you come?"
"Joe," Dan began sternly.

Joe gazed at the ground.

"What am I doing, Danny? How did we come to this?" Joe ran a gloved finger under his nose and wiped up the liquid snot that was dribbling out of it. He wiped the leather glove clean on his oilskin. "Ned tried for so long and hard to shield us from the blame of murdering those traps at Stringybark Creek and now he sends us to do even worse."

"It's like Ned says, this is a war. In war people kill or get killed. Remember why there's traps in Aaron's place. They want us dead, and Aaron is helping them. Don't lose your nerve, old man," Dan responded, reaching across and patting Joe on the shoulder reassuringly.

"I just can't believe that after all we've been through that he'd sell me out. After all I've done for him, all I sacrificed for him for so long!"

Joe's thoughts drifted back over every hare-brained scheme of Aaron's that had landed him in trouble, every idiotic decision that Aaron had made that landed them in court. He recalled the six months in Beechworth Gaol over the cow Aaron roped him into stealing and slaughtering with him. The cold, sleepless nights on stone floors; the aching hunger that hominy and molasses couldn't cure; the humiliation of bathing outdoors in a trough using water brimming with the filth sloughed from the dozen other inmates beside him.

He thought of the months he had laboured on Aaron's selection to bring it up to scratch without thanks so his mate could have a place of his own – something Joe never got a chance to experience himself.

He thought of Aaron swanning down Ford Street in his fine clothes gifted to him by Detective Ward then returning home to his beautiful wife and a warm bed in domestic bliss.

He began to tremble and sweat. The sorrowful expression that had shaped his face was morphed into one of rage. Suddenly he dug his spurs in and the stolen chestnut took off like a rocket.

***

At the Hart selection at the foot of the Warbys, Steve loaded the pack-horses, with help from Wild Wright, with silent industriousness. Close by, Tom Lloyd, his fourteen-year-old brother Jack, and Dick Hart lifted two skyrockets and a keg of blasting powder into a cart with extreme care. Dick draped an oilskin over the explosives and walked over to the barn as Tom continued to load the cart up with rifles and revolvers.

"Stevey," Dick gestured to his brother, "come here."

The brothers went inside the barn and found a spot out of the view of the others where Dick surreptitiously handed Steve two paper boarding passes for a paddle steamer. Steve tucked them into the breast pocket of his Inverness cloak. Neither spoke, worried about what would happen if the others caught wind of the clandestine plan.

It was barely an hour later when Ned arrived. The men were drinking a brew by a small fire beside the barn. There was nothing subtle or subdued about Ned's appearance. He was dressed in his new clothes and around his waist he wore his lucky green sash.

"Feck, Ned, yer makin' me feel under-dressed," cackled Wild Wright. Ned was impassive.

"Is everything ready to go?"

"All good to go," replied Tom.

"Alright, let's get moving. The others should be just about reaching the Devil's Elbow by now."

Abandoning their tea, the men extinguished the small fire and mounted up, Tom took the reins of the cart with Jack.

The brothers went inside the barn and found a spot out of the view of
the others...

***

At the Skillion selection, Maggie and Kate changed into their best dresses in anticipation of the gang's victory. Maggie had a handsome black dress with a scarlet underskirt. She fastened a gold cameo brooch of St. Patrick at her throat and coifed her hair up at her neck. Kate meanwhile dressed in her blue-grey riding habit with black accents; a far cry from the almost uniformly black outfits she usually favoured. She stroked her white silk gloves gently before putting them on, enjoying the smoothness against her fingers. Her hair was held in place with an ornate comb made from tortoise shell, and she draped necklaces that hung low on her chest. On the dining table sat outfits for their younger siblings and Maggie's children for when they awoke in the morning.

Kate twirled for Maggie to show off the outfit.
"How do I look?"
"Beautiful, as always."
Kate paused and frowned. Maggie placed her hands on her hips.
"What is the matter?"
"I'm worried, Maggie. Something feels wrong."

Maggie scoffed and placed the kettle over the fire. She gestured for Kate to sit at the dining table and grabbed a loaf of bread wrapped in muslin from the larder.

"You just need some food in your belly, girl. Reminds me of when we were little, and you'd get so excited on Christmas Eve that you wouldn't eat. Ma would tell Jim to get his boots and coat on in case he had to walk to fetch the doctor. D'you remember?"

"I remember. It's not like that though."

"Sure, it is."

"Maggie, listen to me! Something is not right. Can't you feel it?"

Maggie halted, the bread knife in her hand glinted in the firelight, the orange flames reflected in the blade.

"I'm sure everything will be fine," she said avoiding eye contact.

* * *

Darkness began to envelope the Devil's Elbow as Anton Wick shuffled back from his mate's place, whistling an old German folk song he half remembered. The ale they had drunk sat heavily in his belly, the fruity, bitter taste still coating the inside of his mouth. Wick was a stout old man, his jaw prickly with salty coloured stubble, his head covered by a long mop of silver hair. His gait was an awkward waddle owing to his legs, which bowed at the knees.

Wick knew the road extremely well and could judge fairly accurately by feel where he needed to turn — a useful trait to possess when you didn't have a lamp with you. Wick's ears pricked at the sound of hooves on the dirt road approaching. As he turned, he could just make out the shape of a pair of horsemen leading a packhorse.

"Guten abend," said Wick to the horsemen as they passed him. There was no response. Wick kept moving but soon heard the riders behind him stop and turn back around.

When they returned to his side one of them asked, "Do you know me?"

Wick strained his eyes in the inky blackness but could not recognise any features.

"I do not."

"I'm Joe Byrne."

"I don't believe you!" Wick scoffed.

He was well acquainted with the notorious lad from the Woolshed. They had much animosity in their past and Wick did not like Byrne one jot. He again examined what he could of the rider's face. He certainly didn't look like the thin, well-groomed teenager he remembered, but the long nose and the icy blue eyes were unmistakable, even in such poor light.

Joe shifted his coat and the revolver tucked into his belt glinted in the moonlight.

"Now do you recognise me?"

Wick stammered and shot his gaze from one figure to the other.

"This is Mr. Kelly. Clap the darbies on him, Danny," Joe ordered with a flourish of his hand.

Dan dismounted and approached Wick with a set of handcuffs and locked them on him roughly. He stared into Wick's eyes sternly.

"You are to do everything we say. Do you understand?"

Wick nodded while trembling, "Ja, ja."

***

In Aaron Sherritt's hut, the lone candle in the window blazed intensely. Though in better condition than his previous hut, Aaron's new home was still far from the homely place Belle was accustomed to. The walls inside were wattle and daub, the outside being clad in weatherboard, and only consisted of two rooms, separated by a weatherboard partition with a calico curtain for a door. The most luxurious element of the building compared to Aaron's previous abode was the wooden floor. The dining table was small and old and owing to there being no chairs supplied with it, the seating came in the form of upturned apple crates Aaron had pinched from the back of a grocer's shop in Beechworth.

In the bedroom constables Alexander and Dowling relaxed after a filling supper supplied by Belle; Armstrong dozed contentedly on the bed. The men were in plain clothes and began preparing their gear for that night's watch. Constable Duross, a man with a stern expression and a thick black beard, warmed his hands by the fireplace. Ellen Barry sat nearby in a rocking chair she had gifted the newlyweds, darning her daughter's stockings. In this same chair she had nursed Belle as an infant, and now it was to be the chair where Belle, now noticeably pregnant, would nurse her own infant when the time came.

Aaron sat at the dining table. He cracked his knuckles while Belle whipped around collecting plates to wash.

"There's a chill in here," Aaron said quietly.

"No more than normal, my love," Belle said dismissively. Aaron rubbed his arms to no avail. Belle rubbed her belly tenderly; it felt warm. Her pregnancy was still in the early stages, but Belle felt whole and happy.

"Aaron, darling, when you go into town tomorrow can you fetch some more potatoes for me? We're out."

"Aye, I'll get you potatoes."

The police in the bedroom wrapped themselves in possum skin blankets to fight the cold of winter. The room was cramped, and the men were forced to be far more intimate than any of them had desired, but in the cold, it had its benefits.

***

Joe and Dan moved slowly on horseback, Wick walking ahead

muttering to himself in German. The damp ground was covered in a fine dust that the horses' hooves left clean impressions in. Joe smirked and leaned to Dan.

"Old Antonio here and I go way back. The grumpy old bugger tried to woo my Ma. Took me to court for borrowing a horse of his. Said I was a troublemaker. He'd know; I reckon he's been kicked out of nearly every pub in Beechworth for starting fights."

"Didn't put up much of a fight tonight," Dan replied. Wick tried to ignore the conversation.

"When we get to the place, I'll take this one 'round the back. You hold the front door so nobody can escape," Joe instructed.

He exhaled sharply and fished around in his coat pocket. He withdrew his flask and was about to take a nip when Dan reached across and yanked it out of his hand.

"Careful, old man," Dan scolded.

The outlaws and their prisoner arrived at their destination. The hut sat on a muddy rise about twenty yards from the road, facing downhill to a watering hole. Smoke wafted from the chimney with tiny glowing flecks dancing into the night among the plumes. The hut was obscured by darkness, save for the candlelight emanating from the window.

Joe and Dan dismounted and hitched their horses to a blue gum that grew by the roadside. Joe took his shotgun from the bundle on his saddle and jostled Wick towards the house violently. Dan followed, checking a revolver that he tucked into his belt. He hissed at Joe.

"Oi! What about the armour?"

"Forget it, it'll only complicate things. Let's get this over with quickly. Damn fool idea anyway," Joe replied, continuing to walk. They climbed the embankment, which was soft underfoot thanks to the rains that had moistened the area the past few days.

Joe gestured for Dan to wait at the front door. Dan positioned himself with his back flush against the wall and drew his revolver. Joe and Wick took position at the back door, hidden from the road. Joe cocked the shotgun and stared into the German's eyes.

"Do exactly as I say. These shots are not meant for you, but I can redirect them if I wish."

Inside the hut the occupants heard the sound of Aaron's hound barking as it often did at wombats and possums that paraded through the block at night. There were two sharp knocks at the back door. Duross joined the other police in the bedroom and poked his head through the curtain, but Aaron waved a hand to settle him. Belle looked at her husband with panic, but his calm expression allayed her fear.

"Who is it?" the girl asked.

"It's Anton Wick, I've lost myself," came the reply from outside.

Aaron smiled at Duross in the way he always did that immediately disarmed people.

"Don't worry, he's just a neighbour."

There was another knock and Belle looked at her husband nervously.

"Aaron, would you show him how to get home please?"

Duross quickly went back into the bedroom as Aaron got up. He scratched at the short beard on his chin and unlatched the door. The door swung open easily and before Aaron stood the stocky immigrant with a worried expression.

"Alright, Anton, do you see that sapling over there?"

Aaron knew Wick well enough to be familiar with his drinking habits and read the expression as merely confusion.

"Alright, Anton, do you see that sapling over there?"
Aaron pointed behind the visitor into the blackness, trying to get his own bearings, when he saw the flutter of an oilskin from behind the chimney as it caught the breeze.
"Who's that?"

As if in slow motion, Joe Byrne stood into the light, shouldering Anton Wick aside as he brought his tool of destruction in line with Aaron's chest and pulled the trigger. The shotgun roared. The shot tore through Aaron's chest, shattering ribs and perforating his heart, lungs and stomach in an explosion of scarlet gore. Aaron staggered backwards. The doomed man gasped, too shocked to think of a word and his lungs too pulverised to vocalise anything more dramatic.

Joe placed a foot on the granite block that acted as a doorstep and fired again. The second shot ripped open Aaron's throat. Some stray shot zipped past Belle's head and lodged in the front door. Arterial blood spurted out of the fresh wound in a dramatic arc, landing on Joe's boots as he stepped towards his victim. Firelight cast the shadows of the victim and his murderer like enormous eldritch spectres upon the partition. Aaron blacked out as he fell onto the dining table. He bounced off and hit the floor face down, rolling onto his back in his death throes. Sightless eyes glazed over as blood gurgled and poured out of Aaron's throat and stomach, dribbling between the floorboards. Rivulets of blood snaked out from the pool under Aaron's body and towards the front door. The gushing pulsed with Aaron's failing heartbeat; his handsome face was bathed in so much blood that only one eye remained visible.

The ringing in Belle's ears stopped long enough for her to see the carnage and she let out a hideous scream. She went to the body but knew it was pointless. She shook uncontrollably as she touched Aaron, still warm but unresponsive. Joe loomed over her, his face a furious sneer, his eyes burning like coals; Belle knew who he was immediately. His nostrils twitched at the smell of blood and burnt gunpowder. Belle thought he had the aspect of something demonic about him; an agent of Lucifer sent to take away her beloved husband, the stench of spent powder from his gun like the burning sulphur of Hell.

"That's the man I want. The bastard will never put me away again."

The world seemed unreal to Belle as she tried to process everything. She flailed her arms in jerky spasms, overwhelmed and not knowing what to do.

"Joe, what have you done? What have you done to my Aaron? My beautiful husband!"

"He'll not blow about what he'd do to me now," Joe snapped, ignoring the girl.

Outside, Aaron's hound began howling mournfully from inside his kennel, disturbed by the terrible fate that had befallen his master.

In the bedroom the police hunkered down and listened closely to the events in the next room, fumbling in the dark for their weapons. Constable Duross pushed himself into the corner behind the bed. They waited, hoping that the shots were some morbid joke and that Aaron would come swaggering into the bedroom with a grin. Constable Armstrong took position near the doorway and tried to peek through the curtain. Alexander moved opposite him while Dowling kept low, peeking through a small gap in the slats of the partition, but nothing was visible from his vantage point. Alexander attempted to see over the top of the partition.

Turning, Joe saw Ellen Barry at the far end of the room. She flinched as he approached. The woman was in such a state of utter terror that she was almost unrecognisable as the jolly wet nurse who had helped Joe's mother bring two of his own siblings into the world. She in turn could not recognise Joe in the scowling bearded figure before her. This was not the sweet little boy who was always desperate for a cuddle and demanded to sleep in the bed between her and his mother. Something seemed to flicker in Joe's eyes and the mask of hatred shimmered, replaced momentarily by panic and regret.

"You needn't worry, Mrs. Barry, I don't mean to harm you or your daughter."

This, naturally, did nothing to allay her fears. Joe beckoned Ellen to join him. He managed to keep relatively calm despite everything inside him wanting to burst out screaming.

"Who's in there?" he demanded, gesturing to the bedroom.

"Nobody," replied Ellen, "just a man who was looking for work."

"What's his name?"

"Duross."

"Duross, is it?"

Joe felt aggrieved that the woman would lie to his face when he knew that the room was full of police. He grabbed Belle roughly by the arm and dragged her to her feet.

"Bring him out here," he snapped at Belle. The girl, however, was too scared to move. An urgent knock at the front door quickly redirected their attention.

"Open that door," Joe urged the shaken mother-in-law.

Ellen did as she was ordered, quaking as she tried to step around the blood to open the door, whereupon she was met with Dan Kelly levelling a revolver at her voluminous breast. He stood inside and saw the pool of blood surrounding Sherritt.
He bent down over it and rested his elbow on the table to steady himself. The smell of the blood made him almost gag. His stomach leaped into his throat, and he let out a nervous chuckle at the sight of one brown eye peeking out from a mask of blood. This wasn't the plan and came as a rude shock, but the outcome was nevertheless acceptable in his book. Joe frantically reloaded his shotgun.

"May I be permitted to stand outside?" Ellen asked, feeling light-headed and nauseated.
Joe gave a nod and Dan accompanied the woman outside. Belle lingered, sobbing uncontrollably.
"I want that man," Joe growled as he leaned in close to Belle's face and hissed through gritted teeth, "bring him out now."
Belle sobbed and did as she was told, passing through the curtain into the bedroom where the four constables remained in their positions clutching their revolvers.

"Please," Belle moaned, clutching her breast, "you must come out. Please."
Her voice caught in her throat and came out as a high-pitched whine, her face contorted into a heart-rending expression of incalculable sorrow, pink and glossy from tears. The constables looked at each other, not a single one prepared to make a move. Constable Armstrong, severe and wiry, sucked up some courage.

"Get down or you'll get shot girl," he whispered.

"Bring him out of there," Joe bellowed in the next room.

"He won't come out, Joe," Belle replied sniffling. Belle doubled over, clasped her hands and extended her arms, pleading for compliance from the police, her body shaking violently with shock and terror.

"Out, or I'll riddle the place!"

Joe could feel his control over the situation sliding out of his grasp. Desperate for compliance he pulled the trigger of his gun, launching shot through the wall and sending splinters flying everywhere, narrowly missing Belle's head. Belle screeched, thinking she had been hit, and let out a wail as Armstrong grabbed her and threw her across the room to Constable Dowling, who pushed her to the ground and under the bed with Constable Duross. The pair used their feet to push her and pin her against the wall. The terrified girl was stuck in the throes of a panic attack.

"Let me out! Let me out!" she gasped, her chest tightening with every breath, but she was ignored.

In the next room Joe continued to bellow, "If you don't do as I say I'll shoot you and your mother!" He began to pace wildly, his eyes pinned to the lifeless body of the man who was once his greatest friend. Dan stepped back inside with a look of great concern and clapped a hand on Joe's shoulder.

"What are you doing? We've done enough, let's go!"

"No, Ned told us to clear out the traps and that's what I'm going to do," Joe said, visibly trembling. Dan frowned.

Alexander, who was closest to the door, moved right next to the jamb.

Carelessly he cocked his gun, the loud click of the hammer catching Joe's ear. Joe turned wild eyed to Dan.

"You hear that? They've guns in there. Go watch the window and see they don't try to make a break!"

Dan went outside to stand watch under the bedroom window as Joe panted in fury.

Dan was restless and annoyed. The longer they waited there for the police to come out, the more dangerous the situation became. He aimed his revolver at the wall below the window and fired a shot, hoping it would scare the police out. In the bedroom, Belle gave a muffled scream as a clump of petrified mud was dislodged from the wall and tumbled to the floor near her face.

"Who fired that shot?" Joe boomed.

"It was me," Dan replied from outside. Joe stomped to the door.

"What the fuck are you doing?" Joe snapped.

"Trying to flush the bastards out like the cockroaches they are!" Dan replied.

The police sat in the bedroom, too afraid to move. They shot furtive glances at each other but could not bring themselves to speak or act. They could hear voices outside, but it was not clear what was being said.

"Men," Constable Armstrong said finally, "have you got anything to suggest? Our conduct will be severely commented upon if we don't do something."

There was no response. Armstrong grew weary.

"If I rush them, will you be game to follow?" the constable pressed his companions. They all nodded in agreement, though none of them was truly prepared to act. Suddenly a thump was heard against the wall, then another.

Outside the bedroom, Dan and Joe piled branches against the wall. Close by Anton Wick stood, still in handcuffs, cowering in the shadow of the hut like an injured dog. Dan began to strike wax matches from a case he had in his pocket, but the wind kept blowing out the flames. He turned to Ellen Barry.

"Do you have any kerosene?"

Ellen was aghast at what they were doing. "Please don't do this! Please don't hurt my daughter! I know you, Joe Byrne, you have a soft heart."

"Ma'am, I have a heart, but it's made of stone," replied Joe. His head was a vortex of emotions. In a sudden moment of self-awareness, he realised his well-intentioned loyalty had become his undoing. For as long as he had known Aaron, he had followed him into everything, and it had got him into trouble time and again. Now, he was loyal to Ned Kelly and had a price on his head and blood on his hands for the same reason. He cursed himself.

"Please let me go, you're hurting me," Belle whimpered from under the bed as the police sat motionless, listening to the activity outside.

"Quiet, girl!" Duross snapped. Belle could feel her head getting lighter as her breathing grew shallower and a heaviness spread through her body that caused her to sink into darkness. She fell, limp and senseless, to the floor but none of the men noticed.

"Please Joe, if you kill my daughter, you may as well kill me; let me go to her!" Ellen begged, grabbing at Joe's sleeve. He shrugged her off and tried to get a better view of Dan's handiwork. Dan gave Joe a defeated look and Joe huffed with frustration.

"Be quick about it or we'll roast you too," said Joe.

Ellen promptly ran into the bedroom where she was greeted with guns pointed at her, cocked and ready to fire.

"What are you doing, you cowards! Let me take my daughter or we'll be roasted alive."

"If we let you out, there is no telling what they will do," replied Armstrong.

"You must come out and face them like men or they'll burn the place. Hasn't there been enough death tonight?"

The men ignored Ellen and grabbed her away from the door. They forced her under the bed next to her senseless daughter and hissed at her to stay down and shut up.

Joe whipped his hat off and ran his hand through his hair. His head was slick with sweat. He wiped his boots on the grass to clean the blood off them.

"Why don't we send the German in?" Dan suggested.

"What good will that do? They'll just keep him in there too."

Joe paced around the perimeter of the hut. His mind was a confused mess and tears stung his eyes. Dan stood with Wick, not uttering a word. From the doorway he shouted into the hut, "You must be a bloody coward to protect yourself with a woman!"

Joe joined Dan and Wick, clearly agitated.

"What time is it?" asked Joe. Dan took his watch out and stood in the light from the doorway.

"Nine o'clock."

Two hours they had waited for the police to emerge with no payoff. Joe stood by the door and peered in.

"Gutless bloody mongrels," he spat as he stood on the step.

"Shall we go now?" Dan asked quietly.

"Aye, set the German free and we'll go."

"Alright, pass me the key."

"I don't have the bloody key," Joe replied.

"Well, I don't have it."

"You were the one with the darbies, who else would have the fucking things?"

Dan went to look in the dark around the house to see if he had dropped the keys, and upon finding the key to the handcuffs he released Wick from their grip. Wick rubbed his wrists tenderly.

"Head off and raise no alarm. I have no wish to pay you a visit, but if you breathe a word, you'll receive a present like the one I've given Aaron," said Joe, "Send my regards to your daughter."

Without a word Wick took off, waddling bow-legged into pitch blackness.

Dan and Joe went back to their horses. Joe wrapped the shotgun up in the oilskin that was draped over his saddle.

"Let's go. I need a drink."

Dan did not reply, he merely took the lead of the packhorse in one hand and the reins of his mount in the other and set off with a nod, not once looking back at the scene of the shambolic horror show that had just played out. As the moon rose, drizzle sprinkled down softly from indigo clouds. There was no backing out now.

While the constables continued to cower in the bedroom, smothering the women, in the next room the mortal remains of Aaron Sherritt lay seemingly forgotten in the chaos; a gruesome end to a life defined by suspicion and animosity.

Sherritt had died as a poor, unwelcomed man, a persona non grata. His family spurned him, his colleagues detested him, and his friends turned on him. The one person that had cared for him unconditionally now lay unconscious under their marital bed, crushed by the policemen who had been entrusted to protect them but had instead cowered in hiding, allowing the murderer to escape; it was a cruel irony.

4

To and Fro

The impotent clang of steel on steel rang out in the night at the bend in the track just past the railway station at Glenrowan. Up on the embankment Ned and Steve struck at the bolts securing the fishplates that connected the rails and attempted to pry them away with crowbars, but nothing worked. Steve grunted and swore as he exerted himself before throwing his equipment down in protest.

"It's no good. We don't have the right tools."

"Aye," Ned bent his arm and spat a glob of phlegm over his elbow onto the ground, "But I reckon I know who does."

Just near Ann Jones' inn, on the other side of a chock and log fence, sat a collection of white tents that stuck out like snowy mountain peaks in the moonlight. Faint voices could be heard in several of them, nocturnal murmurings from sleep talkers or sneaky whispered conversations through the calico between colleagues not ready to turn in yet and some rather more interesting sounds emanating from one tent on the end of the line. It was to these tents that Ned and Steve ventured, huffing and puffing in the cold, their body armour weighing them down under their coats. The intention was to bail up the railway workers in the tents and make them pull up the tracks. With guns drawn, they approached the first tent. Some whispers could be heard inside.

"You, in there, come out." said Ned. There was no immediate response. Ned repeated the command, "I said come out!"

"Go to Hell!" came the reply. Ned turned to Steve and the pair exchanged looks of disbelief.

"Uh," Steve improvised, "You'd better put daylight through this one, Strahan!"

A smirk creased Ned's cheek ever so slightly as Steve invoked the memory of one of their sworn enemies, Senior-Constable Anthony Strahan.

No sooner had the words landed than an open hand thrust out of the tent belonging to nineteen-year-old Jack Lowe. A brief look of confusion flashed across the faces of the bushrangers as Lowe extended his other arm but where the hand should have been the empty cuff of a sleeve. Lowe was an amputee; the hand having been removed after a firearm accident many years prior.

"Who are you?" the groggy teen asked.

"I'm Ned Kelly. Bail up."

The outlaws went from tent to tent rousing the occupants; seven men altogether. Besides Lowe there was Jim Simpson, John Delaney, William Sandercook, George Metcalfe, John Maitland and Jack McHugh. They were a motley crew and not too pleased to be up in the middle of the night, freezing cold and held at gunpoint.

"Where's your boss?" Ned asked. The men all shot each other glances and pointed to the tent on the end where earlier some amorous grunting, giggling and moaning had been heard. Ned took young Lowe over to the tent.

"Tell him to come out."

"Ahh, Mr. Piazzi, you must come out," the young man ventured. Some grumbling could be heard inside the tent.

The grumbling gave way to remonstrance heavily inflected with an Italian accent.

"Hey, vaffanculo, I tell a-you not to bother me!"

"Mr. Piazzi, you really must come out this instant!" the man pleaded.

"Coglione!" came the response.

Ned had enough and whipped open the tent flap and pushed his way in.

"Listen here…" Ned began but faltered at the sight of Alphonse Piazzi rolling onto his back, spread eagled with his wedding tackle on full display and a single shot pistol in his right hand. Ned's annoyance turned to fury as Piazzi's eyes widened at the sight of Ned's intimidatingly proportioned revolving carbine pointed in his direction.

"You dare point a gun at me?" Ned roared while attempting to knock the pistol out of Piazzi's hand causing it to discharge terrifyingly close to the foreman's crown jewels, leaving a singed black hole in the bedding.

Outside, Steve Hart bolted towards the tent and cocked his revolver. This was all immediately met with an incredible scream from under the pile of blankets next to Piazzi where a nude woman, all of twenty-three years of age, sat bolt upright and knocked over the empty bottle of gin that she had been drinking from lustily earlier that evening. This night she was Biddy Connolly, Irish barmaid and bed-warmer, but for the right price she could be whoever you liked. Her occupation necessitated a degree of anonymity to avoid a visit from the constabulary, and that night she had been warming Alphonse Piazzi's cockles with the enthusiasm that copious amounts of alcohol and splashed cash often encourage. There was an awkward moment of silence where everyone in the tent paused unsure of what was happening. Alphonse looked at Ned, Ned looked at Alphonse, Biddy looked at Ned, and Ned looked at Biddy. Upon seeing Biddy's nipples erect in the cold breeze that whistled through the open tent flap, Ned averted his gaze.

"Do you know who I am?" Ned said, staring at Piazzi who stared back from under a tangled mop of greasy black and silver curls. Piazzi looked across to Biddy and back to Ned. He had no clue. Biddy failed in her attempt to drape a blanket around her shoulders as she crawled towards Ned.

"I know you," she purred slowly, the consumption of gin having affected a boozy drawl. Ned backed out of the tent and Biddy followed, standing up and clinging to Ned. Her naked skin pressed against Ned's cold steel armour giving her a little shock.

"I know you, Ned Kelly! I have something for you," said Biddy directing Ned's face towards hers. She pressed her lips against his for a drunken kiss, but Ned pushed her away roughly.

"Get dressed," Ned snapped, wiping the taste of cheap gin from his lips. Steve on the other hand made sure to get a good look at everything. Biddy winked at him, and the fearsome bushranger immediately turned into an embarrassed mess.

When everyone had gotten dressed under the watchful eyes of the outlaws, Ned began rounding them up like stray sheep. Piazzi had rediscovered his voice but was mindful not to be too forthright this time.

"I know you, Ned Kelly! I have something for you..."

"What you want from us?" Piazzi asked.

"You're to take your tools and pull up a section of the tracks for me," Ned said. Piazzi looked confused.

"We're quarrymen," the Italian explained, "We don't a-know how to."

Ned's beard began to bristle. His plan was going awry very rapidly.

***

Ann Jones slept in a big iron framed bed next to her fifteen-year-old daughter Jane. Her sons were asleep in the opposite bedroom. The drizzle of rain outside made soothing patting sounds on the bark skillion roof. It had been a typically uncomfortable and fleeting sleep, her neuralgia acting up and causing inexplicable aches in her joints exacerbated by the winter chill. Mouth ulcers didn't help matters much either and then there was the sound outside near the tents that she swore was a gunshot that had woken her. Nevertheless, she had managed a couple of hours of solid shuteye leading up to that. Jane was huddled in close to steal some of her mother's warmth. Then there was a pounding at the door.

It was a pounding that demanded immediate attention. Ann sat up on the edge of the bed, the steel frame creaked sympathetically with her aching joints. Dressed only in a white, frilled shift, she staggered out of the room like her legs were made of wood.

"Ma?" Jane mumbled as she sat up. She joined her mother in the corridor as the thumping continued, now accompanied by a man's voice.

"Open up!"

"Who's there?" Ann asked.

"Open the door and find out!"

"If you're a policeman, go to the tents and find who you want."

"If I was a policeman, I think you'd like me better."

Ann Jones cocked her head. She unlatched the door and saw before her, shrouded in darkness, a tall, bearded man in a pale coat holding a bull's-eye lantern. He was barely visible in the gloom and rain. She strained her eyes and recognised the region's most infamous son.

"Mrs. Jones, you must accompany me to the gatehouse," said Ned. He looked behind the proprietor and saw Jane shivering with cold and fright, "Both of you."

"What about my boys? I can't just leave them here," Ann said.

"Where are they?"

"Why, asleep in their beds of course."

"Then you must lock them in there."

Ann stood in silent apprehension. Ned presented a revolver.

"You're to lock that door right now," Ned snapped. Ann reluctantly took the key that hung around her neck on a string and locked the bedroom door.

"If they awake, they'll be terrified," Ann's voice was shaky with fright. Ned half-cocked the revolver.

"Then you'd better not wake them. Stay quiet, they'll be fine. Get dressed, the pair of you."

The publican and her daughter rushed into the bedroom where Ann hastily lit a candle. Ned followed them in to keep watch. Ann eyed Ned with concern.

"Must you watch?" Ann asked, indignant.

"Mrs. Jones, I have no urge to interfere with either of you, I just need to make sure that you don't do anything rash."

"Come, Janie," Ann hissed as she slid her slip off, doing her best to cover up her womanhood while she fumbled for her chemise and drawers. With an underskirt, overskirt, corset, shirt, and bodice hastily applied, Ann sniffled as she plunged an unstockinged foot into a black leather boot. In the light of the candle, she could see tears running down Jane's soft, round cheeks accompanied by stifled sobs. Her heart sank to see the terror in her daughter but knew that as terrifying as this was, complicity could stop things from escalating. She helped her daughter find her shoes and a shawl and they re-emerged with Ned. Ann's untied shoelaces whipped about the floor like enraged snakes.

As they reached the front of the inn, the two ladies were met with the gravel contractors who were in the charge of Steve Hart. Ann recognised Steve immediately. He tipped his hat.

"Mrs. Jones."

She did not respond. It wasn't far to get to the gatehouse, but it was a distinctly unpleasant walk in the rain, which had intensified while Ann and Jane were dressing. The downpour was heavy enough to tame the notorious frizziness of Ann's auburn hair but gentle enough not to drench everyone.

Ned rapped loudly on the stationmaster's door and heard a commotion inside. Growing impatient he tried the handle and gained entry. He burst into the bedroom where John Stanistreet, was dressing.

"Who are you?"

"I'm Ned Kelly and you'll obey me!"

Moments later Stanistreet was herded outside. Ned beckoned Ann and Jane.

"You're to stay in here. Mrs. Stanistreet and her children are stoking a fire. Stay warm. Don't leave the house."

As mother and daughter went inside Ned approached Stanistreet.

"Now, you are to direct these men to pull up the railway tracks."

"I'll do no such thing!"

"You will," said Ned presenting his revolver.

"I don't even know how to. You'd need the platelayers."

Inside the house, Ann and Jane were very self-conscious as they moved towards the fire. Emily Stanistreet, wife of the station master, who was not someone Ann considered to be a friend by a far stretch, gestured for the woman and her trembling daughter to join her.

"Quickly, hop over here ladies," she said. Ann and Jane were very pleased to feel the warmth of the fire and smell the richness of the smoke from the burning logs.

Ned drew the brim of his hat low over his face as he addressed Steve "Take the men and make them fetch the tools to get these rails up. I'm off to get these platelayers."

"How am I going to keep them under control on me own?" Steve whined.

"Just get in there and do what you're good at," Ned snapped in reply. Steve went to the captive men and Ned popped the collar of his oilskin against the rain.

"Stanistreet!" Ned hollered. The stationmaster moved to the outlaw like a well-trained hound

"Yes, Mr. Kelly?"

"Where are these platelayers?"

"Well, Mr. Reardon and Mr. Sullivan are just down the Benalla Road..." Stanistreet was cut off with a wave of Ned's hand.

"You are to do exactly what my colleague Mr. Hart tells you to do. Any trouble, and he has my permission to shoot you."

Stanistreet nodded.

"Steve!" Ned bellowed. Hart came promptly, herding the quarrymen in front of him through the cold.

"Yes?"

"Have those tools ready by the time I get back. Don't be afraid to use a little lead as incentive for cooperation," said Ned. Steve nodded and turned to the group under his command while Ned strode over to his mount and slung himself into the saddle and spurred off towards Benalla.

"Right, you lot, we need those tools." Steve growled. Stanistreet furrowed his brow.

"But I don't have a key to the tool house," he ventured. Steve drew a Tranter revolver and levelled it at Stanistreet's head.

"Then we'll shoot the bloody lock off," Steve went to the doorway and looked in.

"Jane!"

Jane Jones got up and hurried to the door, trembling. As she stepped out, Steve thrust the bullseye lantern towards her.

"Here, take this. I'm going to have my hands full."

***

In Eldorado the police remained hunkered down in the bedroom of Sherritt's hut. The candle had burnt out and the back door had blown closed in the wind. The fire had been quenched and smouldered. In the bedroom, Constable Armstrong found himself growing frustrated. Standing, he peered out of the bedroom window, hoping to catch a glimpse of the brigands waiting outside for them.

"Do you want to get your head blown off?" said Duross.

"I'm telling you they're long gone," replied Armstrong. To prove his point, Armstrong walked boldly out through the curtain and moved to the front door. He grabbed the latch and pulled it open ever so slightly, waiting for a burst of gunfire but upon there being no such response he opened the door fully.

"What did I bloody tell you?"

"They're probably waiting out there for us to present ourselves. Do you want to take the chance?" Duross hissed. Constable Alexander pushed the door closed gently.

"He's right, we shouldn't venture out until daylight," Alexander said softly.

"Won't be daylight for another six hours. We have to report this," Armstrong complained. He holstered his pistol and returned to the bedroom, stepping over Aaron's hours-old corpse.

"I'm dry as parchment, is there anything to drink, Mrs. Barry?" Armstrong asked.

Ellen sat on the bed comforting her daughter. "There's cold tea in the cups on the table. If you're desperate, drink that," the bereft woman responded in a monotone. Armstrong headed out to get a drink. At that moment Belle leaped to her feet, pushed past the policeman and grabbed the cup from the table. She tossed the contents into the fireplace.

"Dan Kelly might have poisoned them," Belle said.

"Well, if we can't have tea then we'll have to settle for water. Can you get some?" Armstrong asked.

"Aye," Belle replied, "I can go out and fetch you water."

Against her better judgement, Belle went outside and fetched a bucket of water in the dark. When she bought it in, she dumped the bucket on the table on the side closest to the corpse so the men would have to step over it to get a drink. The police did not respond to her passive aggression and Belle went back to the bed and lay down clutching her belly.

****

It was almost half past two in the morning when James Reardon was rudely awakened by his dogs barking outside. His wife Margaret grumbled as the noise had awakened their infant daughter Bridget and set her to mewling after what had been a troublesome evening of getting her to settle. Bridget was not always a disagreeable baby, but something seemed to be in the air that night. Reardon heaved himself out of bed and dressed himself quickly, sensing something was amiss. His heels clomped on the floorboards as he moved to the door and drew the bolt. Outside the night air was filled with droplets of rain that snagged the moonlight. Reardon went over to the kennel and hissed at the dogs.

"Oi, enough of that! Get out of it!" he snapped at the animals, but they took no heed. Then he heard the whinny of a horse down near the train line. He headed straight for where the sound had come from and saw a large bay mare by the tracks. Suddenly the hinges of the railway gate creaked, and Dennis Sullivan came out looking worried. Sullivan was dishevelled and unshaven as if he had been rushed out of bed by some sudden disaster. Reardon waved at him for attention.

"What on earth is the matter, Dennis?"

Sullivan looked over his shoulder at Reardon. "I'm taken prisoner by this man," he said gesturing behind himself. At that moment Ned Kelly came sauntering through the gate. He glanced at Reardon and headed straight for him, holding a Webley revolver aloft. He pressed it into Reardon's cheek and spoke urgently.

"What is your name?"

"Reardon," the platelayer replied.

"Ah," said Ned with a hint of relief, "I want you to come and break the line. I was in Beechworth last night, and I had a great contract with the police; I have shot a lot of them, and I expect a train from Benalla with a lot of police and black fellows, and I am going to kill all the bloody bastards."

Reardon's body surged with adrenaline and the world began to ring like a tuning fork. "For God's sake, do not take me; I have got a large family to look after," Reardon begged.

"I have got several others up, but they are no use to me," Ned replied.

"They can do it without me," Reardon said, his mind racing. As Ned pressed the revolver into Reardon's cheek more forcefully, the platelayer's voluminous sideburns brushed against the steel.

"You must do it or I will shoot you."

Reardon ceased protesting, but he would not make things easy for the brigand.

***

With Mrs. Reardon and her children - Michael, Thomas, Mary Elizabeth, Annie, Kate, Ellen, William and baby Bridget - all deposited safely with the other women and children at the Stanistreet house, Reardon, his boarder John Larkins, and Dennis Sullivan were marched over to the tool shed where Steve was waiting with Jane, the men, Stanistreet and an open tool chest.

"Pick up what tools you want," Ned instructed. Reardon made for two spanners and a hammer.

"I have no more to take," stated Reardon. Ned narrowed his eyes.

"Where are your bars?"

"In front of my place." replied Reardon. Ned pursed his lips. It was Euroa all over again, but Ned was in no mood to fool around.

"Steve," Ned said as calmly as he could muster, "you are to ride down to the Reardon house and get those bars. Take the cretin with you as I've a feeling he's going to make life far more difficult than I am prepared to deal with at present. I want him out of my sight before I put holes in him."

Steve nodded and motioned with his revolver for Reardon to accompany him.

Meanwhile in the house the children were gathered by the fire with the women keeping watch. Biddy Connolly was dressed in ill-fitting clothes, resting her head on her jacket, which she had scrunched up into a pillow. Her boots were off and held loosely in her fingers as she dozed. Nineteen-year-old Michael Reardon sat at the far end of the room with his brothers. The three mothers, Ann Jones, Margaret Reardon and Emily Stanistreet, were seated in armchairs and drinking coffee. Ann could not stop thinking about her little boys back at the inn. They were clever and she had never known them to be prone to panic but if faced with being locked in their room in an empty house anything could happen. Margaret and Emily were more worried about their husbands.

"I'm sure they'll be fine. As long as they don't do anything rash, I don't believe that the bushrangers will do any harm," said Emily, trying to convince herself as much as Margaret.

"Have you met my John?" Margaret chuckled, "I've had half a mind to put a bullet through him myself on occasion."

Outside the house the rain died down. Tiny embers danced from the mouth of the flue as the moon appeared from behind a cloud, bathing the township of Glenrowan in milky blue light.

***

The chip and clang of metal on metal rang out in the early morning darkness as the captive men worked by lantern light. James Reardon directed young McHugh in the proper operation of the spanners while Sullivan directed the other men in the act of removing fishplates and separating the rails with crowbars.

"Old man, you're a long time about breaking up this road," said Ned to Reardon.

"I cannot do it quicker," said Reardon defiantly.

Ned drew his revolving carbine and presented the business end to Reardon, "I will make you do it quicker. If you do not look sharp, I shall tickle you with this revolver."

Reardon crossed his arms in defiance, "I cannot do it quicker. Do what you will."

Ned appreciated Reardon's pluck and concealed a smirk. "Give me no cheek," he muttered.

After a half hour there was finally progress and a length of rail was removed and pushed away. Ned felt somewhat relieved.

"Alright, now another. I want at least four lengths removed."

Reardon's eyes bugged momentarily, "One will do as well as twenty!"

"Do you think so?" Ned asked.

"I am certain," Reardon replied. He hoped that one displaced rail would potentially allow a train going full steam to jump it with only a minor jolt. Fortunately for Reardon, Ned was suspicious but accepted the platelayer's expertise.

Far higher on Ned's list of priorities was returning to the station-master's residence. This whole to and fro business had been a ridiculous waste of time and the sooner he could get out of the rain the better. By the track, Steve Hart rested his head on Jane Jones' lap.

"If you do not look sharp, I shall tickle you with this revolver."

Though Steve was now a notorious outlaw, Jane still saw him as the lanky teenager that used to visit her mother's tearoom to get scones and sensed nothing dangerous in him. For the past twenty minutes he had complained of feeling ill. By the lamp light he examined the boarding passes Dick had given him. He saw Ned moving towards him from down the line and sat bolt upright.

"Alright, we're heading back now. Just leave the tools and get a move on. Look sharp," Ned ordered. As he passed Steve, he saw the lad tucking the passes into his cloak.

"What's that?" Ned asked. Steve shrugged. Ned swept the cape back and reached into the pocket and withdrew a flask. He opened the mouth of the flask and took a whiff. The searing aroma of whiskey smacked him in the face, and he passed it back. He hadn't noticed the papers that had fallen out of the pocket with the flask. Steve quickly tried to cover the papers with his foot. Ned saw the papers on the ground and bent down as far as his armour would allow. He drew the papers out and raised the lantern to get a good look. He shoved the passes back into Steve's chest.

"Not planning on hanging around, eh, Hart?" Ned snarled. Steve was wordless. Ned threw the passes down and stomped off after the workmen. Steve gingerly retrieved them and put them back into his pocket. Inside him a jumbled stew of anger, resentment, fear and disappointment began to bubble. His eyes burned with tears of frustration. With a tap on his shoulder from Jane Jones, he quickly composed himself and pocketed the passes. He looked back over his shoulder at the mangled tracks. Just beyond the sabotaged rail the embankment dropped steeply. He dreaded to think of the horrors that would unfold if the train did not stop in time.

Back at the gatehouse, Ned pulled Stanistreet aside while the others were herded into the building.

"What signals do you give the trains?" Ned asked.

"Well, the rule is that white is right, red is wrong, and green is generally come along," Stanistreet replied.

"I see," said Ned, "Well, this time you will give no signals. We will make sure of that. Now go inside."

As Stanistreet went indoors Ned stared back into the gloom. The rain had stopped and now the clouds rushed past the moon in plumes of purple and navy. Ned sniffed the air. Something wasn't right but he couldn't quite pin it down.

5

Sunday Morning

Dan and Joe rode to a secluded spot on the outskirts of Eldorado where Paddy was waiting under a gum tree. Here the two outlaws had a tent pitched waiting to provide a place for rest. The spot was heavily forested and provided easy hiding spots in the event of a pursuit or ambush.

As Joe dismounted, he grabbed his swag from the pommel of his saddle then unfurled it on the ground. The shotgun came tumbling out at Paddy's feet.

"So, it's done then? The police are dead," said Paddy, picking up the murder weapon.

"No. I changed the plan. I took out that bastard Sherritt instead," Joe said.

Paddy wasn't sure how to process the new information. "Oh," was all he could manage.

Dan dismounted and hobbled the horses by the tree.

"Take that gun and keep it with you while you keep an eye on things around the Devil's Elbow. I expect those bloody traps will be out at any moment. Make sure to give us both time to get to Glenrowan," said Joe, handing Paddy a cartouche full of cartridges to go with the gun. Paddy nodded and fetched his horse.

When he returned, he gave Joe a tight hug. "Please stay safe," Paddy said.

"You too Patsy. I'll be seeing you."

Dan and Paddy shook hands then the younger Byrne mounted and rode into the night. Once he had ridden out of earshot Joe plundered the saddlebags and retrieved a bottle of whiskey which he uncorked and sucked on eagerly. He wandered to the edge of the clearing and took a deep breath. The cold air stung his face, and his eyes began to swim in tears.

"Joe," Dan ventured, "Sherritt got what he deserved. He was in too deep with the traps. It was only a matter of time before he sold us out proper."

"That's easy for you to say," Joe snapped, "it wasn't your mate that got snuffed!"

"He was my mate, but I'm not going to let someone put a noose around my neck because we used to kick around together. Sometimes what's necessary ain't nice or fair!"

Joe stared up into the sky, his eyes dancing as he examined the stars above him. He hoped somehow that this was a dream, but he knew from the sick feeling in his stomach that he was out of luck.

***

Back at the gatehouse the men settled in around the dining table. Stanistreet entered the room with a half-full decanter of brandy.

"I don't suppose I can tempt any of you men into having a bit of brandy to warm your bellies after being out in the cold and wet so long?" Stanistreet said forcing some joy into his voice. The men quietly nodded and Stanistreet counted heads, making a mental note of how many glasses to procure.

In the kitchen, Emily Stanistreet whipped up a platter of bacon, pig's cheek and bread for the men and another for the women and children. She took the food to the men, which they accepted eagerly. As John Lowe reached out for food Alphonse Piazzi slapped his wrist.

"You let the men eat a-first or I take-a the other hand," Piazzi chided. Ned and Steve lingered, waiting for the others to eat before partaking in any themselves. Ned looked at Kennedy's watch, it was almost five in the morning.

"Keep an eye on this lot, Steve, I'll be back." Ned said as he took his leave. The younger bushranger shoved a pistol into the red sash around his waist and eagerly grabbed a piece of bacon from the plate and wolfed it down.

Ned wandered across the tracks to McDonnell's Railway Tavern and entered the building. Inside the lights were low and the sympathisers milled about. Jack was seated by the fire drinking a brandy and ginger beer in a short glass.

"You're a bit young for such hard stuff aren't you, Jacky boy?" Ned joked.

"I can handle it," Jack said petulantly.

"Ah, you wouldn't be the first Lloyd to struggle with a bit of liquor were it to be otherwise." Ned smirked.

"How are things with you, cousin?" Tom asked.

"The track is torn up and we've got prisoners over at the gatehouse. Steve is over there watching them now."

"Who's watching Steve?" said Tom.

"Very funny," Dick replied from across the room.

Ned grabbed the glass from Jack's hand and imbibed a decent mouthful. He winced; the taste of ginger had never been one he particularly enjoyed.

"Now, remember that you are not to set any rockets off until the train arrives. One rocket for a successful derailment, two for danger," Ned said.

"We know," said Jack.

"Did you hand weapons out?" Ned asked Tom.

"Yes, there should be a few sympathisers around the place ready to join us when the time comes. Don't worry Ned."

"I have to worry. We've a lot riding on this."

***

At Maggie Skillion's hut the women took it in turns to nap while they waited for the signal. Kate sat by the fireplace reading Ned's battered old copy of Lorna Doone while Ettie Hart sat at the dining table writing a poem on foolscap paper. In the bedroom Maggie could be heard snoring loudly. Each roaring intake of breath made the women giggle.

"Makes you wonder how Bill Skillion ever managed to get a wink of sleep," Kate laughed. She paused for a moment to consider that as they sat waiting for things to unfold at Glenrowan, Bill Skillion was locked up in a cold, dark gaol cell. She felt keenly that it was a miscarriage of justice, as much as she didn't like him, but she had grown used to the feeling of injustice.

A short while later Ettie and Maggie swapped places and the elder woman took up a spot by the fire and smoked. She held her hand out in front of her and examined her knuckles, which had become swollen and sore.

"Kitty, sweetheart, can you rub my hands for me? You're ever so good at it," Maggie asked.

"Are your hands acting up again? You said you'd see the doctor about this," Kate replied.

"Who has time for doctors? I have too much to do around here to be worrying about that."

Kate kissed her sister's forehead and gently rubbed her aching joints. Time seemed to be moving very slowly and the sisters wondered what was happening in Glenrowan.

****

Ned stood outside the stationmaster's house and filled the bowl of his pipe with tobacco, lighting it with a wax match and puffing gently in the morning light. He checked his watch - eight o'clock. Presently he was aware of the sound of hooves and unslung his revolving carbine from his shoulder. He looked towards McDonnell's tavern and saw Dan and Joe riding towards him. When a few yards from him they dismounted and led their horses to Ned.

"Is it done?" Ned asked.

Joe nodded. He swayed slightly.

"Get inside and have some tucker. You'll need your strength up," Ned instructed. The newcomers hitched their horses to Stanistreet's veranda and went inside.

As Steve gestured for Joe and Dan to join him, Ned walked into the parlour to warm himself. Ann Jones took the opportunity to sidle up to Ned and placed a hand gently on his forearm.

"Why don't you come back to the inn, old man, and have a wash and a bite to eat? It'll do you a world of good."

"I'm perfectly fine Mrs. Jones, thank you for the offer," Ned replied. Ann took her leave of the outlaw and sat down with her daughter, rubbing her aching legs as she sank down onto the sofa. Ned lingered, staring into the flames. He couldn't shake the feeling that things were not going to work out this time.

****

At half past eight the sun had risen enough that it was easy to see outside. For the first time since Aaron Sherritt had been murdered the police felt safe enough to look outside. Constable Alexander took it upon himself to make the move and stepping over Aaron's corpse he pushed the front door open a crack. Everything seemed fine so far, so he stepped outside.

Nothing.

This confirmed Armstrong's supposition that the Kelly Gang had long ago taken their leave. He saw a Chinese man walking by on the road and shouted and waved to get his attention. The traveller was confused but walked towards the hut. Looking past Alexander, he saw the bloody corpse of Aaron Sherritt on the floor and turned to run. Alexander chased.

"No! Police! Police! Police, savvy?" Alexander shouted. The man paused.

"You police?"

"Yes, I'm police. Need your help. You send message?" Alexander said slowly in broken English. The Chinese man nodded, though his comprehension was almost nil.

"Go to police station in Beechworth and tell them murder at Sherritt's."

"Ok, ok. I no going to Beechworf," the Chinese man replied. Alexander took his notebook out and scribbled a message on it, folded it and gave it to the man.

"Please go to Beechworth and give this to police."

"You police," the Chinese man replied, confused.

"No, give to Beechworth police. Very important."

"Important?" the man cocked his head.

"Yes, important." Alexander stressed. As incentive he pressed five shillings into the man's hand. Understanding the universal language of money, the man slid the note into his boot.

"Ok, ok," the man bowed and began walking towards Beechworth. Alexander sighed in relief.

Five minutes later the Chinese man returned and appeared at the door with a knock.

"I no go to Beechworf. Too far. Too far," he said emphatically to the exasperated police. He returned the note but kept the money.

"Please, can you at least go to the neighbour and tell him to come here? We can't go," Alexander begged.

The Chinese man wandered away and almost a half hour later a rider came to the front door. It was a bookish, middle-aged man named Cornelius O'Donoghue. O'Donoghue was a local schoolteacher and had taught both Joe and Aaron. He had followed the unfolding events closely. Constable Duross stood outside to greet him.

"There was a Chinaman sent me here," O'Donoghue said, dismounting, "well, not here exactly; he gestured in this direction. I could barely understand him."

"We need someone to get a note to Detective Ward in Beechworth," said Duross.

"Oh? What's the news?"

"Young Sherritt has been murdered by the Kelly Gang," Duross replied. O'Donoghue went pale.

"How awful. I will do what I can," O'Donoghue said.

***

After Dan and Joe had eaten, Ned sent Joe across to McDonnell's to fetch three of the gang's packhorses. Joe obeyed without a grumble, riding across on his own mare and then taking the three animals from the paddock at the tavern over to Jones' inn.

Meanwhile, Ann Jones took the opportunity to suggest taking the prisoners over to the inn for breakfast.

"Ned," she began in a sing-song tone, "seeing as yer starting to set up at my place anyway why don't I make everyone a nice fry-up for breakfast?"

Ned considered for a moment and his face softened. "Alright," he agreed.

Ann grinned broadly and linked her arm in Ned's. "Oh, I'll fill yer belly up, don't ye worry, young Ned. I have some most excellent ham. I'll send Janie up to stoke the fires and get the boys up."

"I could almost accuse you of being too eager, Mrs. Jones," said Ned with a smirk, "I'll send Joe up with her. He needs jobs to do to keep his mind occupied."

Marching up the gentle slope towards the inn with Jane, Joe got his first good look at the building that would be their prison for the day: a modest weatherboard building, whitewashed and well maintained. The roof was corrugated iron - quite a luxury for such a small establishment. Along the front of the building were three windows - one for each room: the dining room, the bar and the parlour - as well as two doors, one to the bar room and the other to the dining room.

Jane unlocked the door to the bar room and entered, leaving the door open for Joe. The room inside was spacious enough with a long bar stretching across most of the room and equipped with big ale taps that resembled ivory handled bells. A framed portrait of Queen Victoria hung on the wall that separated the bar room from the dining room. Joe sneered at the portrait of the jowly empress in her refinery; lace veil descending from her tiny crown, silk sash over her shoulder and a look of vague disapproval on her face. Sour old cow, he thought.

Jane opened the doors to the parlour and the dining room. Entering the dining room, Jane whipped open the curtains and let the morning light in before trotting over to the fireplace where a dense blanket of ash lay banked up atop the smouldering fire. She took a poker and jabbed at the ashes sending tiny glowing flecks flurrying then took a decent sized log in her tiny hands and plonked it down atop the embers. She did the same with the fireplace in the parlour. Joe stood in the middle of the bar room the whole time watching the girl go about her duties.

When Jane re-entered the bar room, she smoothed down her ebony-black hair and made a move for the back door.

"Where are you going?" Joe asked, reaching for the revolver poking out from under his coat.

"My brothers are locked in their bedroom out the back, I need to get them out and see that they're alright," Jane said.

"Very well, let's be quick about it, there's a couple of dozen hungry bellies out there waiting for breakfast."

Jane led Joe through the breezeway to the skillion and through the kitchen to where her brothers' bedroom was situated. Unlocking the door, Jane pushed it gently open. Inside the boys were all still asleep. She rolled her eyes.

"They'd sleep through the rapture," Jane sighed.

"Reminds me of my brother, Denny," Joe chuckled. He recalled the way his mother would order him and Paddy to wake up their younger sibling, which they did by lifting up one side of the bed and making him tumble out onto the floor. The memory allowed a hint of levity to push aside the gloom that had settled in over him since the previous night.

Jane took a broom from the doorway of the kitchen and used it to swat the boys until they woke up with much grumbling. Owen was the first to become alert and looked straight at Joe and felt uneasy. As Joe brushed aside his coat to rest his hand on his hip, the grip of his revolver was on show and Owen gasped and shrunk beneath his blankets.

"Who are you?" seven-year-old Jeremiah asked, rubbing the sleep out of his eyes.

"I'm Joe Byrne," Joe responded, shifting his weight.

"You mean like the bushranger?" Jeremiah continued.

"I am the bushranger!"

"I thought you'd be bigger," Jeremiah quipped. Jane slapped the boy's shoulder chiding him. Joe gave the boy a greasy stare.

"I'm big where it counts, boy."

"I thought you'd be bigger," Jeremiah quipped.

"Come on, get dressed you lot, we've got work to do," Jane urged the boys. With much whining they complied. Once the boys were in their clothes, Jane herded them out of the bedroom into the bar room where she grabbed a bottle of cognac from the shelf behind the counter.

The group of children, led by Joe, marched back to the stationmaster's house. Entering the abode Dan began to laugh.

"What's tickling you?" Joe asked with a frown.

"I might have to start calling you Nanny," Dan replied.

"Shut up," Joe snapped.

He continued into the dining room where Ann Jones had the bottle of cognac ready and waiting.

"Join me for a drink, Mr. Byrne?" she asked.

"Hard to refuse such a kind offer, ma'am," Joe replied, taking a seat next to her. Ann poured two glasses and raised hers in a toast, Joe did the same but waited for her to drink first before following suit.

"It's a nice drop, that," Ann said looking at the bottle, "I hope the boys weren't too much trouble for ye."

"I've wrangled worse," Joe replied, "one of them was a bit lippy,"

"Oh, that'll be Jeremiah, I'll bet. Got a mouth like a runaway horse, that boy. I shall have to have a word to him about talking respectfully to ye."

"Aye."

Ann threw back the rest of her glass and sucked air in through gritted teeth as the booze left a burning sensation.

"This is the only thing that helps my neuralgia, y'know," Ann said casually. Joe nodded. He absent-mindedly fingered the pocket where he was keeping paper packets of opium powder. Tiny beads of sweat formed on his brow as he tried to force his cravings for the drug down.

***

The morning felt interminable at Eldorado. Cornelius O'Donoghue had returned to the murder scene stating that his wife had refused to allow him to take the news to Beechworth and the police were running out of ideas. Armstrong and Dowling decided to visit the Sherritts' neighbour, a man called Duckett. Dowling knocked on the door with urgency and after a short wait, during which much grumbling could be heard from inside the hut, the door was opened to reveal a scruffy looking young man with mighty sideburns and a clay pipe dangling from his mouth.

"Yeah?"

"We need your help. There has been a murder at the Sherritts', and we need someone to send the word to Beechworth," replied Armstrong.

"Murder, is it?"

"Yes, last night," Alexander said, his voiced was strained.

"Well, I suppose that explains the dog howling all bloody night. I had a mind to shoot the bloody thing so's I could get some sleep."

"Sherritt has been murdered, are you listening to me?" Alexander repeated.

"Yeah, alright. So, you want me to send the word to the police?" Duckett sniffed.

"Yes! Please!"

"Yeah, well, I s'pose I can stop by the police station there when I go into town," Duckett said.

"Thank you," said Armstrong as he handed Duckett an envelope. He took it and slammed the door in the constable's face. Alexander turned to Armstrong.

"He's not going to do it, is he?"

***

As thin fog dissipated in the morning sun, Ned gathered his captives outside the stationmaster's house and stood on the veranda. He rested his hands on his hips, puffed out his chest and prepared to give a speech.

"Ladies and gentlemen, if I can beg your attention for a moment, there are some important points I must inform you of. We are here in Glenrowan with a mission, but we have no issue with its people. You are our prisoners for your own protection as much as ours. We will not keep you locked away, but you are to stay where we can see you at all times or the consequences will be severe," Ned flourished his revolver to drive home the point.

"Remember, we are outlaws. We are desperate men with blood on our hands. Yet we do not wish to enforce our rules any more than you wish to endure the repercussions of violating them. The women and children will remain here under the watchful eye of my confederate Mr. Hart, the rest of you will come to Mrs. Jones' inn with myself, my brother and Mr. Byrne. Mrs. Jones will provide you with a repast. Fetch your things and proceed to the inn."

Ned gestured for his gang to join him. "This train is taking longer than expected. We're going to need to capture anyone who passes through here so they can't raise an alarm or interfere with the train."

"Why do I get stuck on guard duty here?" Steve moaned.

"Because I don't want a repeat of Jerilderie and have to listen to complaints about you pinching cheap watches," Ned snapped.

"Don't worry, Steve. Much nicer things to look at here than we have over there," said Dan encouragingly, gesturing to the women returning to the gatehouse as the parade of workmen began to move towards The Glenrowan Inn.

While walking to the inn, Ann Jones gave instructions to her children, "Listen here my darlings, yer to stay with me in the kitchen this morning and help prepare the breakfast for the men, understand? And no lip from you Jeremiah, treat Mr. Kelly and his companions with respect."

The family headed straight through the building into the skillion where they began stoking the fire and grabbing bacon and eggs and tea to prepare the breakfast.

In the inn, Ned directed the prisoners into the dining room and instructed Joe to keep watch. Ned and Dan then headed out the back.

"Dan, take the armour and weapons into the bedroom behind the bar. That will be our armoury," Ned dictated.

"What will you do?"

"I'll feed the horses,"

"You're not going to help me with this?"

"You can manage."

Ned turned and lifted the sliprail on the paddock fence. Dan shook his head and approached the packhorses which were wandering around the paddock and began removing the saddlebags filled with pieces of armour and placing them at the fence.

As Dan toiled, Jane watched him from the back door of the skillion. She couldn't take her eyes off him. Suddenly her mother's voice rang out from the kitchen.

"Janie!"

Jane snapped to attention and Ann beckoned Jane close to her and spoke in a low voice.

"Jane, listen to me, I want ye to make sure ye do everything Mr. Kelly asks of you. Don't be rude, don't be afraid; just do as yer told."

"But aren't they dangerous?"

"Aye," said Ann, "but they're also men besides. If ye stay in their favour, we may just come out of this the better for it. Their squabble is with the police, and I can't say I blame them after the trouble we've had. Do you understand?"

"I think so, ma," replied Jane.

"Good girl. And don't forget to smile, ye've lovely teeth and a pretty smile can bend a man's will very easily," Ann said tweaking Jane's cheek.

In the dining room Joe paced while some of the men played a game of cribbage. The younger ones opted to smoke and play a round of poker with tobacco as the prize. The room was quiet and sedate.

As he paced, Joe stared out the window. From the dining room he could see the train station, and beyond it, McDonnell's. In his heart he felt like the plan was already a failure. He ran his fingers along the grip of his pistol absent-mindedly.

Behind him one of the boys lost at poker and smacked the table with an open hand. The sound startled Joe and the image of Aaron staggering away from him with his stomach and throat ripped open flashed in front of his eyes. Joe reeled and lost his breath for a second before glaring at the poker players with his pistol drawn. The gamblers immediately settled down.

In that moment Jane entered with plates of food, which she gave to some of the men. Joe approached her.

"Jane, fetch me a bottle of gin, would you? Make sure it hasn't been breached."

Jane nodded and fetched a fresh bottle and a glass. She re-entered the dining room and placed the items on the table before Joe who had taken a seat with his back to the fire. He looked at the bottle and glass intensely. He turned to the girl.

"Go fetch another glass."

"Good girl. And don't forget to smile, ye've lovely teeth and a pretty smile can bend a man's will very easily," Ann said tweaking Jane's cheek.

Jane went to grab the glass in Joe's hand, but he shook his head and gestured to the bar. Jane went to the bar and upon bringing a second glass, Joe poured both of them a drink.

"Bottoms up," said Joe, toasting the girl who understood what was expected. Joe was impressed at how well the girl tolerated the drink. He poured two more but added opium powder to his, which he swilled in the glass to mix into a tincture.

"I shouldn't have another," Jane protested.

"Come, it'll make you merry and life is short so it may as well be merry too," Joe smiled softly. Jane drank her gin and winced at its bitterness. Joe took her hand in his.

"Good girl. Leave the bottle and off you go."

***

Ned rested his foot on the train track near the station master's house, the sunlight gleamed off his polished spurs. He checked his watch - it was nine o'clock. He frowned. Dan approached him, smoothing his floppy black hair down nervously then keeping it contained under his billycock hat.

"When do you think that train will come?" Dan asked.

"Could be any time. Word will have reached Hare by now. Definitely," Ned replied, gazing down the track.

"I don't know if that train is going to come. It's been too long; the longer we wait the more this falls apart. We should leave while we can, let these people go and head for the gap."

"We leave now, it means all of this was for nought."

"No, it doesn't. We've shown the police that we're still here and we're not to be trifled with. Maybe the fear is enough to keep them held back?"

"And what do we do? We run and hide again? I'm tired of running. I'm tired of hiding," Ned snapped, "We stay and see it through. The train will come."

Dan scowled and left Ned to brood over the tracks. Shortly before noon, Ned and Joe rode to McDonnell's. It was a whitewashed, weatherboard building. Squat and broad with a shingle roof and a large sign bearing the establishment's name in bold, ornate lettering, adjacent to the veranda. The outlaws walked past a stack of crates and entered the bar room. They greeted their sympathisers who were tucking into dinner. The mood was almost jovial.

At the bar Paddy McDonnell stood wiping sulphuric acid over the counter with a rag.

"That's a hell of a smell, Paddy," Joe exclaimed.

"Well, it keeps the counter clean. You'd be surprised how many people forget where their mouths are when they're drinking a beer. Speaking of which, can I get you lads something?" McDonnell's face beamed; rosy cheeks plumped by a smile hidden behind a black beard peppered with silver.

"It's a bit early in the day for me," said Ned.

"Got any gin?" asked Joe.

"What sort of establishment would I be running if I didn't have gin?" Paddy replied with mock offence.

"Where's this train at?" Wild Wright growled from across the room.

"Couldn't be far away. Typical of the traps to dally in striking while the iron is hot," Ned declared with a chuckle. If he felt his confidence was misplaced, he was very good at hiding it.

Paddy poured Joe a drink and placed it on the counter. Joe placed coinage down and withdrew a packet of powder from his pocket, pouring it in and swilling the liquid to make it dissolve. In one big gulp he swallowed the tincture.

A short time later they were joined by Hanorah, Paddy's wife. She was a demure woman with a pale eyes and shapely lips. She smiled at Ned who returned the gesture. She greeted Joe by calling him 'sugar' and winking.

"I suppose I'd better get to business, Paddy," said Ned, "we've got to bail you up and take you over to the rest of the prisoners at the Glenrowan Inn. If anyone suspected that you were with us there could be problems."

"What of me, Ned?" said Hanorah.

"Go and fetch the children so we can march you to Stanistreet's house," Ned drew his pistol and rested it on the counter.

Within minutes the McDonnells were heading over the tracks to be lumped with the other prisoners. Hanorah and her children were deposited under Steve's guard with the other women and children. There were suspicious gazes directed at them all as the new arrivals were sent in to join the rest of the captives. The McDonnells' sympathies were an open secret.

Their proximity to the Stanistreets meant that Paddy McDonnell was well acquainted with John's drinking habits and Emily's borderline neurosis. Paddy would say that nobody knows the people better than a publican; people open up to publicans in a way that the police could only dream of, which of course saw local troopers stopping in frequently to ask questions. Between Paddy and Hanorah, the McDonnells had gathered information on everyone in town and knew some juicy secrets that could ruin a few reputations if the McDonnells had been the vindictive, gossipy type.

Ned and Joe headed up to the inn where smoke wafted gently from the chimneys and the captives milled about inside leisurely under Dan's watch. Ned paused to look at the golden timepiece in his pocket. He didn't even check the time, he just felt like it somehow gave him a feeling of control.

***

At ten o'clock Superintendent Hare strode into the general telegraph office in Benalla to see if there was any news. Behind a wooden bench guarded with iron bars, a young man stood dressed in shirtsleeves, a waistcoat and a green acetate eyeshade.

"Good morning, my man," began Hare, "I don't suppose you have any messages for me?"

The telegraph operator handed over a stack of telegrams from the police stations in the district.

"Seems like it was a pretty quiet night, Inspector."

Hare thumbed through the telegrams. He sighed, "Well, in that case I shall return at nine o'clock tonight. If you need me before then, you know how to reach me."

"Very good, sir."

Hare walked leisurely back to his accommodation at the Commercial Hotel and took note of the looming grey clouds that were rolling across the sky. When he returned to his room, he sat on his bed and groaned. His head was dewy with sweat and his heart felt like it was raging in his chest. Normally he would have taken a cab back from the office due to his unusually high blood pressure, but he had decided to get some exercise in.

He doubled over with another groan and took off his shoes before laying back on the bed. He closed his eyes to get a nap in before luncheon. Within minutes he was snoring like a sawblade through a red gum.

***

At the Sherritt hut, Belle awoke with an incredible pain in her belly. She curled up and clutched at the bump with a moan. Her mother launched a verbal barrage at the police.

"You are meant to be men! Policemen at that! Yet you've done nothing but cower and bumble. Will none of you get off your backsides and do something?"

Constable Armstrong got up without a word and marched outside. He marched towards Mount Sugarloaf where he thought Aaron's horses would be milling about the paddock, but not a single one could be seen. Cursing, he began walking down the track towards Beechworth. The gravel crunched underfoot but the damp weather kept much of the track alternating between sludge and slime causing Armstrong to slip when he wasn't getting bogged.

Armstrong estimated he must have been walking for a mile when he saw a rider up ahead. Mounted on a grey horse, the figure was hunched forward and dressed in a grey topcoat and a drab coloured hat. Suddenly the rider turned and galloped towards Armstrong, who immediately reached for the revolver hidden under his coat. As the horse pulled up, Armstrong recognised the ginger whiskers, wide mouth and sunken eyes of Paddy Byrne. Not recognizing the trooper, Paddy sneered and turned off the road, allowing him to pass. Armstrong sighed with relief and continued.

His feet began to ache, and he felt blisters forming on his toes when he saw a rider heading back home after mass on an old nag. Armstrong ducked into his path and waved at him to stop.

"Sir! Stop! Stop there please!"

The man looked up, perplexed, and tugged at the reins.

"What is your name?" Armstrong asked.

"Considine."

"I'm sorry, Mr. Considine, but I must take your horse. Urgent police business!"

Considine dismounted without fuss and Armstrong bounded into the saddle in his place. Turning the horse around, Armstrong galloped away as fast as the mount could take him. Considine stood for a time in the road where the thought struck him that he now had to figure out how to get his horse back.

Only a few minutes had elapsed when Armstrong felt the nag struggling to maintain her pace. Her mouth was foamy, and her breathing laboured. Just as the animal began to slow, Armstrong recognised Duckett who was strolling along the road.

"Hello there!"

Duckett turned, "I thought you was staying back at Sherritt's place?"

"Change of plans. You don't need to go into town now."

As Armstrong rode past, Duckett took out the envelope and attempted to run alongside the beast. He waved the envelope at Armstrong.

"Take this back!"

"No, just tear it up. I don't need it," said Armstrong.

As the trooper rode onwards, Duckett halted. He looked at the envelope in his hands and contemplated the instructions.

He promptly opened the envelope and read the contents of the letter within and gasped.

"Bloody hell!"

ACT TWO

6

Round Up

In the forenoon, the brothers Jack, William and Patrick Delaney had decided that such a quiet Sunday was perfect opportunity to go hunting for "boomahs", the term they used to describe kangaroos. The boys were eighteen, seventeen and thirteen respectively, possessed with the boundless enthusiasm for shooting bounding macropods that seemed to define the teenagers of the region. They walked to the Reardon house with their hunting dog, a greyhound named Lion, to ask young Michael Reardon to go hunting with them as he knew where to get the best firearm for the task. Unfortunately, when they knocked on the door there was no answer. The boys looked in the windows and tried to see any sign of activity inside.

"Not even the old lady is there," William said. As the boys started walking away, they saw seventeen-year-old Tom Cameron, the son of the gatekeeper, who had thought to join Reardon in hunting as well. They all shook hands, clownishly emulating the behaviour of adults in the way teenage boys do.

"Are you coming from the Reardon place?" Tom asked.

"Yeah, there's nobody there," said Jack.

"The whole town is like that, something is up," replied Tom. The boys continued walking along the tracks.

"Hey, Tom, do you have a pipe? I lost mine," Jack asked. Tom handed over his own small porcelain pipe.

"Look after it, will you..."

They were approaching the railway crossing when Ned Kelly rode up on Joe's grey mare. The boys had seen Ned around the area frequently enough that they knew exactly who he was.

"Where are you lot going?" Ned said, pulling the reins gently and bringing the horse to a halt next to the boys.

"We were going hunting but our mate wasn't home," said William.

"Hunting, is it? Well, you shall have to put those plans aside and come with me. What are your names?"

"I'm Tom Cameron, these are the Delaneys; William, Pat and Jack."

Ned ushered the lads in front of him. Ned gave Jack Delaney a side-long stare as they reached Stanistreet's house.

"What's your name again, boy?"

"Jack Delaney."

"You were the one helping the traps, weren't you?" Ned brought Music to a halt and cut the boys off. Percy began to bark.

"What do you mean?"

"I know all about you. Driving the mud-crushers around in your spring cart. I bet you felt like a real somebody didn't you? Carting them around looking for me, you rat!" Ned's eyes burned like fiery coals as he dismounted, "Well, I don't like the sort of people who help the police. You want to be a policeman, do you?" he jabbed his finger into the boy's chest so forcefully it caused him to stagger. Patrick Delaney held Lion by the collar as he growled.

"Please, I didn't do anything," Jack began to tremble violently, crushing Tom Cameron's delicate pipe in his fist as he balled up his hands in terror.

"You want to become a trap so you can shoot me? I ought to blow your head inside out!" Ned was screaming, spittle flinging from his mouth onto Delaney's face.

"Please Mr. Kelly, stop it!" William Delaney begged. Jack sank to his knees, spasming and bawling in terror.

"You want to be a trap and shoot me down like a dog? Here you go," Ned snapped as he took Piazzi's old pistol from his belt and threw it at the trembling boy.

Inside the house, Emily Stanistreet could hear the commotion and walked to the veranda. She saw Jack Delaney fumbling with a revolver while Ned stooped over him shouting.

"Pick it up! I've never done a cowardly thing in my life, but you can shoot me, go on! Claim the reward and live like a king!"

Emily rushed back inside where Joe Byrne was taking a brandy with Steve Hart and tugged on his sleeve.

"Please, Joe, go and stop Ned. He's like to murder a boy out there!"

Joe could see from Mrs. Stanistreet's expression that the situation was serious. He threw back his drink and went outside.

"Aim true. Cock the damned thing you useless bloody milksop!" Ned barked as he stood back, arms outstretched. Delaney aimed the weapon sheepishly in Ned's direction, it wobbled impotently in his limp hand. In his terror Delaney's bladder weakened and he wet himself.

"Ned!" Joe shouted but was ignored, "Ned!"

Ned swung around to look at Joe, his face was bright red and twisted in rage.

"Give it a bloody rest, will you? You've just about killed the boy with fright."

Ned loomed over Delaney and snatched the pistol from his hands. He pulled the trigger, but nothing happened, demonstrating that it was, in fact, unloaded.

"Like I'd waste good ammunition on you," Ned seethed, giving the shuddering youth a nasty shove. He vaulted back into the saddle and from atop Music he ordered the boys inside the house. Joe helped Jack Delaney to his feet, the boy was still sobbing, his trousers damp with urine.

"Bloody hell," Joe said under his breath.

***

Far away from the growing collection of prisoners at Glenrowan, Constable Armstrong finally arrived on the outskirts of Beechworth.

He steered the nag along the coach road until finally reaching the streets, paved with tonnes of soggy crushed granite. Crossing a bridge, squat buildings with facades of yellow, white and red dotted the streets before him, leading up to the churches and the intimidating prison beyond them.

Armstrong rode up Ford Street and headed straight towards the courthouse. Here the telegraph office sat quietly near the Chinese Protector's Office; a reminder of the heady days of the gold rush where men like Robert O'Hara Burke upheld the law despite civil unrest from the gold miners.

He rode to the police stables and interred the horse, which panted and twitched, covered in white foam after such an unusually intense ride for the animal. Armstrong stood a moment to catch his breath alongside the nag. He did not look forward to Detective Ward's reaction.

***

The wheels of a buggy clattered along the road towards the crossing near Stanistreet's. In the buggy rode Thomas Curnow, a twenty-five-year-old Cornishman with a ginger cowlick and wispy beard. Next to him was his pregnant wife Jeannie, holding their year-old daughter, and his sister Catherine. Catherine looked back, her scarlet llama wool scarf fluttering in the breeze. Behind the buggy rode nineteen-year-old Dave Mortimer on a young palomino. The group were headed for the reserve just past Ann Jones' inn for a picnic. As they approached the railway crossing near the Stanistreet house, Curnow could see a considerable gathering around the Glenrowan Inn.

"Ere, what's this then?" said Curnow, "Could Mrs. Jones have died? She has been very ill of late."

Catherine and Jeannie looked at each other for confirmation, neither having a suitable answer. At the crossing, Stanistreet appeared and waved down the approaching party. Curnow yanked on the reins and ground to a halt.

"Mr. Stanistreet," ventured Curnow, "What's all this about?"

"Bad news, I'm afraid, Tom," Stanistreet replied cryptically. Curnow looked beyond and saw a bearded man on a grey horse he didn't recognise, and a tall, tired-looking copper-haired man at the door of the Stanistreet house.

"The whole place has been stuck up by the Kelly Gang," said Stanistreet.

"Giss on!" Curnow replied dismissively. Ned approached the group promptly, his revolvers sticking out from under his coat. Curnow knew at once it was no folly.

"Who are you then?" Ned enquired.

"I'm Thomas Curnow, the schoolteacher. This is my wife Jeannie, my sister Catherine and my brother-in-law Davey on the horse there."

"Well, I'm afraid I'll have to detain you. Take the buggy up to Jones' inn and put it round the back. Ladies, you'll wait in the stationmaster's house with the babe."

Ned turned and signalled for Joe Byrne to escort the women into the house before drawing a pistol, "Gentlemen, accompany me." Ned directed the men with the pistol. They obeyed without further question.

With the conveyances stored safely, Curnow, Mortimer and Stanistreet were marched into the bar. Curnow waddled along, resting heavily on a cane. From birth he had suffered dysplasia that had resulted in excruciating pain in his hip if he walked, rode or sat up for too long. He scanned the room for a familiar face and found it in the form of James Reardon. He hobbled to the platelayer with a greeting.

"Ere, Jim, how is it with you?"

"They snared you too, eh?" said Reardon with a chuckle.

"What on earth is all this about?" Curnow took a seat and thrust his leg out to take some of the strain off his hip. Mortimer and Stanistreet joined them.

"Just quietly," Stanistreet gestured Curnow and Mortimer close, "the Kellys want to knock a special police train off the rails, further on the bend."

Reardon added, "They forced us to break up the line last night."

Curnow was aghast, "And nobody is doing anything about it?"

"If you want to take it up with four armed outlaws, be my guest, but I wouldn't advise it if you like your dome free of holes," Reardon replied, tapping his forehead. "Ned Kelly said they shot a party of police in Beechworth last night."

"When is this train due?" asked Curnow.

"They reckon it's already on its way, but you know how quick the police are to respond."

***

At midday Ned gave a speech laying down the rules to the new captives. It was the same as the one from that morning. Grog flowed much heavier then, and Ann Jones' cash box began to weigh heavily, much to her satisfaction.

Taking a break from tending the bar, Ann walked to the veranda where Ned rested against a post with his arms folded. He wore the quilted blue cap that had been made for him by Kate.

"I say, I ought to have ye lads around all the time. Ye've really drummed up business," Ann said with a wide smile.

"Aye, and I'd give you a hand fixing up the place. The holes in your roof must be a bugger of a thing when the rain hits."

"Something of a tradesman, are ye?" Ann asked, placing her hands on her hips, which was the only full part of her figure.

"Learned to lay bricks at Williamstown; learned how to work bark

"I say, I ought to have ye lads around all the time. Ye've really drummed
up business."

slabs from my Da; I built a house for my Ma and a fort for my gang in the ranges. Aye - I can fix your roof," said Ned.

"I might just take ye up on that when this blows over," said Ann with a sigh. Ned shot Ann a tender look. The idea of doing some honest labour instead of running from the law made him yearn for the quiet days before Fitzpatrick tore his world apart. Ann reached down and ran her hand over Ned's green sash, which rested low on his hips.

"This is very lovely."

"It's my victory sash. Had it for years," Ned beamed.

"Victory sash? Did ye win it?"

"No, not exactly. I wear it to celebrate," Ned was pensive for a fleeting moment then continued. "It was given to me for saving a boy from drowning."

"Well, I don't see them writing about that in the papers!"

"Why would they? Painting me as a monster sells more papers and my enemies are the ones with a voice. I'll give them something to talk about yet."

The pair were silent for a moment.

"I think the men are getting itchy feet, if ye don't mind my saying so," said Ann.

"Well, perhaps some sports are in order. Itchy feet usually get a good scratch from games."

"A contest would be splendid," Ann replied enthusiastically. Ned grunted in reply. Ann studied his face, which was far older than that of such a young man and bore heavy bags under the eyes from sleepless nights from which deep crow's feet splayed out, etched in his flesh by the Australian sun and dry mountain air.

"Soon," Ned said softly. He blinked slowly and swayed for a moment.

"Yer tired. Perhaps ye should have a cat nap?" Ann ventured.

"Aye, perhaps I should," Ned said, wiping his palm over his eyes.

"If you permit me to change first, you can rest on my bed. It's very comfortable," Ann proposed with a twinkle in her eye.

Ned nodded. As Ann left with smile, Ned checked his watch once more.

"Show me to bed, Mrs. Jones."

Meanwhile in the bar room Dan sat against the bar drinking a brandy and lemonade. Jane wiped the bar down and paused as she reached Dan's elbow.

"Sorry," Dan said absent-mindedly. Jane blushed. She wanted to speak but the words would not rise to the occasion. Something about Dan gave her a funny feeling in the pit of her stomach. Was it the sleepy blue eyes? Perhaps his large hands that engulfed the glass he was drinking from? She couldn't pinpoint it, but every time she looked at him, she could feel her skin getting warm.

Dan turned to look at the girl properly, "Have you eaten today, Miss Jones?"

"I... Um, no, not really. I mean to say that I had some bread, but I haven't had the chance for a proper bite. So, um, I suppose not."

"Why don't you fetch me and yourself a bite to eat and come back here," Dan said placing two coins tenderly into Jane's warm and dewy palm, which was enough for two meals. "I'd like to have some company while I eat."

Jane nodded and let out a giggle, immediately clapping a hand over her mouth.

"I'm sorry," she said.

"Don't be. I liked it," said Dan.

Jane promptly went out to the kitchen and began preparing two plates of bacon and eggs. Her heart was racing as she cracked the eggs into the frying pan.

***

Constable Armstrong sat in the office of Detective Ward. Before him, Ward paced with his hands behind his back and a cigarillo poised in his tightened lips. Behind him Senior-Constable Mullane stood by the door. Ward wheeled around, his eyes aflame.

"This happened last night?" he said softly, Armstrong nodded in response. Ward loomed over Armstrong and blew a long puff of smoke in an effort to calm himself, "Why didn't you report this hours ago?"

"We believed that the gang were still outside waiting for us. I suggested a rush, but no man found it advisable. Had I taken the lead and the others followed, they would have all shared my fate. There was no clear way to run it. I thought that by hanging out there would have been the opportunity of following them after."

"Aye, perhaps if you had left sooner you might have," said Ward as he paced.

"With respect, sir, if you had taken my advice to have sentries this could have been avoided," Armstrong said. He immediately regretted the statement. Ward threw his cigarillo on the floor and stormed towards Armstrong.

"What gall to even consider putting this on me, you worm! It was your job to protect Sherritt and you failed miserably. You've put a man in the ground and made a widow of that poor girl by your failure to do your

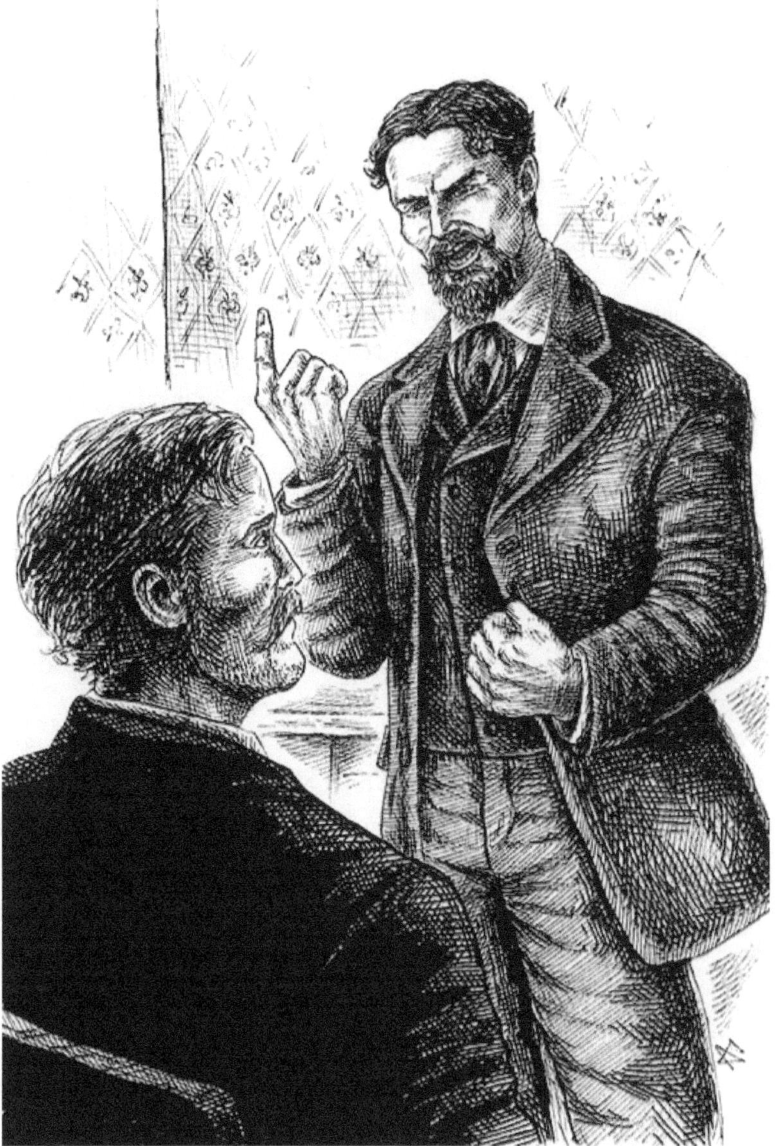

"By God, man, to finish it off you may have just cost us the Kellys!"

duty and you dare to blame me for it? By God, man, to finish it off you may have just cost us the Kellys! Get out of my sight!"

Escorted by Mullane, the deflated constable left the office with a fire rising in his belly. He was determined to make sure that nobody would accuse him of cowardice or incompetence again.

While Armstrong sulked all the way back to Eldorado, Ward strode across to the telegraph office and began the process of sending information to Captain Standish at the Melbourne Club. He scribbled a missive on a slip and passed it through to Henry Cheshire, the manager. Cheshire was a thin, diligent man with keen eyes. He passed the slip through to Osborne, the telegraph operator, who promptly tapped away at the transmitter. Ward waited anxiously to gain confirmation that the message was received.

***

Thomas Curnow limped around the bar room as if lost. Dan Kelly emerged from the crowd and smiled at the schoolteacher.

"Mr. Curnow. Care for a drink?" he asked. Curnow nodded. The teenage outlaw enthusiastically poured a glass of brandy and passed it across.

"Thank you, my 'ansome. Ere, what brings you lads to Glenrowan? We've no banks or the like worth raiding."

Joe turned to look over his shoulder at the Cornishman.

"We're going to wreck a train full of police and black trackers," he said blithely.

"I see," said Curnow, taken aback at such a cold confession of brutality, "a rather audacious plan. What about civilians on board?"

"If there are any on board, we'll gun them down all the same. They've no place on a police train," Joe replied. Curnow hummed.

"Haven't you read the papers? We're vile murderers of the worst kind. Rogues! Brigands! Blackguards!" Dan seemed far more animated than he had all morning, a belly full of grog and his eye on a pretty girl having loosened him up. Joe looked at him with disapproval.

"I've heard that something happened in Beechworth last night," Curnow said.

"Oh, yes, we did some shooting up there," said Dan, taking a drink.

"Well," Curnow chuckled, "It seems you are certainly not men to be trifled with." Curnow raised his glass with a pleasant smile, "To your success, lads."

Dan and Joe raised their glasses in response, clinking the glasses together. The outlaws were wary of Curnow's enthusiasm but still threw back their drinks quickly. Joe winced at the cheap grog.

"Christ. This is like liquid mullock! Jane, where does your mother keep the good stuff?"

***

At one in the afternoon Dan approached Ned with a pleasant expression. The elder Kelly was feeling more refreshed after his brief slumber, though he did not look it.

"Everyone's getting restless," he said, "I reckon I have just the thing."

"What do you want?" Ned replied with more than a hint of frustration.

"A dance. We get some music going, get everyone moving. A right knees-up," Dan swung his arms around in a comical parody of dancing. Ned was incredulous.

"Was this your idea?"

Dan glanced over his shoulder at Jane through the bar room window. "Mine," he answered.

Ned gave Dan a sidelong stare.

"Come on, you know it's a good idea, admit it for once in your life. It's better than everyone wandering around like lost sheep," said Dan as Ned stroked his beard thoughtfully.

"Alright," said Ned, "get things started."

Dan clapped with enthusiasm. He strutted into the bar room and called for attention. Ned didn't linger to hear the announcement, instead he went for a stroll around the back of the inn where some of the prisoners had built a bonfire. He paced around the grounds, scowling at nothing and fretting about the train that wasn't coming.

***

Dave Mortimer sat on a wooden stool by the bar with his concertina. With great gusto he squeezed out an Irish reel. Men danced vivaciously, forgetting their confinement. Dan was buoyant and leapt about like a man with his feet on fire. He pushed through the crowd to Curnow who was still seated in the corner.

"Come along, old man, join in the dance with me," said Dan.

"Oh, my hip... I couldn't possibly,"

"Hip be damned! Dance!"

"Well, I'm not wearing the right shoes. Just my old hobnails, my dancing shoes are at home."

An idea struck Curnow quick as lightning. He hobbled over to Ned who was watching the dance from the back door.

"Mr. Kelly, perhaps you will permit me to go home and fetch my dancing shoes? You will accompany me of course," Curnow said.

"Yes, I suppose that's alright," Ned replied dismissively.

"No, no," Dan interjected, "you stay. I will take him."

Hearing all this, Denny McAuliffe, a cousin of the Kellys, piped up, "Watch out Ned, to get to his place you've got to pass the police station."

"Oh yes," Curnow feigned, "I had forgotten that. Never mind, I shall just make do with these."

As Curnow hobbled to clumsily join in the dancing with Dan, Ned turned conspiratorially to McAuliffe.

"Is that Constable Bracken still at the station?"

"He is. But he's been laid up the past few days with a stomach complaint. He'll be no trouble to anyone if you let him be," McAuliffe said dismissively.

"I shall have to pay him a visit soon to make sure," said Ned.

As the prisoners jigged and jostled, Dan took the opportunity between sets to take a breather. Standing in the breezeway he cooled off. He became aware of footsteps behind him and turned to see Jane Jones.

"Miss Jones," said Dan.

"Mr. Kelly," Jane curtseyed. "I wanted to see if there was anything you needed... or wanted." Jane replied, nervous.

"Well," Dan answered, "I could use a partner for the next set."

"To dance?"

"Aye, to dance."

"Well," Jane averted her gaze, "I haven't really done it properly before. Not with a boy."

"Oh, don't worry, I have plenty of experience dancing. It's easy when you get started. Let me show you the waltz," Dan grinned.

"Alright, but go slowly so as I can learn," said Jane. Dan came close to Jane and took her hands. He placed her left hand on his shoulder and took her right hand in his left. He rested his left hand on her waist and brought her so close they were almost embracing. Jane was trembling.

"How's this so far?" Dan asked.

"It's nice," said Jane with a giggle. She smiled broadly at Dan who returned the gesture, a handsome grin, despite crooked teeth, unfurling beneath his moustache.

"Shall I show you the moves now?"

"Please do."

***

As the dance petered out after an hour and people sat drenched in sweat, Ned was just getting started. He strode to the centre of the bar room and called for attention.

"Gentlemen, we shall be starting some sports outside shortly. Join me in a competition at the front!" he boomed.

Outside in the drizzle Ned Kelly drew a line in the mud with a stick. The men lined up with the Jones boys to compete against the fearsome bushranger king. Among the participants were Paddy and Denny McAuliffe. Finding a Kelly sympathiser or relative around these parts was like looking for apples in an orchard. The McAuliffes by this time were already well on the way to being thoroughly drunk and had taken to obnoxiously laughing at jokes only they understood. Ned was unimpressed.

"Hop-step-jump lads. The rules are simple, whoever goes furthest wins. Don't overstep the crease or you're out. Let's begin," Ned said, champing at the bit. He was finally in his element. Not even the excruciating pain in his back could stop him. One after the other, contestants bounded over the crease. Some stumbled, some lunged. Johnny Jones took his turn, running as fast as his spindly legs could go. Hop - step - JUMP! Johnny positively flew nearly four feet from the crease. The group erupted into cheering, Jones standing up with a huge grin. Next Ned Kelly took a turn with a revolver in each hand for balance. He wobbled slightly on his larrikin-heels but got traction. He bounded off the crease but fell short of Johnny's mark.

"No fair! I've too much weight," Ned complained, "Joe, take these,"

Ned thrust his revolvers out and Joe took them with a smirk. Getting another run, Ned jumped from the crease. He landed even shorter. The group laughed, including Ned who ruffled the Johnny's hair.

"Ah, you've bested Ned Kelly right and fair, my boy. Well done!"

From the veranda, Ann Jones watched the proceedings with a broad smile as Johnny was lifted aloft by the men and carried on their shoulders. At the rear of the inn Dan led a group of men in a game of quoits, tossing coiled rope with one hand while holding a brandy in the other and not spilling a drop. All the while the Jones children flitted about running errands and serving the prisoners as if they were all welcome guests having a party.

For a spell, Owen, Jeremiah and Heddington sneaked out near the paddock and played marbles. Jeremiah was particularly proud of his Tom Bowler. A shiny sphere of ruby-coloured glass that he used to thump his brothers' marbles out of the circle. He got on his knees in the mud and flicked it as hard as his thumb would allow, sending the marbles flying. Old Red was victorious again!

***

At half past two, Hare woke from his nap and struggled to his feet. His back gave him grief as he sat on the edge of the bed. Checking the time on his watch, which sat on his side table, he decided lunch was in order. Hare made his way to the dining room and placed an order for a beef steak and some cognac.

He sat as the drink was brought to him. The cognac filtered through his silvery moustache and left a sweet burning on his tongue. A general maid arrived at his side carrying a memo slip from the Benalla railway station. He took it tenderly from the girl and thanked her. He read the slip, which informed him that an important message was waiting for him at the general telegraph office. Annoyed as much as curious, Hare put down the memo with a cough and a sniff.

"Shame," he grumbled to himself, rising from the table. He downed the rest of the cognac, coughed, and returned to his room to prepare for a walk. Outside the soft drizzle created a fine mist. He took out a handkerchief and blew into it with a trumpeting sound. After a quick once over in the mirror he donned a great coat and his hat and set off for the telegraph office. He did not notice the crow scrutinizing him from the gutter with keenly intelligent corvid eyes.

7

The Wait

While the sports took place outside the inn, the women and children in the gatehouse continued to occupy themselves with chatting until the conversation ran dry.

In the front room, John Stanistreet waited with his instructions to watch for the police train and to signal it to pass freely through if it came. Steve Hart hovered by the window sulking with a bottle in his hand, swigging big mouthfuls from a bottle of Hennessy that Joe had brought down from the inn. He gazed over his shoulder at his prisoners.

Margaret Reardon nursed her baby while Emily Stanistreet read to the children from a novel. Tom Cameron and the Delaneys played cards and surreptitiously passed a bottle of gin between themselves. Steve scowled and finished his bottle then started looking around the house for more. The alcohol he had already consumed was taking effect and he wobbled slightly. He felt very light and uninhibited.

"What does he take me for? A damned nanny?" Steve grumbled to himself. Emily Stanistreet's eyes bugged with shock.

"Could you mind your language please?"

"Oh, I'm sorry my bloody language was so damned offensive," Steve replied with a sneer and a hiccup, prompting the children to giggle loudly. Emily was not impressed. Steve eyed the liquor cabinet in the lounge and made a beeline for it.

"Oh, hello..."

He yanked open the doors and laid his eyes on the collection of bottles: brandy, gin, even a jar of proper Irish whiskey.

"What are you doing?" Emily asked.

"I'm getting a drink, Mrs. Stanistreet," Steve replied, grabbing a bottle of brandy, "Seems to me you could use one too."

Biddy Connolly giggled. Steve took a seat on the sofa and unbuckled his spurs before extending his legs out. His feet ached terribly as they had swollen inside his boots over the two days straight that he had worn them. He uncorked the brandy and took a swig.

Meanwhile, Biddy Connolly had determined to make herself more familiar to the outlaw. He appealed to her in a way the rough and crude quarrymen didn't. Steve was handsome, with almost delicate features despite his attempts to cultivate a fearsome "bushrangery" look. There was a vulnerability to him, but with a dark edge that flashed from time to time. Underneath the vulgar language and the heavy drinking, she sensed something tender. She approached him slowly. He pointed his revolver at her and sat up midway through a drink.

"Where do you think you're going?"

"I just wanted to talk," Biddy said, raising her hands.

"Talk?"

"Yes; to the notorious and handsome Steve Hart. Is that so strange?"

"Well," said Steve putting his weapon down, "you're only human."

Biddy sat next to him on the sofa and there was a moment of awkward silence. She was first to speak.

"I suppose you have lots of girl admirers around the place then," she said. Steve smirked.

"What makes you say so?"

"Well, you're easy on the eyes and you've got a big gun. May I hold it?"

Biddy ran her fingers along the barrel of Steve's revolver tenderly. He allowed her to take the weapon in hand. Her eyes were green like absinthe and her long features were tarnished by pock marks in her cheeks, yet Steve thought she was the most alluring woman he had clapped eyes on in a long time. As she held the revolver and felt its heft she smiled slightly, revealing a snaggletooth. With her free hand she touched Steve's thigh and gently moved her fingers higher. She looked Steve straight in the eyes as he jolted at her forthrightness. Biddy had been with enough men to know what she wanted as much as what they wanted.

Steve looked over Biddy's shoulder at the older women staring at him aghast then rapidly averting their gaze. Steve put his mouth near Biddy's ear. "Now's not ideal," he whispered. Biddy pouted. As Steve sat back, he gave Biddy a wink before directing her to return to the others, pretending to boss her around. Nobody was convinced.

***

Superintendent Hare entered the Benalla telegraph office and removed his hat, hanging it on the stand by the doorway. He shook off the drizzle he had collected with a cough. He walked to the desk with a confident stride.

"Good afternoon, I received a memo stating that there was an urgent telegram waiting for me here," Hare boomed. Within a moment Hare held in his hands the tragic news of Aaron's murder. He went silent and froze. Though the words on the telegram made perfect sense, somehow, they just seemed unreal. Hare braced himself against the desk. He peered into the room where the receiver was buzzing.

"I need someone to go to the police station and summon Superintendent Sadleir at once."

Hardly any time had passed before Sadleir arrived. A wooden pipe hung from his mouth, and he made a beeline for Hare, who was morose.
"What's the matter?" Sadleir asked.

Hare handed him the telegram and waited for the "I told you so," but even though Sadleir desperately wanted to throw Hare's stupidity back at him he understood that it was not appropriate in that moment.

"Why have we only heard about it now?"
"Your guess is as good as any," Hare replied.
"We must form a plan immediately. What have you done while you have waited?"
"I have decided that we should head to Beechworth at once and join Detective Ward in the pursuit while there's still a good chance they're in the area. We should be able to pick up their tracks from Sherritt's hut," Hare said.
"Yes, I concur. The weather will be a nuisance, but this is an opportunity we can't waste. We need to get O'Connor and his boys back straight away," Sadleir responded.

"I'll need four or five men to go up with me." Hare continued,

"Constables like Barry, Arthur and Gascoigne if we can get them. And our black trackers, Spider and Moses. I'll lead the party."

"You're hardly in any condition to get in the saddle, Hare."

"I'm perfectly fine."

"You don't look it."

"I am, I assure you," Hare declared as he rose to his full height and puffed out his chest. "There's not a chance that I will stand by after I've waited a year for the Kellys to resurface. I'm not bowing out of the hunt over a damned cold."

"For God's sake, man. This is not some game hunt. These are men, not beasts to be shot for their pelts," Sadleir snapped.

Hare thundered, "Aaron Sherritt was my friend. I was to protect him from the Kellys, and I failed. As his friend, I will have these blackguards brought to justice."

Sadleir stood silent, as Hare's lip trembled imperceptibly behind his mighty beard.

"Very well. O'Connor and his boys are in Melbourne. I'll send word for them to join us as well."

"O'Connor and his blacks will not be necessary, but I suppose their numbers will bolster any efforts to capture the bushrangers without too much disruption to the number of officers on duty in the district. If you wish to notify him then have at it," said Hare. Promptly, Sadleir began drafting a telegram while Hare stood by the fire, pensive.

***

"We must form a plan immediately. What have you done while you have waited?"

At Jones' Inn, Thomas Curnow began to fret. He hadn't heard from the women since they were taken with his baby to be guarded by Steve. He worried about Jeannie's health as she was almost three months pregnant and very fragile. He saw Dave Mortimer smoking by the veranda and joined him.

"A most interesting afternoon it has become, wouldn't you say?" Mortimer said, not looking up. He pinched the ends of his moustache.

"You can certainly call it that," Curnow replied, fixing his own pipe for a smoke. He began to speak more quietly, "We have to find a way to warn that train, David."

"There's no leaving this hotel without being shot, you know that."

"Doesn't mean we ought not to try."

"Unless you want my sister to become a widowed mother, I'd leave it well alone," Mortimer replied sternly.

Standing at the fence that separated the inn's courtyard from the railway reserve, Ned took a drink from Jane Jones and sniffed it. He held the glass to the light and passed it back to her.

"Have a sip," Ned ordered. Jane put the brandy to her lips and allowed a small amount to pass into her mouth before returning the glass to Ned. The outlaw seemed satisfied and allowed Jane to return to the inn. When he looked up, he saw Curnow and Mortimer looking at him. Curnow waved with a friendly smile. Ned replied with a disinterested nod.

"I can't in good conscience allow this murderous plot to go unhindered, David," Curnow snapped. He looked towards the Stanistreet house then approached Ned.

"Mr. Kelly," Curnow began, "I wonder if I might be permitted to go across to the stationmaster's house?"

"What for?"

"I'd like to see my wife. I'm worried about her. You see, it's her condition."

"Well," Ned paused, "I don't see any harm in that. Stay where Hart can see you and I shall be along directly."

"Thank you, Mr. Kelly. You're a good man," Curnow responded and took his leave. Ned watched him with one hand ready on his revolver.

The place was quiet when Curnow walked into the gatehouse. Women and children were scattered throughout, many napping, while Steve Hart was seemingly asleep on the sofa. Much to Curnow's surprise the dormant outlaw raised a hand bearing a revolver and with a mechanical click aimed it straight at Curnow's heart. Steve had not flinched or opened his eyes.

"More cautious men have been shot trying to catch a Kelly, you know," Steve drawled. He took a quiet pride in his delivery; he had been practicing the line in his head for a long time and was glad for an opportunity to use it. Curnow raised his hands.

"Now, now, I've only come to see my wife. Ned gave me permission to come over."

Steve opened one eye and looked the schoolteacher up and down. He relaxed his arm.

Recognising her husband's voice, Jeannie Curnow rushed over to him. "Tom!"

She hugged her husband tightly.

"Jeannie, are you alright? How's your condition?" asked Curnow, his fresh, friendly face lit up.

"I'm fine Tom; are you alright? What is happening? Why are they keeping us here like this?" Jeannie said, her voice full of panic and desperation.

"Stay calm. Everything is alright," Curnow replied, kissing his wife's forehead.

"I just want to go home," Jeannie said softly.

"Don't we all?" Steve grumbled.

"Are you alright, son?" Curnow said, redirecting his attention.

"My damned feet are swollen. I've been wearing these boots for days."

"Jeannie, go and fetch a bowl of warm water," Curnow directed, "Let me help you off with those boots."

Steve sat up and extended his left leg and Curnow grasped the boot. Steve kept his pistol trained on Curnow but gasped in relief as the boot was pulled from his foot. The boots were the ones plundered from Gloster's wagon. Steve had barely worn them, saving them for special occasions such as this. The second boot came off with a little more struggle. It didn't help that Steve wore no socks.

"My lad, you'd best get some stockings, or your sweat will rot those pretty boots," Curnow ventured, reeling from the smell of sweat and damp leather.

"Who are you?" Steve asked.

"Thomas Curnow," he paused, "I'm the schoolteacher." Curnow looked across to the children and winked. It surprised them immensely to see their teacher helping the outlaw soothe his swollen and blistered feet.

"Well, thank you, Thomas Curnow," said Steve.

There was an awkward lull.

"Much quieter over here, isn't it?" Curnow ventured.

"Aye, it's that. Say what you like about the fairer sex," replied Steve, "they're nothing if not dull."

"Oh, that's nice of you," said Biddy from across the room with a glare.

"With some exceptions, of course," Steve blurted with a sly wink.

Shortly Jeannie returned with the bowl and Curnow eased one of Steve's feet into the water, his wife assisting with the other. The relief was enough for Steve to let his guard down.

"Ooooh..." he moaned. This was met with a wry smile from Biddy.

"That'll put you to rights in no time," Curnow said, straightening.

***

At the bar of Jones' inn, Joe held his glass tightly as he tipped opium powder into his gin. Just as he swilled the tincture, Dan Kelly entered and frowned.

"You'd better steady on with that, mate."

"Mind your own business," Joe snapped.

"We need you straight," Dan snapped back.

"I'm straight as a bloody arrow," Joe slurred.

"I'll be sure never to try archery with you in that case. I'm going to visit Steve over the way. Watch this lot while I'm outside. Can you manage that between drinks?" Dan grumbled and headed for the back door.

"Bloody Kellys," Joe growled to himself then sank the opium tincture in one hit with a wince. He plucked his revolver out of his belt, half-cocked it and spun the barrel. He contemplated turning the weapon on himself but thought better of it.

In the stationmaster's house, as Steve soaked his feet and watched the prisoners, Curnow spoke in hushed tones with his wife and the Stanistreets at the dining table.

"John," said Curnow, "do you still have a revolver in your desk? I have an idea."

"Don't be doing anything foolish, Thomas," Jeannie scolded.

"I'm not. I'm just thinking," Curnow replied calmly

As they spoke Dan Kelly approached the group from behind. He seemed anxious and looked under the table.

"What's the matter?" Emily Stanistreet exclaimed.

"I'm looking for a small bag; I must have it," said Dan, almost breathless.

His search fruitless, he left the room and headed to Steve. The Curnows and Stanistreets sat in silence, listening carefully to the muffled dialogue between Dan and Steve from the next room.

"What the bloody hell did you put it in there for?" Dan could be heard shouting from the other room. Moments later he walked back outside looking through a small purse. Inside it was a wad of banknotes, coins, a ladies watch and a small bottle of strychnine.

***

At half past four, Captain Standish returned to the Melbourne Club to take a brandy and was greeted with telegrams from Benalla declaring that Aaron Sherritt had been murdered the previous night and the police required the services of O'Connor and his native police. Such news was disheartening for the embattled commissioner, but there was no time to dally so after finishing his brandy Standish made way to the nearest telegraph office.

He sent a letter to the Chief Secretary Robert Ramsay detailing the situation and sent another letter by hansom cab to Sub-Inspector O'Connor in Essendon requesting his assistance. As much as Standish was loathe to see the sun-baked Irishman again, he had to admit that

O'Connor and his "boys" would be useful with fresh tracks to work with instead of the usual stale leads. He sent a message to Hare in Benalla to let him know that he was awaiting a response from O'Connor.

With dusk approaching, Standish returned to the Melbourne Club where Robert Ramsay was waiting for him. Ramsay was a stout man with curly brown hair and a thick beard. His face was puffy, and there was some aspect of the pugilist in his features that made him fearsome.

"Standish, what on earth is going on?" Ramsay intoned in his gruff Scottish burr as he shook Standish's gloved hand.

"Ramsay, my dear, it is all a terrible mess. The Kellys are back, and they have committed another murder right under our noses. I have just come from the telegraph office."

"What's your plan?"

"I have not formed a plan myself yet," said Standish, "but I intend to send O'Connor and his blacks over to my men to help them pick up the trail."

"How quickly can he reach Beechworth?" Ramsay asked.

"I shall try to get him there by Monday morning, but I need a special train organised for them."

Ramsay knew exactly how to procure such a train and the pair headed out immediately, not yet knowing whether or not O'Connor would be available.

***

After an early supper at his accommodation in Flemington, Sub-Inspector Stanhope O'Connor retired to pack his things with his wife Louisa. He closed up his luggage as Louisa stacked her own near the door.

"Just think, my darling, this time tomorrow we will be making our way to Queensland! Aren't you excited to be going back?" Louisa chirped. She was young and blessed with the sweet face of a porcelain doll: full cheeked, shapely lips and large eyes with long lashes.

"At this time of year, certainly," O'Connor replied, his thick Irish brogue muffled further by the stiff upper lip that bore a huge moustache. He did not look up from his task.

Louisa walked to her husband and embraced him. O'Connor was a man yet to get used to displays of affection. It seemed like yesterday he was on the beach at Cape Bedford looking out to sea waiting for the Aboriginals he had chased into the water to either drown or swim back to be shot. Wholesale slaughter was just part of the job, not one he enjoyed but one he was expert at, and a 'slaughterman' did not make for an affectionate lover. He withdrew his pipe and tobacco from a pouch on his belt.

"Oh, Stan, put that away - you know how Catherine is about smoking."

O'Connor rolled his eyes and there was a knock from the front door followed by the faint murmur of voices. The Catherine of whom Louisa spoke was her sister, Catherine Prout-Webb, the lady of the house.

At that moment Catherine sang out to the couple.

"Stanhope! There's an urgent message for you."

With reservation, O'Connor walked to the front door where he was handed the letter from Standish. Looking outside he observed the black hansom cab waiting.

"What is it?"

"How am I to know?" Catherine replied.

O'Connor read the manuscript silently and frowned.

Melbourne Club, 27th June 1880. —My dear Sir, —I have just received telegraphic information that the outlaws stuck up the police party that was watching Mrs. Byrne's house and shot Aaron Sherritt dead. The police, however, appeared to have escaped. In the urgent position of affairs, could you return to Beechworth with your trackers by the early train to-morrow, or by a special train, if that can be arranged. If you can oblige us in this way, could you manage to come in at once to see me at the Club by the hansom which I send out with this?

Louisa joined the pair and noted her husband's dour expression. "What's the matter?"

"Standish wants me to head back to Beechworth immediately to follow a fresh lead on the Kellys."

"Then you must go, surely?" Catherine said.

"What about out plans?" replied Louisa.

"Dash it all," Catherine said, "We will come with you to Beechworth. I could do with the change of scenery."

O'Connor's brow furrowed with misgivings. He was in no mood for another of Hare's wild goose chases and certainly not keen on a day longer than necessary with his sister-in-law. Still, duty called, and O'Connor was not one to shirk his duties.

"I must go into Melbourne to consult with Standish. Stay here until I return."

With that, O'Connor donned his greatcoat and top hat and climbed into the cab.

***

Ned pushed his way inside the stationmaster's house and was met with the scattered group of prisoners sitting around the lounge area. Steve was still seated on the couch with his feet in the water bowl.

"Hart," Ned barked, "put your boots back on!"

With a slight grumble, Steve complied. In the corner Jack Delaney hid behind his brothers.

"Right," Ned announced, "I want everyone to come up to the inn with me. The Stanistreets will stay here."

At that moment John Stanistreet sidled up to Ned with a strained look on his face, "Mr. Kelly. The next train is due at nine o'clock tomorrow. Those rails must be replaced."

"There will be no trains tomorrow, I can assure you of that," Ned waved a finger in front of Stanistreet's face. He then turned to the collective.

"Everyone but the Stanistreets come back with me to the inn now," Ned repeated.

"How much longer until this bloody train arrives?" Steve complained, tugging on his boots.

"Won't be long now."

"Aye, you said that six hours ago."

"Shut up and put your damned boots back on!" Ned turned to Biddy who was lingering by the sofa. "Miss, you're coming too."

"Can't I stay here, please?" Biddy responded. Ned viewed her suspiciously.

"Why?"

"They don't much like me over there. They cast a lot of aspersions,"

I can't imagine why, Ned thought to himself. "Fine; Hart should be capable enough to keep you under control," Ned sighed. Biddy grinned in reply.

When the group stood outside, Paddy and Hanorah McDonnell approached Ned.

"Shall we go with you as well?" Hanorah asked.

"No, I think you can take the kids across to the tavern, but the old man will stay with me," Ned said with a soft smile.

The small army of women and children moved into the inn quietly – or at least as quietly as a group of children had the capacity for. Dan kept the door open for everyone to enter, his revolver tucked prominently into his belt and a vermilion silk sash.

Ned peeled away from the group and strode across the veranda to the whitewashed sign that proudly proclaimed that the tiny inn had the best accommodation. He looked beyond and saw Joe resting his elbows on a fence rail behind the inn near the paddock, puffing thoughtfully on his pipe. Ned shifted the slip rail and walked past the bonfire where prisoners warmed their hands against the biting cold.

"This train is running awful late," Joe said without looking up as Ned joined him.

"Aye, but Hare won't miss the chance to take another crack at us with a fresh trail. As sure as mud after the rain, he'll be coming," Ned reached into the pouch on his belt that held his pipe and a cake of tobacco.

"What's he waiting for, then?" Joe's lips pursed and he fell quiet.

Ned used his clasp knife to shave a plug of tobacco, catching the shavings in his palm. He'd never gotten used to cut tobacco since leaving Pentridge. It felt like a needless luxury, and it spoiled too easily while the gang were on the run. He put away the cake and knife and rubbed out the shavings in his hand. The rich aromatics of the tobacco, like wine, cherries and wood, wafted through the cold air from his warm hands. Joe's silence began to make Ned uneasy.

"What's up?" asked Ned. Joe didn't respond immediately.

"I'm just thinking," said Joe behind tiny curls of smoke that unfurled from his lips. Ned concentrated on plugging the bowl of his pipe and attempting to light it with a match. The cold air made Ned's fingers less useful than he'd like. It was just another annoyance in a long line of annoyances since Saturday.

"I never imagined I'd be a murderer. It sits with you, doesn't it? The blood, the screaming," Joe trailed off. He bore a rosy complexion from his almost constant consumption of booze since his arrival. Joe wrestled in his mind with the fact that however much the events of Saturday night had been traumatic, he felt a kind of thrill from pulling the trigger on Aaron and watching him explode. He wondered, is this how Ned felt after Stringybark?

Ned was defiant, however, clasping Joe's shoulder, "This is war. People die in wars," he said. Tiny plumes of smoke carried each syllable from his mouth into the ether.

"Aye, and so shall we if this plan of yours fails."

Silence fell briefly between the pair.

Joe cleared his throat and spat on the ground. "Do you ever think about them – the police you killed?" he asked.

Ned's eyes glazed just for a moment as the echoes of gunshots from Stringybark Creek filled his head. He envisioned Kennedy's watch and the letter, smeared with bloody fingerprints, which would never reach Kennedy's widow. He felt his own hands releasing the clasp on Lonigan's gun belt and wrapping the leather around his own waist. He remembered the way the pages of Kennedy's letter had curled and turned black in the campfire and how that last fatal blast from his shotgun had left a hole the size of a fist straight through Kennedy.

"Every day," Ned said calmly, "I never forget that my own liberty has not come cheaply. After today we'll never have to look over our shoulder again. I promise you that."

Joe pointed to the looming peak beyond the inn, totally covered with trees except for a bald patch that created a cleft at the pinnacle.

"That mountain up there, see?" he said softly. Ned nodded.

"Morgan's Lookout. What of it?"

Joe shifted to lean against the fence with his back, sucking the last of the smoke through his pipe and letting its woody tones paint the inside of his mouth. "Remember why it's called that?"

Ned looked at Joe with befuddlement, "That's where Dan Morgan hid after he crossed the border from New South Wales. He bailed up every-one from here to Benalla."

Ned bore a smirk of admiration. He'd always had a soft spot for Morgan growing up. He would read the papers with his father to learn of the latest of Morgan's depredations and occasionally his father would come back from the pub with the latest news on the grapevine. He idolised Morgan for his one-man war on rich bullies and the police. To him, as a child of poverty, nothing was more romantic than an outlaw challenging the very people who kept people like his family struggling. The thought of highway robbery took him back to his days riding with Harry Power.

Harry Power: remembered by those who didn't know him as a funny old rogue and a teller of tall tales; the self-proclaimed friend of the poor and reliever of burdensome purses; the tutor in crime of the notorious Edward Kelly, referred to in the papers in those days as "Young Kelly".

How much had changed in the ten years since those days when Power taught him how to smoke a pipe or change a horse's brand with iodine? He didn't speak of the other side of Power that would curse at his young offsider and hurl whatever was at hand at his head because his stricture was playing up, or force Ned to sit in the bedroom of his mistress while he rutted with her so the boy could look out for traps. The smirk faded.

"What then?"

"Eh?" Ned snapped to attention.

"What happened to him then?" Joe repeated. He tipped the ashes of his spent tobacco out of his pipe with a dour expression.

"What are you driving at?" asked Ned impatiently.

"Don't you remember Peechelba Station? They shot Morgan down like a mad dog without a fight, then they skinned his face for a trophy, cut off his head and anything else that made him a man before dumping what was left in an unmarked grave to be forgotten."

"Aye, and if I ever find that Quinlan who put the bullet through him, I'll return the favour," Ned rumbled. Joe scowled.

"This is the problem, Ned. Here we are at the foot of the monument to Dan Morgan's final days about to do something so horrendous even he would never dream of it, and you're shooting your mouth off about killing more people. Don't you see how that makes us look?" Joe's voice trembled slightly. He'd never gotten angry like this at Ned before – not to his face.

"Do you doubt me?" Ned eyebrows knitted and his jaw clenched behind his dirty red beard.

"Ned, I've soaked my hands in blood for you, don't you understand that? Where does it end? What we're doing here is almost unspeakable. If that train comes…"

"It will come."

"If it comes and our plan works, what does that make us? It's murder on a scale unseen!"

Ned sighed.

"The traps and politicians declared war on us. They've made it a crime to know us, and they've shown there's no depth they won't drop to in order to destroy us. It ends when we win. They want a war? We'll show them how we fight wars in Kelly Country!"

"Kelly Country," Joe scoffed, "You idiot, Ned, this is not a war; we have no army and you're no general. We have a quarter inch of steel between us and the might of Victoria's Empire. You've not courted a fight, you've engineered a slaughter," Joe's eyes hardened, he felt the fire in his belly. That itch in his trigger finger returned. I could end this all right now with one bullet, he thought.

He and Ned locked eyes like territorial stags. Joe was the first to look away.

"Maybe we really are the monsters the papers make us out to be," he said.

Ned snarled and swung a fist at Joe, striking him in the chest and causing him to lose his footing.

"Step up; be a man!"

Joe struggled to his feet, his chest aching like he had been struck with a mallet. He prepared to crack Ned's skull with his fist but remembered his place. He had one more departing barb as he retreated to the safety of the bar.

"Whether at the end of a rope or the end of a bullet, we'll have to pay the piper for what we've done – and what we're about to do," Joe said as he adjusted his tatty, crocheted scarf, "and if I have a date with death, I'm going to get some more drinking in first."

Ned sulked at the fence. In his head he raged. The cold air condensing against the breath jetting from his nostrils lent him the appearance of a furious dragon. As he gazed at the mountain a crow swooped low and landed on the fence next to him. He stared at the bird with its shiny black feathers and cold blue eyes. It stared back at him, unafraid.

Cawww, the crow exclaimed.

Ned recalled his granny telling him stories of the Morrigan when he was a little boy; the Celtic goddess of war and death who could transform into a murder of crows and protect warriors in battle – or claim their souls in defeat. The appearance of the Morrigan's crows before a battle could be good luck or a curse depending on the goddess' judgement of the warrior. With a flurry of its midnight wings, the crow left as suddenly as it had appeared. Ned felt cold.

***

The whole afternoon Hare and Sadleir had been sending messages to all of the police stations in the district to warn them of the danger of the re-emerged Kelly Gang, all the time waiting for some kind of response from Melbourne. Sadleir and Hare had briefly made a trip to the train station to organise a special train to take the police party to Beechworth that evening.

It was six o'clock by the time Hare received an update from Standish stating that O'Connor had been reached and consented to cancelling his plans to return to Queensland.

"Everything is coming together," said Sadleir, returning from his errands procuring supplies for the mission, "Have you heard from Captain Standish yet?"

"Only this," Hare handed the message to Sadleir, "he says that

O'Connor and his boys might not arrive until Monday morning. I have returned a message asserting that if they are not here by midnight, we must go without them. We cannot wait that long," said Hare.

"But we need his trackers," replied Sadleir.

"We have Spider and Moses, they'll do fine. O'Connor and his boys have produced no more than our own men have. We can't afford to let the tracks go cold."

At that moment Hare's attention was called for at the front desk. He strode over and received the news that O'Connor was to leave Melbourne at 10pm by special train.

"Sadleir," Hare called out. Sadleir joined him and read the message.

"What do you think?" Hare asked.

"I think if Standish is sending up another special, we should use our engine as a pilot," Sadleir replied.

"What do you mean by that?"

"I mean something like a scout to go ahead and look for danger. You know as well as I do of the rumours circulating that the sympathisers are planning to sabotage the railway. Some have said they plan to lay logs on the tracks or break the rails. A pilot engine can detect any such hazard before it's too late."

"Ah, yes, of course," said Hare, "I shall let Standish know."

As Hare scribbled out the new message, he sniffed in an attempt to stop his nose from running. He had felt exhausted all afternoon, but it was starting to wear him down.

"Damn these Victorian winters. What I wouldn't give to be back in Cape Town right now."

***

Tom Lloyd watched the commotion at Jones' inn from the rear of Mc-Donnell's tavern as Dick Hart and Wild Wright played cribbage inside. On the couch lay Jack Lloyd, sleeping with his straw hat over his eyes.

"What in the hell's going on over there? Where's this damned train?" Tom fretted to himself as he returned to the warmth of the bar.

"Take it easy, Tom," Wild responded from behind him.

"Get some sleep if you need it. We'll holler when it shows up," said Dick.

"If it shows up. Something's wrong. I can feel it," Tom frowned, anxious. Dick tried to focus on moving his peg on the cribbage board, but he felt the same.

* * *

Over the course of ten minutes Ned, Joe and Dan rounded up their captives and herded them into the inn. The crowd took position in the bar, where the most floor space allowed them to stand and be counted. Dan attempted to lock the front door in the dining room, but the key wouldn't fit. Ann Jones came to his aid.

"No, dear, that's the key for the cabinet. I'll be needing that," she handed Dan a larger mortice key, "Take this one and I'll take the other."

Dan locked the door and placed the key on the mantle as he crossed to the bar room.

"Dan, take a headcount," Ned instructed as he moved into the armoury. Dan handed one of his revolvers, a small Belgian pistol, to Jane.

"Just in case anyone tries to sneak away, you point the long bit at them and pull the trigger."

"I know how a gun works, Dan," Jane sighed. Dan poked his tongue out at her and began moving through the crowd counting. Meanwhile

Joe stood on the bar doing the same from overhead, wobbling slightly on his tall heels.

"I make it fifty-one," shouted Dan.
"I count sixty-five," replied Joe.
"How the hell did you get sixty-five?"
"I bloody well counted!"
"I'll count again. I bet you're wrong," Dan said as he pushed through the crowd again, counting as he went. Joe climbed down from the bar, almost slipping.

"It's bloody fifty-one, you drunk bastard!" Dan exclaimed as he took his pistol back from Jane. Ned re-entered wearing his body armour with his oilskin over the top. The sleeves strained against the steel plates that hugged his biceps and created the illusion that his shoulders were far broader than they really were.
"What's all the shouting about?"
"I counted fifty-one and Joe counted sixty-five," Dan replied.
"Well, as long as we don't have less than fifty-one, that's near enough ain't it?"
Dan looked incredulous at his brother as he stood before the crowd.

"Ladies and gentlemen, I regret to inform you that we must detain you further. However, you can thank the gallant Victoria police for it. I must say they've positively outdone themselves. They'd be late for their own funeral. Though, I suppose in a sense they already are."
The crowd did not as much as titter at Ned's poor-taste joke. Ned continued unabated, "Mrs. Jones will provide you with food and drinks, but you must remain inside until further notice."

***

In the dining room, Dan and Joe played Euchre. Dan dealt the cards with Jane on his lap. Joe's pipe hung lazily from his lips as he examined his hand. His eyes narrowed and he glared at Dan. Dan arched an eyebrow. Joe reached across the table and grabbed Dan's cards.

"Oh, come on!" Joe moaned.

"What?"

"You stacked the bloody deck, you sharp cove!"

"Me? Sharp?" Dan feigned offence.

"I'll deal. Pass me the bloody deck!"

Dan slid the cards across the table and looked up into Jane's face.

"Jane, can you go and make sure everyone's accounted for?" Jane stood up and took Dan's revolver from the table.

"If I'm doing your job, I'll need this, won't I?"

"Please don't shoot anyone. Unless it's Tom Cameron, he's been looking daggers at me all night. I think he's a bit jealous," said Dan with a broad smile. Jane left and entered the bar room leaving the door open.

Joe glared at Dan for a moment.

"I'd be careful with that one, mate," Joe said, his pipe waggling as he spoke.

"Isn't it you that's always saying barmaids are the perfect lovers?"

"Dan, my boy, truer words were never spoken. However, you might want someone with a little more experience," Joe winked.

Ned entered the bar room, slightly unsteady on his feet. He saw Jane counting heads with Dan's revolver and his beard bristled. He strode into the dining room and up to Dan and Joe, leaning down hard on the table. Dan could smell brandy on his breath.

"You're supposed to be watching this lot. Not playing cards while Jane wanders about with your pistol."

Ned swayed slightly.

"I see you kept your wits about," Dan replied averting his gaze. Ned's face twisted with rage, and he grabbed Dan by the collar.

"I gave you a bloody job to do!"

Dan pushed Ned away roughly, "What's the point? The train isn't coming, and you know it."

"Ned," Joe interrupted, "for chrissakes, go blow off at someone else."

Ned looked at Joe with watery, furious eyes. He released Dan and hobbled away.

***

It was just past eight and getting profoundly dark when Edward Reynolds and Robert Gibbons went looking for little Alec Reynolds who had not returned from Sunday school. The boy was not one to wander off and had always been as reliable as clockwork, but as dusk approached the family had begun to panic. Reasoning that the Sunday school was held near the train station and Alec may have followed the Stanistreet children back, Edward and Robert headed to the stationmaster's house.

When they knocked on the door, they were greeted by Mrs. Stanistreet who led them in. They were soon shocked to be met by Steve Hart brandishing pistols.

"Who are you?"

"We're looking for Alec Reynolds," Edward replied.

"Well," Steve said, cocking his revolvers, "I don't know about him, but you've found me."

"Who the devil are you?" said Robert Gibbons.

"I'm Steve Hart, and I'll trouble you to get inside!"

***

After the food had settled and the crowd began to feel merry, a second dance was called for. The small table was carried out onto the veranda to clear room. Now Dave Mortimer's concertina was joined by John Simpson's fiddle in a rousing performance of The Wild Colonial Boy. It was a fitting tribute to the outlaws; the ballad was just as outlawed as the gang were and the decision to perform it raised a few eyebrows but, after all, who was going to get them in trouble for performing it? The floorboards thumped and shuddered under the weight of the dancers and the lights hanging from the ceiling swung furiously. On the dance went with the Salamanca Reel, and Dan Kelly took to the dance floor with Jane. The pair hopped and twirled to the music.

At the bar, Ann poured Ned a drink. He and Joe exchanged wary glances.

"Might I have one as well, ma'am? No need to breach another bottle," Joe winked.

"Trust me now, do ye?" Ann replied.

"If you were going to poison me, you'd have done it by now. Besides, I'm too parched to give a damn either way," Joe placed his empty glass on the counter, but Ned slid the glass away before it could be filled.

"Reckon he's had enough."

"He's no fun at all, is he? Spiteful bugger. If he was any sourer, I'd call him Lemon," Joe said, staring sidelong at Ned and moving his glass back into place. Ann poured reluctantly and Joe snatched the glass up and sank the drink in one hit, keeping his gaze unflinchingly fixed on Ned. Ned seethed. Joe stood and extended his hand to Ann.

"Would you care to dance, Mrs. Jones?"

"I'd be delighted, Mr. Byrne," Ann replied taking his hand as he led her out from behind the bar. They moved to the dance floor and joined in.

For the first time since the murder of Sherritt, Joe allowed himself to feel some joy...

Ned watched the festivities with a dour expression and drank. How does he do it? Ned thought, how does he go from the depths of misery to wooing the hostess as if he had not a care in the world? He saw the grin on Joe's face with his uneven, smoke-stained teeth and blackening gums on show. For the first time since the murder of Sherritt, Joe allowed himself to feel some joy, not merely drowning his feelings in drink and drugs. He whirled the publican around in a whimsical waltz.

As the song ended the pair pulled away from the group and moved back to the bar.

"Oh Joe, you dance superbly. Where did ye learn to move like that?" Ann beamed.

"Well, whenever you get a new dancing partner you learn some new moves - but you never forget the best footwork."

"Is that right? And who might this lovely lass with the fancy footwork be, Mr. Byrne?"

"A gentleman never tells."

"Oh, come now, at least give me a little something to sate my curiosity."

"I'll tell you what, you pour us some good whiskey and I'll tell you."

Ann gave Joe a cheeky wink. She moved behind the bar and grabbed two glasses and a bottle of Irish whiskey and poured. The pair toasted.

"Sláinte, Mr. Byrne!"

The amber liquid left Joe's mouth tingling.

"Her name is Maggie," Joe began, "it's not her real name though. She has a smile like the kiss of sunrise on the Woolshed and eyes like turquoise. She makes my heart sing."

"Very romantic."

"Aye, she's something special. Special indeed. There was another girl who had my heart before, but I was too late to make my intentions known. I made sure not to let the ship sail ever again."

"And so, where is the lovely Maggie now?"

Joe went quiet and fingered the keepsake hidden under his shirt. He tried to drown his thoughts with whiskey and changed the subject.

"Has anybody told you that you have beautiful eyes, Mrs. Jones?"

"Oh, be off with ye, Byrne. Ye make me feel old!"

"Old? No young slip of a girl could hold a candle to you. Where is that husband of yours at any rate?"

"Oh, last I heard he was working the rails with my eldest over in Gippsland. I'd be lying if I said it bothered me not having him around. I've worked myself near to death getting this place going, no thanks to him."

"A fine job you've done of it too," Joe declared and raised a glass in toast.

***

As Ned wandered through the inn, Thomas Curnow grabbed his attention.

"Mr. Kelly, erm, Ned, I feel I must raise something with you."

Ned shifted his weight and gave the teacher his attention, "Yes?"

"I need you to know I'm with you heart and soul and there is something else. The stationmaster keeps a loaded revolver in his desk. I thought perhaps it was wise for you to be aware of that."

"Very good, Mr. Curnow."

"You're most welcome. While Mr. Stanistreet would not think of using it, I can't vouch for others here who might also know about it."

Ned excused himself and headed straight into the gatehouse, where Steve still sat on the sofa playing with his revolvers.

"Hart, go and fetch the pistol from the stationmaster's desk," Ned ordered.

Steve returned with a railway issued Webley revolver, capped and loaded. Ned was impressed by Curnow's truthfulness.

"When can I go up to the inn with you lot? I'm bored to madness stuck in here," asked Steve.

"Your job is to keep an ear out for the bloody train, and you'll stay here until I deem it no longer necessary."

With that, Ned made his way back to the inn, accompanied by Steve's newest prisoners Reynolds and Gibbons. The lamp on the post at the front of the building had been lit for the benefit of the men who needed to head out for a smoke.

Upon returning, Ned stalked through the grounds at the rear of the inn. A small flick of his tangled brown hair curled up from under the quilted skull cap. He took up a spot on the fence behind the kitchen where he lit his pipe and stood in thought for some time. The cold in the breeze reminded him of the nights he spent in Pentridge on a thin mat of woven coconut fibres as the cold seeped into his bones. The relentless chill of a prison cell was no place for a boy of sixteen, let alone a mother of young children.

"A penny for yer thoughts?" said Ann Jones, from behind the pensive outlaw, "ye look like ye have the weight of world on yer shoulders."

"Often feels that way."

"What's on your mind?" Ann asked, putting a hand gently on Ned's shoulder.

"I was thinking of my Ma, locked up in that gaol cell in Melbourne these past two years. On nights like this you can't get warm in those cells, no matter what."

"Terrible what they did to her," Ann tutted in disapproval.

"It was me and Dan the traps wanted, but they took Ma instead. And all over the dirty lies of a policeman. I even offered to give myself up, if they let her go. D'you know what they said?"

Ann shook her head. Ned gazed deep into her eyes.

"They said nothing. They ignored me. Well, after tonight, they won't dare ignore me again!"

Ned's vehemence almost rattled Ann. There was something in his eyes so desperate like a wild beast backed into a corner. She took his hand and kissed his knuckles.

"Come inside and have a drink, sweetheart. Does no good stewing about it out here. In the cold, no less! Shall I organise supper?"

"Do you have food for the prisoners?" asked Ned.

"Let the bloody buggers mind their own business. I have got plenty, but I want it all for ye, Ned, old man," Ann said, putting her arms around Ned's neck affectionately, "What shall I make? There's plenty of fat dogs about," Ann joked. This prompted a wry smile from the troubled outlaw.

Just as the pair were speaking, Edward Reynolds walked along the fence line looking for a place to relieve his bladder. Finding a secluded spot, he unbuttoned his breeches and flopped out his member, looking over his shoulders for witnesses as he began to urinate. He was almost done when Ann Jones took notice.

"Look Ned, he's going to escape," the publican shouted with an accusatory pointing gesture. Reynolds froze as Ned craned around to see.

"What are you playing at?" Ned growled.

"No, I just..."

"Get over here!"

Reynolds panicked as he tried to figure out how to obey the directive mid-stream. He raised his hands but remained with his back to the others.

"Did you hear me? Get here now!"

Reynolds closed his eyes, took a breath and shook off the last drops, tucking himself back into his breeches. He turned and walked to the furious outlaw.

"When I give you an order you bloody well do as I say, boy," Ned rumbled like a storm cloud.

"I'm sorry, but I... Well, I just couldn't. I asked Dan for permission," Reynolds mumbled.

"Get inside, mongrel," Ned waved Reynolds away. He turned to Ann.

"I'll be heading out to fetch Constable Bracken shortly; I was wondering if we could borrow Jane to coax him out."

"I'd rather you didn't put Jane in any situation that could harm her. Besides I need her here to help," Ann replied.

"No," said Ned with a nod, "Of course. I apologise."

"It's alright. I'll get supper started."

Ann turned and headed for the kitchen with a lascivious wink. Ned spotted Thomas Curnow lingering by the breezeway between the inn and the kitchen and made his way across.

"Thank you for letting me know about the pistol, Mr. Curnow." Ned said, clapping a hand on Curnow's shoulder.

"Of course, friend," Curnow began, "Pardon my impudence, but I couldn't help overhear that you planned on bailing up Constable Bracken and you needed someone to lure him out of the barracks."

"Aye," said Ned.

"Well, if you don't mind my saying so, my brother-in-law Dave Mortimer would be perfect to take along. He's practically Bracken's neighbour and the constable would recognise his voice easily. He would trust Davey."

Ned thought carefully about the new information and nodded appreciatively.

"That sounds like an excellent idea."

"I want to make sure you succeed any way I can," Curnow said as he smiled broadly.

"I shall have to think of a way to repay your support," Ned mused.

"Well, with my wife's delicate health might I be permitted to take her home? At your earliest convenience of course! I just worry what the stress might be doing to her and the baby."

"Fine," Ned replied, "Make sure you're all ready to go in the next few minutes."

They returned to the inn where festivities were continuing unabated.

***

Thomas Carrington, journalist and illustrator, had been at a friend's house for supper and tales from India when a note arrived. Only an hour earlier he had been in the offices of The Argus where he learned that the Kellys had struck again. He had left his friend's address with the editor in case he was needed.

In the message, Carrington was asked to head to Beechworth on a special train to depart from Spencer Street. No doubt his well-known artistic stylings were seen as important for the Chief Commissioner, who was under the pump for the inability of police to catch the outlaws and presumably wanted favourable press coverage, or so Carrington reasoned as he donned a floppy felt hat, a pair of fingerless woollen gloves and pocketed three pounds in borrowed cash before making his way towards Spencer Street railway station on foot. With him, he carried his sketchbook and pencils.

The city of Melbourne was like most any city in Victoria's empire - wide streets, telegraph poles everywhere and handsome stone and brick buildings formed the central business district.

Of course, it also bore the same palette of smells: horse droppings mingling with smoke from the chimneys and the earthy scent of the damp dirt on the roads. It was claustrophobic and filthy compared to a less industrious city like Beechworth, but Carrington preferred it to anything rural Victoria had to offer. He often complained that the further away from the city you got, the worse the coffee tasted.

As the wind whipped along Spencer Street and nipped as his nose, he considered how welcome a cup of coffee would be at that moment.

At nine o'clock the journalists piled into the special train at Spencer Street amid clouds of steam rolling down the platform from the engine. Thomas Carrington, representing The Australasian Sketcher, was joined by Joe Melvin, John McWhirter and George Allen representing the Age, Argus and Daily Telegraph respectively. As they sat, Melvin checked a revolver he kept in his jacket to see if he had loaded and capped it correctly. These men had no inkling of what lay ahead of them as the train pulled away. The whistle screeched ominously.

***

In the makeshift armoury, Ned assisted Joe into his body armour, tightening the bolts on the side plates. Joe groaned under the weight as he held the breastplate still for Ned.

"I was hoping this bloody armour would feel lighter."

"Better than being shot, isn't it?"

"Marginally, perhaps."

The pair grabbed their helmets and moved to walk out. Ned paused.

"You're missing the leg armour."

"If you want me to ride a bloody horse, I need to be able to get into the saddle," said Joe, picking up his discarded apron and demonstrating the leather loops that would help it hang off the breastplate. Ned grunted.

"It's meant to protect your thighs."

"I care more about what's between them," Joe sneered with a drunken giggle.

As they moved into the breezeway Ned saw Dan leaning against the wall of the kitchen with Jane Jones. He whistled at his brother for attention.

"Keep an eye on the place."

"Where are you going?" Dan asked.

"We're off to make an arrest," Ned replied with a cheeky grin. Ned and Joe disappeared into the darkness towards the paddock. Jane looked befuddled.

"What in blazes were they wearing under their coats?"

"Let me show you," said Dan with a broad smile.

In the armoury, Dan lifted a sheet to reveal his iron breastplate.

"What is it though?"

"Bulletproof armour. We made it ourselves; with some help of course."

Jane reached out and tapped the steel. "Is it very heavy?" she asked.

"You'd have a bit of trouble carrying it, but I can manage fine."

"So strong are you, Dan Kelly?"

"I could lift you with one arm."

"I bet you can't."

"What's the wager?" Dan cocked an eyebrow.

"If you can lift me with one arm, I'll give you a kiss," said Jane.

"Alright. What happens if I can't?"

"Then you'll have to kiss me," Jane said with a smirk.

Suddenly, Dan scooped her up with his right arm. She screamed, then giggled as he spun her around effortlessly.

"You win, you win! Just put me down!"

Dan lowered Jane and she stood before him, blushing. Rising on her toes, Jane kissed Dan softly on the lips. Dan placed his long-fingered hands on her face and went in for another kiss. The kiss lingered and lingered. As Jane sunk to her true height she smiled.

"Sorry. I can't stand on tippy-toes longer than that."

***

Ned and Joe rode their horses ahead of Dave Mortimer and Edward Reynolds on theirs respectively as they left the grounds of the inn. On the buggy sat Jeannie and Catherine Curnow with the baby, Alec Reynolds and Thomas Curnow at the reins.

"Mind you stay as quiet as can be and don't make a break for it. My associate Mr. Byrne can shoot the eyelashes off a harlot from fifty yards."

"Uncle Eddie," Alec began innocently, "what's a harlot?"

"I'll show you when you're older, lad."

Meanwhile, at the stationmaster's house, Steve watched from the veranda as Ned, Joe, and their little troupe disappeared into the darkness. He turned to what remained of the captives in his charge and called from the doorway.

"To hell with this; come on, we're all going over to the inn."

With that the tiny group got up and walked across to the inn and joined the festivities.

"Did Ned send you up?" Dan asked Steve as he reached the bar.

"No, I got sick of waiting for the train over there. I was losing my mind. There is no bloody train and Ned knows it. He's just trying to punish me," Steve replied.

"Well, you know how he's going to be when he gets back and you're up here. I hope you're not too attached to those teeth," said Dan passing Steve a drink.

"Let him have a go and we'll see how many people call him as a natural leader with a "thorough command of his gang" afterwards. I take it he left you in here to keep all of this lot under control on your own then."

"Yeah, just like at Jerilderie," said Dan.

"I'm surprised none of them have had a go at you for the reward. Aren't you the one they keep calling the most bloodthirsty?" Steve joked.

Dan scanned the room to make sure he could see all of the prisoners. Apart from Mortimer being noticeably absent with no more concertina to be heard, Dan could not see the Curnows.

"Steve, when you saw Ned and Joe leaving who did they have with them?" asked Dan.

"I saw a couple of chaps on horses, and a buggy with the schoolteacher and his family in it. Why do you ask?" replied Steve.

"Ned is a bloody fool. That schoolteacher is up to some mischief, I know it!"

"Well," said Steve as he drained his glass, "I suppose we shall find out in due course."

8

The Train

Darkness had well and truly fallen over the Glenrowan police station and all was quiet. The land the station was built on was leased to the police by Hillmorton Reynolds who lived next door, and the wide frontage of the building was handsomely embellished with a veranda awning held up by a series of lathed, whitewashed posts. This was clearly a building intended to house a half dozen officers but instead held only one - Constable Hugh Bracken. The station spoke volumes about the state of affairs in the police force. Living at the station with Bracken were his wife and son, who were both asleep in another room. This evening had seen him in bed with a fever and gastroenteritis. He was glad that there was a latrine outdoors for the sake of his family, but he had not relished the frequent trips through the cold and wet to empty out what felt like half his body weight from his bowels. He was glad, however, for the cold air, which helped to soothe the fever somewhat.

Bracken had resigned from the police some years earlier but reenlisted to help hunt the Kellys after he had heard of the murders in the Wombat Ranges. He had been hand-picked by Superintendent Hare to be stationed in Glenrowan due to its proximity to Greta and Wangaratta. Hare had secretly tasked him with venturing into Greta at night with several of Sergeant Steele's men from Wangaratta to spy on Maggie Skillion's hut in the hope that the outlaws would visit her, but they never seemed to show up when the party was watching the place. Glenrowan otherwise was a quiet place to be the lone representative of law and order in. The most trouble Bracken usually had to deal with, apart from livestock escaping their enclosures, was the Kelly sympathisers harassing the Stanistreets at all hours to open the crossing gates.

Just after nine o'clock the group from the inn arrived at the barracks. Ned dismounted and put his helmet on. His restricted vision forced him to walk more cautiously and stoop.

"Mortimer," he barked, "knock on the door and rouse Bracken."

Dave Mortimer dismounted and complied. He knocked and called for the constable to come to the door but there was no response.

"He must be asleep," Mortimer said to Ned.

"Where's his room?"

"I would assume at the rear. I've never been inside."

"Alright," said Ned, "Joe, get your helmet on. I want you to keep this lot around the front in case our brave man in blue makes a break for it," he pointed to Edward Reynolds, "this one will come with me around the back."

In the bedroom, Bracken began to stir as he heard knocking and shouting outside. He sat up with considerable effort.

"Mr. Bracken! Mr. Bracken!" Reynolds shouted.

Bracken recognised the voice but could not place who it was.

"Who is it?"

"It's Edward Reynolds. Please come to the door now!"

Bracken struggled to get up. He slid his legs into a pair of trousers and his stockinged feet into his boots then shuffled to the door. He took his shotgun from the rack by the door and strapped on his pistol belt as he stood at the threshold.

He opened the door only to be greeted by Ned Kelly brandishing his colt revolving rifle dressed in his crude armour. Bracken staggered back in shock.

"What the devil!"
"I'm Ned Kelly. Bail up or you're a dead man," Ned demanded.
His voice was thin and metallic. Bracken raised his hands, unsure if his antagonist was serious. Something about the strange helmet that resembled a malformed nail can convinced him it was a ruse.
"Ned Kelly be blowed. You're someone from Benalla sent to test my pluck!"
Ned promptly pulled off the helmet to reveal a face seething with frustration.
"Throw down your arms Bracken or I will shoot you."
Bracken quickly obeyed and laid his shotgun down on the floor.

Moments later Ned reappeared, leading Bracken and his horse to where Joe waited on horseback.
Joe removed his helmet with a sigh, "Well, that was easy enough."
"Aye," replied Ned, watching Bracken mount his horse, "but watch this one carefully. I heard he can ride cross-country as well as we can."
Ned made his way to the buggy and helped young Alec Reynolds down.
"Now, you run along to your father and straight to bed, young man," Ned said, "Hasn't this been more fun than Sunday school?"

"I'm Ned Kelly. Bail up or you're a dead man."

Alec nodded while rubbing his sleepy eyes. Ned chuckled and sent him on his way next door, watching to ensure he went inside. Ned then turned his attention to the Curnows who waited in the buggy.

"You can go home now, Mr. Curnow. But someone will be along later to make sure you're all accounted for."

"Bless you, Ned," Thomas Curnow replied.

"Go straight to bed. And don't dream too loud!"

Curnow extended his hand to Ned, and they shook warmly. Sitting up straight, Curnow flicked the reins and set the horses to a canter. As the buggy headed away, Ned and Joe ordered Bracken, David Mortimer and Edward Reynolds to head back to the inn.

***

In the bar room of the inn, the prisoners danced to the squawking sound of Simpson's fiddle. Steve sat in the parlour with Jane Jones, complaining of a stomach-ache. Having barely eaten, unlike those at the inn, his hunger was mounting an insurrection against him and combined with his fatigue from almost twenty-four hours without a proper sleep, he was a wreck. Jane listened to his moaning but kept her thoughts fixed on Dan. When Biddy Connolly returned from relieving herself outside, she took over comforting the outlaw. Steve's face lit up.

Ann Jones poured out liquor and ale like it was her last chance. Her cash box full, she started planting the money straight into the pocket of her apron. Everyone, though tired, seemed jubilant.

Outside, Dan greeted the returning party in the breezeway. As the fever-ridden Bracken shuffled inside, herded by Joe, Dan looked around for the rest of the group.

"Where's Curnow?" he asked Ned.

"I let him go home."

"You did what? Curnow's been up to something all day, or hadn't you noticed that?" Dan scowled as Ned stepped inside, throwing his helmet onto the bed in the armoury.

"I know what I'm doing," Ned mumbled.

"Do you? Then where the hell is this train that you've been saying is on its way?"

"For the last bloody time, it's coming!"

"How many more hours you expect us to guard these people?" Dan's voice grew louder, "The longer we stay the more dangerous this becomes. And we are in no condition for a fight anymore!"

"He's right, Ned," Joe interjected from the door to the bar room, "we should forget about all this and ride out while we can."

"No! We've come this far, and we are not bolting now," Ned growled.

"What if they're not even coming by train? What if they're coming down here from Beechworth on horseback?" said Joe.

"How would they know we're here? We've bailed up everyone that would have spread word that we are in Glenrowan and there's no telegraph," said Ned.

"You don't know that," Dan shouted. "What about the lot you've just sent off? What's stopping them from interfering?"

"Christ almighty, I am so tired of your bloody griping," Ned snapped. He brought his face up close to Dan's, attempting to stare him down. Dan refused to be cowed.

"You're a thick-headed Irish cretin and a bully, just like Uncle Jimmy! If you'd listened to me about Fitzpatrick, none of this would've ever happened," Dan snarled back.

"Listen to you Danny? If you hadn't been gallivanting around stealing horses with Jack Lloyd, Ma would never have been arrested!"

"I never stole those damned horses, and you know it! Besides, I wasn't the one that put a bullet in Fitzpatrick then let him go free! I'd have gone quietly and proved my innocence, but you had to go off half-cocked like you always do, and now we're all suffering for it!"

Ned shoved Dan back against the wall, pressing his hand into his chest.

"I was trying to save your neck you bloody ingrate!"

"I didn't need saving. You were the one pinching Whitty's horses and selling them over the border. Who was saving you from yourself?" said Dan. Ned slapped Dan across the face. It stung like the stroke of a cane.

Dan spat at his brother, "This is why Ma's in gaol - because of your damned temper. You blame everyone but yourself, and I'm sick of it!"

Ned's eyes burned with untameable fury as he grabbed Dan around the throat and squeezed, dragging him into the open. Dan's face began to turn red as he flailed, his fists ineffective against Ned's armoured body. As Ned slammed Dan into the wall of the skillion, Dan grabbed Ned's beard and yanked it up, using his free hand to strike the exposed throat. Ned loosened his grip and Dan seized the opportunity to ram into him with a hip-and-shoulder. The pair wrestled clumsily, tripping over bags of provisions. Ned used his weight, now almost doubled by the armour, as a weapon to pin Dan to the ground where he choked him mercilessly. Joe ran in and tore them apart.

"You're a fucking mongrel, Ned. I wish you had never come back to Greta," Dan wheezed, massaging his throat, "We were all better off without you!"

"Alright!" Joe shouted, "Simmer down, you bloody idiots."

Ned paced furiously, "Now you listen to me, that train will come. And when it does - we will be here waiting! There'll be no running and hiding anymore, do you hear me?" Ned stared Dan straight in the eyes, "No more running. Not if you have any Kelly in your blood."

"Go inside, Ned. That's enough," said Joe.

Ned stormed back inside. Joe turned to Dan who began to tear up in frustration.

"I'm done, Joe," said Dan, "Talk to him before he gets us all killed. He listens to you."

"He used to. Not anymore," Joe sighed.

"Then why are we staying with him?"

"Because," said Joe, "we're not Sherritts. Loyalty still means something to us."

At the bar Ned grabbed a bottle of brandy and a glass and poured a drink, knocking it back with a wince. He saw the Stanistreets sitting in the dining room and Steve Hart keeping watch. Ned growled and rolled his eyes. He marched across to Steve.

"What are you doing here?"

"What use is there being over in the stationmaster's house? I'm more use over here. You had Dan guarding all these people on his own."

"Take the Stanistreets back now."

"What for?"

"Just do it, damn you!" said Ned, reaching for his revolver. Steve grumbled but did as he was told. He rounded up Emily, John and their children and marched them back to the gatehouse. Meanwhile Ned took position in the corner of the dining room and sulked. Dan and Joe slunk back inside, keeping their distance from Ned. As all this unfolded, Constable Bracken watched everything very carefully, making mental notes.

***

At Essendon Station, O'Connor waited for the train beneath the dim glow of a lamp. His wife and sister-in-law were seated on a bench while the native police huddled together for warmth nearby. Jimmy, Johnny, Barney and Hero were all dressed in heavy greatcoats and billycock hats, each carrying a rifle. In the gloom, O'Connor checked his expensive timepiece.

It was ten o'clock when the train arrived, the luggage loaded on, and the passengers led into the carriage. O'Connor was particularly unimpressed to see the party of journalists in the booth behind him. Joe Melvin popped his head over the seat and began interrogating O'Connor with a soft Scottish burr.

"Evening, sir. Would you be Superintendent Hare?"

"No, I'm Sub-Inspector O'Connor of the Queensland police."

"Can you give me any information on the outrage near Beechworth?"

"No. Now leave me alone."

Melvin sat back down and checked his pistol again. McWhirter, an older man with tremendous sideburns and handlebar moustache, frowned at him as the train began to move along.

"You shouldn't be carrying that. You're a reporter," McWhirter said.

"Aye, so should we receive a report from the bushrangers, I'll give them a report back," Melvin replied with a smirk beneath his downy moustache.

The train hurtled along the tracks from Essendon, steel wheels gliding along the rails. The journalists sat in their booth chatting amiably while the women talked about visiting the garden and the museum in Beechworth. The trackers dozed as the train carriage rocked and gyrated.

On the engine, the driver, Alder, looked out ahead of them. As they approached the crossing at Craigieburn the gates across the tracks suddenly caught the light from the engine lamps.

"Jesus!" he screamed. Alder made for the brakes, but it was too late. The engine ploughed through the steel gates with a loud crash. The mangled metal took off a lamp, damaged the engine brake and sheared off the footplate on the carriage where the occupants watched the debris fly up and hit the windows.

"Bloody hell, what was that?" Melvin shouted, ducking for cover. The train slowed just beyond the crossing and came to a halt after what seemed like an eternity. Alder and the guard, McPhee, hopped down to inspect the damage with a bull's-eye lantern.

"Damn it all. The brakes are well-fucked, but I reckon we can get them patched at Seymour," Alder said, wiping his forehead with a sleeve as filthy as his language.

In the carriage, Barney was very unhappy about his rude awakening.

"What we stopped for, Boss?" he asked O'Connor. O'Connor opened the window and peered into the gloom. He could see the mangled remains of the footplate hanging off the side.

"The train seems to be damaged, but don't worry, we'll be on our way soon. Try and get some rest. We need you in tip-top shape for the hunt, boy," he replied. Everyone waited anxiously for the engine to start again with the familiar chugging and the screech of the whistle.

***

At home, Thomas Curnow fed his horse outside while Catherine prepared some supper. Jeannie put the baby down in her cot and sat at the dining table wringing her hands. Thomas soon entered and sat next to his wife as Catherine dished up ham and eggs.

"I must tell you both something tremendously important," Curnow said, "I have a plan to stop the train from derailing."

"Don't be a fool, Tom," Cathy scolded.

"It's perfectly safe. Ned Kelly trusts me. After all, he let me bring everyone home."

"No. That is absolutely out of the question," Jeannie snapped.

"Jean, please! I must do this."

"What happens when they return and find you gone? We'll all be murdered, Thomas!" Jeannie said and began to sob in terror.

"How many fathers and husbands will be murdered tonight if I don't try? I must do this, or I am no sort of a man," Curnow thundered.

"I forbid you to leave this house. I forbid it!"

Catherine saw this moment as ideal to intervene, cuddling her sister-in-law while staring at her brother. "It's alright Jeannie, Tom won't do anything stupid."

Curnow knew better than to press the point and sat silently.

***

At Benalla station, Hare paced furiously in an attempt to keep warm. Having had two hours of sleep to make sure he was not worn out by the time they reached Beechworth; he was feeling energized, but the bite of the winter chill was intolerable.

Assembled on the platform were his party: Senior-Constable Kelly and Constables Barry, Phillips, Canny, Kirkham, Arthur and Gascoigne. While Hare and the less proficient marksmen carried shotguns, the others were armed with Martini Henry rifles. While they weren't exactly the newest technology, they were the best available and had proved very effective for the British infantry in the Anglo-Zulu War, which had ended almost exactly a year earlier. Hare had read with great interest about the conflict, wondering if his brothers back home in South Africa were involved as he had not heard from his family in some time. Here, however, he was not concerned with annexing tribal lands for the British Empire, merely the application of law and order.

At the edge of the platform stood Charles Rawlins, a civilian who had gained permission to head home on the special train.

"Where is this bloody locomotive? I'm frozen stiff out here," Hare grumbled. He checked his timepiece which read that it was midnight. In the depot, another engine was raising steam in preparation for the journey. Attached to it were several carriages including a guard van and horse trucks. Hare was just about to give the signal for the train to take up position at the platform when the squeal of a whistle could be heard. Finally, the train rattled to a halt at the platform, gouts of steam jetting out of the engine.

Hare immediately sought answers from the driver who informed him of the misadventure in Craigieburn. Hare did not feel at all confident to have the train hauling the carriages after such an incident.

"Senior-Constable Kelly, a word please?" Hare said with a beckoning gesture.

"Yes, Superintendent?" Kelly asked.

"I'm aware that there may be hazards on the tracks, we need to have eyes up front to warn us," said Hare.

"What do you have in mind?" asked Kelly.

"I suggest we get something to strap one of the men to the locomotive with a lantern to keep a lookout," replied Hare. "I'm thinking Constable Barry might be an ideal candidate. He's robust and has the eyes of an eagle."

"I'm not so sure that's a very practical suggestion, sir," offered Kelly, "The driver will be able to give a better idea."

Hare repeated the idea to Alder who broke out into peals of laughter.

"You mean to tie some poor bastard to the front of a locomotive screaming along the tracks at top speed? He'll freeze to death," said Alder.

"What about if he stays on the side of the boiler?" replied Hare.

"You're mad! The poor bastard will drop dead long before we arrive, even if he manages to hang on."

"Very well," said Hare, "I'm open to other suggestions."

"You've got two perfectly good engines steamed up and ready to go, I reckon we'll go ahead as the pilot. Shunt the carriages from ours to the one you have waiting and that'll do the trick," suggested Alder.

"Yes, that sounds reasonable. Good thinking Mr. Alder. Let's make it so."

***

Things were calm at the Glenrowan Inn. The tired crowd mostly talked quietly or dozed in their chairs. In the dining room, Jane sat on Dan Kelly's lap resting her weary head on his shoulder giving him tender kisses on his neck. Ann Jones sat beside Joe at the bar, staring lovingly at her son Johnny as he sung 'Cailín deas crúite na mbó', a beautiful Gaelic song about infatuation that translated to 'The Pretty Girl Milking Her Cow'. Joe affectionately tugged at Ann's hair as she played with Scanlan's topaz solitaire ring, which was stuck on Joe's pinkie finger. Nearby, Ned drained another glass of brandy. Silence fell over the inn when the song reached its end.

"Johnny, give us something a little livelier." Ned boomed.

"I think I'm all sung out, Mr. Kelly."

"Sing us 'Farewell to Greta' and I'll give you sixpence," said Ann. With that promise, Johnny broke into song with David Mortimer on concertina:

Farewell my home in Greta, now my sisters fare thee well;
It breaks my heart that we must part but here I dare not dwell.

The brand of Cain is on my brow, my hands are stained with gore;
So, I must roam the forest wild within the Australian shore
Even now the price is on my head and bloodhounds on my trail;
All for the sake of gaining gold my freedom they assail.
You know the country well dear Ned, go take your comrades there;
And profit by your knowledge of the wombat and the bear.
See yonder ride four troopers, one kiss before we part;
Now haste and join your comrades Dan, Joe Byrne and Stevie Hart.

Everyone applauded the boy as he took a bow, but not Ned. Rather, the outlaw threw back another drink and staggered down the passage, his eyes watery.

Outside, he gazed up at the stars and thought to himself. These were the same stars that had guided Brian Boru in his great cattle raid and had twinkled above Ben Hall as he lay down to rest before being shot to pieces by the police. And it was these same stars that had looked down upon his father in Ireland as he stole a pair of pigs, which had condemned him to a life in exile. They made Ned feel small like nothing else could.

***

Meanwhile on the other side of Glenrowan, Thomas Curnow had been putting his plan into effect. With Jean finally settled and down to sleep, he had grabbed a candle and matches. He walked to the front door carrying the items in one hand and his shoes in the other to allow him to walk more quietly. Suddenly he felt a hand on his shoulder and whirled around to see Catherine with a concerned expression.

"Are you sure you should do this, Tommy?" Catherine said, her soft Cornish accent almost soothing Tom's racing heart.

"I'd never sleep at night knowing I didn't at least try. I may just be a schoolteacher, but I am no coward, and I can do this. I must do this!"

Catherine hugged him tightly and kissed his forehead.

"Don't get yourself killed. I'll never hear the end of it."

Thomas allowed a weak smile. Hanging on a coat hook was his sister's red llama wool scarf. He took it down before quietly slipping outside. He put on his boots and rushed to his horse. Mounting, he set his sights towards Benalla and galloped off.

***

On the police train the men sat anxiously, gripping their weapons. Hare tried to snooze but the violent oscillation as the train hurtled down the line made it quite impossible. There was tension in the air, but nobody could quite pinpoint why. Something about this re-emergence of the Kelly Gang felt different. Outright murder wasn't their usual style. After Euroa and Jerilderie, it seemed like the days of the gang as blood-thirsty bushrangers had passed, but now all bets were off.

Poor Tommy, Hare thought, I failed him. His mind drifted back to those icy nights in the caves watching the Byrne house. Aaron's cheeky smile as he recounted his misadventures with Joe Byrne. Hare couldn't comprehend what would make someone turn on a friend like that. He sighed.

In an adjoining carriage, the journalists chatted about the publishing industry and their gripes with their editors. McWhirter ribbed Carrington about a cartoon he had done depicting The Age newspaper as a little old lady dancing with the premier and Ned Kelly around the flag of Communism. Carrington defied him to prove it wrong.

The trackers chatted in Butchulla. The conversation was peppered with laughter. If they feared the Kellys, they were putting on a good show to hide it.

The train rumbled into the night, with Glenrowan rapidly approaching with every passing second.

***

The Glenrowan captives entertained themselves with games of cards and soft conversation as midnight came and went. Mrs. Reardon nursed baby Bridget in the corner of the dining room by the hearth as Dan Kelly moved slowly from room to room, pistol in hand and a rifle slung over his shoulder. Ned was still outside and to Dan's knowledge had been skulking around the kitchen for the past half-hour. Joe sat at the bar idly swilling gin, almost slumped on the counter.

Outside, Ned stalked past the horses, watching them as he shuffled like a condemned man waiting for his trip to the gallows. He entered the paddock carrying a bag of chaff and fed his horse Mirth a handful. The animal's huge lips plucked the food out of his palm greedily. With his free hand he stroked her face, the short bristly hairs, coarse even against his calloused fingers. As proud as he was of Mirth, he was perhaps prouder of Music though he didn't like to admit it.

She was Joe's mare but whoever had broken her in had done a lousy job. Ned had made her the perfect mount; loyal and gentle. A beautiful horse, he thought, deserves to be trained properly. Joe had been grateful at first but soon realised that Ned had now effectively taken her as his own. It was Ned's way. He strode to her and fed her as well. He ran his hands along her flank and could still feel where her skin was healing from Joe's overuse of spurs when pushing her. Music was the best horse of the bunch, but Ned considered himself the best horseman.

I could mount her right now and ride away, Ned thought but his pride overtook his thoughts and he buried them down deep. He wanted to see this thing out.

***

The thunder of hooves could scarcely match the racing of Thomas Curnow's heart as he reached an elevation overlooking the train tracks. He saw distant plumes of steam catching the moonlight, dragged behind the relentless chug of an engine. He turned and rode back down the line to a spot where he would be seen better. Realising there was not enough time to enact his original plan, he dismounted and ran to the tracks, his horse taking the opportunity to dash off into the scrub.

He took out the candle, scarf and matches. His hip was burning with pain and his laboured breathing was illustrated by puffs of condensation spitting from his mouth as he got on his knees and tried to light a match. The engines grew louder, but the match would not take and snapped under Curnow's frenzied strikes.

Another match. The engines were louder still, he could feel the vibrations in the rails. Strike, strike, strike and a flash - the match was alight! He touched the flame to the candle wick and held it until it took hold. The rumble of the wheels and the relentless chug of the locomotive filled his ears as he stood, held the red scarf in front of the candle and prayed to God that it would work.

***

Margaret Reardon tried to soothe Bridget, but the babe would not stop grizzling. She bit her lip and got to her feet then strode across to Dan Kelly.

"What is it?" asked Dan.

"Can I please take my baby home? She's fierce disagreeable. She needed to be in her own bed hours ago."

"Aye, I reckon that about sums things up," Dan said before he moved to a spot where his voice could carry and shouted for attention.

"Everybody, listen up. We're sending you home. Get up and head out the back. Go quietly to your houses!"

Ann Jones flew into a panic. Ned hadn't mentioned anything about letting everyone go and God help anyone who disobeyed Ned Kelly! She flew out from behind the bar and blocked the door with a wild expression unconvincingly stretched into a friendly grin.

"Wait, don't leave yet, Mr. Kelly is to, err, give a lecture," she lied.

Everyone groaned and looked to each other with the same weary look. Dan's eyes were wild with confusion and frustration. What is this madwoman doing?

Presently the door to the passage creaked open behind Ann Jones and Ned Kelly towered over the tiny publican. He was unsteady on his feet and looked like he could keel over at any moment.

"Lecture, eh? Yes, well I suppose I ought to be letting you all go so I won't detain you long. Thank you for reminding me, Mrs. Jones," said Ned.

Ann sighed in relief. Ned planted a hand between her shoulders, it was warm and firm through her jacket. He dragged a chair across the floor and tried to stand on it. His legs, weakened by brandy and the weight of his body armour, would not support him properly and he slipped twice before giving up and simply holding the back of the chair.

"I thank you, people of Glenrowan, for your good company and patience. You must be sure to thank your gallant Victoria Police for responding so promptly to our most recent outrage, resulting in your long detention these past nights. It's good to know that when the Kelly Gang strike, they can do as they please then get clear away before the traps stop scratching their arses long enough to pursue. After all, the longer we're at large the longer they're on double pay and what trap is going to lift a finger when they can get extra money for doing nothing at all."

Ned wobbled and pointed to Sullivan the platelayer.

"You're Sullivan, aren't you?"

"I am."

"Were you ever in New Zealand?"

"No," Sullivan replied.

"Then you're not Sullivan the murderer?"

Sullivan shook his head. Ned smirked.

"Now, there's a scoundrel I'd like to shoot. I will pay £1000 to whoever brings that dog to me, so I have the pleasure of putting a bullet between his eyes. And Quinlan! That coward who shot Dan Morgan in the back. I'll give him the same while we're at it."

Ned's watery eyes scanned the room. The crowd was silent, deflated.

"There's no man in the force that is a match for Ned Kelly, even those man-eaters from Queensland," Ned slammed the chair, "Ha! Why, I can track twice as well as them - and in their own country too. Those little black demons. But you see, I don't really mind a policeman. They have their duty to do, so long as they don't overdo it."

"Tell you what, Ned," Bracken interjected, "If you were an honest man, you couldn't get by without the police!"

Ned scoffed, "Am I not an honest man?"

"I'll be damned if you are," Bracken snapped. Ned feigned offence, fanning his face with his hand like a lady of quality, prone to swooning. The crowd giggled and Bracken fumed silently.

"I am an honest man! What's more, I'm more honest than any Irishman in a police jumper who denies his heritage so he can sleep at night, knowing that he's exchanged the wit, wisdom and beauty of Ireland to dance to the tune of his English masters, who would sooner starve him to death for entertainment than hold him up as an equal!"

"Tell 'em, Ned!" shouted Denny McAuliffe.

"Bracken, are you sworn not to spare father, mother, brother, or sister?" Ned asked.

"No," said Bracken, "our oath is not that; it is to protect life and property, which you or any other man can see in written form."

"Bah!" Ned replied.

There was silence again. Several people checked their watches, shifting uneasily, and baby Bridget grizzled. Ned turned to see where the baby was.

"Oh, everyone's a critic," Ned sneered.

Dan cursed under his breath and walked out to the veranda for fresh air. He could still hear Ned droning on inside, but he no longer had to listen to it. He kicked at a post and sat down on the squat table that had been dragged out to clear the dance floor and sighed. The bar room door creaked open and for a moment Ned's voice rang loud and clear into the night before Joe pulled the door shut behind him.

"Needed a breather too eh, mate?" said Joe.

"I'm tired of him blowing hard all the time. I was this close to getting them out of there and home where they belong, and that daft biddy had to go and ruin it all. Give Ned a chance to talk and he'll be there all bloody night," moaned Dan.

"It'll be over soon. At least he's agreed to let them go," said Joe, fondling his pipe and debating about having a smoke, he tongued the smooth groove in his teeth made by the neck of his old clay pipe. He felt Maggie's ring under his shirt and brushed his hand over it briefly.

***

CHOONGA-CHOONGA-CHOONGA-CHOONGA

The train came into view, piercing the night. Curnow had never seen something so big move so fast, but he kept on holding his small signal.

McPhee, the guard, saw a flash of red on the side of the tracks and leaned into his colleague Alder.

"Stop the engine, there's something ahead!" he screamed. The brakes squealed as they slowed down but shot past what they took to be as a man with a lamp shouting at the train. McPhee only caught a snatch of the man's voice screaming about the Kellys.

As the locomotive ground to a stop, the draft blew out Curnow's flame. Curnow rushed to the cabin where the occupants were now leaning out.

"Hullo?" McPhee called out.

"The Kellys, the Kellys are ahead!" Curnow shouted back. McPhee jumped down and strode into the darkness where Curnow was thinly outlined in moonlight.

"Eh, what's this?"

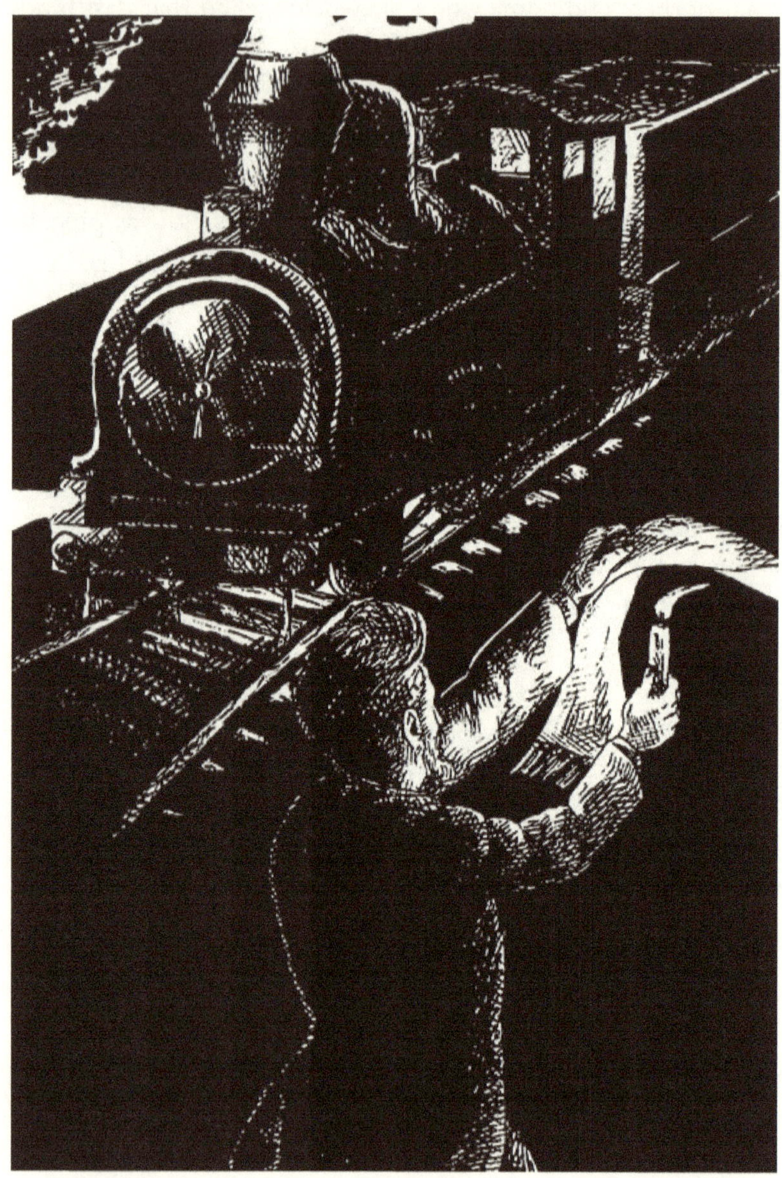

The train came into view, piercing the night. Curnow had never seen something so big move so fast, but he kept on holding his small signal.

"The Kelly Gang are in Glenrowan, they've broken up the line ahead," Curnow gasped. With his eyes wide, McPhee jumped back into the engine.

"Sound the bloody whistle, the rails are out ahead," McPhee shouted.

"What do you mean the rails are out?" Alder replied.

"The Kellys have broken the rails. Just sound the fucking whistle, would you!"

While McPhee lit the three red emergency lanterns that were mounted on the rear of the engine, Alder sounded the whistle, which screamed into the night like a wailing banshee to warn the incoming police special that was gaining on them.

***

In McDonnell's Tavern, Tom Lloyd sat bolt upright, roused by Dick Hart who shook him.

"Tom, something is going on out there. I think I heard the train whistle," said Dick.

"Did you see anything?"

"No, I only heard. I can't see any sign of the train from here, but I swear I heard it."

Tom was quiet and nodded. He got up and grabbed a rifle and headed outside where he peered into the gloom towards Benalla. There was nothing he could see clearly from his vantage point. Frustrated, he stomped back inside.

***

Meanwhile from the veranda of the inn, Dan and Joe heard the faint sounds of an engine rolling down through the chill of night. They looked at each other for confirmation. Dan stood up and walked to the southern end of the veranda.

"You must be joking," Dan groaned.

As if in answer, the hideous peal of the train whistle tore through the silence of the night yet again.

Joe ran to the door and almost yanked it off its hinges.

"The train is coming!"

Ned stood bewildered, "Are you sure?"

"Yes! I just heard the whistle."

"Send Dan out and make sure!"

Joe poked his head out of the door.

"What is it?" asked Dan.

"Go and get a closer look. Ned's not convinced," replied Joe.

Dan glared at Joe momentarily but obeyed. He unslung his rifle and ran down the railway reserve as fast as his feet would take him. He halted on the tracks gripping the rifle tightly. He saw pinpoints of lights in the gloom ahead of him.

He ran back to the inn and pushed past Joe and into the bar room.

"It's not half a mile off!"

Joe followed Dan in and slammed the door, locking it. He threw the key onto a shelf above the hearth in the dining room and followed the others who had dropped everything and were scrambling about quenching lanterns.

"Mrs. Jones, put out the fires!" Joe shouted. Immediately Ann and Jane fetched buckets of water to throw into the fireplaces.

Dan and Joe went straight into the armoury.

Meanwhile Ned rushed to the paddock and fetched Music. He put on her saddle and bridle as quickly as he could manage.

The horse seemed unwilling to cooperate with the extra weight on her back, but Ned asserted himself, galloping down to the stationmaster's house where Steve was waiting at the door, having also heard the whistle.

"Drop everything, the train is here. Take Stanistreet to the inn to make sure he doesn't try to interfere but leave the others. Quick!" said Ned.

As Steve took John Stanistreet to the inn, Ned rode back along the tracks to the station platform. He sat erect in the saddle and saw the steam from the engines fluttering into the night in the distance. The engines were halted. They knew what lay ahead. The plan had failed.

***

The police special had now ground to a halt and, unaware of what was happening, Hare opened the carriage door and plummeted to the ground.

"Barry, Phillips and Gascoigne, come out please," Hare called out. The three constables hopped down from the carriage, landing heavily on the gravel. They had been much higher off the ground than they assumed.

"I need you men to get up on that ridge and keep an eye out while I speak to the engine-driver. If you see the outlaws, you know what to do," Hare ordered. As the constables hiked up the embankment, Hare half-jogged to the engine where he was informed of what had transpired.

While Hare was learning the news, the journalists started speculating on what was happening. Carrington looked outside and noted that the cutting they were situated in was a perfect vantage point for the outlaws to fire upon them from. Evidently this was not lost on the others either.

"I'd wager there's danger. If the bushrangers are about, we don't want to bring attention to ourselves," Joe Melvin said. He tested the doors, but they were locked from outside. He opened the window and squeezed out, pulled the lamp in from outside the carriage and extinguished it. The journalists pulled up the bench cushions and put them against the windows to hide behind. They were now in a cold, dark carriage with no news. For journalists, this was the worst kind of uncomfortable.

The women began to panic. Constable Canny reached over and gripped Mrs. O'Connor's hand.

"Don't fret," Canny said with a soft smile. O'Connor gripped his rifle and slid across the seat to look out of the window. He sensed there was big trouble ahead.

Hare ordered the constables on the ridge to come to him. "Gentlemen, the Kellys have pulled up the rails just past the station. I need you to ride on the pilot engine with me in case there's an ambush," Hare explained. The men obeyed without question.

***

In the bar room, the captives talked quietly, confused as to what was happening but knowing it wasn't good. Steve Hart had entered and ushered John Stanistreet into the crowd before joining Dan to get into his armour. The bedroom was alive with the clanging of iron as Steve prepared. He grumbled about the weight and the large apron that made walking a strain. The boys, now armoured, paused to catch their breath then put their coats over the top, Steve's cloak proving far easier to fit over the steel than Dan's oilskin, which he draped over his shoulders instead.

Certain that the gang were out of sight, Bracken slunk over to the hearth in the dining room and grabbed the front door key, dropping it into the cuff of his trouser leg.

There was a commotion at the back door as Ned returned and gestured for Joe to come outside with him and the pair walked around to the veranda. They watched as the pilot engine slowly trundled along the tracks. Close behind was the police special. Joe's heart sunk.

"Someone warned them," said Joe.

Ned simply nodded.

The pilot engine came to a halt just past the station in a cloud of white steam.

McPhee and Alder stared at each other, lit by the fiery glow of the furnace. Both men were anxious but could find no words to express it. Looking back, they saw the police special line up at the station platform.

Bracken stood at the threshold of the back passage keeping note of where the gang were. When he heard Ned and Joe at the back door, he was satisfied they were occupied and quietly moved through the crowd to the front door.

"Everyone," he said in a loud whisper, "stay low to the floor, do not stand up for anything. This will be over soon enough."

The prisoners sunk low as Bracken unlocked the door, placed the key on the window ledge then quietly slipped out. He ran across the railway reserve, his weak stomach protesting against the activity. He felt like his insides would rupture but his eyes were firmly clamped on the station where the semi-luminous steam billowed around disembarking figures. It was imperative that the police knew where the gang were, and although the short distance felt interminable Bracken soldiered on, there was too much at stake if he failed.

9

Besieged

Thomas Curnow, upon imparting his knowledge to Superintendent Hare, had dashed off into the scrub to fetch his horse then rode the short distance back to the house. He put his horse behind the house and gave it chaff. He removed the saddle and placed it on a railing, wiping the dew off before heading inside. He breathed deeply to try and settle his heart. He removed his boots and walked inside where Catherine waited for him. She greeted him with a tight hug. She felt his clothes, which were soaked from the drizzle he had caught on the return trip. He quickly disrobed and Catherine hid the wet clothes.

Thomas headed to the fireplace where he saw Jeannie standing with tear-stained cheeks. Without a word Jeannie moved to her husband and slapped him across the face with as much strength as she could manage. "You bloody fool, Thomas Curnow; you've killed us all!"

***

By now the sympathisers at McDonnell's were keenly aware of the commotion, signifying the fact that after such a long wait the plan had failed at the most important step. All they could do was watch impotently from the darkness.

"I knew we shoulda left by now," Wild Wright grumbled.

"Shut up; this is not the time," Tom snapped. His heart was racing, and he could feel his chest tightening. He prayed that the gang were making a move to escape.

***

At the rear of the Glenrowan Inn, the gang stood around their leader, each one dressed in his homemade suit of armour.

"What the hell is going on, Ned; why has the train stopped?" Steve asked.

"They know we're here. Someone must've stopped them," Ned fumed.

"What did I tell you? It's that bloody schoolteacher," Dan fumed.

"They'll be all over us like ants. There's still a chance we can get away. They don't seem to know we're here yet," said Joe.

"No! We stay and fight," said Ned stamping his foot petulantly.

"The plan has failed. It's all over. We have to get away or everyone here is as good as dead," Dan said, his voice strained.

"Please, Ned - we don't stand a bloody chance," said Steve. Joe began to laugh.

"What's so funny?" Dan barked.

"This is so absurd. Look at us," Joe pointed to Steve, "Whippet can barely walk with that armour, and I can hardly see in front of me with this daft helmet on. This was never going to work. We're fools. Absolute fools,"

"Hold your tongue, Joe," said Steve in a hushed voice. Ned's face was bright red, and his eyes burned with the fury of wildfire.

"Then go. Run away, you cowards. Hide in the mountains and leave it all to me, like always. I was a fool to think a single one of you was man enough," Ned snapped. He put on his helmet and moved past the side of the hotel, dislodging the sliprail violently and throwing it aside. The gang were dumbfounded and couldn't find the motivation to speak or move.

***

At the station, the troopers filtered out on to the platform accompanied by the trackers and the journalists. Superintendent Hare shouted orders over the din. He gestured for Barry, Gascoigne, Phillips, Rawlins and Senior-Constable Kelly to join him.

"I saw a candle in the window of one of the houses over yonder. Do you have any idea whose place it was, Rawlins?"

"Yes. There's Jones', that's the stationhouse, and there is McDonnell's."

"What is the name of the stationmaster here?"

"Stanistreet, sir," Rawlins replied.

"Alright, I think we'd better pay a visit to Mr. Stanistreet. You men will join me of course, O'Connor will hold the fort here."

***

In her bed, Emily Stanistreet lay unable to sleep. With her children sleeping around her, she had kept a candle burning on the off chance that the Kellys would allow her husband to return home. She struggled to keep her eyes open, her depleted body fighting her mind for dominance. Suddenly there was a heavy knock at the door. Emily felt a cold chill wash over her and settle in the pit of her stomach.

Another knock.

She refused to get up, instead endeavouring to pull the covers over her eyes. A moment later a knock at the window forced her to look. She could see shadowy figures moving outside then a voice, muffled by the glass.

"Stanistreet, are you in there?"

She recognised the voice but couldn't place it. Attempting to avoid waking her children she slid out of bed. Her naked feet pattered along the floor as she went to the front door where the police were standing. For a moment her knees weakened.

"Who's there?"

"Police," came the reply from outside. Emily opened the door hesitantly.

"Ma'am, I am Superintendent Hare. Where is your husband?"

Emily released all of her tension and broke down into a blubbering mess in the doorway. Hare looked to the others with discomfort.

"My good woman do be calm for a minute; tell me, where is your husband?" said Hare.

Emily sniffed, "They have taken him away."

"Who do you mean by 'they'?" asked Hare.

"The Kellys. Steve Hart was here only a few minutes ago."

"In what direction have they taken him?"

Emily pointed towards the inn and began sobbing again. Hare thanked her, then as soon as they had arrived the men were headed back to the station. Hare took long-legged strides as he tried to formulate a plan of attack.

"If the woman is to be believed the outlaws have headed into the Warby Ranges with a hostage. We must act fast," said Hare.

"Inspector, may I assist you in the hunt? I know the Warbys well and can guide your men," said Rawlins.

"Do you have any supplies? A weapon?"

"No, but I was hoping one of your men could spare a rifle."

Hare paused and took his service revolver from its holster and passed it to Rawlins.

"Take my revolver and I will stick to my gun," said Hare, "Do you know how to use it?"

"If it's a Webley revolver, I know how it works," replied Rawlins.

***

Dan, Joe and Steve stood silently, ashamed and uncertain.

"What shall we do?" asked Steve.

Joe frowned, grunted and donned his helmet. His pale blue eyes were barely visible through the eye holes. He marched off to the veranda grumbling to himself, the sound became a muffled rumbling inside his helmet. Dan and Steve looked at each other. There was nothing for it.

Dan slid his helmet on.

"A short life," said Dan.

"And a merry one," Steve said. He put his helmet on and took a moment to adjust. Dan and Steve pushed past Ned and joined Joe on the veranda, fanning out across its width. Ned took a moment to observe his brothers in arms.

The gang brandished revolvers and cocked the hammers ready for action, Ned was armed with his revolving carbine. Steve's breathing was audibly shaky from within his helmet. Ned felt he should say something, but nothing came to mind. The gang could hear the whinnying of the police horses at the station and the noise as people disembarked from the train and began unloading equipment on the platform.

Dan closed his eyes and prayed. He hoped there would be no bloodshed, but he knew it was inevitable. He took deep breaths to try and settle his nerves. It didn't work.

***

"Get the horses unloaded, the Kellys will likely be heading to the War-bys, and we must be on their tails as quickly as possible!" Hare ordered as he strode onto the platform. The doors of the horse trucks were opened with much clanging and the horses, seventeen in total, stirred within.

A short distance away, Constable Bracken was trying to run to the station. He tripped on the stump of a sapling and fell but picked himself up and continued as fast as his feet could move. As Bracken reached the platform of the station there was utter chaos as horses were being unloaded and policemen scattered about the place. Sub-Inspector O'Connor was doing his best to direct people, but the constables seemed to ignore him. Bracken headed to the trackers who stood at the corner of the station passing a small bottle of brandy around.

"Boss? Boss? Where's Boss?" Bracken asked, breathless and stumbling. Barney looked around and saw Hare and pointed in his direction.

"He's over there," said Barney.

Bracken stumbled towards Hare and waved for attention, "Inspector!"

"Constable Bracken?" Hare replied

"The Kellys. They're at Jones' Inn," Bracken gasped, "Not five minutes ago. Don't let them escape!"

Hare was suddenly invigorated, "Men, they're at Jones'. Follow me!"

"What shall we do with the horses?" came a voice from the crowd.

"Let go the horses and come as quick as you can!"

Bracken steadied himself against the station wall and eyed off the police horses running free from the trucks as the troopers ran to join Hare. With his arm raised, Hare charged into the night followed by a handful of his men. They rushed down from the train platform gripping their weapons tightly. Hare ran at the front, his huge frame acting as a beacon.

"Fan out!" Hare shouted as he pushed through a steel gate. Immediately they were joined by the rest of the men including O'Connor and his trackers who threw themselves down into a drainage ditch directly in front of the inn.

The gang watched the police getting into position. Ned tightened his grip on his carbine.

Dan struck his pistol against his breastplate, "Let's pink the bastards!"

Ned kept his eyes trained on the figures barrelling towards them. As Hare ran through the gate, his arms were thrust out in front of him ready to fire. Ned fired first. The bullet struck Hare's left wrist causing him to spin. The bullet had smashed the bones and nicked an artery, causing blood to flow freely immediately. Hare was in such shock he didn't feel any pain, he merely returned fire, emptying both barrels, single-handed. Hare staggered as his brain tried to work out what had happened.

"Fire away you bloody dogs, you cannot hurt us!" Ned hollered.

The remaining police scattered and threw themselves into cover as Joe, Dan and Steve opened fire. Attempting to regain equilibrium, Hare sat on a tree stump and planted the gun in between his knees. He raised his left arm, unable to move his fingers.

"God! I'm hit - and in the first bloody shot," Hare exclaimed as the police around him opened fire.

Bullets punched through the weatherboard walls of the inn and shots glanced off the gang's armour without effect. The gang blazed away at the police, firing aimlessly into the darkness, hoping to hit something – anything – or at least drive the attackers back. The clouds began to roll away from the moon, bathing the police in light and casting more profound shade over the gang, which was only broken by the muzzle flashes of their weapons.

From his seat, Hare reloaded his gun with one hand, a trick he had perfected as a boy growing up on a farm in Cape Town. He raised his gun and blasted at the inn again.

"Don't be foolish, throw down your arms and we can discuss your surrender," Hare called out. His arm throbbed.

"Surrender be buggered," replied Dan.

Joe Byrne strode out from the veranda with a pistol in each hand. "We don't want to speak to you," he said before firing at the superintendent. Bullets continued to ricochet and flatten against the gang's armour.

Ned laughed defiantly, "Fire away, you bastards!"

Hare swept his gaze over the battlefield. His heart was pumping so hard that it seemed like it would explode. His breathing was laboured, and he was sweating profusely. He tried to stand but his legs had become weak. His head was throbbing, but he continued to move, the percussive sound of gunfire marbling with the rushing of blood in his ears.

The bushrangers' bullets kicked up dirt and took chunks out of the trees as they fired blindly into the night. Each blast from their weapons illuminated the veranda, briefly revealing the stocky, block-headed silhouettes of the outlaws through the clouds of gun smoke. The police weapons were far more powerful, and their shots penetrated the inn as if its walls were made of cardboard. The captives inside screamed and hugged the floor as disaster unfurled around them. Bottles and glasses exploded and rained shards down on the captives. Women and children screamed in fear and confusion.

Dan and Steve pushed past Ned and joined Joe on the veranda, fanning
out across its width.

Fuelled by adrenaline, brandy and overconfidence in his armour, Ned Kelly walked proudly into the railway reserve. Bullets whizzed around him and ripped at his coat. He took no heed.

"You bloody cocktails can't hurt me. I'm in iron!"

In response to the taunting, a fusillade was directed at Ned. A shot lodged in Ned's right thumb, crushing the ball joint and making it almost impossible to grip his weapon effectively. He swapped his grip to his left hand and gritted his teeth as he attempted to mockingly laugh at his attackers. Constable Gascoigne heard Ned's taunts and recognised the voice. He took careful aim at the lumbering silhouette with his Martini Henry rifle.

BANG!

The shot caused Ned to stagger as it struck him below the wrist of his left hand, travelled a short distance down the forearm and exited the flesh before smashing through the upper arm just above the elbow joint. The lucky hit had smashed his arm, leaving it fairly useless. Within a moment, as more fire was directed at him, a bullet hit Ned's left foot above the big toe, ploughed through the bones, tendons and nerves and lodged at the instep near his heel. Ned buckled slightly and nearly collapsed on his side, roaring in frustration and pain. It felt like his foot had been skewered with a red-hot spike. He mustered what little control he could exert over his left trigger finger and returned fire, the bullet striking the post where Gascoigne had ducked for protection.

Breathless with pain, Ned staggered away back toward the inn as more bullets and shot hit his armour through his oilskin with a dull chink sound. He moved through the gap in the fence and past the sign, retreating like a wounded dog and leaving the rest of the gang on the veranda to fight.

Hare, meanwhile, held his shattered wrist up to his chest, breathing stertorously as he sought Senior-Constable Kelly in the chaos.

"Kelly," Hare shouted, "I'm hit. I have to go back!"

Kelly barely heard Hare over the din. Hare approached closer.

"Keep everyone spread out and for, God's sake, stop them from escaping," he ordered.

"Right, sir."

He retreated to the station, passing O'Connor who seemed to ignore him. As he reached the platform, Hare saw a pile of saddles stacked next to the wall of the building.

"What are all these here for?" he asked.

"It's a barrier for our protection," said McWhirter. Hare moved into the light of a lantern where Rawlins helped him to sit.

"The inspector is injured; does anyone know first aid?" Rawlins called out. Thomas Carrington stood forward.

"I know some first aid; might I take a look?"

Hare's gear and jacket were removed and his shirt sleeve, now sopping wet with blood, was unbuttoned and pushed up his arm. The wound presented a most frightful, gory spectacle with raw, torn flesh swimming in bright red blood that spluttered from the wound.

"I need cloth and something to pad this with," said Carrington.

In the main carriage of the train, Louisa O'Connor and Cathy Prout-Webb sat on the floor, cowering between the benches as bullets struck the thin wooden walls. Suddenly the door to the carriage was opened by Rawlins who gestured for the women to come out.

"Do you have any cloth? We need something to bind this wound," Carrington said.

"Yes, we're perfectly fine. Thank you for asking," Cathy said sarcastically.

Louisa offered up her silk handkerchief and a pair of scissors from a sewing kit in her purse. Carrington promptly cut the handkerchief into strips and used them to dress Hare's wound, plugging the entry and exit wound with cotton waste Melvin had found in the station building.

As Hare was being patched up, he addressed the women.

"Ladies, I must implore you to find cover. The Kellys are in the hotel over yonder and the firing is only going to get worse until we can get on top of them. We will get them soon enough," said Hare. He rose to his feet and began looking around him, "Where's my gun?"

"Sir," said Rawlins, "you're not going back out there, are you?"

"I will do what I must, my men need me," replied Hare, snatching up his shotgun. He began walking down towards the battlefield, tailed by Rawlins. Hare almost made it to the fence line, when suddenly he lurched and stumbled.

"Catch me," Hare whimpered as he toppled over like a felled tree, with Rawlins grabbing him in the nick of time, breaking the fall.

The battle raged on, though the gang soon found themselves out of ammunition and began to make a move around to the rear of the inn to reach the armoury. Joe began shuffling along the veranda, cursing under his breath as the Colt revolver he was using jammed. As he stood fiddling with the weapon, a bullet tore through the calf of his right leg, shearing through the Achilles tendon. His ankle went slack, and he lost balance, falling against the wall. He hollered in pain and confusion.

"Boys! Help me, help me!"

Dan and Steve moved to Joe's side as quickly as they could and carried him away from the veranda.

"Where the hell has Ned gone?" Joe said with a grimace. The pain in his leg was like nothing he had felt before. It was as if his foot was stuck in a fire.

Once clear of the frontline, Joe was let down and the other two went into the bedroom to reload. He could not put weight on his injured leg but made an effort to crawl into the breezeway and haul himself onto a pile of sacks. Sliding his helmet off, Joe felt the chill of night on his sweat drenched skin. Tears rolled down his cheeks and he moaned as he attempted to find a comfortable position for his maimed leg. He tugged at his scarf and drew the long end of it out from under his breastplate and wiped his face with it. He paused and stroked the wool.

Presently he became aware of movement as the police moved around the inn. His apron dug into him as he sat. He unhooked the leather thongs and set the plate down.

Joe grumbled to himself, "Bloody Ned. 'This will set everyone's ears a-tingle', he says. 'Trust me, Joe', he says. Stupid bastard."

With the gang disappearing behind the inn the focus of the police's fire became the building itself, but they too found themselves short on ammunition. Rawlins was soon sent out to distribute ammunition from the guard van to the men who promptly reloaded and resumed.

Inside the inn was a cacophony of screams and prayers as bullets zipped around the terrified captives. They stayed low to the floor with hands over their ears while shards and splinters sprinkled over them. In the mayhem, Johnny Jones had begun to panic and stood near the bar looking for Ann amid the darkness.

"Where are you, Mother?" Johnny cried. A bullet crashed through the building and struck the boy. It shattered his pelvis and tore through him, bursting out under his arm. Johnny squealed and collapsed. Ann heard the awful sound from the bedroom and ran to her boy as he fell. With his last ounce of strength, he clutched the red velvet folds of Ann's skirt.

"Oh, mother, I've been shot," he whimpered before slumping unconscious to the floor. Ann wailed and grabbed the boy's shattered body and held it close to her bosom. A bullet whipped past her head, dislodging her coiffured hair, another tore at her sleeve but she did not care.

"My beautiful boy!"

From behind the bar, Martin Cherry could hear everything. He nudged Jack McHugh who lay beside him.

"Come on, we can carry him out!" Cherry said.

Cherry and McHugh picked up Johnny, and carried him through the breezeway, past Byrne. They laid him down in the kitchen by the fireplace, miraculously avoiding injury themselves. Here they were joined by Ann who sobbed inconsolably. Unable to help her boy, she cradled him. As McHugh lingered in the doorway, Joe called out.

"What are you all doing? Get down or you'll be shot!"

"Little Johnny Jones has copped it," McHugh replied. Joe had no words to give, merely giving a stoic nod before he returned to his self-pity.

Steve and Dan had been remarkably unscathed during the initial volleys compared to the others, but the armour was proving prohibitively heavy and the helmets too restrictive on their vision. They went into the bar room, now equipped with rifles. They took position by the windows and looked out. The battlefield was almost completely hidden by a wall of gun smoke and fog. Most of the window glass had been shattered and the smell of spent gunpowder wafted in through the holes.

Steve cocked his rifle, pushed the muzzle through a hole in the window and fired at where he supposed there were targets. As the rifle kicked back into the steel breastplate it made a dull thud. He put his back to the wall to reload. In response police bullets peppered the wall and window around him. Lead and wooden splinters bounced off his armour, shredding his cloak. The force of the blows threw him off balance.

Elsewhere in the inn, a rifle bullet struck the fireplace behind which George Metcalfe cowered. The bullet chipped a brick and the ceramic shards hit the labourer in the face, badly lacerating the flesh around his eye. He hit the floor hard with his hands clapped to his face, screaming.

Outside, with his foot and arm in incredible pain, Ned staggered through the grounds of the inn. Dazed and wounded, he had been looking for a way out. He limped to the breezeway where he saw Joe slumped against the wall.

"Is that you, Joe?"

Joe peered into the gloom at the figure hobbling to him.

"Yes, is that you Ned? Come here!"

"Come here be damned! What are you doing there?" Ned sunk to his knees beside Joe, "Come, load my rifle. I'm cooked."

"So am I," Joe replied, "I think my leg is broke."

Ned removed his helmet and gasped for air, sweat streaming down his face.

"Leg be damned! You've got the use of your arms. Load for me and I can pink these buggers," Ned ordered as he presented his carbine and cartridge bag to Joe. He begrudgingly took them and began the complex process of reloading, fumbling with the moving parts in the dark. Ned held his crippled right hand up. He could not move his thumb.

"Don't be so excited; the boys'll hear. It'll dishearten them," Joe grumbled as he removed the column that held the carbine's barrel in place.

"I'm afraid it's a case with us this time," Ned said in a low voice. He was only just realising what a colossal failure he had manufactured.

"Well, it's your fault. I always said this bloody armour would bring us to grief," Joe snapped.

"Don't you believe it," Ned snapped, "Old Hare is cooked, and we'll soon finish the rest."

"Of course, Ned," Joe replied dismissively.

"Listen, I reckon I know a way to escape. I found a spot where the bastards haven't got us covered. We can slip out behind them, and they won't even know."

"Now? You want to escape now?"

"Do you have a better idea?"

"What would it matter if I did?"

The pair were silent as Joe finished reloading. He thrust the gear back to Ned. Suddenly Dan appeared at the back door.

"What are you two doing? That bastard Bracken has bolted."

Joe laughed, "Ah, you can't trust 'em, can you? When I find him, I'll make a bracken out of him."

Joe crawled on his hands and knees into the inn.

"Listen, Dan," said Ned as he rose to his feet, "I want you boys to create a distraction at the front so I can make sure it's clear for us to get out the back here. When I come back, we can just slip past the police and head for the ranges."

Ned staggered into the armoury and grabbed his revolvers. With considerable difficulty, and assistance from his brother, he managed to get Lonigan's pistol belt around his middle, and shoved Devine's Colt Navy into his cartridge bag. Finally, he pulled out his old pocket Colt, the same one that wounded Fitzpatrick. He donned his helmet and disappeared into the darkness.

Venturing into the paddock Ned attempted to grab Music who shied and whinnied. She could smell blood and had already been spooked by the gunfire. Ned grabbed at her bridle and attempted to get his foot into the stirrup but found his shattered foot too weak to support the weight. He then tried to put his injured foot into the stirrup on the other side but found that he still could not vault into the saddle. From a slope overlooking the rear of the inn constables, Arthur and Gascoigne saw the movement in the paddock. Gascoigne took aim at the figure attempting to mount and fired. The shot struck Ned in the shoulder, cutting the straps that secured his right shoulder plate. The plate slid to the ground and Music bolted. Ned roared inarticulately and made a move for the fence as Music burst through the sliprail and out into the bush behind the inn.

***

On the platform, Hare took brandy to soothe his pain as Joe Melvin ventured to the pilot engine and spoke to Alder.

"My good man, how quickly do you think you can get the inspector to Benalla?"

"Given the time I reckon we can get there about three o'clock."

"Alright, let's make it happen," Melvin replied.

Within moments the pilot engine began to pull up to prepare for the journey. Suddenly the engine was struck with bullets from the direction of the inn with a startling pinging.

"Bugger this!" shouted McPhee and the engine headed off without Hare.

Arrangements were quickly made for the special train to take Hare to Benalla and bring back reinforcements. As Hare sat in the guard van, he contemplated just how quickly his glory had been snatched away. So much build up to the moment of swift victory had been met with calamity. Hare felt ashamed. With a ghostly whistle, the train pulled away slowly. On the platform a commotion erupted as Cathy Prout-Webb and Louisa O'Connor realised the train was leaving them behind.

"Why are they leaving us here? We're not safe," Cathy complained.

"The train will be back with reinforcements, there's no need to worry," Melvin told the women as he guided them into the shelter shed to take a seat. Louisa buried her tiny face in her delicate, lace-gloved hands. Cathy, however, was more angered than despairing and took a swig of brandy to calm herself. She nudged her sister and shoved the flask into her hands. Hesitantly, Louisa took a sip.

"Oh, don't act like you don't take mouthfuls of the stuff when nobody's looking. Drink the blasted brandy, woman," Cathy chided. Louisa allowed a thin smile to creep across her face.

***

At McDonnell's tavern, Tom Lloyd felt every nerve tingling with fear and excitement.

"What do we do, Tom?" asked Dick. Tom did not reply.

"To Hell with it! We have to help them, come on," growled Wild Wright as he grabbed his rifle from behind the counter of the bar.

"No! That was not the plan. You go out there, you'll be riddled," Tom shouted.

"We have to do something, they're clearly outnumbered," said Dick

"They won't be outnumbered for long," said Wild as he shook Jack Lloyd awake, "Come on, Jacky boy. We've work to do."

"Wild, what are you doing?" said Tom as he pressed his hand into Wild Wright's chest to stop him. Wild brushed him aside and went outside where he and Jack headed over to where the signal rockets were positioned.

"Gizza match, Jacky boy," Wild whispered, extending his hand. Jacky dug a matchbox out of his pocket, dropping it gently into Wild's outstretched paw. Wild lit the fuses and stood back. The rockets fizzed and shot off into the night sky over Glenrowan and exploded. A bright scarlet bloom unfurled across the inky blackness with a loud crack.

As Ned moved through the bush in search of the horse, he saw the signal rocket and cursed. Knowing there was nothing he could do about it he continued to blunder through the trees where he caught sight of Music ahead of him like a ghostly beacon, headed for a clearing.

Nearby, Arthur and Gascoigne saw the signal too as the second rocket exploded.
"What the hell is that?" gasped Arthur.
"It must be a signal of sorts." replied Gascoigne.
"Where did they come from?"
"Other side of the tracks, I suppose." Gascoigne said dismissively. He slid another cartridge into his rifle and fixed his gaze on the inn.

In the kitchen, Jane Jones crawled to her mother and Johnny. Heddington, Owen and Jeremiah had all done the same, accompanied by John Stanistreet.
"What's happened, Ma?" asked Owen.
"Those curs have shot Johnny!"

There was no time to register the information before a shot entered the skillion wall and ricocheted off the fireplace. The bullet struck Jane across the forehead and lodged behind her ear. Dazed and in pain, Jane shrieked uncontrollably.

"Jane!" screamed Ann. Stanistreet rushed to the girl's aid. He cradled the hysterical girl's head and examined the oozing wound in the dark. He found a large lump behind her ear.

"Hold still, my dear. I can see the bullet."

Stanistreet pinched the lump, working the lead out from under the skin. Within a moment the deformed bullet was free along with a lot of blood.

"There it is. You're alright, dear. Stay low and I'll get a bandage," said Stanistreet. Jane nodded and sobbed as she clutched at the wound.

In the bar room, Dave Mortimer rose to his hands and knees and scurried towards Dan Kelly who was at the bar reloading his Colt revolvers. His helmet sat on the counter surrounded by broken bottles and dented pewter steins. He looked down at Mortimer.

"Dan, Dan, will you please let us go?"

"You'd be mad to try. Those bastards are out for blood, and I doubt they care whose. Just stay low. We'll get you out as soon as we can," said Dan, striding through the room and out into the breezeway. He entered the skillion where he was met with sobbing and commotion.

"Is everyone alright?" Dan asked. Jane clutched at Dan's leg.

"They shot Johnny, and they shot me," Jane wailed. "Please, Danny, do something!"

"I will get you out. Get behind something and stay calm. I will try to get them to stop shooting long enough for you to escape."

"Please be quick, Johnny is dying," said Jane.

Dan stroked Jane's freshly bandaged head and crossed back into the inn. His heart was in his throat. He stood at the window and cupped his hands around his mouth.

"There's women and children here, hold your fire!"

His reply came in the form of a shot striking the last pristine piece of glass in the window. The bullet zipped close to Joe's face.

"Fuck me!" Joe said in surprise. He looked around the room and called out to the McAuliffe brothers.

"Oi, you McAuliffes reckon you want to be a part of the action? I'll give you some rifles and you can have a crack at the traps with us."

"Fuck off, Joe!" Denny McAuliffe shouted back. Joe smirked. He knew exactly the sort of support he could expect from Kelly sympathisers when the going was tough.

As John Stanistreet observed the carnage around him, he realised that if there was any chance to convince the police to stop and allow the captives free, he must take it.

"Sit tight everyone, I'm going to try and get out. I'll tell the police there's women and children in here."

Stanistreet emerged from the kitchen, listened to the gunfire and made his way to the fence. He vaulted over it and ran for the tree line. Bullets zipped past him, singing frightfully close to his ear but by dumb luck or providence he reached safety unscathed. Before him stood Senior-Constable Kelly with his gun raised.

"Stand! Who goes there?"

"Don't shoot, I'm the stationmaster," Stanistreet cried as he raised his hands. Kelly lowered his gun and rushed the newcomer away from the siege.

"Who's inside the hotel? Are the outlaws accounted for?" the trooper asked.

"The Kellys are in there alright, but there's some forty-odd captives as well. Men, women and children. Please, you must stop this shooting, some are badly wounded!"

"I will do what I can. Your wife will be glad to see you. Clear the scene quickly," replied Kelly. With that, Stanistreet ran home.

Joe awkwardly pulled himself up on the bar, putting his weight on his one good leg. He saw Dan by the window.

"We have to get these people out of here before anyone else gets shot."

"I know, damn it, I know!" Dan hissed. He leaned close to the window repeated his plea but was again greeted by firing.

"You bloody bastards, give them a chance to escape!" Dan screamed.

Something in his mind snapped and, in his rage, he fired wildly out of the window.

"Did that work?" Joe asked snidely.

"Shut up."

Meanwhile, the sense of desperation was mounting in the kitchen. Jack McHugh looked at the mortally wounded Johnny Jones, limp and bleeding from the mouth.

"There's no more time for this," McHugh said. He lifted Johnny gingerly and draped the fragile boy over his shoulders. "I'll look after him, missus," McHugh said to Ann Jones before heading outside.

He retraced Stanistreet's movements and ran from the hotel like a man chased by starved wolves. Bullets narrowly missed him, but McHugh made it across the paddock. Constable Gascoigne noticed him heading straight toward the police line and raised his gun.

"Stop or I will shoot!" he barked. McHugh stood still.

"Please, sir, this boy's been shot! Let me save him."

After a moment's contemplation the trooper allowed McHugh to pass.

He continued across the train tracks to McDonnell's where he called out for help. Paddy McDonnell opened the door and allowed McHugh in. Seeing the horrific state the boy Jones was in, Hanorah fetched pillows and McHugh was able to lay the dying boy down in safety. As he looked at Johnny, he did not think there was a hope in Heaven for him.

***

Finally, the police staggered their fire; an hour had elapsed since the opening volley. While the police had riddled the inn with bullets and shot, the outlaws had scarcely fired more than a couple of dozen shots between them.

Joe rested at the bar with his disabled leg, Steve sat sullen in the parlour reloading. Dan went out to the breezeway, away from prying eyes and bullets, where he cried. He attempted to stifle the sobs, but Jane, who was sitting at the door to the kitchen, saw him and took pity on him.

As everything was unfolding at the inn, Ned was bumbling around the bush in a daze. His mind focused on escape and the shame of his failure. He tried to find any excuses that didn't put him at the root, but none were forthcoming. As Ned staggered into a clearing, his mind became a battlefield as intense as the one he had escaped. His pride vied for dominance over his empathy for those he had left in the Colosseum to fight or die.

The world around him lurched and heaved and he sank to his knees near a huge fallen gum tree; its ghostly, spindly, branches twisted into a mess, providing a support for the exhausted outlaw. He stooped to remove his helmet and clawed his skull cap off his head in a fit of exhaustion. He shook uncontrollably, his teeth chattered, and he blacked out, slumping to the ground senselessly.

10

Death in the Night

Unnoticed by his colleagues, Constable Bracken had taken the reins of one of the loose police horses and shot off like a rocket for Wangaratta, hoping to get back-up. The jostling and bumping of the horse under him made his gizzards ache, but he squeezed his legs tighter and hunched over his steed's neck. The night air stung his face, but the distant sound of guns kept him motivated.

***

Inside the inn, Dan and Steve took advantage of the decreased firing to move women and children to the back away from the heaviest fire. Steve stood in the breezeway looking out at the shadowy figures lurking in the scrub. A blast of shot bounced off his breastplate as prisoners moved behind him into the kitchen. As Margaret Reardon passed the bar her skirt became tangled with Joe Byrne's rifle, which had been resting near the doorway.

"Oi, Byrne, move that damned gun before someone shoots themselves," James Reardon barked. Joe hopped over and took the rifle up and laid it on the bar.

Wild with grief, Ann Jones crawled down the passage to the bar, feeling sick with sorrow and anger. She saw Joe slumped at the bar, loading his pistols among debris. In her fury she walloped her fist into Joe's injured leg, causing excruciating pain.

"Argh, you mad bitch!" he screamed. Ann was unrepentant.

"Get out of here, ye cowards! Go and fight like men or run like mangy curs. Just go before my whole family is murdered!"

Joe tried to shrug her off. Several bullets smashed through the walls of the bar room, barely missing Ann.

"Get up and die instead of hiding! Get out of my place - look what ye've done!"

"Get back in the kitchen before you get hurt too," Dan said from across the room. Ann staggered into the breezeway.

"Ye bloody bastards!" Ann screamed at the police. She went back into the kitchen, eyes dancing like embers caught on a draft.

"Damn the lot of them. Janie, we're getting the children out this instant!"

With her head still bleeding under a makeshift bandage, Jane began to gather as many women and children as she could, rounding up the smaller children just the way she did at Sunday school.

"Alright, little lambs," Jane said calmly, "take each other's hand and stay close behind me."

Jane took the lead, holding a lit candle aloft. Among the women making a move for the exit was Biddy Connolly. She searched in the dark for Steve who remained by the fence in the breezeway. She quickly moved through the gap to his side.

"Steve," she said, "we're going to make a break for it."

Steve removed his helmet and stepped into the shadows.

"I'll cover you from here and draw their fire away. Move like lightning. Get to safety as fast as you can and don't stop," Steve said. Biddy kissed Steve tenderly before she turned and joined the group at the back door. As Steve moved back into position a blast from a Martini Henry rifle struck his breastplate. The force of the blow cracked his collarbone and the steel around the shoulder strap. He staggered but remained standing. With difficulty he put his helmet back on. His left arm felt weak and limp.

As Ann lined up the group, including the entire Ryan and Reardon families, Dan made a beeline for Jane.

"What are you doing?" Dan asked.

"We're getting out of here," replied Jane.

"Are you mad?"

"It's madder to stay here and get shot."

Dan bowed his head and sighed, "It wasn't meant to be this way. I'm so sorry."

"There's no time for sorry now. Help us."

Jane held Dan's cheek and kissed him, lingering as long as she could. Dan felt her tears wetting both of their faces. He pulled away.

"Until we meet again," Dan said as he tried to smile. Ann grabbed Jane's arm and dragged her away from the outlaw. Ann glared at him. Dan turned and walked through the building to the veranda. Shouldering the bar room door open he gazed out at the smoke haze.

"Hold your fire, there's women and children coming!" Dan screamed.

The firing seemed to pause, and the group headed for the railway. Guided by Jane, the prisoners moved swiftly past the sign. The movement caused a new burst of gunfire. Steve fired from the breezeway to create a distraction. Toddlers bawled in the confusion. Little Patrick Ryan, waddling in short pants, hesitated and stumbled around near the fence wailing and rubbing tears from his eyes with his tiny, pudgy hands until his mother doubled back and grabbed him. The women screamed as they snatched up some of the slower children and ran to safety.

In the confusion, Margaret Reardon flew into a panic. "Where's Catherine?" she screamed, looking around wildly for her daughter. The Reardons doubled back to the inn rather than risk getting shot, where they found Catherine on the floor of the bedroom unable to get up due to leg cramps.

Ann and Jane continued to guide the escapees while shouting at the police to stop firing. Their hands were raised high as they moved down the paddock toward the police.

"Please! Do not shoot! We are women and children!" Jane screamed as hard as her lungs allowed. The cries fell on deaf ears.

"Mongrels! Sons of bitches! Baby killers!" Ann cursed at the police.

From the tree line Senior-Constable Kelly watched anxiously. "Oh my God, what are they thinking?" Kelly gasped before screaming at the men in his proximity to hold their fire. Within a moment the group reached the train station where they took cover with the journalists.

***

"Please! Do not shoot! We are women and children!" Jane screamed as
hard as her lungs allowed.

By this time Hare had finally arrived in Benalla. Utilising the telegraph at the station, he sent word to Violet Town, Wangaratta and Beechworth to organise all the police they could muster and converge on Glenrowan.

Following this he called on Doctor John Nicholson, assisted by a man named Lewis. Lewis knocked on the door to rouse the doctor, who responded quickly, jumping out of bed and throwing clothes on.

"My apologies, doctor, but I will be needing your services," said Hare weakly.

Nicholson looked at Hare's arm, which dangled at his side, dribbling blood on the ground like a leaky faucet. Nicholson grabbed his bag and accompanied the two men to the Benalla telegraph office.

At the telegraph office, Hare dictated a message for Captain Standish to Mr. Saxe, the manager, before laying down on a mattress that had been put there for the telegraph operators to nap on during the night. Doctor Nicholson finally had an opportunity to examine the wound, removing Carrington's well-intentioned but ultimately useless bandaging. The misplaced cloth was drenched with blood and Nicholson immediately knew how dangerous the wound was. Grabbing an old book, he tied it to the wrist as a splint and bandaged the injured limb correctly.

"You got quite a nasty injury there, inspector. The bullet looks to have severed an artery. That, combined with your bad heart, could have ended a lot worse. You're very lucky."

Hare barely responded before passing out.

***

Ann and Jane frantically searched for Johnny, asking the journalists for his whereabouts. Constable Kirkham, who had returned to the platform to fetch ammunition directed them to McDonnell's Tavern. The two rushed across the train line towards the tavern. Ann and Jane burst inside and spotted Johnny under a blanket on the billiards table, drenched in blood. Ann hurried to Johnny's side, pushing the McDonnells and Jack McHugh aside.

"He hasn't woken since I got here. Someone's gone for a doctor," McHugh said quietly.

"Johnny? Sweetheart, can ye hear me? It's Ma. I'm right here," Ann said holding the boy's hand. It was cold and his pulse was weak. Ann began to bawl bitterly. Behind her Jane was wrapped in the comforting embrace of Hanorah McDonnell. The other boys had remained with the other children at the station

Dick Hart stepped forward but kept his distance, "Mrs. Jones, do you know what's happened to the outlaws?"

"Damn the bloody lot of them!" Ann exploded. "They brought this upon us, they can burn in Hell!"

Dick wisely backed away. From the corner of the room Tom Lloyd looked on with tears in his eyes. He could scarcely fathom how incredibly, spectacularly everything had fallen apart.

***

Several miles away in Wangaratta, Sergeant Arthur Loftus Maule Steele stood by the train tracks, sniffing the air like a bloodhound. Steele was a stout man of aristocratic blood with a large moustache and an imperious face. Born in France and raised in Ireland, he was a soldier without a war. He had been educated in a military academy and just missed the Crimean war before coming to Australia; a vexation that dogged him daily. He joined the police force expecting some kind of glory and status but spent his first years doing paperwork. He was intimately acquainted with the Kellys and Harts, having arrested or pursued members of both families on numerous occasions over a myriad of offences, most of them equine related. Steele had sworn to avenge the murder of his friend Sergeant Kennedy and had prayed nightly for God to deliver Ned Kelly to him so that his vengeance could be exacted.

Steele had received his instructions from Superintendent Hare and the distant cracks of gunfire from the direction of Glenrowan made him restless. He jerked his ear towards the sound of approaching hooves. Suddenly a horse came into view with Constable Bracken mounted atop.

"Who goes there?" Steele hollered.

"Constable Bracken. The Kellys are in Mrs. Jones' inn, and they've torn up the railway line. Superintendent Hare is badly wounded, we need you there right away."

Steele immediately sprang into action to gather the rest of his men with all the swiftness of Hermes.

***

As he lay against the tangled branches of the fallen gum, slowly regaining consciousness, Ned heard the gunfire echoing into the night. He also heard voices and footfalls approaching his position and grabbed his helmet, crawling away into the bush. He left his carbine and cap behind and sought cover. From the protection of the trees and scrub, Ned observed shadowy figures moving up toward him. Senior-Constable Kelly darted from tree to tree, with Constable Arthur close behind him. They were scouting the perimeter of the inn for better vantage points.

Reaching the clearing, Constable Arthur knelt by the fallen tree. He grabbed the revolving carbine and the skull cap.

"Look here, sir!" Arthur cried out.

Kelly rushed over, taking the cap. It was damp with blood and frost. He looked around nervously.

"Some of them have escaped!" Kelly gasped. Arthur passed him the carbine.

"Must have been recent, this is sticky with blood."

"Hold this position and make sure nobody else comes through here."

Taking the items, Kelly hurried back to the police line leaving Constable Arthur to find a comfortable spot to wait.

Breathing a sigh of relief, Ned left the scene as quietly as possible and miraculously avoided detection. He wore his helmet and hobbled painfully, deeper into the bush to take the long way back around, each step excruciating on his injured foot. Blood squelched as he walked. Barely able to see, he bumped into a tree and lost his equilibrium, falling backwards. With a heavy thud Ned landed hard on his back, the crushing weight of the armour knocking the wind out of him.

He lay in the bush wheezing. Sapped of energy and strength, he could not move. He used what little effort he could muster to take the helmet off and breathed as deeply as his lungs could manage. Ned tried to roll over, but the weight of his armour prevented it. He strained until his body gave up and he passed out once again.

***

Exhausted, Dan Kelly sat by the window trying to get some light from outside. He reached into the pocket of his jacket and withdrew his pocketknife and the strychnine powder he had been carrying since the previous afternoon.

"Stevey!" he called out. Hart crossed the room to join him.

"Here, let's have a heart-starter to keep us going until Ned gets back," said Dan. The pair proceeded to indulge in the jockey's trick of taking a tiny amount of poison powder on the blade of the knife and ingesting it. The effect was one of an instant energy boost and the two bushrangers suddenly seemed to perk up as their hearts raced.

In the bedroom with the Reardons, Martin Cherry lay on the floor and propped himself up on one elbow when a bullet passed through the building and struck him in the belly. The old man curled up in agony, groaning pathetically as the projectile forced its way into his stomach. Larkins, the platelayer, crawled toward him.

"What's happened, Mr. Cherry?"

"I've copped a bullet. I'm done for," Cherry replied.

Larkins immediately called out for assistance and Cherry was carried into the skillion with the aid of Dave Mortimer. Cherry was laid on the ground and covered with a mattress as he began to tremble with shock and vomit blood.

Meanwhile, Dan and Steve resumed shooting, joined by Joe who crawled on his elbows and knees through the glass and splinters to take pot-shots from the window. Between shots he would put his head in the window and taunt the police.

"Come on you bastards; you're the worst shots I've ever encountered in my life!"

"Pull your head in, Joe," Dan hissed. Joe grew tired of the pointless shooting and attempted to crawl back to the bar, bullets pinging off his back plate.

"What happened to Ned? He's been gone for ages." said Dan.

"Maybe he didn't make it? Or maybe he escaped and left us?" Steve replied. Dan wanted to deny the possibility of abandonment, but he couldn't completely discount it.

Joe plunged his hand into the pocket of his coat in search of his opium powder and managed to find a laudanum bottle he had forgotten about. He pulled the cork and gulped the remaining dregs down. He cursed in disappointment.

"Ned Kelly," said Joe, "is many things, Steve, a fool, a hothead, a madman. One thing he is not is disloyal. If he's alive, he'll be back. Then he can die with the rest of us trapped here like rats. When has he ever let us down? Good old reliable Ned," Joe said looking across at Dan with watery eyes.

***

There was incredible clamour at the Benalla telegraph office when Superintendent Sadleir arrived. Sadleir burst inside and approached the telegraph booth where he saw Hare talking to Saxe, then turn to face the new arrivals. Hare looked like he was two breaths away from death.

"Dear God - what happened, Hare?" Sadleir asked.

"Ned Kelly, the blackguard, shot me," Hare responded softly.

"I've been told the outlaws are in Glenrowan."

"At Glenrowan, yes," said Hare, "I'll be going back just as soon as I hear from Captain Standish."

"Don't be foolish. Who did you leave in charge?" asked Sadleir.

"Oh, I think O'Connor or Kelly... I can't remember. Until I get back there, they can manage," Hare mumbled. "You must fetch as many men as you can and head to Mrs. Jones' inn."

Hare's eyes rolled back in his head, and he passed out, flopping onto the mattress. Sadleir immediately turned to Doctor Nicholson.

"What's the situation?"

"He's lost a lot of blood. Looks like an artery is severed. We might have to amputate but I can stabilise him for now," Nicholson said with a sombre expression. Sadleir winced.

"Do your best for now. I will need you to accompany me to Glenrowan."

***

Senior-Constable Kelly moved through the police lines monitoring the progress and morale of the men. On his head, in place of the floppy felt hat he had been wearing he was now sporting the skull cap. Constable Gascoigne stopped him.

"Sir, why are you wearing that?"

"I lost my hat. It must have blown away."

Gascoigne produced Kelly's hat and handed it over.

"One of the blacks found this. It must be yours," said Gascoigne.

"Yes, it is. Thank you," said Kelly, visibly disappointed to have to remove the outlaw's cap. The quilting had kept his head quite warm.

In the bush on the far side of the inn, Ned Kelly stirred awake. He became aware of voices and the sound of horses pushing through the scrub. He looked up and saw several mounted police riding past - Sergeant Steele and his party. He tried to sink low behind a bush.

As the men rode past, they thought they heard the clanking of metal but dismissed it as a stirrup iron. They were completely oblivious to the fact that Ned was laying down behind a bush so close that, if he wanted, he could have reached out and touched them.

Sergeant Steele could almost smell the burnt gunpowder in the air and began to canter towards the action.

Senior-Constable Kelly resumed moving among the men on the battlefield, making his way around the northern side of the inn. He became aware of the thumping of hooves moving down from the direction of Wangaratta. Within a moment, Sergeant Steele came into view with his troopers Dixon, Cawsey, Healey, Moore, Mountiford, and Johnston as well as Constable Bracken.

Steele bounded out of his saddle and handed the reins to Cawsey to hobble away from the line of fire. Senior-Constable Kelly approached Steele, hand extended, but Steele had his gaze fixed on the inn. He unslung his shotgun and looked for a good position.

"Wangaratta police. Who's in charge here?" Steele snapped.

"I suppose it's me and Sub-Inspector O'Connor at the moment - he's in front of the hotel in the ditch. The outlaws are inside the house, but there's civilians too," said Kelly.

"My men will see that nobody can get out. I have foot constables Dwyer and Walsh coming down by train as we speak," Steele stated brusquely. He took position close to the fence line and aimed at the inn. The smell of gun smoke seemed to arouse a kind of bloodlust in Steele, like a lion catching the scent of fresh blood. He began to fire at the inn without a target, prompting strange looks from the men around him.

In the drainage ditch, O'Connor and his men took a lull in the firing as an opportunity to reload and relax. O'Connor stuffed his pipe with tobacco and lit up. Barney and Jacky did the same. The cold air was starting to seep into their bones, and they shivered. O'Connor did not say a word, merely smoked and contemplated.

***

Barely ten minutes after the arrival of the troopers from Wangaratta, Superintendent Sadleir stepped onto the platform at Glenrowan, accompanied by Sergeant Whelan, Senior-Constable Smyth, trackers Moses and Spider, and Constables Graham, Ryan, Wallace, Wilson, Stillard, Reilly, Milne, Hewitt and Kelly – the last of which had the charming nickname of "The Fat Bastard". Also amidst the number were Doctor Nicholson and Jesse Dowsett, a railway guard of diminutive stature with a thick beard and long greatcoat. Senior-Constable Kelly rushed across the platform to greet them, slightly frazzled but composed.

"Where is Mr. O'Connor?" Sadleir asked Kelly.
"He's down here in a hole," Kelly replied.
"Take me down and show me where he is,"
"Come this way; keep the men in single file as we go," said Kelly.

Kelly led Sadleir and the new arrivals to the battlefield. In the drainage ditch, Sadleir spotted O'Connor on his belly clutching his rifle.
"O'Connor, come here," Sadleir ordered brusquely.
"No, you come here," O'Connor snapped in reply. Sadleir was unimpressed, but not surprised. He turned to Senior-Constable Kelly and Sergeant Whelan.
"You go and replace the men wherever you think they are required."
Kelly and Whelan proceeded to direct the police to spread out around the inn. Sadleir made his way to the drainage ditch.

"The bushrangers are trapped in the hotel. Kelly seems to think one or more may have gotten out already," O'Connor said, barely acknowledging Sadleir.
"How did you let that happen?"

"Where is Mr. O'Connor?" Sadleir asked Kelly.

"We couldn't surround the hotel with our numbers. Besides, there's a concern the bullets from the Martinis would go straight through the building and we'd end up shooting ourselves. I have instructed the men to shoot high to avoid hitting any civilians."

"How many civilians are inside?"

"Thirty or forty we've been told. I suspect many of them are sympathisers and probably armed. It's impossible to know at this stage. There have been casualties."

As the men spoke several bullets came from the inn and hit the ground at their feet, spraying them with gravel.

"Alright, O'Connor. Discretion is the better part of valour, I suppose. Let's keep them at bay until daylight."

Margaret Reardon kept her children low to the floor in the bedroom opposite the armoury. Through the open door she saw Dan Kelly pacing up and down the passage holding a carbine and looking bewildered, his floppy fringe hanging over his left eye and lank with sweat. The Reardon matriarch was by now frantically waiting for a cease in the firing to allow her family to escape. She clutched baby Bridget snug in her swaddling cloth and moved into the corridor and grabbed Dan's hand.

"We're leaving," she stated, Dan looked at her with confusion.

"What do you mean?"

"I'm taking my family and leaving."

Dan nodded and stuck his head out of the back door. There was more firing at the back now. He turned to Mrs. Reardon, planting a hand on her shoulder.

"Here is what you must do: when you go outside, wave your handkerchief and make the children all scream. Say that you're women and children, and when you get clear you tell Superintendent Hare to stop the firing until daybreak, understand? Tell him once we've let the prisoners out, he can fight us until judgement day if he likes."

Margaret beckoned her children, "Now, did you hear what Mr. Kelly said? When we go outside you must scream as loudly as you can so that the policemen know not to fire. Can you do that my darlings?"

The children nodded in the gloom. When Margaret turned once more to Dan, she saw the gleam of moonlight on the tears that streaked down his cheeks.

"I'm sorry," he said.

"I know, dear. Now make it right."

Dan held open the door and screamed into the night as he had done earlier, "Hold fire! Women and children!"

The Reardons began to pour out. Nineteen-year-old Michael took his three-year-old brother William by the hand, the sisters all linked arms. The children screamed as they ran through the breezeway. Mrs. Reardon echoed Dan's words.

Sergeant Steele saw the commotion and took aim with his shotgun.

"Come no further or I'll shoot you!" Steele bellowed.

When the children ignored him, he discharged his gun. Shot flew through the night spraying the bark wall of the kitchen, a fragment piercing Bridget's swaddling cloth. The baby gave a terrifying scream of pain such as Margaret Reardon had never heard before. The woman panicked and turned on her heel, adrenaline overtaking logic.

"You've shot my child! You've shot my child!" she wailed. The children scattered. Michael turned back with William and retreated to the breezeway rather than stand in the open to be gunned down by the police.

"Stay where you are!" Steele bellowed again. When his order was ignored, he fired at the teenager, the shot striking him in the back and piercing through his shoulder blade. Just as Margaret turned to see what had happened, Michael fell like a sack of potatoes. James Reardon dragged him inside. Margaret, mad with fear, ran shrieking hysterically out past the inn's sign towards the train station.

Behind the fence, Constable Arthur shouted at Steele, "You fire again, and I'll be damned if I don't put a bullet in you myself!"

Steele merely shrugged the constable away and continued reloading.

"I don't care. I shot Mrs. Jones in the tits!" he chuckled.

"Proud of that feather in your cap, are you?" Constable Phillips shouted mockingly in reply from further down the line.

As Margaret ran through the night, Bridget's screaming fell silent. A coldness that far surpassed the winter chill filled every part of the terrified mother. A bullet passed through her shawl, cutting across her shoulder but miraculously not cutting her flesh.

"Come towards me," came a sudden voice from the direction of the tents.

She peered through the gloom and smoke, and saw the small, stout figure of Jesse Dowsett, the railway guard. He extended his arms as if going in for a hug. Margaret approached with trepidation. She shook violently from shock and terror; her hair had come loose and lay across her back down to her posterior. Dowsett guided her to safety with firm, yet gentle hands.

"They... shot... my baby," Margaret said, trying to catch her breath between sobbing and shivering as shock was setting in. Dowsett guided the woman into the light at the station. Margaret pushed aside the bloodied folds of the swaddling cloth slowly, expecting to see the infant with its brain blown out, but as she opened the cloth up, she could see her bloodied baby shaking violently, crying without sound but still alive. The shot had merely clipped across her forehead. Margaret almost collapsed at the sight, but Dowsett caught her. He held her up and she sobbed into his shoulder.

Distraught, James Reardon carried Michael inside with William and his daughter Ellen who had doubled back in confusion. He laid Michael down carefully.

"They've shot my boy! Oh Christ, help me!"

Several others crowded around to tend to the wounded boy.

Infuriated, Dan screamed wordlessly and punched the wall. The framed portrait of Queen Victoria fell from its mount.

"Oh dear. You've gone and toppled the Queen, Danny." Joe chuckled.

"You think this is a big joke, Joe?"

"Aye, Danny. We're clowns in a circus. Look, Steve can be the dancing monkey!"

"Shut up, you drunken idiot!" Dan snapped, hurling a fallen candlestick at Joe. It bounced off the breastplate and landed by the bar. Steve sat silent and morose by the parlour fireplace.

"Daniel Kelly, you're a hell of a man," Joe slurred, raising his glass in a mocking toast. He was no longer in complete control of himself.

***

The minutes felt interminable with the remaining prisoners dotted across the floor of the inn. Joe Byrne, using the bar and the walls to keep himself upright, stuck his head around the doorways of the bedrooms to see how people were getting on. He saw Jack Delaney against the iron-framed bed cradling his greyhound. The poor animal had been shot by police fire and was dying. Joe had no particular affection for dogs but found it affecting that the police had literally shot a dog down.

"Stay low everyone. We'll get you out of here as soon as we can," he said.

Joe hopped into the bar room. A bullet nipped at his coat sleeve. The bar room was littered with people, spent cartridges and bullet casings, broken glass and any number of liquids of diverse origin.

"Everyone, stay where you are; you're a great deal better off than we are," said Joe.

Grabbing a miraculously unscathed bottle of whiskey and a half-emptied glass he licked his lips. Tipping the liquid in the bottom of the glass out, he refilled it with the whiskey. Resting against the bar to take the weight off his useless right foot, Joe held his glass inches from his nose and contemplated. He felt the prayer book in his pocket and a memory flashed to the fore of his mother making a fuss over him of a Sunday, urging him to make a good impression on the priest. He recalled the uncomfortable wooden pews and the lingering smell of incense. He always squirmed when the priest's eyes lingered on him a little too long. His mind settled on the mad dash through the bush from Sunday school when he couldn't bear it anymore, and the thrashing his mother administered for making her look bad to the rest of the church. He chuckled to himself. Not much has changed.

He thought about Maggie and the ring he kept on a chain around his neck - another broken promise. He felt a lump rise in his throat. He looked around at Dan and Steve slumped against the walls, despondent and exhausted, Ned now long gone. The armour carried with it a much greater weight now. He pulled out the prayer book and a pencil. He flipped to the last available scrap of paper and began to write laboriously and clumsily in the darkness with what focus he could muster:

Neddie is gone. Abandoned us. The traps have us pinned in the pub. My leg is broke and so are our spirits. At least I can die with the taste of wisky on my lips. Thus ended the rein of Joey Byrne and the Kelly gang.

His fingers gripped the glass firmly and he turned to Dan.

"What do you reckon Danny boy? Was it a grand old lark?"

"What are you on about?"

"I think we deserve a toast to showing those sow-faced blowhards out there what happens when you take on the Kelly Gang."

"Joe, stop please," Dan pleaded.

Joe felt an odd calm come over him. A smirk tickled the corner of his mouth.

"Here's to many more long and happy days in the bush, boys," Joe declared as he raised his glass high. He threw the whole drink down in one hit and slammed the glass down on the counter. He savoured the burn of the booze and the smoky hint of flavour that lingered. He turned to face the front wall, resting his back against the bar. Another volley of bullets spat at the inn, punching through the walls. Joe felt an intense pain, like he'd been stabbed with a red-hot poker in the groin. The pain pushed up into his body and his leg went numb. It was then he became aware of a feeling of damp in his trousers - had he wet himself? He heard liquid dripping onto the floor as he looked down. Blood gushed from under his breastplate, pulsing. He clamped his hand over the wound but could not put enough pressure on it.

He looked forlornly at Dan as he felt dizzy. Dan returned an expression of confusion, whereupon Joe felt his head go cold, his sight ceased, and he fell, senseless, managing to land on William Sandercook who shouted in pain at the weight. Dave Mortimer was mere inches away and could hear the gushing of blood slow down to a complete stop.

"Here's to many more long and happy days in the bush, boys," Joe
declared as he raised his glass high.

Behind the bar, Ann Jones' clock chimed incessantly due to it being struck by bullets in the burst of fire.

Within two minutes Joe Byrne - the Alan-A-Dale to Ned Kelly's Robin Hood; bank robber, murderer, wayward son - was dead.

Dan cried out and rushed to Joe's side, but nothing could be done. In a fit of confusion Dan attempted to move the body to the back door but failed, the immense weight of the body and the armour proving just too much to shift on his own. He released the body and sobbed. At that moment, Dan despised Ned for dragging them all into such a mess and forcing them to stay while he disappeared into the night. He grabbed Joe's Tranter from the counter and stormed to the window, discharging all of the shots until it clicked impotently. He fell back against the wall and slid to the floor sobbing, cursing the police and his brother.

ACT THREE

I I

A Deep Breath

Wind rustled the canopy above Ned as he slowly regained consciousness. He opened his eyes, but everything was a blur, like seeing the world through a puddle. The sound of gunfire continued to crackle in the distance, though more sporadic than before. Suddenly there was a voice right next to his ear.

"Ned; get up, mate."

Ned snapped his head around to see a figure standing over him with a hand extended. In the moonlight, he recognised the chestnut hair and golden beard of Joe Byrne though his face was shrouded in shadow, save for his piercing ice-blue eyes that seemed to be glowing.

"Joe?"

"The boys - get them out of there."

Ned reached up to grab Joe's hand but couldn't seem to grasp it, merely snatching at thin air.

"Help me up, Joe, damn it. Help me..." Ned slurred as he heaved himself into a sitting position. He looked around but Joe had vanished. There

388

seemed to be a flutter of tar-black feathered wings in the tree overhead. He sat in confusion for a moment. At first, he tried to dismiss it as a dream, but it didn't feel like a dream, and he was awake. What was that apparition? In his gut he knew Joe must be dead.

He used his good arm to support himself against the tree and slowly stood. He stumbled and snatched up his helmet with considerable difficulty. In the distance, he could almost see the flashes of gunfire through the trees.

Joe's message still rang in ears, "Get them out of there."

He began to move toward the inn the way he had come, moving as fast as his trembling legs would take him and sticking to the bush so that he wouldn't be spotted.

****

Constables Walsh, Kirkham and Dwyer walked to and from the station and relayed information from Sadleir to the police on the battlefield. Morale amongst the troops seemed to be high and many of them chatted whenever they weren't taking pot-shots at the slightest movement they perceived inside the building. Constables shared tobacco and took mouthfuls of brandy from a bottle being shared around by Dwyer in order to fight the winter chill. It seemed as if it was all a fun excursion to them, none paused to acknowledge the implications of the screams from inside the inn.

Tom and the other sympathisers stood near the train tracks and watched the flashes of gunfire in the darkness.

"Enough of this," Tom said as he rushed inside to collect his rifle. "Wild, Dick, follow me. We're going to try and get around the back to get the boys out."

The trio scurried across the train tracks, giving the battlefield a wide berth, and headed for the bush on the far side of the inn.

Meanwhile, Ned stumbled around half-conscious for what seemed to him to be an eternity. His foot snagged on a tree root, and he tripped. His helmet flung off as he hit the ground. Crawling along on all fours he heaved the contents of his stomach onto the ground. The smell of brandy and bile seared his nostrils. He rolled over and lay on his back looking up into the canopy. He lay stricken and drifting in and out of consciousness. He felt as if the whole world had stopped being real and he was in some horrible nightmare.

***

Dan stood at the back door calling for his brother, but there was no response. Defeated, he returned to the dining room and drew a chair so that he could sit next to the window, which had been completely shattered. Peering out into the murky blue of the pre-dawn he observed dozens of troopers lying in wait around the hotel. He wondered how many were out there. To him it felt like a hundred.

Directly opposite the veranda, he could see O'Connor and his trackers poking their heads out from the drainage ditch. Seeing an opportunity to pay them back for Joe's demise, Dan took careful aim with his rifle and fired. The bullet zipped across the reserve and sliced Jimmy across the forehead. Jimmy dropped down into the ditch, stunned and in pain. Dabbing blood from his brow, he felt anger boil up within him and he popped up again and fired five shots from his revolver rapidly.

"Take that, Ned Kelly!" he shouted as he blazed away. The other trackers laughed at the outburst.

"Bama! Better get down before them Kellys shoot you again!" said Barney, laughing hard.

Sadleir waited nearby beside a thick blue gum and puffed on his pipe. His leather gloves creaked as his tightened his fingers around the bowl, his thumb covering the opening while he sucked the smoke in. A strong breeze kicked up that made the leaves shake and shifted much of the smoke lingering over the battlefield. He approached Senior-Constable Kelly.

"I'm going to check in on the men. Keep an eye on things."

Sadleir made his way through the police lines, checking in on each trooper as he went. He reached Gascoigne who seemed agitated.

"What's the matter constable?"

"I saw Ned Kelly following a horse out into the bush earlier. I fired at him, and it took no effect," Gascoigne answered.

"What do you mean?"

"My shot didn't seem to affect him at all, he just kept walking. He must be wearing some form of protection."

Sadleir remembered the report from the Diseased Stock Agent that Hare had dismissed out of hand. Perhaps it wasn't poppycock after all, he thought.

With the police running low on ammunition and taking a moment to have bread and brandy, an uneasy calm began to settle over Glenrowan for the first time in hours. Police stamped their feet to avoid being frosted over like the grass. Smoke mingled with the rising mist creating an eerie atmosphere as the moon sank and the sun began to climb.

***

Far behind the police lines, Tom, Dick and Wild had managed to sneak into the bush without being noticed. Their eyes were accustomed to the gloom after having strained to see what was happening in the dead of night. They darted through the bush, crouching to avoid being spotted. The forest was dense in this part and foggy, like wandering through a dream. Suddenly, Tom saw Ned's helmet lying on the ground. He ran over quickly to find Ned slumped against a tree. The normally proud and sturdy bushranger was now a shattered, bloody mess; his face ashen and waxy, his hands drenched in blood. He stared blankly into nothingness.

"Ned? Are you alright? Where are the others?" Tom whispered, shaking his cousin by the shoulder with no response, "Ned, can you hear me?"

Ned took a moment to regain his senses, his eyes were bleary and unfocused. In his daze he recognised the voice.

"Tom..."

"Where are the other boys?" Tom gently moved Ned's face to allow him to keep eye contact.

"The boys... they didn't follow me," Ned mumbled.

"Come on, we have to get you out of here, the place is swarming with traps," Tom insisted as he gestured for Wild and Dick to help heave Ned to his feet.

"No! I'm not leaving. Gotta go back. Gotta get them out."

Ned removed his cartridge bag and pistol belt, tossing them at Tom's feet. "Load my pistols, Tom. I can't do it. My hands are scrammy."

"You're in no state to be going back. We'll get you to safety," said Tom.

"Just load for me, damn you. I need to see this thing out."

The normally proud and sturdy bushranger was now a shattered, bloody
mess...

Tom frowned but proceeded to fulfill his cousin's demand, divvying the pistols and ammunition up with the others to speed up the process.

Ned propped himself up on a tree and tried to catch his breath. His thoughts drifted to his mother, her thin lips and hazel eyes that were fierce yet imbued with weariness from her hard life. He imagined the tears she would shed if she ever found out he'd abandoned his baby brother. Ned resolved not to allow her to think she'd raised a coward.

"I have to go back. I have to get Dan and Steve out of there," Ned muttered.

"How? That inn is completely surrounded. You can't take them all by yourself," said Tom.

"I'll draw their attention away. Give the boys a chance to get out."

"They'll shoot you to bloody pieces!" said Wild pointedly.

"They will try," Ned said as he patted his breastplate. He attempted to stand, painfully swaying like a tree in the wind. Tom tried to steady him. Ned brushed him away.

"Please, Ned. Don't go back there."

"I got them into this mess. And I'll get them out."

"Right, then I'm going with you," Tom snapped.

"No!" Ned's voice cracked, "This is not your fight, Thomas. You just wait here for the boys. I'll see it right."

Tom nodded and fetched the cartridge bag, which he looped over Ned's shoulder.

"Wait," Ned interrupted. He worked his left hand under his breastplate painfully and withdrew the golden fob watch and chain he had taken from Sergeant Kennedy. He grabbed Tom's hand and thrust the watch into his palm.

"What's this?"

"My time's up. I need you to do one more thing for me. Make sure this gets back to the widow Kennedy. I don't need it anymore."

Tom nodded solemnly. Ned grabbed Tom by the back of the neck, pulling him closer and pressing their foreheads together.

"You take care of my family," Ned whispered.

"You know I will, Ned. Always."

"Don't let Maggie push you around."

"I can only promise so much," Tom chuckled.

"Good lad."

"Ned, please, you can't win this one," Tom pleaded.

"I know that. Such is life."

The two men stared into each other's eyes for a moment and understood one another. Tom draped the oilskin over Ned's shoulders and placed the helmet on Ned's head slowly and obsequiously. Ned drew his Pocket Colt, trying hard to grip it in his crippled right hand. He turned towards the sound of gunfire and began to hobble through the bush, disappearing into the mist. Tom wiped tears away from his cheeks as he turned back towards McDonnell's.

"Someone needs to let the girls know what's happened."

"I'll go to Greta," Wild volunteered.

"Be quick and quiet. If the police find out what we've been doing it's the rope for the lot of us," said Tom.

***

At the station, Superintendent Sadleir contemplated how to get the bushrangers out of the inn without police casualties. On the platform were a set of thick hemp ropes that he had brought with him to loop around the chimneys to pull them down. The brick fireplaces, he had reasoned, would be excellent protection from bullets and therefore ideal hiding places. He seemed to imagine that the police could simply tear away the chimneys like lifting a stone from atop an ant nest and send the outlaws scurrying out. However, it had since dawned on him that this was a very risky manoeuvre and speculated that an artillery cannon could blast the building wide open and allow a swarm of lawmen to overwhelm the outlaws. At any rate, any move was impossible to execute safely until daylight.

The special train had already headed back to Melbourne, taking Louisa O'Connor and Cathy Prout-Webb with it. A team of line repairers was en route to Glenrowan but were still a way off. Sadleir was furious that he had finally gotten his chance to lead the effort to catch the Kellys, but what he inherited was such a mess that no matter what he did there would be critics waiting in the wings to pounce. He checked his watch and noted that it was almost half past six in the morning. He hoped that there would be a resolution before passenger trains began running.

****

As Ned wandered towards the battlefield, he paused to catch his breath again. The hundredweight of armour was proving extremely cumbersome. He felt sluggish and could not concentrate. He reeled and slumped against a tree. He felt nauseated and his head ached. He became aware of a presence in front of him that he could almost discern through the eye slit of the helmet. He strained his eyes and seemed to discern the form of a woman hunched over washing something in a rivulet. He knew he was hallucinating as she rose and showed Ned his own green silk sash, stained with blood. Ned closed his eyes and mumbled an approximation of the Lord's Prayer. When he opened his eyes, all he saw was a wall of mist. He ran his hand over his hip and felt the fringes of his sash. He tried to bury the spectre at the back of his mind. He took a deep breath and continued on his way.

12

The Last Stand

At the Kelly selection everything was quiet. The lamp burned in the dining room and Kate slept in her mother's bed. Maggie remained awake with Ettie Hart, and both sat in silence. Grace was asleep in the old hut with the youngest children. Maggie took out her "witch pipe" and prepared it to smoke.

"I don't think the plan worked," Ettie whispered.

"Why would you say that?" Maggie responded abruptly.

"If it had worked, we'd have been told by now. I just have this feeling that it's gone horribly wrong. You've heard the gunfire as well as I have."

Maggie did not answer. She knew Ettie was right but didn't want to think about it. The faint sound of gunshots could still be heard in the distance.

As she puffed on her pipe, Maggie became aware of the sound of hooves approaching the homestead. The women stared at each other, wide eyed. Maggie quietly rose and reached into a bag of flour by the stove and withdrew a small valise. From the valise she took a small revolver and checked to see if it was loaded. Once satisfied, she kept it close.

Suddenly there was a rapping at the door.

"Who's there?" Maggie called out. Ettie held her breath.

"It's Wild," came the voice on the other side. Ettie exhaled as Maggie laid the revolver down and opened the door where she was met by Wild Wright's grim expression. She knew it was bad news.

***

The battlefield was hidden in a sea of fog. There was no report from the inn and the men outside found it increasingly difficult to see. As the first hint of sunlight painted a deep blue hue upon the landscape the sun rose slowly from behind the forest.

Constable Arthur reloaded his rifle then laid it across his lap as he prepared his pipe. Striking a match, his face was briefly lit up with a splash of yellow from the flame, then a wash of orange as the tobacco caught alight and he sucked through the pipe lustily; the woody, oily smell of the tobacco smoke permeated his nostrils.

Presently he sensed movement among the trees. At first, it was the merest glimpse of a strange shape moving between the trunks and he dismissed it as a passing animal. He puffed on his pipe, but his attention was once again drawn to the bush where he could see the figure moving into a clearing. His blood ran cold and the hair on the back of his neck pricked up. His smooth face crinkled as he strained to make out what he was actually looking at through the fog. It moved like no animal he'd ever seen, wobbling unsteadily on two legs, and appeared to have a broad head and neck with great white wings close to its body like a bat. Arthur watched the queer vision obscured by fog and the weak half-light of sunrise. When it staggered into the clearing, he saw it was a man wearing a cloak and a strange mask.

"Get back, you fool, or you'll be shot!" he yelled. The reply was a rumbling metal voice, accompanied by the presentation of a revolver. As fast as he could, Constable Arthur aimed his rifle at a light patch where the figures eyes ought to be and fired.

BLAM!

There was a clang, a spark and a rasping grunt as the bullet struck Ned Kelly in the face. He staggered, nearly losing his balance. Inside the helmet blood gushed out of his freshly broken nose.

With his crippled left arm, he made a prop to help him steady his aim and rested his revolver on his forearm. He fired but the bullet merely kicked up dirt in front of the constable. Arthur pushed the lever on his rifle and ejected the spent cartridge, replacing it with a fresh one. He aimed and fired again, this time the bullet left a huge dent in the breastplate. Again, Ned staggered, the blow like a well-placed punch briefly knocking the wind out of him. He recovered his equilibrium and attempted to fire again.

"Phillips!" Arthur yelled as he doubled back. Constables Phillips, Healey and Mountiford turned towards the new outbreak of gunfire. Phillips reeled off two shots in rapid succession.

"Watch out boys, he's bulletproof!"

With his crippled left arm, he made a prop to help him steady his aim
and rested his revolver on his forearm.

On the train station platform, the journalists had become bored. After sitting up in the dark and freezing cold for hours with nothing more than the sound of gunfire to report they had begun to take turns napping against the wall of the station building. The one member of the press party who had remained alert was Thomas Carrington who rested against the shed with a lamp to provide light while he sketched in the dark. His ears pricked up at the sound of renewed fire and shouting just behind him and he got up to look. He saw gun blasts peppering the fog and gloom, the silhouettes of the plainclothes police running around like black birds closing in on a bread crust. He walked as close as he could and began to discern the pale cloak and cylindrical head as Ned Kelly stumbled towards the station in the half-lit morning, pausing to prop his foot up on a tree stump.

"Christ almighty, what is that?" Carrington exclaimed. His colleagues got up and joined him at the edge of the platform. Carrington's fertile imagination began to throw up scenarios to describe the vision, he considered that it was some avenging phantom in winding sheet with no head, only a long thick neck.

From the bar room, Dan and Steve could hear the firing but were confused that none of it was coming through the walls. The prisoners cautiously raised themselves up to see what was happening.

"No, no, stay down everyone! We'll check it out," Dan said. He gestured for Steve to join him as he moved to the back door.

From the breezeway they saw the police buzzing around the dense bushland behind the inn. Steve strained his eyes and peered into the cobalt dimness.

"I think that's Ned," Steve said.

"Surely not," Dan began but trailed off when he realised Steve was correct. He ran past Steve into the armoury and fetched a pair of rifles and a pouch full of ammunition. Dan loaded the rifles and handed one to Steve.

"Come on!"

"But I can't aim properly." Steve bemoaned.

"That's never stopped you before," Dan said with a smile.

Onwards Ned staggered, bullets raining down on him, blow after blow knocking him about. Bullets nipped and tore at his clothes; his oil-skin was almost tatters. Ned struggled with his pistol, his broken thumb proving useless for cocking the hammer or even holding the weapon steady. When he found the strength in his hand lacking, he took to beating the butt of the revolver on his chest to maintain the intimidation.

Senior-Constable Kelly headed to the action and upon seeing the queer figure shouted, "It's a bunyip, boys!"

At his side Jesse Dowsett fiddled with his railway issue revolver, "Looks like Old Nick himself," he mused.

"Come out, come out lads! We'll whip the beggars!" Ned shouted to Dan and Steve in the inn. However, he was too far away for them to hear. Ned found himself struggling to breathe from exertion and slowed down by a tree and tried to shelter from the firing. He attempted to reload the Pocket Colt, but he had neither the visibility nor dexterity so merely tossed it aside.

He put his right foot on a log and drew Lonigan's Webley. Adrenaline surged through him as he held his broken arm to his chest and attempted to fire at a trooper that was ducking and weaving through the scrub. He had emptied almost all of the chambers when a bullet struck the gun out of his hand and damaged the cylinder making it inoperable.

He fumbled in his satchel and pulled out the largest of his weapons, the Colt Navy. This weapon signified the end of Ned's relatively good fortune; it was a reminder of the days when careful planning had seen the gang earn their place in the pantheon of bushrangers alongside Ben Hall, Frank Gardiner and Matthew Brady. The weight of the pistol made it far more difficult to hold aloft, let alone aim. Ned's wrist was limp, his right arm on fire with the pain from his wounds, so he kept moving, slowly and wobbly on his damaged feet. Still the police swarmed.

From the station, Constable Dwyer ran down with his shotgun at the ready. He cut an odd figure with a thin moustache and a smoking cap and gave out a strange whooping noise as he charged into battle.

On the verge of deliriousness Ned stumbled. He fired without aiming, his shots went nowhere. He stood with his legs apart, bracing himself, and bashed the revolver sloppily into his helmet.

"You can't hurt me. I'm in iron," he slurred and panted.

From the breezeway of the inn, Dan and Steve took shots in Ned's direction, attempting to pick off the police. Daylight was beginning to wash over the battlefield and the darting silhouettes in the fog became tweed-clad huntsmen. Steve put his rifle down and pulled a pistol out of his pocket and began to squeeze the trigger.

"What's he trying to do?" Dan thought aloud as he watched Ned staggering around near the outlet of a stream.

"Is he coming back here or heading to the station?" Steve asked.

"Just keep those traps away from him, give him some room to move," Dan instructed.

The surge in activity had roused Superintendent Sadleir's curiosity and he moved towards the commotion, borrowing a shotgun as he moved around the police line. He saw Dan and Steve firing from the breezeway and aimed the gun in their direction and fired. The shot whizzed past Steve's head, forcing the pair to fall back.

Ned reached the clearing where earlier he had collapsed and left his carbine and cap. He tried to rest briefly while he fiddled with the revolver, which had jammed. He jerked his upper body around and saw movement. Without thought, he fired at it. The movement had been Sergeant Steele as be approached the fracas, and as the aimless bullet struck a branch of the tree the sergeant was sheltering behind debris flicked into his eyes and he hit the ground clutching his face.

"I'll put daylight through you, you damned curs!" Ned screamed, his voice was hoarse and breaking. Bullets were now coming thick and fast, one striking the pistol and taking a chunk out of the walnut grip and the tip of Ned's little finger. He grunted and recoiled and pulled his hand in close to his side as blood dribbled from the mangled fingertip. His body was so exhausted and wracked with searing pain that he barely reacted.

At that moment, there was a commotion from the bush and Music came thundering out from the tree line, flushed out by wayward bullets missing the outlaw and penetrating the scrub. She was still saddled and bridled and galloped through the crossfire, pausing by Ned to rear up as a bullet clipped her flank. Her eyes were wide in terror and pain, and she continued to bolt past the inn.

This distraction, combined with no peripheral vision or the ability to hear clearly meant Ned did not notice the approach of Jesse Dowsett who began taking pot-shots at his head that bounced off ineffectually.

"How do you like that old man?" Dowsett shouted above the din loud enough for Ned to hear.

"How do you like this?" Ned replied, firing at Dowsett. He turned and stumbled over the branches of the fallen tree, struggling to right himself.

It was at this moment that Steele found himself in the perfect position. He could see clearly that the armour did not protect the assailant's legs and promptly aimed at his knees and fired.

Ned's right knee exploded in a burst of blood and shredded corduroy, causing him to buckle. Steele fired again, this time slightly higher. The shot tore through Ned's hip and became buried in his groin behind the iron apron. Ned roared like a wounded bull and sank to his knees.

"I'm done! I'm done!" he cried as he slumped over into the tree.

The police wasted no time in descending upon Ned. They piled on like vultures on a carcass. Ned wheezed under the weight of officers laying across his chest. Senior-Constable Kelly removed the helmet and stood agape.

"My God, it's Ned Kelly!"

This was all Steele needed to trigger his fury. He shouldered the other police away and straddled Ned, grabbing his wrist so violently blood oozed out from the wounds in his hand. Ned reflexively squeezed the trigger of his Colt, its last remaining round going off by Steele's face, blowing his hat off and leaving powder burns on his cheek. Steele immediately grabbed Ned's throat. Dowsett planted a foot on Ned's bicep and yanked the revolver away, twisting the finger that had gotten stuck in the trigger guard.

"Don't break my bloody fingers," Ned complained, his voice reedy and strained. Steele's concentration was broken by Dowsett liberating the revolver.

"Don't touch that, it belongs to me!" Steele roared. He grabbed Ned by the beard and stared into his eyes with malice. Steele drew his own revolver and pressed it hard into Ned's forehead, cocking it.

"Look at me you bastard. I swore I'd be at your death and now I am!"

"I've got my gruel," Ned said softly. Suddenly, Steele's vision was interrupted by the twin barrels of a shotgun pointing inches from his face. Steele lifted his head to look up at Constable Bracken.

"You shoot him, and I will shoot you," Bracken stated calmly. Steele sneered and wisely rolled off Ned's chest.

Bracken stood over Ned, turning his gun towards the police now swarming towards them. "Get back! I will shoot any man that tries to interfere."

"Please," Ned whimpered, struggling to breathe, "let me live as long as I can."

The police attempted to lift Ned as he slipped into unconsciousness but had underestimated the weight of the armour and the limp bushranger came crashing down on top of Steele, pinning him down as he struggled to push the weight off.

Re-emerging from the breezeway in full armour, Dan just barely saw the police around Ned on the ground. Have they killed him? He screamed and began firing recklessly with the Spencer repeating rifle. He ran to the fence and began firing with his pistols.

"Look at me you bastard. I swore I'd be at your death and now I am!"

The police ducked as the shots sang past them perilously close to where Ned lay.

"Get down, they mean to kill us," Senior-Constable Kelly said.

Dan quickly ran out of ammunition and retreated to reload.

As Ned lay prone, the jostling having roused him slightly from his stupor, there came from the crowd a loud whooping sound as Constable Dwyer ran toward him at top speed. He took a swing with his right foot at Ned's crotch but bashed it on the steel apron. Dwyer whimpered and promptly hobbled away.

Steele and Dowsett attempted to carry Ned, but the weight and differences in height proved to be problematic.

With an officer on each limb Ned was carried close to the railway reserve where Doctor Nicholson came running brandishing a small knife. With the blade, he slashed the straps and cords that held the armour on Ned's body so that it could be removed.

Bullets began to zip past the group from the veranda of the inn. Dan stood by the dining room door blasting away, Steve stood in the window doing the same.

"Drop him, you bastards!" Dan screamed. The police directed a fierce volley at the veranda, Dan now much more clearly visible. The shots hit low and a bullet from a Martini Henry struck Dan's left kneecap, causing him to buckle and slam into the door jamb, which cracked under the weight. Steve rushed to Dan's aid and helped move him inside. Dan gasped and groaned from the extreme pain from his pulverised knee.

With the two remaining bushrangers back inside and no more shots coming from the inn, Ned was carried over a fence to the train station where he was laid in the guard van of the police special, which had only just arrived. Sadleir entered the van to get a look at the prize as a gang of platelayers poured out of the train to repair the line. Before Sadleir was not some vicious brute like Dan Morgan or a wild-eyed tramp like Captain Moonlite, but a bush dandy half shot to smithereens, his fine clothes and boots ripped, punctured and shredded, stained with blood. On the floor, Ned was drifting in and out of consciousness and bleeding freely from his wounds.

Without warning, the wall of the van was perforated with bullets. Dan and Steve had resumed shooting from the window of the dining room in a last-ditch attempt to prevent the police from stealing Ned's body.

"Get him into the station," Sadleir said urgently to the men around him. The outlaw was carried across to the station building and laid on the floor.

On the platform, Ned's armour was planted next to the wall of saddles and the journalists gathered around to marvel at it. Joe Melvin poked his finger into the inch-deep dents where the armour had been struck at close range. McWhirter made an effort to pick up the helmet and gaze into the eye slit. He felt a strange kind of energy emanating from the iron.

A mattress was soon procured and as Ned was laid out Sadleir, Steele, Dowsett, Kelly and Bracken all lingered, accompanied by the journalists, as Doctor Nicholson entered the room to get an initial assessment.

"We need these boots and spurs off," Nicholson said. John McWhirter proceeded to unbuckle the spurs and slice the handsome leather boots vertically from the top of the pipe down to the toe with a penknife. When the left boot was removed blood poured from it like a jug. The foot that was inside was deformed. Ned wore no socks, so the wounds were very much on show, blackened clots of blood clung to the skin where it wasn't awash with fresh blood. Ned was stripped of his jacket, from which several unused cartridges fell, and his green sash, smeared with blood, which Nicholson absent-mindedly tossed into his bag. Senior-Constable Kelly promptly searched Ned's garments and extracted threepence in silver and a Kate Lloyd's Geneva watch.

Ned's face was swollen, his eyes puffed up and purple, and the bridge of his nose bore a gash where it had been broken by the percussive force of Constable Arthur's bullet on his face plate. Nicholson rolled Ned's shirtsleeves up and bound his left bicep with a cloth to act as a tourniquet so that the bleeding would stop long enough for the wound to be cleaned and dressed. He inspected Ned's right hand and noted a deep laceration across the back of the hand but most importantly, the mangled thumb. The ball joint had almost entirely been destroyed, giving the thumb a slightly shrivelled appearance. The whole hand was awash with blood. Nicholson sighed at such carnage.

***

The interior of the inn was quiet as Dan and Steve sat in the dining room ruminating. Dave Mortimer felt game to sit up and rested his back against the wall while stretching his legs out.

"Do you think we'll be able to get out now?" he asked.

"Perhaps. It's no matter," Dan responded gloomily. Mortimer noted that the colour had drained from the boy's face and the fire in his eyes was snuffed. All the fight was gone, replaced with sadness and pain. On the other side of the room, Steve attempted to remove his armour with some difficulty.

"We're not keeping you here, you know that," Steve said to Mortimer.

"Aye, but it is daylight. Surely, they'll let us out now," Mortimer replied.

"Do you really want to test that idea?" said Dan. Mortimer went quiet.

***

Tom Lloyd and Dick Hart had observed Ned's capture from afar. Realising the plan had failed, Tom went inside while Dick fetched the horses. Tom shook Jack Lloyd to wake him.

"Huh?" Jack shouted, bleary-eyed.

"Get up, we need to ride to Greta. Come on!"

Outside Dick had three horses waiting. They all mounted and headed towards Greta. As they rode Jack asked what had happened.

"The plan's fallen through, you must stay quiet and pretend you know nothing. You'll be staying at the Kelly place with the little ones."

"Aww, why do I get stuck there?"

"Do as I damn well tell you and don't complain or I'll shoot you myself!" Tom barked.

"I tried to set the packhorses loose but only one would budge," Dick interjected.

"Which one?"

"The one with the keg of blasting powder."

"Good, if they found that we'd be in strife. Just focus on the girls for now."

***

"What do you make of things, Doctor? Will he live through it?" Sadleir asked Nicholson.

"He's in a delicate state. It's too early to say if he'll pull through well enough to hang. I presume that's where your line of questioning was headed, Superintendent," Nicholson said dourly.

"That is not up to me," Sadleir replied.

Ned rested with his left arm in a sling, his head propped up on the rest of the cotton from which the journalists had taken a small amount to patch Hare's wound. His face bore a gentle expression such that everyone around him could hardly imagine him being the monster that they had so feared. Sergeant Steele stood nearby on constant watch lest someone try to lay claim to his prey or take any souvenirs without his approval.

At that moment there was a new arrival: Doctor Hutchison, a Benalla surgeon who had been brought in on Nicholson's request. Immediately, Nicholson ushered everyone out except for Jesse Dowsett.

"Why does he get to stay?" Steele snapped.

"Because he's the only one I can trust not to put a bullet between my patient's eyes, now move along!" Nicholson barked in reply, closing the door.

Gently, the doctors undressed Ned in order to get a detailed view of his injuries. Nicholson noted the nasty bruises all over his torso that gave him a purple, blotchy appearance. Between the two doctors they counted twenty-five bullet wounds, mostly superficial. Nicholson took particular note of the injury in Ned's left elbow. He extracted shot from Ned's thumb but knew that the joint was too damaged to properly heal. Ned's right knee was almost pulped with shot, the second blast from Steele left deep gashes across Ned's thigh and pelvis, the shot having become embedded in his leg muscles and just beneath the skin right by his privates. Beyond the blood and sweat, Ned's skin was remarkably clean for a man who had spent eighteen months living in caves and tents. The wounds were bandaged, and Ned's clothes put back on loosely.

Ned continued to drift in and out of consciousness and was barely aware of what was happening. Rather, whatever lucidity he had was focused on his failure. His lofty dreams of war and conquest dissipated as quickly as the morning mist had. For the first time in his life, he had certainty - he knew that the long arm of the law would not allow him to go free. He would never again know liberty.

13

Last Rites

The inn was calm now as shafts of daylight stabbed through the bullet holes in the walls. There were no more than thirty prisoners still trapped inside. In the dining room, Dan slumped against the wall with his leg elevated on a chair. He was sweating bullets and breathing shallow, barely coping with the pain. He looked to Steve mournfully, who stared back with a weary expression.

"Steve, see if you can find any of Joe's powder."

Steve nodded and headed to the bar. Several tiny paper packets of opium powder remained unopened on the counter. He snatched them up with a glass of whiskey and took them to Dan.

Dan mixed the powder into the drink and gulped it down. Within a few moments he felt everything ease up and the pain in his leg faded to a more bearable ache. He looked to Steve with a half-lidded expression of relaxation.

Steve held Dan's hand. He could see that Dan's knee was deformed from the shot. Even if by some miracle they could get out, that leg would have to come off. Steve tried to distract himself.

"What are we going to do, Danny?"

"The first thing we need to do is get everyone out of here," Dan replied weakly.

***

With Ned in a rare moment of lucidity, Sadleir took the opportunity to question him. He crouched low next to the mattress and Ned turned gradually to face him.

"It was as good as Waterloo, wasn't it?" Ned mumbled.

"What is his condition, Doctor? Is there a chance I can question him?" Sadleir asked, "Ned, can you hear me?"

"Brandy," Ned whispered. Sadleir turned to Constable Dwyer who hovered outside the door.

"Fetch some brandy, Dwyer."

Dwyer nodded and went in search, returning a moment later with a bottle. Dwyer poured the liquid into Ned's mouth, some dribbled into his beard. With his limited strength, Ned lifted his beard to suck the brandy out. The drink seemed to relieve him slightly, but it was not enough.

"Can I have some bread please? I'm so hungry."

"Of course," Sadleir said.

"Well, this is more kindness than I thought to ever get from you," said Ned, his voice hoarse.

'You'll have all the care and attention we can give, but the fate of your companions is now certainly sealed unless you send them word to surrender. Would you do that?" Sadleir asked.

Ned grunted, "They won't listen to me. The heart's gone out of them. They're only boys."

"The first thing we need to do is get everyone out of here," Dan replied
weakly.

He turned away and was quiet a moment. He then turned back to Sadleir.

"When I saw my best friend dead, I knew it was over. I just wanted to see it through. I could have got away."

"Why did come you back? Why didn't you get away when you could have?" Sadleir asked.

Ned considered his response.

"A man would have to be a nice sort of dingo to walk out on his mates."

***

Outside, the police were becoming agitated. The repair of the train line had seen an influx of fresh arrivals from the nearby districts; rubber-neckers, gawkers and lollygaggers keen to watch the show, as well as many Kelly sympathisers who had got wind of the unfolding siege. Beyond the larrikin motifs of the chinstrap under the nose, the bright sash around the waist and low crowned felt hats, what set these arrivals apart was the grim determination with which they conducted themselves and the firearms many carried openly upon their person. Many of the faces were easily recognised by the police as prominent troublemakers and miscreants.

Among their number, gathered at McDonnell's, the police spotted Henry Perkins with his hollow cheeks, small, piercing eyes and large, hooked nose; Joe Ryan with his bright blue eyes, gentle blonde waves and prominent double-lip; Kate Lloyd with her smooth, handsome features and jet-black curls coiffured beneath an ostentatious Gainsborough hat, trimmed with green ribbon and ostrich feathers. The police anticipated a fight to break out from within the crowds.

Further consternation was aroused with the arrival of a cart bearing

Tom Lloyd, Maggie Skillion and her sisters. Not far behind, Wild Wright and Dick Hart rode in, all dressed in their finest clothes, though the men had taken the precaution of wearing gaiters over their trouser legs to hide the mud from their trek through the bush in the early morning. Maggie held her chin up imperiously from her perch on the buggy next to Tom Lloyd. Her black Gainsborough hat with white plumes, sleek black dress and bright red underskirt caught the eye of everyone in attendance. Many wondered why she was so dressed-up, but none were keen to ask.

Maggie, Kate, Grace and Wild Wright were let in to see Ned. The room was quiet as a tomb as the sisters walked in. Ned did not respond to the entrance as so many people had come and gone already that he felt he would rather conserve his energy than greet each one.

Wild was the first to make a move and stooped to kiss Ned's forehead.

"Ye showed 'em a good fight, old boy," Wild said.

As Maggie came closer, she covered her mouth with her hand and her eyes burned with tears, but she remained silent. Kate, however, could not suppress her sobs and cried openly, sinking to her knees beside the mattress. Grace lingered by the door, afraid to move closer.

"Is he dead?" Grace blurted.

"Ah, it'll take more than some lead to kill me," Ned groaned unexpectedly. Grace shot Maggie a worried expression. Through tears Maggie gestured for Grace to come close to her brother.

"Oh Neddy, it's all gone wrong," sobbed Kate. She held his bandaged left hand against her cheek, the cloth soaking up her tears.

"What's done is done," Ned replied.

"We've been told the boys are inside the inn," said Maggie.

"Aye," There was no emotion in Ned's delivery. Kate wept uncontrollably.

As the train services had begun running along the line again, word had passed around quickly between stations that there was something dramatic afoot in Glenrowan. Among those hearing the news was the Very Reverend Dean Gibney, vicar-general of Western Australia. Gibney was a tall, traditionally handsome man of the cloth, with silver hair and a warm Irish brogue. He had come to Victoria from Perth on a tour of the wealthier parishes in the colony with a view towards obtaining funds for the Subiaco Boys' Orphanage. The orphanage had been struck by lightning and badly damaged, leaving one boy dead and others injured. Gibney had left Kilmore that morning to visit Albury but upon learning that there were casualties at Glenrowan he quickly altered his plans.

The Lord's work was never done.

***

Just before nine, a party of police sallied forth from Beechworth under the leadership of Senior-Constable Mullane. Among their number were the police who had cowered in Aaron Sherritt's bedroom and whose hesitation to act had unintentionally caused Ned's plan to fall apart. Constable Armstrong in particular was determined to do all he could to seek justice and retribution and clear his name of the yellow stain of cowardice.

Accompanying them, and well-armed, was Jack Sherritt, who had sought out the police after learning of his brother's murder and demanded to join the hunt for Joe Byrne. Whereas his motivation in informing the police of any news of the gang he found had originally been money, he now had a personal reason to pursue them actively. Though he felt much remorse for how he had treated Aaron prior to his death, Jack also knew that if the outlaws had suspected Aaron enough to gun him down it was only a matter of time before they came for the other informants. This was a matter of self-preservation as much as revenge.

Accompanying the police on the train were Cheshire and Osborne, the telegraph men from Beechworth. Cheshire had formulated a plan to create instant telegraphy to Melbourne from Glenrowan using a miniature telegraph machine, thus compensating for the lack of a telegraph station in the town.

Once on the platform in Glenrowan, Cheshire gave the equipment to Osborne and instructed him to climb a large telegraph pole to connect the machine to the line. As Osborne climbed, he felt bullets zip past him from the direction of the inn, though it wasn't clear if it was from the outlaws or police. He reached the ground with a broad grin, shaking like a leaf. Cheshire immediately began sending messages to Melbourne for the Chief Commissioner, updating him on events in real time from the battlefront.

***

The noon train pulled into the station with the typical hiss of steam, and as the carriage doors were swung open the occupants scurried out like tiny spiders hatching from a nest. In the sea of gawkers, Gibney stood tall, his black clothes rendered his appearance very sober in amongst the dirty browns and greys of the farmers' clothes.

Gibney followed the crowd and soon reached where Ned was being kept. He forced his way through with timid apologies, holding a Gladstone bag in one hand and his rosary and bible aloft in the other to calm any tempers that flared up by his movements. At the doorway, he got Doctor Nicholson's attention with a wave and a flourish of his hand.

"Please, I'm the vicar-general of Western Australia, I have been told there's a dying man in here in need of spiritual aid," Gibney pleaded. After a moment he was permitted to enter. It was an effort to stop the onlookers from forcing their way inside as Gibney entered.

As Gibney approached Ned, the captive outlaw opened his black, swollen eyes and gazed at him with relief.

"My son, I am told you're in a very bad way. Would you permit me to help you?" Gibney said, his accent refined and smooth.

"Of course, father."

"Do you confess your sins?"

"I have killed and robbed, I confess," Ned replied flippantly. Gibney went quiet for a moment.

"Say 'Jesus have mercy on me' and pray his forgiveness," the vicar instructed.

"Father," Ned said, "I have done that many times before today."

"That's good, my son. Very good."

***

With the sun well and truly on show, the early morning clouds having dissipated soon after Ned's capture, the police continued to fire sporadically. It no longer seemed like they were attempting to shoot the outlaws, but rather that they were merely firing for the fun of shooting a high-powered firearm or merely out of boredom. Even the journalists joined them with borrowed firearms. Joe Melvin appeared to be enjoying himself immensely.

Sadleir and Rawlins walked to the drainage ditch to join O'Connor who was leaning against a tree reading the newspaper. Yonder, the inn was dark and dormant.

"Hard at work I see," Sadleir quipped.

"What are your orders, sir?" O'Connor replied haughtily, without looking up from his paper.

"Our first and most important priority is to get the captives out of the house. I suggest we call on them to exit."

"And what if the gang is hidden amongst them?"

"We shall have them all lie down so that we can inspect them one by one. No doubt it would be impossible for the outlaws to escape with so many eyes on the inn and some of the most famous faces in the country."

O'Connor nodded and put away his newspaper.

Nearby the native police were sitting on the ground eating bread. Jimmy's head wound had been bandaged but not without some grum bling about it being a waste of medical supplies.

"After the hostages are released, we give a few more rounds of fire, which ought to soften them up. If not, I've sent for a cannon from the Royal Garrison to blast them out," Sadleir stated with more than a hint of pride in his decision making. O'Connor was sceptical about the effectiveness of the plan.

"Well, sir, we had better start getting those inside the inn out," Rawlins said.

Sadleir stood on the embankment above the ditch facing the inn.

"All those inside, if you are a civilian, you've ten minutes to come out and lay on your belly on the grass, after that time we will resume firing," Sadleir shouted but his voice was too soft and was barely audible in the inn.

Rawlins interjected, "Sir, with respect, your voice will not carry. I've much experience at the cattle auctions, allow me to speak."

"Very well, go ahead." Sadleir replied. Rawlins stood up and cupped his hands around his mouth.

"To all those inside the hotel, you are to come out and surrender at once! You have ten minutes," he boomed, giving some of the nearby police a little fright, "After that firing will resume."

Inside, bushrangers and captives alike listened to the directive. Dave Mortimer looked straight to Dan for consent to leave. Dan's face was ashen, and his expression showed his exhausted resignation, but his eyes still danced with a flicker of hope.

"Now is your chance everyone. Go," Dan said.

The captives quickly stood, lifting their wounded comrades and heading for the front door. Dan remained seated. He painfully extended his hand to Mortimer. They shook hands firmly with a nod.

Mortimer followed the survivors outside. As they shuffled out, some of the men took turns to shake Dan's hand in farewell. Dan accepted every gesture graciously but felt a painful guilt that such respect be given to the man who had helped put them in this situation in the first place.

A white handkerchief waved from the door as Mortimer stood out at the front of the group, hands raised high. Before him stood no less than half a dozen plainclothes troopers pointing Martini Henry rifles at him. He hesitated. A bullet zipped past the group, but they continued all the same.

"Do not fire, for God's sake! We are all coming out!"

"Get a move on!" barked the trooper known as "the fat bastard". The opportunity to take pot-shots at the bushrangers had excited him immensely and he stood abreast of his colleagues dressed in a tweed cloak, bandolier and pith helmet. He rested the stock of his gun against his shoulder and aimed at Mortimer's head.

Immediately, the thirty-odd remaining captives spilled from the hotel. Without a further word uttered, they ran into the railway reserve, the rabble of confused civilians being herded poorly by the police.

Dave Mortimer bolted straight across the reserve and ducked into the drainage ditch, where he was greeted by the rifles held by the native police.

"What we gonna do with this fulla, Boss?" Jackey asked O'Connor.

"Keep him covered and take him to the others. If he tries any funny business, you can shoot him," O'Connor replied. The trackers cocked their guns and Mortimer raised his hands.

Meanwhile, the police had rounded up the captives and yelled for them to lie flat on the ground. They stalked back and forth, examining the prone civilians with firearms pointed, ready to fire at the first sign of disobedience.

Michael Reardon struggled to breathe next to his father in the grass.

"Please, my son is badly wounded, let me take him to safety," James Reardon begged as he got up on his knees and cuddled his terrified toddler, but he was ignored.

Portly Constable Kelly recognised the McAuliffes and jabbed his rifle in their direction, "Well, I reckon we can shoot this lot right here!"

The McAuliffes were promptly handcuffed and informed that they were under arrest as sympathisers. They went quietly; happy to be away from the firing.

* * *

Meanwhile, Father Gibney continued to administer the last rites to Ned. The ancient words washed over the weakened outlaw as the priest made the sign of the cross. Gibney halted and rested a hand on Ned's shoulder.

"Son, would your companions surrender to me?"

"No. They will shoot you if you go near."

"Even a clergyman?"

"They will not know what you are. They are lost."

"Nobody is ever truly lost," replied Gibney.

Ned examined Gibney's kindly face and believed in his earnestness, if not the truth of his words. He looked over Gibney's shoulder and could see faces pressed against the window as the onlookers tried to peer inside the station to see the outlaw.

Outside on the platform people stared in awe at the armour. This crude collection of cobbled together steel was peppered with shiny flecks where shots had chipped at the patina and was smeared with blood and dirt. Constable Dwyer attempted to hold people back as one enthusiastic gentleman attempted to pick up the helmet. Dwyer pushed him away with the stock of his gun.

"What's the matter?" the young man complained, "It's not like he's going to need it where he's going!"

"It's police property now. Keep your hands off it if you intend to keep them," Dwyer replied in as menacing a tone as he could muster with his pinched, nasally voice.

***

Dan watched from the dining room window as the prisoners were allowed to go free. As much of a relief as it had been to see the people free and safe, their rough treatment by police grated on him. He turned to Steve who nursed a glass of whiskey.

"Well, that's the end of it," Dan sighed.
"What happens now?"
"I suppose it's the end for us as well."

Steve attempted to maintain his composure by looking away, but everywhere around him was decimation. The floor was a mosaic of shattered glass, splintered wood and bullet-damaged gallimaufry. The walls were all bullet holes and shredded wallpaper. On the dining room table, the cards with which some of the labourers had been playing the night before were strewn about; all Steve could see were aces and eights. Seeing the extent of the damage in the light of day made everything more real. He squeezed his eyes shut, trying to hold back tears as it all seeped in.

Dan peered outside and just beyond the tents he saw a man setting up a camera. He gestured for Steve to come to the window.
"What is it?" asked Steve.
"See that photographer? What do you say I make him rethink where he sets up?"
Dan picked up the Spencer and aimed it near the photographer's feet. He pulled the trigger and his shot kicked up the dirt beneath the camera. The photographer, Oswald Madeley, seemed to jump a foot in the air, causing the two trapped outlaws a moment of entertainment.

"We won't let them take us, will we?" said Steve.
"Of course not," replied Dan.

***

As the Kelly sisters crossed the platform through the crowd, Senior-Constable Kelly approached Maggie.

"Mrs. Skillion, wait," Kelly called out. The group slowed to a halt. "Would you go to the hotel and ask your brother and Hart to surrender?"

"Surrender to you lot? I'd sooner see them burn," Maggie sneered defiantly. The girls promptly turned around and headed for McDonnell's.

With the captives freed, the troopers got closer to the inn. Had the bushrangers inside been so inclined they could have picked them off like bottles on a fence now that the fog and the gloom was gone. Yet, there was no discernible movement inside the building. A deafening explosion erupted as the police began their promised assault, firing wave after wave into the inn in sequence.

Meanwhile, Steve carried Dan into the armoury and closed the back door. Dan sat on the iron-framed bed and loaded and capped his revolvers. The odd bullet sang past his head, but he took no notice, the firing having become little more than background noise to him. Steve put his helmet back on and tried to look out the window. He could see the troopers closing in. He pushed the muzzle of his revolver through a hole in the glass and fired, narrowly missing Constable Cawsey who hit the ground.

"Nearly got one, Danny," Steve laughed.

"Well, I suppose that's my turn then," Dan replied. With Steve's help, he hopped across to the window with great effort and fired out at the constables, his bullets clipping their hat brims and nipping at their clothes.

"Well, you can't always get a bullseye," Steve said. He saw Dan grimace at the pain in his leg, now that the drugs had worn off. He took Dan to the bed and helped him to sit.

The police were at the fence now and could hear the movement in the back room in between the blasts. Constable Dwyer took cover behind a fence post and checked his watch. It was now one o'clock. He was hungry but there were more important things to worry about in the moment than lunch, though he was struggling to keep focus.

The police unleashed a heavy torrent of fire at the back of the inn, bullets punching through the weatherboards as Dan sat with his helmet off and his back to the onslaught, bullets ricocheted off his back plate. In amongst the shower of lead, a single bullet scraped the top of the steel and lodged in Dan's neck, paralysing him. He gagged and fell backwards. The crash of his armour and the toppling bed could be heard outside.

Steve raced over to Dan and grabbed him under the arms. He attempted to drag him away from the bed, but his own shattered collarbone made him weak. Dan slipped from Steve's grip and lay on the floor drowning in his own blood. Steve panicked and grabbed one of the tarpaulins to craft a makeshift pillow. Dan began to lose consciousness, his eyes fixed on the calico ceiling flapping gently as a breeze slipped through the shattered window. His mind was a jumble of pain, confusion and his memories doing a mad scramble as if aware they were about to disappear into oblivion.

Steve clasped Dan's hand tightly and watched as Dan gasped his final, futile, crackling breaths. He pressed his forehead against Dan's and sobbed.

"Dan, please don't leave me here. Please," Steve whispered into Dan's ear. Dan took a few last, sharp gasps and then was still. His face softened, his eyes lost their glint, his mouth hung open as his last lungful of air escaped with a wet, bubbling sound. Steve wept uncontrollably as the next barrage of bullets sent splinters flying about his head.

***

By two thirty in the afternoon, the inn lay eerily dormant. Despite no shots having come from inside for an hour, the police remained poised for the gang's retaliation. Sadleir stood at the edge of the battlefield calmly puffing on his pipe, O'Connor beside him doing the same.

"Should we prepare to rush the inn?" asked O'Connor.

"Don't trust this silence. When you have a rat in a trap, you don't reach your hand inside," Sadleir remarked. As they spoke, Senior-Constable Charles Johnston sauntered up to them. He was a friend of Sadleir's, burly and endowed with a greying beard, and was known as a man of action. The waiting had been grating on his nerves.

"Hullo, gentlemen." Johnston called out as he approached.

"Johnston, good to see you," replied Sadleir.

"Looks like we finally have the buggers where we want them but we're not striking. What's the hold up?"

"I don't want to risk lives unnecessarily by storming into an ambush," Sadlier said folding his arms.

"Sir, if you'll permit me, I have a simple idea. Let's smoke them out."

"Smoke them out?"

"I can get close enough to set fire to the wall. It's only whitewash on weatherboard, it'll go up like kindling. All I need is some kerosene, matches, straw and covering fire from the men," said Johnston.

"It's a good idea, Sadleir. Either they flee into the line of fire, or they roast. Simple but effective," O'Connor interjected.

Sadleir thought for a moment then nodded in agreement, "Fetch what you need but don't allow anyone to find out what you're about. That should give me time to relay the instructions to the others."

Johnston saluted and ran to fetch his tools, taking a wide berth of the inn. As he moved along the path on the Benalla side of the inn, he saw a quartet of men dressed in the larrikin style, carrying rifles. He slowed his pace.

"What's going on?" asked one of the armed sympathisers.

"They've got the Kellys trapped in the house," Johnston replied. The sympathisers all looked at each other in bewilderment.

"You're not a trap, are you?" another man asked. Johnston felt his heart racing.

"Oh no, not I," Johnston bluffed, "I'm just passing through and thought I'd look at the commotion."

The sympathisers were satisfied and allowed Johnston to pass. Once he was clear he increased his speed while thanking his lucky stars that things had not escalated.

***

The inside of the inn was a shattered tomb. From outside, voices could be heard clearly. Occasionally a shot would go off as if to remind the occupants of the building, living and dead, that they were there on the police's terms. Steve wandered from room to room in a state of confusion. He hoped one of the police bullets would end him. He was bereft and his chest ached. He clutched at his revolver and stared at it. He felt its heft in his palm.

Just one click at just the right spot on the temple or below the chin, that's all it would take, he thought. He ran his thumb over the hammer.

Just one click. He looked up and caught his reflection in what remained of the mirror behind the bar. His hair was a tangle of greasy black curls, clinging to his brow with sweat. His face was pale and waxy save for the eyes that appeared dark and sunken, and his two-day growth of stubble was coarse. Steve considered he seemed more a ghost than a man.

He stepped over Joe's corpse, the expression on the face serene despite his sudden and painful death and entered the armoury where he lingered by Dan's body. The corpse bore a look of sadness as it stared upwards with sightless eyes. By his feet was the dead greyhound. Steve held two bottles: one of strychnine taken from Dan's pocket and another of carbolic acid he had found under the bar. He examined the labels. Both were poison. Both were utterly deadly. He held them as he returned to Dan and moved an oiled canvas tarpaulin into position close to Dan's head. He piled it up as a pillow as he lay at a right angle to his late companion. He had no escape. No hope. No friends left. All he wanted at that moment was to join Dan. Life without him was no life at all. He popped a cork and raised the bottle to his lips.

***

Among the sea of onlookers by the train station, Tom, Maggie and the others continued to watch the last stages of the siege. Presently, Tom noticed Johnston move past carrying kerosene and straw and trained his eyes on him as the police momentarily ceased fire. Something was up and he knew it, but he wasn't sure what it was. Father Gibney approached them quietly and singled out Kate. He touched her shoulder and she jerked around.

"Excuse me, are you Kate Kelly?"
"Yes?"

"My girl, will you go and tell your brother there's a Catholic priest here anxious to see him and to let me in?" Gibney asked, taking Kate's hand in his.

"Of course, I will go to my brother," Kate answered. She hitched up her skirts and ran towards the inn, straight through the police lines, the lace from her hat trailing behind her, fluttering. She made it into the railway reserve before Sadleir ran her down and grabbed her.

"Where are you going?" Sadleir demanded as he struggled with the girl.

"I'm going to get my brother, please let me go to him!"

"Girl, it's too late. He had his chance to surrender, and you had yours to save him. It's too dangerous now; stand back," Sadleir growled as he pushed her away.

"You never gave me a chance you bloody cur! You have to let me see my brother! He's still in there! Let me go to him!"

Sadleir grew tired of Kate's hysterics and directed two constables to drag her back behind the police lines. Kate staggered back to her sisters weeping uncontrollably.

"Present arms!" O'Connor commanded. The police stood and raised their rifles in unison. Johnston stood at the ready. Suddenly his motives were clear to the onlookers.

"That son of a bitch is going to burn them!" Dick Hart roared as he grabbed his revolver from his pocket and tried to take aim. Tom grasped Dick's forearm and lowered it.

"Don't do it. There's been enough bloodshed."

"Fire!"

The police unleashed a Mexican wave of gunfire that circled the inn.

Johnston kept low and ran to the inn as fast as he could, planting the straw against the parlour chimney, dousing it with kerosene and hurling the bottle at the wall. He lit a match and set the mess alight. With a great fwoosh flames licked the boards and Johnston hastily retreated back.

Maggie suddenly rushed toward the inn, her bright red underskirt kicking up around her ankles. She was abruptly pulled back by a constable.

"I have to see to my brother! Let me go, for pity's sake!" Maggie shrieked. The police paid no heed. The fire spread hungrily, fanning across the wall like ivy. Smoke billowed through the front rooms. Gibney was incensed that the outlaws had not been allowed a surrender and rushed toward the inn as if with winged feet.

"Father! Get back here now! I order you, in the name of the Queen!" Sadleir yelled. Gibney paused to look at the superintendent.

"I am not in your service," he yelled back, "I serve a higher authority!"

Gibney took out his crucifix as he reached the veranda with his hands held high. Onlookers crowded the inn and applauded as if watching some exciting theatre performance. The heat inside was intense, a raging furnace. Smoke choked the priest as he recited The Lord's Prayer and entered the bar room.

Unable to bear the thought of some foolish priest burning alive on his watch, Sadleir signalled to constables Armstrong, Dwyer and Arthur to follow him.

Gibney staggered through the bar room looking for signs of life. His face glistened with sweat. It seemed as if he'd rushed into the very fires of Purgatory.

Smoke choked the priest as he recited The Lord's Prayer and entered
the bar room.

"My sons, I am a priest, please come to me! I'm here to help you!" Gibney called, his voice quietened by the roar of the fire.

He saw Joe Byrne's body next to the bar and quickly checked it. The skin was cool to the touch, the vessel devoid of life. He blessed it and moved on.

Behind him, Sadleir and the constables tried to enter from the front. A falling portion of the burning ceiling stopped Sadleir and Arthur from entering but Dwyer and Armstrong made their way to the back.

As Gibney moved from the dining room to the bedrooms, Armstrong entered through the back door brandishing a revolver.

"There's no need for that," Gibney said, pushing Armstrong's arm down. The constable moved to Joe's body. The left sleeve was now on fire as a chunk of the roof had landed on the forearm. Armstrong stamped the flames out. The face was blackened by smoke, the arms rigid. The left arm was bent at the elbow and pointed straight up, the other bent with the hand over the crotch, caked in blood. Dwyer joined Armstrong and held the feet of the corpse and Armstrong grabbed under the shoulders, carrying the body outside. All around them flames undulated and spat. Thick clouds of black smoke tumbled and drifted, filled with glowing embers that danced like fireflies.

Gibney discovered the bodies of Dan and Steve. He moved fast, venturing close enough to tell the boys were devoid of life. Both had their heads propped up, neither showed any visible sign of trauma, but Gibney did not hang around to make detailed observations.

"They are dead!" Gibney hollered as he went through the back door into the kitchen. Flames shot out from under the iron sheets on the roof and snagged on the bark roof of the skillion.

Dwyer ran back into the bedroom and headed for the bodies. By now, a significant portion of the exterior wall had burned away and through a fiery ring Dwyer saw the scores of gawkers staring in.

"Get back, it's a fire!" Dwyer yelled at them through the hole. He got close enough to the bodies to recognise Dan. He noted the deformed knee, and the way one arm was outstretched. There was blood on the neck and the burning floor caused the skin to swell and frizzle, the limbs had begun to tighten and bend at the joints. Smoke curled from under the iron breastplate.

Steve on the other hand was almost unrecognisable by this point. His body was on fire from his toes to his waist, his legs bent up and his feet resting by the iron bed frame. Already the flesh on his face had begun to bubble and boil like streaky bacon. His arms were curled up at his sides and his handsome red sash, the proud symbol of his allegiance to the Greta Mob, no more than a scrap of burnt silk fluttering away in the updraft. Dwyer bolted outside, followed by Armstrong. Through the burning hole in the wall, Thomas Carrington sketched the bodies as quickly as possible.

Elsewhere in the inn, Steve's shredded cloak was consumed by flames, and the boarding passes he had tucked away in the pocket burnt to nothing.

Within moments, the wounded Martin Cherry had been liberated from the kitchen by a small group of civilians who had rushed in to save him. Cherry was alive but barely conscious as he was carried a safe distance from the fire.

"How are you doing, Martin?" one of the rescuers asked.

"Oh, you know me," replied Cherry. Presently, Gibney went to his side and began to administer the last rites. Upon the conclusion of the ritual, Cherry closed his eyes and quietly passed away.

Unnoticed by the onlookers, Thomas Curnow watched the fire from close to the gatehouse and wondered if he had done the right thing after all. His heart was heavy as he considered the ramifications of his act. Curnow had not slept a wink and was terrified that the Kelly Gang or their sympathisers would come around to exterminate his family should word slip out that he was the one who had warned the police. He pulled the brim of his cabbage-tree hat low over his face and slipped away.

***

While he could not see what was happening, Ned could hear the commotion and smell the smoke wafting through the gaps in the window frames. Nicholson watched from the window, flanked by Steele and Dowsett.

"That's finished then. I don't suppose they got the outlaws out of that," Dowsett said.

"Good riddance," Steele said bitterly.

Ned heard it all but remained silent. Just on the edge of his hearing he swore he could hear Dan's voice by his ear.

***

Finally, the inn and skillion collapsed with an almighty crash of steel and wood. Embers floated away into the sky. Some of the onlookers cheered. It was not clear what they were cheering for. As the flames began to settle, only the two brick chimneys remained standing as a sadly ironic sight along with the sign still boasting about the accommodation.

The onlookers closed in on the smouldering ruins desperate to get a good view. While most were merely curious in a general sense, some of them were keen to see any bodies that were trapped inside the fire. They'd never seen a burnt corpse before.

Joe's body had been left against a fence and a couple of bored little boys threw pebbles at it, watching them bounce off the armour with little plink sounds.

Some of the police began poking around in the ruins. Constable Phillips shifted some charred roofing at where the back rooms once stood using a pole. He paused and craned his neck to see the black lump he had uncovered.

"Sir, I've found them," Phillips shouted.

One of the bodies was dragged out with the pole. The action caused the lower limbs to crumble away. The remains were placed on a sheet of bark and left for people to gawp at. The legs were missing from the knees down, the arms also missing below the elbow, though the left hand had apparently fused with the hip. The body was little more than a crunchy black lump with bone fragments stuck to it. People stood around the horrific sight as photographs were taken. A young boy sat on the table that had been carried out to make way for dancing the previous night. He waggled his feet as he stared at the corpse.

***

Henry Cheshire sat by the telegraph transmitter waiting to send further news when there was a commotion behind him. He turned and saw some very grubby looking policemen, blackened by ash and smoke, carrying the corpse of Joe Byrne, stripped of its armour. For a lack of room, they were forced to lay the dead body at Cheshire's feet. Naturally he recoiled in horror as he beheld the smoke blackened features. He noted the knuckles, cracked and blistered from the heat of the fire, the enormous stain that soaked the outlaw's lap from where he was shot, and the forearm burned to the bone. He was disgusted at the horrendous mingling smell of singed flesh and the various bodily fluids that had since evacuated the body postmortem. He dry-retched.

"Good lord!" the telegraphist said clapping a hand over his mouth.

"Merry Christmas," said one of the constables with a wink and a morbid chuckle.

Without further word, the police left, and Cheshire sat staring at the horrendous sight at his feet. He took in everything: the grey striped Crimean shirt, the brown tweed waistcoat and riding trousers, the handsome blue sack coat now shredded and burnt. His boots were far too small and gave his feet a comically misshapen appearance. Cheshire also noted the rings on his fingers and something peeking out from under the ragged scarf around Joe's neck. He moved the scarf gingerly and saw it was a lady's silver ring with a diamond set in it and suspended around the neck on a leather thong. Cheshire's horror had well and truly given way to curiosity and now as he studied every contour, every crow's foot, he began to feel a growing sympathy. He was surprised at how well dressed this murderous brigand was. The only indication that he had lived a hard life on the run was the emaciated look of his features. His fingers were thin, the knuckles prominent. His smooth face was drawn and haggard now, yet serene. Cheshire wondered if the other outlaws had been comparably genteel in their appearance.

He reached down and grabbed the diamond ring, yanking at the thong until it snapped. He looked around for witnesses. Satisfied he was in the clear he secreted the ring in his coat pocket. After all, he thought, is it really immoral to steal from a thief?

In another part of the station, hidden from the public, a sheet was draped over the earthly remains of Dan Kelly and Steve Hart. Sadleir approached them with Maggie Skillion and Kate Kelly. The sisters struggled to maintain composure.

"May we see them please?" Maggie said coldly.

"I'm not sure that would be wise. You will not be able to recognise them," Sadleir replied.

"He's our brother. We have the right to see him," Kate insisted. Sadlier regretfully nodded and Constable Phillips removed the sheet slowly, revealing what remained of the bodies.

What was once two handsome young outlaws was now nothing more than black lumps of charcoal flesh and shrivelled, charred organs holding together bits of bone. The Kelly sisters grasped each other in utter shock. Overwhelmed by the horrific sight, they collapsed to their knees, wailing loudly in their grief. Men around them lowered their eyes and removed their hats. Sadleir walked away, allowing them to grieve alone.

As the girls mourned, the crowds closed in, pushing the police roughly in their morbid lust to get a look at the charred corpses and the wailing women. Gascoigne fretted and started to unload his rifle for fear the crowd would cause a misfire with the violent jostling.

"Don't be so quick to unload, son. Look what's coming our way." Senior-Constable Kelly said gesturing to a small army of Kelly sympathisers amassing around McDonnell's.

Men and women of a myriad of ages and backgrounds, marched to the platform bearing arms and wearing chin straps under their noses, with coloured-scarves and sashes on show. Had Ned's plan worked, they would have been the people celebrating in Benalla by now. But instead, they were in Glenrowan and furthermore, they were confused and angry.

Tom Lloyd rushed to the sympathisers, waving for them to gather by him. Though sceptical, the mob complied and stopped. In hushed tones, Tom explained what had unfolded.

***

Sadleir brooded from inside the station building near Ned. Sergeant Steele continued to sit vigilantly next to the wounded man with his shotgun at the ready, his face still black and stinging from powder burns. Sadleir contemplated how to diffuse the tension with the sympathisers and decided on the only gesture he considered to be effective.

Finally, he strode outside and made a beeline for Tom Lloyd and Maggie Skillion who were attempting to comfort Dick Hart, whose face was red and glistening with tears.

"May I have a word?" Sadleir said gesturing for the trio to join him. They followed.

"What do you want?" Dick said.

"I have decided to allow you to take the bodies of Dan Kelly and Steve Hart. No doubt Captain Standish will demand an inquest but there's nothing that we can find from the bodies in the state they're in. Take them quietly and bury them quickly," said Sadleir.

Maggie teared up but maintained a stiff upper lip. Dick barely suppressed his own tears, his lips pursed and his eyes red. He nodded his thanks. Tom Lloyd extended his hand to Sadleir and the men shook hands. Tom looked deeply into Sadleir's eyes.

"Thank you," was all Tom could muster.

The relatives of the deceased promptly made way to procure their buggy and retrieve the remains. Sadleir lingered a moment and contemplated. He reasoned that a little kindness could go a long way in keeping retaliation suppressed, and he was prepared to wear the criticism from his superiors should they not share his enthusiasm for peace. If it really mattered to them, they would have been in Glenrowan instead of sipping expensive port in the Melbourne Club. All Sadleir cared about at that moment was that he had avoided escalation.

He eyed the army of sympathisers as they dissipated. With the conclusion of the siege there was nothing left for them to do except return to their farms. There would be no celebrations.

***

At five o'clock Captain Standish arrived in Glenrowan. Most of the police were at that point milling around the station debriefing. One of the first people Standish saw was O'Connor. O'Connor extended his hand and Standish shook it weakly.

"Capital show," was all Standish could muster before he sought out Sadleir to get an update from the horse's mouth. O'Connor fumed at Standish's dismissiveness.

When Standish was taken to see Ned, the outlaw was unconscious. Standish took no small amount of glee in seeing the bane of his life in such a horrid condition.

"He's positively brutish," Standish said to nobody in particular.

"I hope you will stand by my decision to give the bodies to the families," Sadleir said.

"Oh, of course," Standish replied dismissively, "I have arranged for the surviving outlaw and the other bodies to be taken to Benalla. Now the excitement has passed, let us get on with the work of enforcing law and order."

Sadleir nodded and left. As he stood on the platform, he looked across at the smouldering ruins. The white sign still stood untouched, and Sadleir read it aloud to himself.

"The Glenrowan Inn. Ann Jones. Best accommodation."

<h1 style="text-align:center">14</h1>

The Ashes of Glenrowan

The Wangaratta hospital room that held Johnny Jones was dim, the blinds drawn shut as Ann Jones sat by the bed of her son, still in the dress stained with his blood. She struggled to stay awake. She held the boy's hand, but he was unresponsive, his breathing shallow and laboured. Across from them, the other Jones children were cuddled together asleep. Jane's cheeks were still tear stained, but her wound had been freshly cleaned and bandaged.

Suddenly Johnny took several heaving breaths and just as suddenly ceased. Ann waited for a reprise, a sudden burst of life as if to say it was merely a ruse. The reprise never came.

Ann had paid a price for her attempts to exploit the gang's needs for her own gain that was incalculable. She was homeless, her business gone, and her possessions just the same. Now on top of that she had another child to bury. She could not understand why she had been punished so severely by misfortune. As she wailed at her boy's side, she wondered what was left to be taken away from her.

***

Ned Kelly lay half-conscious on the blood-stained mattress in the guard van of the Benalla-bound train. His wounds stung and everything else ached mercilessly. He was quite unable to move any extremities and his feet were icy cold.

There was movement at the door and several troopers shuffled on carrying the corpses of Joe Byrne and Martin Cherry, which they flopped onto the floor next to Ned. The smells were horrendous, filling the van with a reek of decay and singed flesh.

Sadleir briefly entered the guard van, where the dead and dying laid together, to check on the prisoner. The driver and fireman joined him to get a look at the infamous cargo and stood over Ned as he slowly awoke. He looked up into a coal-black face and was struck with terror.

"Get that black bastard away from me!" he exclaimed as he tried to move away having mistaken the soot covered face of the fireman for one of the trackers.

The train soon lurched to life and began to trundle towards Benalla. Ned had known that his fate was to hang as soon as he was in the clutches of the long arm of the law, but his injuries made things uncertain. He spitefully wished to die from his wounds to deny the traps the satisfaction of ending his life on their terms. Ned considered it shameful to die a prisoner of his enemies and not in battle against them.

He lay wallowing in self-pity as the quiet battlefield was left far behind. Every jostle and bump in the line sent a surge of pain through his body, keeping him awake.

***

At the Kelly selection Kate and Grace entered the house where Ettie had just put the children down to bed. Jack Lloyd napped in Ellen's rocking chair by the fire. Ettie looked up at the girls who were sombre. She felt a profound coldness wash over her. Grace burst out crying and ran to the bedroom to compose herself. Kate tried her best to hold herself together as she sat at the dining table. She reached out to Ettie, who stood before her, and held her hand. She spoke slowly.

"The boys didn't stop the train. They got into a big fight with the police."

"What happened?" asked Ettie who refused to be seated.

"Ned has been captured alive, but the others..." Kate fell silent and trembled violently. Ettie already knew how the sentence ended. As the realisation hit her, she buried her face in her hands and sank to her knees.

***

Superintendent Sadleir spent the night unable to clear his mind. He drank glass after glass of French cognac, but it barely took the edge off. In the few hours after returning from Glenrowan he had already received word on the grapevine that Captain Standish was furious at his decision to surrender the burnt bodies to the families, despite his expressed indifference when Sadleir had informed him of the decision in person. He'd also been made aware of Standish's distaste for the hesitation to send police into the inn to capture the outlaws, dead or alive. Sadleir maintained that he had been right in his decisions and felt the criticism to be unjust. Like all combatants who fate had led to Glenrowan, he would not come away unscathed.

***

The parlour of the Vine Hotel had been blocked off to customers that day to allow for the inquest on Aaron Sherritt to take place. In the centre of the room sat a cheap wooden coffin that had recently been brought up from the cellar. The top remained open as Maggie the maid entered, sneaking so as to avoid suspicion.

She approached the coffin and peered inside at Aaron Sherritt's corpse, his face completely drained of colour and life. She reached out and pulled the edge of the sheet covering his body down just enough to reveal part of the hideous wound in his neck. Suddenly she heard people approaching outside and quickly exited the room.

Once clear of the parlour, the realisation of what she had seen hit Maggie and she began to sob uncontrollably. She had not yet learned Joe's fate.

Inside, John Sherritt and his teenage son Willie were directed to the coffin. John looked down at his son without a shred of emotion making itself visible on his face. Willie, however, began to tear up. He wiped his eyes with the back of his hand. His father looked across at him sternly.

"Pull yourself together, boy."

"Sorry, Da," Willie said meekly.

****

Two small coffins were hastily arranged by Tom Lloyd and taken to McDonnell's Railway Tavern where the remains of Dan and Steve were waiting. The bodies were gently transferred into the coffins.

She approached the coffin and peered inside at Aaron Sherritt's corpse,
his face completely drained of colour and life.

"They barely weigh a thing," said Wild Wright absent-mindedly. Dick Hart glared. The coffins were loaded onto the cart where the undertaker sat at the ready; the black veil on his top hat fluttered gently in the breeze.

A small crowd had gathered and were posing for a photograph before being accosted by Tom Lloyd.

As the crowd dispersed Tom looked at the rain clouds swirling across the sky. He knew they had to get moving back to Eleven Mile Creek to beat the rain.

***

Ann Jones, flanked by her surviving children, sifted through the charred, smouldering remnants of her inn. She shifted a pile of debris from what was once her bedroom. Miraculously intact was her bronze jewellery box, slightly warped but relatively intact.

She opened it hoping to find her few precious accessories unscathed. Her heart sank at the emptiness that greeted her. She broke down and hurled the box at the iron stove, which stood mockingly unharmed amongst the charred rubble. It had only remained because it was too heavy for souvenir hunters to carry away. The children watched their mother forlornly.

Jeremiah kicked a bit of rubble hoping to find his marbles in the remnants of his room. He found the charred box he kept them in and found the marbles inside burnt, cracked or melted into useless glass and ceramic lumps. Even the Tom Bowler didn't make it. His lip quivered and he cried pitifully.

Jane wandered aimlessly around her former home. The nasty gash across her head itched. She seemed to be looking for something, but her mind was clean of motivation.

She thought about Dan and Steve dying alone in the guest room, where the partially melted steel bed frame protruded from under a tarnished sheet of corrugated iron. She had heard rumours that they had taken their own lives rather than be captured, or burned to death in the inferno, and hoped that whatever ended their lives was quick and painless, despite the continuing pain the outlaws had brought them.

She stood still in the wreckage, numb and confused. She missed her bed, her books and her brother.

Ann, in a moment of lucidity, pulled herself back together and rounded up her children.

"We're going," she said.

"We haven't got anywhere to go, Ma," replied Jane.

"We're going to ask the McDonnells for help. Just for tonight," Ann said as she held her youngest boys close, running her fingers through Jeremiah's hair in a vain effort to soothe him.

As they left the smouldering wreckage, souvenir hunters moved in and began to rummage. A young man went straight for the jewellery box and pocketed it. Some boys found bullets and carried them in pannikins, the metal making a thin rattling as they stalked the ruins. Not once did anyone question the morality of picking apart the carcass of Ann Jones' home and livelihood like crows on a dead kangaroo.

Lumps of burnt wood, the cracked head of a porcelain figurine, doorknobs, anything that seemed unique or relevant, no matter how tangential, was pilfered.

Even Doctor Hutchison was not averse to the ghoulishness and returned to the inn where he managed to find Dan Kelly's foot. He took it home wrapped in a handkerchief and secreted in his bag.

Another ghoul managed to find Steve's hand, still wearing his signet ring. They cracked open the charred fist like a nut and removed the ring. After giving the jewellery a wipe on his trousers to clean off the traces of the finger left behind, he placed it on his own finger and admired it.

***

Ned lay in darkness in the holding cell of the Benalla courthouse. He had been here only a few years earlier after his confrontation with the police in King's boot shop. A part of him was amused at the fact that, quite inverse to that incident, this time his testicles were about the only part of him that the police hadn't injured during their clash.

He had been drifting in and out of consciousness, increasingly reliant on the little, infrequent mouthfuls of brandy he was given to cope with the pain he was in.

There was movement outside and the cell door was opened. Ned strained his eyes to see the figure silhouetted in the doorway. It was a thin man, not overly tall, with a long beard and Derby hat cocked slightly on a broad skull.

"Do you recognise this man?" said Senior-Constable Kelly from outside. Ned squinted.

"It's Flood, is it not?"

"You made that mistake last time we met," the silhouetted man replied. He took a few steps closer, and Ned refocused. He quickly recognised the visitor.

"Oh yes, it's McIntyre," Ned said bluntly, "I suppose you've come to say your piece about what happened."

"I have some questions," said McIntyre, "I have suffered a great deal over this affair. Tell me, was my statement correct?"

"Yes, it was," Ned replied.

"You remember the last time we met; didn't I tell you I would rather be shot than tell you anything about the other two men if you were going to shoot them?" McIntyre continued.

"Yes," replied Ned who turned to the doorway to address the Senior-Constable, "McIntyre said he would rather be shot than bring the others into it if they were going to be shot."

"When I turned around, I saw you had my chest covered."

"Yes, I had."

"And when I held out my hands you shot Lonigan."

"No," said Ned indignantly, "Lonigan got behind some logs and pointed his revolver at me. Didn't you see that?"

"No, that is only nonsense," McIntyre said dismissively. Ned glowered.

"Did Kennedy fire many shots at you?"

"Yes, he fired a lot," said Ned. He grew weary of the interrogation and dropped down onto his bed with a sigh.

"I never saw him fire a shot. I suppose you had a shot at me as I was getting away?" McIntyre continued.

"I don't think I had. We never thought you could get away, or we would have shot you at once."

"Why did you come near us at all? You could have kept out of our way when you knew where we were."

"You'd have soon found us out. If we hadn't shot you, you'd have shot us," Ned said with bitterness. This bloody trap, he thought, the trouble I'd have been saved if I were half as ruthless as they made me out to be.

McIntyre averted his gaze momentarily. There was one thing above all else he needed to know.

"Tell me, did I ever show cowardice when you bailed me up?"

"No," Ned replied bluntly. McIntyre nodded; he had his validation.

He turned to leave, and Ned quickly found himself once more enveloped in darkness.

****

Captain Standish had been keeping a low profile in Benalla all morning when he permitted a pair of photographers, Burman and Lindt, to capture images of the body of Joe Byrne. Standish, wily as ever, had seen this as a way to kill two birds with one stone. He immediately arranged a special train to take Ned Kelly to Melbourne at the same time Byrne's corpse was to be displayed. This would enable the police to remove Kelly without crowds of people interfering. It would also be a final indignity for Byrne to have his remains become a curiosity.

Ned was quickly transferred to the holding cell in the courthouse to await the train's arrival while the police at the station fetched ropes.

The consternation at the Benalla police station that afternoon was incredible. Dozens of people milled about in the tiny paddock behind the station hoping to catch a glimpse of the notorious Ned Kelly. Police officers in plainclothes, still buzzing from their previous day's battle in Glenrowan, strutted about with their Martini Henry rifles in hand as if expecting the conflict to break out again.

Just after noon the second cell was opened by the constables on duty.

The men entered carrying ropes and proceeded to tie loops around the chest and waist of Joe Byrne's corpse. One policeman grabbed the corpse under the shoulders and the other by the legs, then carried the body outside where they hooked the ropes through the bars over the cell door and heaved until the body was more or less erect.

There the mortal remains of Ned Kelly's lieutenant, left arm wrapped in the shredded remnants of his handsome blue coat, knees buckled, and ankles rolled in, dangled like a ham in a delicatessen. His hands were caked in blood and balled into fists. Lonigan's and Scanlan's rings were prominent on his fingers. The face was blackened with smoke and the hair and beard seemed matted and feral.

Lindt approached the grisly sight and set up his camera. He looked at Joe and decided that the blackened face just wouldn't do. Taking his handkerchief, he dunked it in the dog's water bowl on the ground near the door, then wiped the face clean. Scorching had made the left brow blackened and crusty, but Joe's face appeared serene despite the evidence of violence.

As the exposures were made in the box camera, the crowd composed of police, trackers and civilians gawped and gossiped. Little boys stood baffled by the lifeless bushranger as their fathers stood chatting with the police.

"Made short work've the blaggard, didn't they?" said a rough looking local rhetorically. His largely toothless mouth broke into an ugly smirk as he eyed tracker Jacky suspiciously, "You lookin' fer a nibble orf the old feller, is yer?"

At the back of the crowd stood the artist Julian Ashton in his black pea coat and Derby hat with his sketchbook tucked under his arm. Having shortly before spent time in the cell sketching the corpse by candlelight for a newspaper illustration, he was glad to be done with the miserable assignment.

The body had been on display for almost twenty minutes when a young woman pushed through the crowd. Joe's betrothed, Maggie the maid, had heard rumours of something afoot in Benalla and had travelled all the way down from Beechworth. As she pushed through the gathering the grim reality assaulted her. The body of the man she had hoped to run away with was before her, the scene was surreal. Only a few days earlier she had been in his passionate embrace. She half expected Joe to spring to life and flash her a smile, or to see his eyes open with a twinkle the way they did on those stolen nights he visited her. She stumbled back through the crowd and found a more secluded place where she broke down in tears.

***

The train for Melbourne was steaming along the line with Super-intendent Hare on board with Ned Kelly. Hare's left arm was covered in bandages and held in a sling. He had made specific arrangements to ac-company Ned Kelly to the Melbourne Gaol and thence to Sunbury with his wife where he would meet with her relatives at the Rupertswood Mansion.

Finally, Hare came face to face with the young man who had made him a target of scorn for the press for almost two years. Ned lay on a mattress buried in blankets. The two combatants locked eyes in silence, but Hare was the first to break the tension.

His hands were caked in blood and balled into fists. Lonigan's and
Scanlan's rings were prominent on his fingers.

"You're a lot smaller than people say, you know?" Hare said. Ned did not respond. Hare lifted his maimed arm, "You struck me well; I am impressed. Almost lost the hand, they tell me."

"If only I'd aimed a couple inches lower," Ned quipped.

Hare smirked. "But you didn't and now here we are. Your companions are dead, you are shot to pieces and headed for the gallows if you live that long. I wouldn't feel quite so clever in your position."

"I suppose you're here to gloat then?" said Ned.

"No; that would hardly be sporting. Do you remember the first time we met all those years ago when you were arrested for helping Harry Power?"

"I do. Nicolson did all the talking while you stood behind me trying to look dangerous. You're grey now and fat too," Ned chuckled.

"I have a beautiful wife who keeps me well fed. You, on the other hand have spent the past two years in the bush, begging for scraps from relatives and friends. I know which I'd rather," Hare replied, "I recall you sitting there in the office at Kyneton, a half-starved bush urchin with a mouth like a London gutter. I thought you no more than a ragamuffin, as I'd seen your type countless times before. But Nicolson saw potential in you. It's a shame you proved that optimism to be foolish."

"I never had a chance to be anything other than what I am. Your lot would never allow it," Ned smiled wryly, "Still, you put on a good show, old man," Ned said mockingly. Hare allowed himself a smug half-smile in return.

When the train arrived in Melbourne, Hare stood back as Ned was unloaded and placed on a handcart. He looked across at two uniformed constables talking with a young woman. She was of an average height and build with a cascade of raven black curls down her shoulders and delicate features, the most notable of which were her turquoise eyes that were red rimmed with tears.

The constables nodded and the girl was allowed through. It was Kate Lloyd. She could not contain herself as she reached the cart. She reached in and clasped Ned's head, bringing it towards hers. She planted a sweet kiss on his lips.

"Oh, Ned," she sniffed, "What have they done to you?"

"My dear, sweet Kate, why are you here?"

"For you, you fool. I thought for sure I'd never see you again!" Kate said before she kissed the outlaw again as tears ran down her smooth cheeks.

"Kate, the traps took your watch. They took it from me."

"I don't care a farthing about a watch," Kate drew her handkerchief and wiped it along her cheek to collect her tears. Unceremoniously she was jostled aside, and the cart was pushed away. Ned stared mournfully back at Kate as he disappeared from view.

***

Father Peter Aylward was a young man who worked at the Melbourne Gaol giving spiritual aid and counselling to the inmates. His lanky build and smooth features were paired with his soothing temperament to create an island of calm in the sea of tumult that many prisoners endured. For this reason, Aylward was tasked with breaking the grim news to Ellen Kelly of the fate of her two outlawed sons.

Mrs. Kelly entered the chapel with her face impassive except for a sadness in her eyes. Aylward gestured for Ellen to have a seat.

"If it's all the same, Father, I prefer to stand," Ellen replied. Aylward nodded.

"I'm sure you've heard whispers about the place that something has happened to your boys," Aylward began.

"I've heard nothing, but I had a dream that I saw my boys fighting like soldiers against trooper police," Ellen replied.

"There was a conflict. That is correct. Your son Ned was captured alive but his companions Byrne, Hart and your son Daniel, were all killed. I'm sorry."

"Yes, I understand," Ellen mumbled. She felt numb and her thoughts bubbled in her head like the water in a boiling kettle. She barely heard what Aylward said from that point.

"Mrs. Kelly?"

"I'm sorry, Father. Could I be permitted to return to my cell now?"

"Yes, of course. Let me just rouse the guard," Aylward said. He was surprised not to have seen the wailing and collapsing and curses to the heavens he expected, but Ellen Kelly weathered the blow like a rock.

On the way back to her cell, Ellen was escorted by the Governor of the gaol, John Buckley Castieau. Castieau was a small man with thick black hair and oversized muttonchops that gave him an appearance reminiscent of some kind of spaniel. Ellen did not speak on the way except to ask a favour.

"I'd like to see my boy, Ned. May I go to him?"

"Unfortunately, at this stage Ned's injuries are severe and the doctors worry that even the slightest distress could exacerbate his condition. He's simply not well enough yet to receive visitors. I'm sorry."

"I understand," Ellen replied as she slunk into her cell with a bowed head.

As the door was bolted and locked, Castieau could hear Ellen on the other side sobbing. He wondered how much hardship one woman could endure before it finally broke her.

***

With the grisly circus outside the lock-up completed, Joe Byrne was taken for his postmortem examination. Two constables were given the unenviable task of shifting the corpse from the lock up to a table for the coroner. Decay was setting in, though the mix of winter cold and the brick holding cell had slowed the process down.

The body was stripped, the boots were removed with some effort revealing the calloused and narrow feet that had been squeezed into them. The one from his injured right leg was full of blood. The blood-soaked underwear was discarded, and the coroner noted, just above Joe's genitals, a deep entry wound where the fatal bullet had entered the groin and pushed up into the body.

The corpse was washed and examined, very few notes were made. Some of the police who remained behind to watch jeered and made tasteless comments about the body from outside of the room, much to Doctor Reynolds' distaste. Reynolds had been told by Captain Standish that the postmortem was merely a formality, and no considerable detail was required, so it was completed quickly without a full autopsy.

Once the examination was done the naked body was left on the table. A woman entered the room with a large bag. This was Harriet Watts, fiancée of Maximilian Kreitmayer the proprietor of the Bourke Street waxworks in Melbourne.

The Kreitmayer museum had acquired exclusive access directly from Captain Standish to make a cast of the bushranger's head and hands. With a straight razor Harriet took away the clumped beard and the greasy hair, revealing the smooth and handsome face of the Woolshed lothario.

She began mixing plaster and preparing wax. In the warm light of a hurricane lamp, she laid a string down the centre of the face and poured hot wax over it. As it set, she admired Joe's proportions.

A glance at the fatal wound reminded her of her husband's collection of casts of private parts afflicted by venereal diseases, relics of his previous occupation providing anatomical models to surgeons. Apart from the bullet hole, however, everything appeared pleasantly normal down there.

She fancied that under different circumstances the outlaw would have been quite attractive; it was difficult to imagine him being a brutish bushranger with such delicate features.

She laid bandages soaked in plaster over the wax and proceeded to cast the hands. She winced at the horrific burns on his arm and knuckles, unaware that they occurred postmortem.

Once the casting was done the moulds were carefully loaded onto Harriet's cart, wrapped in sheets. She had also managed to steal Joe's blood and mud encrusted boots, which she hid in her bag.

With the casting taken care of, Joe's remains were stitched up in a canvas bag. He was then hauled outside to a cart, dumped in a wooden box and shoved into the cart to be taken to the cemetery.

***

At dusk the fading light obscured the party of constables and the undertaker on the outskirts of the land standing around an open grave in Benalla cemetery. Next to the non-consecrated grave was the cart on which were the mortal remains of Joe Byrne. The makeshift coffin was dragged off the cart and dumped unceremoniously into the hole. The undertaker shot the constables a disapproving look.

"Don't give me that look. A shallow grave is better than he deserves. Should have fed him to the wild dogs; make him food for his own kind," said one constable, spitting into the grave.

Earth was piled on top of the body until the grave was filled. With that, those in attendance left the cemetery. The clandestine burial had successfully prevented the Kelly sympathisers from acquiring yet another body to mourn over. As darkness settled over the unmarked grave there was a profound silence and stillness.

***

At the Skillion selection the remains of Dan Kelly and Steve Hart lay on the dining table in the house beneath a calico sheet. Maggie had made sure that little Nellie, Jack and Alice had not been confronted with the gruesome sight and assigned Grace to keep them in the main house over on the Kelly selection.

Outside, a mass of relatives and sympathisers, close to two hundred people, had flocked to pay their respects to the deceased bushrangers. Many were already horrendously drunk as they descended upon the hut and jostled to gain entry.

So absorbed were they in their own grief or curiosity that they paid no heed to Maggie's cries for them to stop. More and more people pressed inside, filling the tiny room with more than a dozen people so tightly packed that there was scarcely room to raise a hand let alone doff a hat in respect for the fallen.

Maggie felt weak in the crush and overwhelmed as her cries were drowned out by the collective murmur. She pushed her way through the crowd with no inconsiderable effort to the hearth above which a shotgun hung on hooks. It had gathered a lot of dust but was still in working order. Maggie yanked it down and thrust the barrels over the corpses and cocked the hammers.

"Everyone, get out of here," she screamed. The crowd all stared in bemusement.

"I bloody well said get out!"

As the crowd moved slowly back outside Maggie sobbed bitterly. When the crowd had cleared, Tom Lloyd pushed his way inside where he was met with Maggie pointing a gun at him.

"Put it down Maggie, what's going on?"

"They were going to crush me to death, Tom," Maggie's voice trembled, her hands shook violently. Tom wrapped his arms around the terrified woman and kissed the crown of her head.

"Let me go and speak to them, I don't think I'll need a gun to get their attention."

Tom summoned the crowd and informed them that they would admit only two at a time, with family first.

The first to enter were Richard and Bridget Hart. The outbreak had taken its toll on Richard, his hair now silver. Bridget had a delicate countenance but her piercing grey eyes were glossy and pink from tears. They approached the table with great trepidation.

"May we see?" Bridget asked Maggie. Maggie returned a solemn nod and tenderly removed the tarpaulin.

Upon seeing the grisly remnants of their son, Bridget's face went pale, and she reflexively put one hand to her mouth and the other to her belly, unable to make a sound. She could not recognise the body, but she somehow knew that her son was laid out before her. She felt a pain in her heart greater than any pain she had ever experienced and wailed.

Maggie looked on helplessly, her own grief rising again for another round.

Unbeknownst to the sympathisers, a small band of police was riding out from Glenrowan at that moment. Led by Senior-Constable Kelly, these men were tasked with retrieving the charred bodies. Kelly carried a copy of the magistrate's orders in his pocket as they rode, Martini Henry rifles slung on their shoulders, the troopers all in mounted police uniforms with handsome blue jumpers, skin-tight white jodhpurs and polished boots and helmets.

As they approached the scene of the wake, they became keenly aware of the magnitude of the undertaking. Suddenly a sympathiser shot a pistol into the air. The shot spooked the horses and Kelly began to rethink the plan.

"Men, we must turn back, this is unwise. If Standish wants the bodies so badly, he can fetch them himself," Kelly said.

The police turned tail and left without the mourners being any the wiser apart from Tom Lloyd who had been scouting the perimeter in anticipation of police interference. From under his cloak a hint of iron plate was visible. In his free hand he carried Ned's prized rifle "Betty". Fortunately, he didn't need to use it.

Upon the last visitor leaving, Maggie sat and fell asleep within moments; her body and mind were completely exhausted.

Tom Lloyd re-entered the hut and found her there asleep, resting her head on the table. He ran his hand tenderly over her head, Maggie groggily opened her eyes and looked at him.

"Kate has fed the little ones. You need to go to bed."

Maggie nodded and forced herself to stand. Every movement seemed to take almost superhuman effort, with her joints aching. She proceeded to the bedroom and with Tom's assistance she removed her clothes.

The pair climbed into bed and Maggie looked up into Tom's eyes with a sorrowful expression.

"Tom, can you hold me?"

Tom kept Maggie in his embrace until she fell asleep. He, on the other hand, could not stop thinking about everything that had recently unfolded. He was desperate for enough drink to drown out the thoughts, but eventually sleep caught up to him and he fell into a troubled slumber.

***

In the aftermath of the siege, Thomas Curnow applied for a transfer to Ballarat. The sound of trains going through Glenrowan filled him with terror and every knock at the door was anxiety inducing.

He rode to Wangaratta where he purchased a revolver along with bullets and percussion caps. He spent his evenings practicing loading and capping the pistol by candlelight. The weapon felt heavier in his hand than he imagined, having seen the way Ned and his gang waved theirs about like toys.

Jeannie Curnow still found herself unable to sleep, bursting awake from nightmares of the Kelly Gang rising from the dead to grab her. With her health already delicate due to her pregnancy, Thomas grew increasingly worried, barely functioning until the news reached him that his transfer was given the all-clear. As soon as they could leave, the family exited Kelly country and never looked back.

15

The Rule of Law

In the gaol hospital, Ned had been drifting in and out of sleep. He felt uncomfortable, not only from his extensive injuries but also from his unfriendly surroundings. He began to come around but was severely disorientated, the world fuzzy and painfully bright even in the poorly lit bluestone hospital. In front of him, slowly coming into focus, was a familiar face. He believed he was hallucinating, but sure enough beside his bed was his mother dressed in prison greys. She was stoic and silent.

"Ma?"

"Yes, it's me Neddy," Ellen said as she reached out and took Ned's crippled right hand in her own. She held it tightly, tears began to well in her eyes. "I dreamed of you. And I knew something was going to happen," she said.

"Ma..." Ned began. Ellen shook her head to silence him.
"I know about Danny."

"I dreamed of you. And I knew something was going to happen."

Ned squeezed his eyes shut in shame, "I tried to get him out, but he didn't follow. I couldn't save him. And I couldn't save you."

Ned had ruminated on his failures for days, but to speak of them aloud to his mother was more painful than all his wounds combined. Bullets were like the butterfly kisses of cherubim compared to the sting of breaking his mother's heart.

"You tried, son, I understand," said Ellen, a lump rising in her throat.
"I would've taken your place, Ma. But they wouldn't have it. All I wanted was to get you out of here," Ned said, averting his eyes.
Ellen gently turned Ned's bruised face back towards hers.
"Tell me, was my Danny brave?"

Ned looked into his mother's searching eyes. He wanted to tell her that Dan was a coward and a fool, too paralysed with fear to escape the inn when he had the chance. He wanted to tell her that there was no fight in him and that he had let the traps end him. He truly believed these things but understood that no matter how much he wanted to scream those thoughts, his mother deserved to remember her boy as a brave warrior, so he nodded solemnly.

"Aye. He died like a Kelly, Ma."

Ellen broke down at that moment. Somehow, knowing her youngest son died a fighter was not as comforting as she had hoped.
"Oh, poor Danny," Ellen sobbed, "He was only a boy. Those bullies have robbed us of our happiness, they have."

"There's still fight in me, Ma. I'd burn this wretched city to the ground to cleanse the earth of every one of them if it would free you or bring the boys back," Ned said through clenched teeth. Ellen leaned over her son and held his head to her bosom until the guard approached to return her to her cell. Ellen was removed hastily, holding Ned's hand until the guards dragged her away and left Ned alone once again.

***

July came and went and with it the Felons Apprehension Act lapsed. The legislation that had branded the gang as no more than dangerous native fauna ripe for extermination expired without fanfare. Ned knew that it was so and reflected on the what-ifs.

How could his life have been different if he'd only just waited a few more weeks? He supposed that it meant nothing to a policeman though. Glenrowan had demonstrated only too well that the average trap would shoot you until there was nothing left but a fine red paste if they could, outlaw or not.

Part of him wished that Steele had pulled that trigger and blown his head inside out. Instead, now he had to wait for the government to go through the motions to get him dancing on the air.

This whole time, family members and sympathisers had been attempting to reach Ned, but every application was refused. Even attempts by Maggie Skillion to get Ned new clothes and arrange his solicitor were thwarted. No reason was given but everyone knew that this was a power play. The police had their prize and things would now be done on their terms.

Some expressed concern that poison might be smuggled to him to cheat the hangman but, more disturbingly, this refusal to allow visitors also seemed to restrict the capacity for Ned to be given an effective defence for his trial. Ned and the boys had made the authorities a public laughingstock and now was their time for payback and they weren't going to risk it, even if it meant being underhanded or breaking their own laws if necessary.

In New South Wales when the police had ambushed Ben Hall, they had summarily executed him, pumping his unprotected body full of holes thirty times over as years of frustration and public backlash put strength in their trigger fingers. Ned's armour had not allowed Victoria's police that same satisfaction, so now his suffering was extended as much as possible. Ned considered what hope remained for him and came up with nothing.

***

At the beginning of August, Ned was deemed fit to stand trial. On the appointed day of transfer, he was escorted to a wagonette from the gaol hospital by Castieau, where Sergeant Steele waited in a tweed hat and topcoat. He seemed uncomfortable without a gun and ammunition pouch on him.

"Now, Kelly, it is your game to be quiet. Don't do anything foolish," said Castieau as Ned took his seat.

"Damn it, ain't I always quiet?" Ned replied with a grin.

Ned was no longer in his bloodied and shredded outfit from Glenrowan or in ill-fitting prison greys, but rather had finally received the handsome outfit Maggie had sent for him to wear in court - a neat white shirt with a dickie; checked waistcoat; brown corduroy trousers; a navy-blue serge coat; ostentatious fob chain; and handsome Chelsea boots with undercut heels, custom made to slip his mangled feet into. Ned had taken to parting his hair on the opposite side to normal as he could not properly grip the comb in his right hand. It seemed as if the sunlight invigorated him, and his finery brought out the larrikin in him.

As they trundled down Russell Street, outside he saw a trio of teenage boys riding past. One of the horses threw its head around wildly, gnashing against the bit, and seemed unwilling to move. Ned leaned out of the window and cupped his hands around his mouth.

"I'm the man who can show you how to ride properly," he hollered.

The boy on the disagreeable nag responded by jabbing two fingers up at Ned and instructing him in as few words as possible to proceed and copulate with himself.

The occupants of the wagonette rode in awkward silence to the train station in Newmarket where they were greeted by several plain-clothes constables including Constable Bracken and Constable McIntyre who had shortly before arrived from the police depot in Richmond. A moment later a group of senior police arrived accompanied by none other than the chief commissioner himself. Standish walked up to Kelly and despite being a much shorter man began to eye him up.

"You seem to be recovering admirably, Kelly," Standish said.

"Who are you again?" Ned said sarcastically.

"I'd show a bit more respect if I were in your position, lad."

"Oh yes, I have the utmost respect for British law and its officers. Isn't that obvious?" Ned sneered, looking down his nose at Standish.

Standish gestured for the constables to remove the prisoner. With a constable grabbing each of his arms, Ned was assisted to the train, which comprised of engine, first class carriage and guard van just like the one Standish had sent to Glenrowan months earlier. Ned hobbled across the platform to the guard van and struggled inside. He took a seat by the window and kept his crippled legs extended. It was not long before the train was on its way.

As the train rattled along on its journey, Ned chatted with the constables but made no bones about his feelings towards two of his guards, Steele and Constable Dwyer. He dared not look at Steele except to scowl. Such was his contempt toward the man. He looked at Dwyer, however, with utter disdain.

"You're the bastard who kicked me when I was down, aren't you?" Ned asked Dwyer, who turned his back and refused to respond.

As the train passed through Donnybrook, Ned gestured out of the window.

"That's where I was born," he declared to the assemblage. Truthfully, he didn't know if it was or not, but his mother had often pointed to the same hills and told him as such. He didn't even know how old he was anymore; the years having blurred together.

Every now and then Ned would give commentary on the journey, like a guided tour of his life. He seemed assured that not only were his stories incredibly interesting, but that the half-dozen police escorting him were riveted. In truth, the talking was as much for Ned's own reflection on his journey to that point in his life as anything else, which became clear as he spied the Strathbogie Ranges coming into view.

He rested his head in his hand and sighed. They seemed more majestic from the ground.

"There they are. Shall I ever be there again?" he asked himself. Several of the police gave each other knowing smirks.

Occasionally Ned would break into song, but he would only sing the tunes about his own exploits. His singing voice was flat and unrefined but what he lacked in ability he compensated for with enthusiasm.

"My whole family is musical, you know," Ned explained, "I'm the least gifted singer in my family but music is food for the soul they say. I know a good one, but I best not sing it, or I'll hurt McIntyre's feelings."

It was not long before they approached Glenrowan. The spot where his companions had perished was now marked by a pile of black rubble bookended by chimneys. Ned stiffened and pointed to the fallen tree north of the inn where his freedom had come to an end.

"A great man fell there," he said mournfully.

"What a shame you were the only man out of the lot of them. I expected a proper fight," said Steele.

"Byrne and Hart were plucky and reliable fellows," Ned said.

"Hart was a mere lad. A brat. Not one of you were such good shots as you claimed," Steele said. Ned's eyes burned with a fiery hatred, and he leapt to his feet, yanking his coat off and throwing it in Steele's face.

"I'll have you, Steele. You'll have to run to India to be safe from me," he roared, "Come, take a swing. My chest is one mass of bone. I'm unbreakable!"

He wobbled violently on his damaged legs and was forced to sit. Steele simply turned away. Still wound up, Ned pointed at Bracken.

"There's one man I did not have the heart to shoot."

Bracken shifted uncomfortably and felt Steele's baleful eyes upon him. In fact, he soon realised that all of the police were staring at him. His threat to Steele that fateful June morning had not gone unnoticed or been forgotten by his colleagues.

"Perhaps you ought to have," said Bracken.

"It's a pity about Sherritt," One of the constables said as they drew nearer to their destination.

"What about Sherritt?" Ned asked.

"About Byrne shooting him."

"No, Joe would never do that," Ned responded.

"My oath he did. Blew Sherritt away right in front of his wife and mother-in-law. Could hardly believe it when I heard. I hate to think what will come of his widow."

Ned was unwilling to believe that Joe would destroy his friend rather than follow his orders but saw no point in disputing it further.

"I expect that there will be a provision for her from the reward money," said Ned.

"Unlikely. No, that poor girl has a lot of heartache ahead of her for sure. The place is sitting empty now. They can't sell it - couldn't even give it away because of what happened. Nobody will go near it."

One of the other chimed in, "I heard the girl lost her baby because of what happened. The fright must have been too much for her and she miscarried."

Ned was silenced. This trip had forced him to face the consequences of his war against the police and he did not like what he saw.

When the train arrived in Beechworth, Ned was feeling particularly agitated. As he was jostled towards a cab, he kicked one of the escorting police horses in the leg. The horse responded the way horses do and jumped forward. The horse almost bowled Sergeant Steele over and the trooper riding it tried valiantly to calm the beast while retaining his position in the saddle. Steele grabbed Ned roughly by the arm and clapped the darbies on his wrists as tightly as he could manage.

"Pull a trick like that again and you won't live long enough to hang, I promise you that," Steele seethed.

***

Ned was taken through the massive wrought iron gates of Beechworth Gaol in a cab. These gates had been installed at great expense to the government to prevent the Kelly Gang from breaking out their sympathisers who had been remanded there, but now would be used to prevent the sympathisers from reaching Ned.

Close behind was another cab bearing Constable McIntyre, who was to be the key witness for the trial. It had been decided that the safest place for McIntyre was in the gaol - specifically in the condemned cell. There had been word filtering through the district that the sympathisers intended to kill McIntyre to prevent him giving evidence and the condemned cell offered safety that no other building in Beechworth offered.

Ned was ushered into an office and stripped of his fine clothes down to his underwear. The governor glowered at Ned.

"Come on, off with those. I need to do this examination."

"I refuse," Ned replied defiantly. He folded his arms across his chest. They still bore bandages stained with blood where wounds had refused to heal properly. The governor rolled his eyes and proceeded in spite of Ned's lack of cooperation.

Kelly and McIntyre were interred in their respective cells, Ned below the gallows and McIntyre beside them. McIntyre was anxious about how he may be perceived by his peers and his lodgings only added to his discomfort. Ned, meanwhile, ruminated on the foregone conclusion of the hearing.

As Ned lay in his cell dozing, he was awakened when his solicitor was ushered in. Thin and intense with grey-green eyes and a pointed ginger beard, David Gaunson was something of a renegade in the legal world and exactly the man Ned needed for any chance of success. Ned studied Gaunson for a moment.

"Good evening," Ned said. Though he had not seen this man before, he knew that Maggie had organised a solicitor for him as she had gotten a letter to him via Castieau.

"Well, Kelly, I do not want to keep you up too late tonight; I have come up to know what you wish done in the morning about a remand. I myself think a remand ought to be applied for, as I know nothing of the facts of the case, and I do not think I can defend you until I have heard from you a full statement of the facts. Moreover, it is very necessary to thoroughly understand that whosoever is to defend you, there must be implicit confidence between you and them."

"That is very true," Ned said thoughtfully.

"Your eldest sister and Lloyd asked me to act for you, but am I to understand that it is with your full concurrence and wish that I step in?" Gaunson said as he sat on the end of Ned's bunk.

"Quite so. I can depend my life on my sister, and as soon as I got her letter today, strongly recommending you, I put confidence in you directly."

Ned sat up with some effort, "Until today I have had no chance to get their advice or exercise a choice on their recommendation. I have been kept like a wild beast. If they were afraid to let anyone come near me, they might have kept at a distance and watched, but it seems to me to be unjust, when I am on trial for my life, to refuse to allow those I put confidence in to come within cooee of me. Why, they won't so much as let me have a change of clothes brought in. When I came into the gaol here, they made me strip off all my clothes except my pants, and I would not do that."

Gaunson nodded his understanding and proceeded to take out his notebook. Ned spoke at length about his exploits and Gaunson made his notes, capturing his client's words to the best of his capacity in order to understand him.

"All I want is a full and fair trial, and a chance to make myself heard. Until now, the police have had all the say and have had it all their own way. If I get a full and fair trial, I don't care how it goes; but I know this: the public will see that I was hunted and hounded on from step to step. They will see that I am not the monster I have been made out to be. What I have done has been under strong provocation."

***

The morning of the committal hearing arrived quietly. Ned was nervous but made an effort to hide it. Roused by the guard, Ned stood in the doorway of his cell as it was opened. He walked forward and looked up to where McIntyre stood against the railing outside the condemned cell. Between them the gallows loomed ominously.

"What a pity they should hang a fine fellow like Ned Kelly up there," Ned mused aloud. He returned his gaze to McIntyre who looked haggard and pale. Ned smirked. "Still; better than a wombat hole, hey, McIntyre?"

McIntyre frowned at Ned who was amused at his own poor taste in humour. McIntyre retreated into the condemned cell to freshen up. As he stood by the hand basin, he felt his chest tightening and his breathing became shallow. He tried to slow his breathing down, but his heart was pounding so hard he could hear the blood rushing in his ears. He gripped the edge of the basin and closed his eyes in an effort to regain composure. It was going to be a difficult day.

***

As the players took their positions in the courtroom there was a buzz in the air. The gallery was full, and still more people clamoured outside for a chance to get in. The inner circle of sympathisers filled up as many of the seats as possible near the dock. Maggie Skillion sat with Tom Lloyd; nearby Kate Lloyd sat with Kate Kelly. Beyond them were figures such as Dick Hart, Wild Wright, Henry Perkins, Joe Ryan, the Delaneys and McAuliffes. Sergeant Steele stood by the dock in full uniform waiting for the arrival of the magistrate and the prisoner.

When Ned was brought out from the holding cell behind the dock, he was given a stool to sit on and assumed an imperious pose with his left hand clutching his lapel and his mangled right hand resting on the banister of the dock.

As silence was called for, Ned caught the sound of a gentleman with squeaky shoes trying to move surreptitiously from his seat and failing. He grinned at the man who in turn blushed with embarrassment.

The proceedings began in earnest with Gaunson and Smyth, the prosecutor, duelling like gentleman warriors; the witnesses were their point of attack. Gaunson felt he was beginning to get ahead, and things were proceeding smoothly but had he known his client better he would have known not to assume the smoothness would continue.

Constable McIntyre moved hesitantly into the witness box and clasped the rail tightly while giving evidence. He spoke at length about the events leading up to and including Stringybark Creek and also noted how he had watched Mrs. Kelly breastfeeding while she stood trial for aiding the attempted murder of Constable Fitzpatrick. Ned took smug satisfaction as McIntyre alluded to Fitzpatrick's lack of moral character.

As the proceedings unfolded, Ned became aware of the artist Julian Ashton sketching him from within the audience. Ned took umbrage at his likeness being captured without his permission and decided to put a stop to it.

He asked his guards for a possum skin blanket to protect him from the cold. Within moments a scarlet-lined fur blanket was given to Ned who immediately draped it over his head. This absurd behaviour caught everyone's attention and murmurs began to rumble through the crowd. Ashton got the hint and vacated his position. It was no matter to him as he was a fast worker and already had enough down to finish the piece later. Meanwhile, Gaunson massaged his forehead in frustration. It was his first indication of things to come.

***

A recess was called and as the crowd dispersed, Tom and Maggie pressed through the mess of people to the dock where Maggie thrust out her hand. Ned grasped her fingers.

"Neddie, I've tried so hard, but they won't let me see you!"

Ned was promptly dragged away by the constables.

"It seems they won't let me see you even now. Goodbye," Ned replied sadly.

"They're just a bunch of curs!" Maggie shouted as her brother disappeared behind the door to the holding cell.

Ned's voice rang out from out of view, "There's one native that's no cur and he will show them that yet!"

During the recess, Gaunson ploughed through a stack of newspapers trying to get to grips with the case. He sighed as he looked at the clock knowing it was not enough time. He knew that the case had been sabotaged. The authorities had done everything they could to make sure Ned Kelly went to the gallows, but they underestimated Gaunson's tenacity. This was no longer a simple murder case to him; this was about the bigger picture of the abuse of power, and he was determined to lift the stone and set the roaches scurrying for all to see.

***

When court resumed, McIntyre was recalled to answer questions about the discrepancies in his testimony. Ned watched keenly.

"May we fetch a chair for the witness please, he has been unwell the past few days," Smyth asked.

"No, no I'm fine to stand," McIntyre responded. He couldn't risk the ridicule that would be levelled at him if he was unable to stand up to give his evidence, no matter how much he really needed to be seated.

The questioning began in earnest and McIntyre responded as ably as he could, but the more he tried to recall his evidence the more he shook and the more he shook the more he questioned his own memories. Thinking of the carnage brought back to his mind the feeling of absolute terror and the fight or flight response that had made him act fast enough to survive and raise the alarm. If not for that instinct, he would be buried with his comrades in Mansfield now. By the time the constable stood down, Gaunson was convinced that he had struck a nerve and McIntyre was on the ropes.

At the conclusion of the evidence, he stared McIntyre square in the eyes.

"Well, sir, I'll leave you to the hands of a gentleman in the Supreme Court far more able to turn you inside out than I am."

***

When news had reached Sydney, that Ned Kelly had been captured alive and was to face trial, his brother Jim Kelly had been working as a bootmaker and keeping a low profile, having only just gotten out of gaol in Wagga Wagga. Jim had waited for news from his sisters before acting and as Ned's case was about to be examined in Beechworth, he had decided to return home to support his family.

The journey back across the border was a long one but Jim, like his brothers, was an excellent bushman and knew the best ways to get back to Greta. In the time since his release, he had cultivated a short beard and cut a dramatically different figure when he arrived at the Kelly selection in Greta. As he passed through the gate, he could not recognise much of what lay before him, but he knew in his gut this was home. A seemingly tame kangaroo munched on grass beside the kitchen garden where he spotted vegetables growing poorly.

Inside, Kate hovered around the window looking out at the new arrival unable to recognise him, but as he turned the Kelly features were unmistakable. Kate rushed out and embraced her brother tearfully.

"Steady on, old girl," Jim exclaimed. Kate guided him inside and brought him up to speed on the happenings of the past few months over bread and butter. Jim sat in stunned silence, unable to comprehend a word of it.

In his mind, he half-expected Dan to come waltzing in carrying a 'roo over his shoulder, proud as punch, or his mother to come bustling about with a broom to shoo him off to get to work mending fences or tending the farm.

In the time he'd spent in gaol his whole family had been torn apart. He felt incredible guilt that his stupidity had seen him taken out of the equation for so long. He vowed to remain and protect his sisters.

***

The committal continued in Beechworth for several days in August before a ruling was given. At the conclusion of the hearing, Ned's fate was sealed. Committed for a trial in Melbourne, away from his friends and family, Ned still held onto the faint hope of a fair trial where the jury would see his side of events, but the writing was on the wall.

Gaunson felt dejected at the outcome at this stage as much as he was frustrated at the veritable circus he had been brought into but knew there was more to be done.

Meanwhile, Jim promised Maggie he would stay in Greta to look after Kate and the little ones so that she and Tom could be in Melbourne for Ned. It was a gesture that the elder sibling appreciated, but her mind was so burdened already that it made little difference.

Maggie and Tom tried everything they could to raise money to get Ned the best legal defence and save him from the noose, but it was impossible. There was no more money from the bank robberies, and it seemed no sympathisers were willing to donate.

Maggie sat at the dining table in her hut across from Tom with her head in her hands. Her children were on the floor nearby playing with boiled sheep knuckles.

"I don't know what to do Tom," said Maggie, "they were all happy to take the money from Euroa and Jerilderie, no questions asked, but not one of the sympathisers is prepared to throw in a pound when Ned needs their help the most."

"You know how it is, Maggie," Tom replied, "most of them are all talk and the ones that matter don't have much to give. Gaunson wouldn't just let Ned hang, not after all the work he's put in. I'm sure he has a plan."

***

Since the end of the committal, Gaunson had been attempting to procure Hickman Molesworth for the defence. Molesworth was a battle-hardened legal veteran, but his fee was more than what could be raised, not that Molesworth had even entertained taking on such a case in the first place. Gaunson had three days to come up with an alternative plan.

"Could you not appear for Ned again?" asked Maggie Skillion.

"I'm afraid I am not qualified to appear in the Supreme Court as Ned's barrister. I am only a solicitor," Gaunson replied. Maggie's heart sank and she stared at the floor of Gaunson's office. Her joints ached.

"What's to be done? We don't have a lot of money and I doubt the crown is going to dole out any more funds for Ned," Tom said.

"Of course," Gaunson replied, "I can't in all good conscience allow the continuation of the abuse of power we have seen, nor do I believe Ned should hang, but I can't be the man at the front. Now, I know of a junior barrister named Henry Bindon. He's pretty green, but that's good for us because it means he's pliable and cheap. My recommendation is that you employ him as the barrister, and I will stay on as counsel and guide him through the trial."

"Has he ever done a case like this before?" asked Maggie.

"No, not of this magnitude, but Bindon's lack of acquaintance with the case will give us a perfect excuse to adjourn and build the case up. If they're going to rush things to hasten their desired outcome, then we must do all we can to stall them."

****

Henry Massey Bindon was stout and bearded and overconfident. He was thirty-seven and had only been practicing as a barrister for ten months, yet he entered the Supreme Court with complete optimism in his abilities. He had with him a document of more than eighty pages provided to him by Gaunson detailing the case and the suggested approach to the defence. Ned took up his place in the dock, the jurors sat in their box and all in the court except the defendant rose for the judge, Redmond Barry.

It seemed fate had brought them to this moment; one last battle between Ned Kelly and the man who had helped lay the path to guide him here. As a child, Ned had watched Redmond Barry place the black square on his bewigged head and sentence his uncle Jim to death for burning the family's house down and nearly killing them all. The experience of giving evidence against kin was difficult for a young boy who had recently lost his father. Ned felt that, regardless of the fact that he was a victim in the matter, Barry was casting judgement upon him just as much as his uncle.

But then more importantly, Barry had committed the ultimate offence in Ned's eyes years later - that of gaoling his mother for three years with an infant at her breast.

Ned had been told that at the conclusion of his mother's trial that had he been there, Barry would have given him fifteen years for attempting to murder Fitzpatrick. This judge was a man Ned had fantasised about doing unspeakable things to and now, here he was. But Barry was not as Ned remembered him. Now he was aged, fat, and jowly and his stern eyes were adorned with long, white brows that curled up like a wizard's.

As Barry took his place, he seemed to struggle to breathe somewhat, exhausted by the mere act of walking up a few wooden stairs. Barry glared at Ned who was seated due to his injuries. As Barry settled into his throne the rest of the court were also seated and proceedings began.

Witnesses were brought out in quick succession through the trial, ranging through all of the Kelly Gang's career: prisoners from Euroa; bank staff from Jerilderie; police from Glenrowan and so on. All stood in the box to have their say and each one that had conversed with Ned about the death of Lonigan demonstrated that his story was consistent throughout each retelling. When he had called on Lonigan and McIntyre to bail up, Lonigan had gotten behind cover and was about to shoot when Ned fired, killing him. There remained a niggling doubt that it was a wilful murder as time and again it was reported that Ned stated that "if I had not shot them, they would have shot me". This seemed like a reasonable point to build a case of self-defence upon.

***

There was one piece of evidence that could change the course of the whole trial and prove Ned was innocent of wilful murder: the letter Ned had written in Jerilderie with Joe Byrne. Within it was Ned's account in, mostly, his own words of the shootings and his motivation for pulling the trigger. David Gaunson knew this was the key to the trial and called Bindon into his office.

Bindon had taken his cues from Gaunson throughout proceedings but was confident in his capacity to helm such a huge case. He had grown resentful of Gaunson's interference, especially as out of the two of them Gaunson was the least qualified.

"David, have you actually read this thing?" Bindon said, "if the jury were unsure if he was guilty already then this would make it a certainty. It's full of threats of torture and revenge against police officers and any-one helping them. If we allow this to be admitted, then our case is dead."

"This is the only chance we have for Ned to tell his own account of what happened!" Gaunson snapped.

"If this is the best you can come up with you may as well put his head in the noose yourself."

Gaunson fumed but concluded the meeting by instructing Bindon to see him the next day for a meeting. He assumed that after sleeping on it Bindon might change his mind.

Bindon, however, did not heed the call to meet Gaunson and sub-sequently, when the letter was raised in court Bindon rose to his feet.

"Your honour, I move to suppress this document as it may act as self-incrimination against my client and pervert the course of justice," Bindon stated. He intended to fight based on the inconsistencies in McIntyre's statements. Smyth offered no resistance to the suppression of this evidence, knowing that the prosecution case was stronger with only one side of the events being examined.

"I will allow this," Judge Barry responded. The last hope for Ned's plea of self-defence to be heard vanished like a gambler's paycheque.

It seemed fate had brought them to this moment; one last battle between Ned Kelly and the man who had helped lay the path to guide him here.

Ned shook his head and gazed into middle-distance. He felt as if he had been cheated by fate or at the least sabotaged by ineptitude. As much as Ned was dismayed, so too was Gaunson who made no secret of his feelings, holding his head in his hands for all the court to see. Smyth the prosecutor smirked.

***

It seemed as if it were deliberate that the trial would be reaching its conclusion on the anniversary of the Stringybark Creek tragedy. Two years to the day, Ned Kelly resumed his place in the dock and waited for the inevitable. In the gallery throughout the trial had been a handful of his close sympathisers, Maggie and Tom, Dick and Ettie Hart, Denny McAuliffe and Kate Lloyd among others. If nothing else, Ned took comfort in their presence. However, by the last day the numbers had dwindled, and visibly so.

On the last day the prosecutor and the defence gave their final speeches to the jury. Smyth argued that Ned's behaviour demonstrated a habitual criminal who would think nothing of looting the bodies of those he had murdered in cold blood. Bindon, however, stuck to his plan of laying doubt upon McIntyre's testimony and went further to state that all information about Ned's actions following the death of Lonigan were irrelevant to the charge his client was facing.

Ned's supporters gradually left the court as the inevitable became too painful to bear. Only Kate Lloyd remained in the end. Ned tried to hide the hurt that his sisters and Ettie were not there to show support in his moment of crisis. The jury were sent out to deliberate and returned after half an hour with the guilty verdict.

Ned was overwhelmed with disappointment and anger. Barry turned to the defendant and asked if he wished to make a statement.

"Well, it is rather too late for me to speak now," Ned replied snidely, "I thought of speaking this morning and all day, but there was little use, and there is little use blaming anyone now. Nobody knew about my case except myself, and I wish I had insisted on being allowed to examine the witnesses."

Barry looked at Ned with disdain. This was the kind of response he had expected - a tirade of self-aggrandising and fatalistic ramblings. Barry had lost count of the number of men like this he had encountered in courts over the years.

"If I had examined them, I am confident I would have thrown a different light on the case. It is not that I fear death. I fear it as little as to drink a cup of tea," Ned continued with barely a moment spared to catch breath, "On the evidence that has been given, no juryman could have given any other verdict. That is my opinion, but as I say, if I had examined the witnesses it would have shown matters in a different light, because no man understands the case as I do myself. I do not blame anybody - neither Mr. Bindon nor Mr. Gaunson - but Mr. Bindon knew nothing about my case. I lay blame on myself that I did not get up yesterday and examine the witnesses, but I thought that if I did so it would look like bravado and flashness."

Barry remained unmoved. It was time for him to say his piece.
"Edward Kelly, the verdict pronounced by the jury is one that you must have already expected."
"Yes; under the circumstances," Ned interrupted.

"No circumstances that I can conceive could have altered the result of your trial," Barry bit back.

"Perhaps not, from what you can now conceive; but if you had heard me examine the witnesses it would have been different."

Barry scowled. "I will give you credit for all the skill you appear to desire to assume."

"No, I don't wish to assume anything. There is no flashness or bravado about me. It is not that I want to save my life, because I know I would have been capable of clearing myself of the charge, and I could have saved my life in spite of all against me," Ned said. Barry's face began to go a noticeable shade of scarlet, his lips tightened to an impatient scowl.

"The facts are so numerous and so convincing, not only as regards the original offence with which you are charged, but with respect to a long series of transactions covering a period of eighteen months, that no rational person would hesitate to arrive at any other conclusion but that the verdict of the jury is irresistible, and that it is right!" Barry barked in his mangled Irish brogue, dulled from years of mingling with the higher end of society. "I have no desire whatever to inflict upon you any personal remarks," he said, "It is not becoming that I should endeavour to aggravate the sufferings with which your mind must be sincerely agitated."

"No, I don't think that. My mind is as easy as the mind of any man in this world, as I am prepared to show before God and man," Ned said with a smug half-grin. He was rather enjoying making the judge squirm.

"It is blasphemous for you to say that. You appear to revel in the idea of having put men to death!"

"More men than me have put men to death, but I am the last man in the world that would take a man's life two years ago, even if my own life was at stake; and I am confident if I thought a man would shoot me, I would give him a chance of keeping his life, and would part rather with my own. But if I knew that through him innocent persons' lives were at stake, I certainly would have to shoot him if he forced me to do so, but I would want to know that he was really going to take innocent life," Ned declared as he gesticulated wildly, like an impassioned preacher.

"Your statement involves a clearly proved charge of perjury against a phalanx of witnesses."

"I dare say," Ned replied, unfazed, "but a day will come at a bigger court than this when we shall see which is right and which is wrong. No matter how long a man lives he is bound to come to judgment somewhere, and as well here as anywhere. It will be different the next time they have a Kelly trial, for they are not all killed!" Ned paused to allow the chamber to echo dramatically. "It would have been for the good of the Crown had I examined the witnesses, and I would have stopped a lot of the reward, I can assure you; and I do not know... but I will do it yet if allowed."

Barry leaned forward and glared at Ned intensely.

"An offence of this kind is of no ordinary character. Murders had been discovered which had been committed under circumstances of great atrocity. They proceeded from motives other than that which actuated you. They have had their origin in many sources. Some have been committed from a sordid desire to take from others the property they had acquired, some from jealousy, some from a desire for revenge; but yours is a more aggravated crime, and one of larger proportions for with a party of men you took up arms against society, organised as it is for mutual protection and for respect of law."

"That is the way the evidence came out here," Ned responded, returning Barry's glare, "It appeared that I deliberately took up arms of my own accord and induced the other three men to join me for the purpose of doing nothing but shooting down the police."

The two combatants stared each other down. Barry leaned back to address the court.

"In new communities where the bonds of society are not so well locked together as in older countries, there is, unfortunately, a class which disregards the evil consequences of crime. Foolish, inconsiderate, ill-conducted, unprincipled youths unfortunately abound, and unless they are made to consider the consequences of crime, they are led to imitate notorious felons, whom they regard as self-made heroes! It is right, therefore, that they should be asked to consider and reflect upon what the life of a felon is."

Barry paused to catch his breath.

"A felon who has cut himself off from all decencies, all the affections, charities, and all the obligations of society is as helpless and degraded as a wild beast of the field. He has nowhere to lay his head, he has no one to prepare him the comforts of life, he suspects his friends, he dreads his enemies, he is in constant alarm lest his pursuers should reach him, and his only hope is that he might use his life in what he considers a glorious struggle for existence. That is the life of the outlaw or felon, and it would be well for those young men who are so foolish as to consider that it is brave of a man to sacrifice the lives of his fellow creatures in carrying out his own wild ideas to see that it is a life to be avoided by every possible means, and to reflect that the unfortunate termination of your life is a miserable death," Barry boomed as he returned his gaze to Kelly.

"New South Wales joined with Victoria in providing ample inducement to persons to assist in having you and your companions apprehended, but by some spell which I cannot understand - a spell which exists in all lawless communities more or less, which may be attributed either to a sympathy for the outlaws or a dread of the consequences which would result from the performance of their duty - no persons were found who would be tempted by the reward."

Ned looked into the audience at Kate Lloyd as Barry spoke. The girl was barely holding back tears as Barry's rant continued.

"The love of country, the love of order, the love of obedience to law have been set aside for reasons difficult to explain, and there is something extremely wrong in a country where a lawless band of men are able to live for eighteen months disturbing society. During your short life you have stolen according to your own statements over two hundred horses."

"Who proved that?" Ned snapped indignantly.

"More than one witness has testified that you made the statement on several occasions," Barry replied dourly.

"That charge has never been proved against me, and it is held in English law that a man is innocent until found guilty," Ned protested petulantly.

"You are self-accused!" Barry howled in frustration, he felt his patience running out, "The statement was made voluntarily by yourself. Then you and your companions committed attacks on two banks and appropriated therein large sums of money amounting to several thousands of pounds. Further, I cannot conceal from myself the fact that an expenditure of £50,000 had been rendered necessary in consequence of the acts with which you and your party have been connected. We have had samples of felons and their careers, such as those of Bradley and O'Connor, Clarke, Gardiner, Melville, Morgan, Scott, and Smith, all of whom have come to ignominious deaths," Barry said, invoking the names of some of the most notorious bushrangers Australia had ever produced, many of them tried by himself.

"Still, the effect expected from their punishment has not been produced. This is much to be deplored. When such examples as these are so often repeated society must be reorganised, or it must soon be seriously affected. Your unfortunate and miserable companions have died a death which probably you might rather envy, but you are not afforded the opportunity."

"I don't think there is much proof that they did die that death," Ned said, imagining Dan and Steve cowering in the burning inn with guns in their hands pointed to their own heads. A coward's death.

"In your case, the law will be carried out by its officers. The gentlemen of the Jury have done their duty. My duty will be to forward to the proper quarter the notes of your trial, and to lay, as I am required to do, before the Executive any circumstances connected with your trial that may be required. I can hold out to you no hope. I do not see that I can entertain the slightest reason for saying you can expect anything. I desire to spare you any more pain, and I absolve myself from anything said willingly in any of my utterances that may have unnecessarily increased the agitation of your mind. I am now to pronounce your sentence."

Barry placed a black cloth square atop his white horsehair wig. The collective went instantly quiet, the altercation now over.

"Edward Kelly, you shall be taken from here to a place of incarceration. There, on a day appointed by the executive council, you shall be hanged by the neck until you be dead. May the Lord have mercy upon your soul."

Barry brought his gavel down with considerably more enthusiasm than normal. If Barry had thought that was the end of it, he was mistaken. Ned Kelly had one more barb for the hanging judge.

"I will go a little further than that and say I will see you there where I go!" Ned boomed from the dock. Barry scowled and waved a hand at the dock as the crowd erupted into astounded chatter. Kate Lloyd began to weep.

"Remove the prisoner," Barry ordered over the din of the excited crowd.

Ned's last defiant act was to blow Kate Lloyd a kiss as he was dragged out of the court by two constables.

****

The return to Melbourne Gaol was crushing. Though the court neighboured the gaol, it felt like an eternity returning behind the cold, bluestone walls. Ned was taken to the baths, stripped of his fine clothes, and ordered to bathe. His nakedness revealed the full extent of his injuries, puckered and puffed scar tissue was all over his arms and legs, his knee and pelvis were mangled from the shots that brought him down at Glenrowan. He attempted to cover his manhood but quickly realised he needed to focus on maintaining his balance on his weak legs as he stepped into the bath.

The water had already been used by innumerable convicts prior and filth floated about him as he dunked his arms. He wanted to cry but refused to allow the guards the satisfaction of seeing him broken.

When he was dried, he was handed his prison greys - the last outfit he would ever wear. Soon his legs were bound in iron shackles, riveted shut by a blacksmith. The heavy chains between his ankles were suspended by a cord tied to his belt to stop them scuffing the floors. His already laboured walking became agonisingly slow as he was marched into the old section of the gaol and to his new cell. In here he had no bed like he had when he was in the hospital, just the usual coconut mat and moth-eaten wool blanket.

With the closing of the cell door, Ned closed his eyes and prayed. He begged God to intervene but knew he could expect no answer.

16

The Last Days

Ned Kelly's death sentence was not taken as a last word by his supporters. Maggie Skillion sought out David Gaunson and demanded assistance to have the condemned man reprieved. Gaunson, a staunch abolitionist of capital punishment, agreed. Within days, a coalition had been formulated with David Gaunson and his brother William, a taller, darker likeness of his brother, as the spearhead.

In early November, a huge meeting of reprieve supporters was held at the Hippodrome in Melbourne. Four thousand people were crammed inside and dozens more were outside vying for a way in. The result of the meeting was a resolution in favour of a petition for reprieve, on the grounds that Ned was not guilty of murder as he had fired on the police at Stringybark Creek in self-defence.

In the days following, Melbourne was chaos. Huge protests marched through the streets as a demonstration of the sentiment against the hanging. Police were ill-equipped to handle the thousands of angry pro-testors and merely stood on the footpaths that flanked the processions to protect the rest of the population from any potential conflict.

Meetings were had with government officials as the Executive Council deliberated on the matter of when Ned was to be hanged, rather than if. Kate Kelly became a prominent member of the effort, the pretty seventeen-year-old marching around Melbourne with William Gaunson, meeting with politicians, all the while clad in her black mourning wear in deep grief for the untimely death of her beloved brother, Dan.

While the deliberation met with the government, petitions were doing the rounds throughout the city. Ettie Hart, Kate Lloyd and Maggie Skillion gathered signatures on hastily printed bills from anyone who would stop and give them. They believed that with enough signatures they could prove public sentiment was against the execution and force the Executive Council to change its mind. It was optimism bordering on delusion.

Jim Kelly and Wild Wright ventured into the city and joined the women. They had a very different approach to gathering goodwill, opting to shake hands with as many pub patrons as possible. One young man also made a point of showing off a small collection of cards he had bought to the men. They were carte de visite photographs depicting a replica of Ned's armour and his last stand at Glenrowan. The teen with the cards seemed excited to show them off.

"Where did they come from?" Jim asked.

"There's a bloke selling them from his studio on Burke Street; Burman. He says he was really there at Glenrowan. Look how close he got!"

"That's not my brother," Jim frowned.

Ettie Hart, Kate Lloyd and Maggie Skillion gathered signatures on hastily printed bills from anyone who would stop and give them.

"Sure, it is, look," the young man insisted, showing one of the cards. On the presented card two men dressed as plainclothes troopers appeared to be grappling Ned Kelly, prone and still dressed in his body armour, wearing an unconvincing false beard. There was a tarpaulin draped over the log beside the men and the background was clearly a backdrop, with a support beam from the wall of the studio visible at the edge of the photograph.

"And this photographer is selling these?"

"Yeah, only a few shillings for the lot."

Jim said no more about the offensive articles but resolved to make his displeasure known to this Burman character at the soonest opportunity. It was apparently not enough to merely recreate such a moment, but to try and profit from it to wit. As far as Jim was concerned it was unconscionable.

The family rented rooms at the Robert Burns Hotel on Lonsdale Street and used the pub as a base of operations. There were unlikely companions here that the family were surprised to encounter. Ann Jones and her children had been staying at the hotel since the week before, still homeless from the siege. The Kellys, upon discovering this fact, made a point of giving her their sympathies for her losses. This kindness was meaningful to Ann who had received nothing but scorn and suspicion from everyone in Glenrowan following the siege, but especially from the police who had been keeping tabs on her movements.

That night Kate Kelly and Jane Jones chatted by the fire about what had happened at Glenrowan. Kate wanted to know about what happened to Dan.

"He was sweet," said Jane.

"Had you under his spell, did he?" Kate asked warmly with a little smirk.

"Oh yes, and I don't think I was the only one that was sweet on him. I was just the lucky one he was sweet on in return."

"Dan always had a way with the girls. I can remember one morning when Ma got up early and found him with a girl from Wangaratta asleep in the stable. She made the girl get dressed while she chased Danny around the selection with her broom. You should have seen him running like a headless chook, naked as the day he was born!" Kate laughed and Jane blushed. For the first time in almost six months, she smiled. However, it soon gave way to tears and the two girls consoled each other.

***

Every day thousands of signatures were added to the petition, but the press looked upon the movement with disgust and disdain. It was reported that the signatures were merely those of the criminal classes, the illiterate or those with a political axe to grind rather than those sympathetic to Ned.

Ettie had struggled to maintain her energy to campaign and elected to briefly return to Wangaratta with Dick to recharge then return to fight. Moreover, the gaol continued to deny her access to Ned. Her letters were blocked and her requests to visit him were rejected. The emotional toll as much as the physical one had left her completely burned out and she barely uttered a word on the trip home. Such needless cruelty had cut deep.

Agitation for the reprieve continued despite the press condemnation, with a procession of ladies led by Maggie Skillion, and Kate Kelly on the eighth of November starting from the Robert Burns Hotel. They marched to government house but were refused entry. Upon this news spreading through the network of supporters, another demonstration of two hundred marched to the Town Hall. The demonstration was hardly peaceful with the protestors bursting inside. Police descended upon the elegant stone building, waving batons around as they subdued and ejected rowdy protestors, many of whom, it was believed, had no idea what the demonstration was even about.

The demonstration continued and the protestors were joined by William Gaunson, Jim Kelly, and Wild Wright. They set course for Government House; a sea of angry men and women, some bloodied from the violence at the Town Hall, stomping over the Princes Bridge unhindered like the Gauls marching on Rome. The police rushed ahead on horseback to seal the Domain gates. The deputation of Maggie, Kate, Jim and Wild, led by Gaunson, rode to the Domain in a hansom cab, breathless and anxious.

When the crowd reached the Domain gates they were held back, but Gaunson and the deputation were permitted. They walked with furious pace to the house, Jim Kelly and Wild Wright carrying bags full of signed petitions. They were met with the private secretary of the governor, Captain Le Patourel.

"Quite an entrance you've made!" Le Patourel said with a chuckle.

"We've come to see the Governor," said Gaunson. The secretary shook his head.

"I'm afraid his Excellency cannot receive any deputation here today."

"We have petitions for the reprieve of my brother. There's more than thirty thousand signatures," Kate Kelly said gesturing to the bags.

"You can forward the documents to his Excellency who is at the treasury building until two this afternoon. That is when the Executive

Council will be meeting. My dear, I wish you the best of luck. I will meet you there," Le Patourel said planting a hand on Kate's shoulder.

As the group returned to the cab William Gaunson gave a plan of action. Maggie complained that her knees were in too much pain to continue on.

"Jim and Isaiah, you two go back to the hotel with Margaret, lead this group away so we can get to the treasury safely and quickly. Kate and I can handle the bags."

The plan was agreed upon and Jim, Wild and Maggie led the demonstration with much fanfare. Uncouth men from the slums grabbed the men and shook their hands uttering phrases like "bloody champion" and "fuck those coppers", which were not exactly helping raise the tone of the affair. When they reached the Robert Burns Hotel, the horde was not satisfied to end things at the door and dozens of them pushed their way inside, searching the rooms for the pair. Wild absolutely adored the limelight and happily accepted every drink that was bought for him, the earnings from which almost made up for the wreckage caused by the unwanted visitors.

Meanwhile, Kate and Gaunson arrived at the treasury building and walked up the sandstone steps with heavy hearts and sweating palms. By the building another thousand people had caught wind of their movements and gathered to gawp. Kate mused quietly to Gaunson.

"You know, I don't think I'd mind all this quite so much if it weren't for the fact that any number of that mob would be just as eager in wanting to watch Neddy hang as save him. I hate them."

William Gaunson looked ahead and silently prayed that their efforts were not in vain. Once inside they were taken to a waiting room where

Le Patourel collected the petitions. They remained there until after the Executive Council had made their decision: Ned Kelly would hang on the eleventh of November.

* * *

The following morning, as Ned lay on his coconut mat humming a hymn, he was roused by Governor Castieau. Ned sat up painfully anticipating good news in response to the reprieve efforts.

"I have important news from the Executive Council, Ned."

"Oh, yes?"

"They have decided to uphold their decision. I'm sorry," Castieau said softly with a sigh.

Ned gazed back at him impassively.

"I see. When?" asked Ned.

"The morning of the eleventh," Castieau replied.

"What day is it today?"

"The ninth."

"Well, it is short," Ned said, "Such is life."

Castieau left Ned to consider his fate. However, rather than ruminate on the turn of events, Ned occupied himself with reading the scriptures and praying. He had accepted his time in this world was over, he had to focus on preparing for the next one.

* * *

On November the tenth, Charles Nettleton adjusted his camera in the courtyard of the Melbourne Gaol. Before him stood Ned Kelly, his rumpled and ill-fitting grey woollen uniform making him almost camouflaged with the bluestone wall of the hospital building. His beard was longer than he'd ever let it grow before, his hands were far too crippled to hold a razor or clippers. His long hair had been painstakingly oiled into a sort of pompadour, coiled up on top of his skull. Around his neck, a pale blue handkerchief embroidered with flowers covered the apparatus from the stand that allowed him to stay upright, a device commonly used by photographers to take memento mori portraits of the recently deceased.

His legs wobbled under the strain of holding up his body, but there he stood with his feet out turned to show off the handsome boots Maggie had bought him for the trial. The leather belt that stopped his chains from dragging held up his trousers. Ned lifted the cord that ran from the belt using his weak left hand to elevate the iron chains between his feet. His crippled right hand rested on his hip, his mangled thumb tucked out of view, a plain ring visible on his middle finger. He puffed out his chest and held his breath as long as he could to steady himself until Nettleton gave him the all clear to relax.

With that Ned collapsed, two warders clutching the condemned man under the armpits to prevent him toppling. They assisted him back inside the gaol, his legs barely able to move for the weight of the irons. Ned said not a word as he passed Nettleton, he merely shot him a weary expression and a nod. Nettleton removed the plate negative from the camera and stored it with the two other exposures he had taken.

He paused for a moment to consider how this man had changed since he photographed him as a hardened eighteen-year-old six years prior. He remembered how intimidating he looked with his broad, chiselled features and his piercing hazel eyes, how he said not a word but took directions from the photographer precisely. He remembered the haunted look in the boy's eyes as he entered the room and sat next to the window, looking out at a freedom he had not tasted in months.

Now he was here waiting to be put down like a sick animal. Taking portraits in prison was a thankless task for Nettleton, so often reading years of trauma and broken spirits in the faces of the individuals that sat before him, very often wondering if they'd ever again see the world outside of prison walls. He felt a sinking feeling as he realised that the man who had just stood before him was hours away from death and would never know freedom again.

He shook his head and focused on clearing away his equipment.

***

His appearance still groomed; Ned met with his family for the last time in the condemned cell. One after the other, he bade farewell to his kin through iron bars.

When Jim arrived, accompanied by Kate and Grace, Ned hardly recognised him. As they spoke Ned's face was stern. He held Jim's hand tightly.

"Jim, make sure you look after Ma and the kids. You're all they've got now. Keep them safe."

Jim nodded and wiped away a tear.

Kate tried to speak but no words came. Ned kissed her hand and told her he wished he could be around to see her marry and give him nieces and nephews.

"I'm sorry I wasn't there when you needed me to protect you, Kitty. Can you forgive me?" Ned said solemnly. Kate stood on her tiptoes and kissed her brother's cheek.

"When you see Danny, tell him I miss him," Kate whispered.

Ned reached out and stroked Grace's head. "Farewell, my sweet baby sister. Please, let the people know and understand how the police have treated you. Don't let this have all been for nothing."

Next, he saw Tom Lloyd. Tom was a mess, his eyes red from crying before he'd even seen his cousin. They held hands tightly and Ned instructed Tom where to find his hidden treasure - a stock saddle concealed in a tree stump. He wished Tom the best with Maggie.

"What do you mean Ned? It's not like that..."

"Of course, it is. I've seen the way you two are with each other. Be happy. Live the life I never could. I want my nieces and nephews to grow up strong and smart like their mother."

"Alright, Ned. Alright."

When Maggie Skillion came, she held her brother through the bars as tight as she could.

"I did everything I could, Neddy!"

"I know, I know. Calm yourself, old girl!"

"I'm so sorry I failed you," Maggie said.

"Here, now. I haven't seen you this upset since Mr. Patrick," said Ned.

"Mr. Patrick?"

"Don't you remember? You found a little currawong chick out of his nest when we was all little and you carried him around all day looking for his Ma. You called him Mr. Patrick. You cried for so long after he died, Ma tried to get the priest to tell you at school he was in heaven with the angels just so you'd calm," Ned said with a chuckle. Maggie allowed herself to smile.

"You're a mite more important to me than a bloody currawong! What will my Ellen and Jack ever do without their uncle Ned?"

Ned gave a weak smile. "Have you seen Ettie?"

Maggie shook her head, "They won't allow her to see you. We tried. She's in Melbourne but those bastards..."

"I can't ask more than that," Ned said. He slid the ring off his finger and passed it through the bars to his sister.

"What's this?" Maggie asked.

"Can you give this to her for me? She'll understand," said Ned. Maggie stared into Ned's eyes mournfully.

By the time Kate Lloyd arrived, Ned was almost completely drained. Yet, seeing his cousin filled him with a happiness that was almost electric.

"Hello Ned," Kate said from the afar.

"Don't be daft, come to me girl. There's bars in the way."

Kate was hesitant but complied. Ned reached out to her.

"What would I do without you, Kate? You were there right to the end."

"Of course. I'd do anything for you, Ned."

"Alright," Ned paused, "in that case there's something I want you to do for me."

"Yes?"

"Find a good man, raise a family and get away from this misery. Have a happy life where the Kelly name won't get you in trouble. Can you do that for me?"

"I can try."

When Ellen was finally brought to see Ned, he was seated on the edge of his bed with his head in his hands. Castieau had promised to let her into the cell so long as she kept it secret. Ellen nodded and the door was opened slowly so as not to elicit a creak. Ned struggled to stand and moved painfully and slowly to hold his mother. He buried his head in her shoulder and she felt him trembling.

"What's this then, Ned Kelly?" Ellen chided.

"I'm scared," Ned whispered. Ellen put on a brave face but knew that Ned didn't need a matriarch now, he needed a mother.

"Neddy, have you made your peace? Have you done your rosary?"

Ned nodded.

"Is your conscience clear?"

Ellen pulled Ned away from her to look into his eyes. They were red and watery, a far cry from the dark and brooding gaze that they usually presented.

"Ned, is your conscience clear?" Ellen repeated.

Ned shook his head.

"I broke the commandments, Ma. How could I ever wash that away? I'm a sinner."

"You listen here my boy; do you have faith in Lord Jesus?"

"Yes."

"Have you done your penance?"

"I have, Ma."

"Then the Lord will take care of the rest."

Ned nodded with a sniff. Ellen held her son as tightly as her arms would allow. If she could have, she would have fought like a lioness to protect him. In any other scenario it would have taken an army to drag her out of that cell, but she knew that she had to knuckle down so that she could go back to what was left of her family. Ned sobbed.

"Hush now, no more of that. I love you so much, Ned."

Ned's crippled legs struggled to keep him upright, but he fought his weakness.

"Mind you die like a Kelly, son."

"I don't want you to go," Ned said.

"I must Ned. I can't help that. But we will be together again. We will." Ellen pulled away. "Look at me."

Ned stood erect and Ellen ran her hand down his cheek and over his bushy beard.

"You remind me so much of your Da," Ellen's eyes began to sting, "Mind you die like a Kelly, son."

***

Ned Kelly's last night on earth seemed interminable, yet it was mercifully brief. Inside his cell two armed guards kept watch, two more waiting outside. Ned turned to his guards with a curious sparkle in his eye.

"What purpose do you have for so many men to guard me?" he asked. The guards looked at each other.

"To make sure you don't try to escape or do yourself in," said one, a portly gentleman with a five o'clock shadow.

"Aye, I suppose they wouldn't want to miss out on the satisfaction of watching me dangle like a worm on a hook," replied Ned.

For a time, he had another prisoner in his cell dictating his final missives. Ned had considered how to address the plan at Glenrowan and had come to the conclusion that in order to protect his sympathisers the best course of action was to lie.

Once his scribe was gone with the letters signed with a defiant and wonky X, he comforted himself with songs, at once stoking the fire in his belly by reciting 'Farewell to Greta' then moments later contemplating his fate to 'In the Sweet By and By'.

There's a land that is fairer than day,
And by faith we can see it afar;
For the Father waits over the way
To prepare us a dwelling place there.
In the sweet by and by,
We shall meet on that beautiful shore;
In the sweet by and by,
We shall meet on that beautiful shore.
We shall sing on that beautiful shore
The melodious songs of the blessed;
And our spirits shall sorrow no more,
Not a sigh for the blessing of rest.
To our bountiful Father above,
We will offer our tribute of praise
For the glorious gift of His love
And the blessings that hallow our days.

When dinner was delivered to his cell, the scent of roasted lamb wafted and gently filled the small stone room. Ned savoured each mouthful of meat and green peas and allowed the taste of the claret that was given to him to wash the interior of his mouth and linger. Castieau had ensured this special meal be given to the condemned man personally, particularly the wine which was one of his personal favourites. The flavours seemed incredibly intense after months of gruel and molasses. The wine seemed to relax him somewhat and after the meal he slunk over to his bed and rested. He tried to sleep but his mind was restless, sleep seemed pointless. As he stared at the stone above him, he began to reminisce.

Ned stood in front of the fireplace in the back room of the Shelton family's store, drying slowly after that morning's drama in Hughes Creek. Mrs. Shelton fussed over young Dick whose plump-cheeked face was pink with embarrassment. Earlier, Ned had dragged the clumsy child out of the creek where he had been thrashing about in the water, nearly drowning, after tumbling in when reaching for his hat.

Mrs. Shelton was not a conventionally beautiful woman. Ned considered her features somewhat masculine and odd, but he felt jealous of the motherly tenderness she lavished on the young boy he had rescued.

"I should be off," Ned said finally, "I've got jobs to do."
Mrs. Shelton looked over to the soggy little boy. Her face softened.
"You're still soaking wet," she exclaimed.
"Ma's very particular about where I get to without Da around the place."
"Oh? Where is your father? Is he travelling for work?"
Ned averted his eyes.
"He's in the gaol, missus."

Mrs. Shelton's face dropped, and her eyes darted between the boys.
"I'm sorry to hear that, Edward. That must be very difficult."
Ned didn't respond.
"At least let me take you home. We can't have you walking back like that."
Ned nodded. He did not relish the thought of walking back to the selection in wet bluchers.

"Edward, you are a very special boy, I am so thankful for what you did. Wait here a moment," said Mrs. Shelton as she ducked into another room. When she returned, she was holding a green silk sash with gold fringes. She handed it to Ned.

"What's this?" asked Ned.
"A gift. To say thank you," Mrs. Shelton replied. Ned looked at the

sash with a mixture of awe and confusion. "It's a sash to wear around your waist," Mrs. Shelton explained. She draped the sash around Ned's hips and tied a loose knot to keep it in place. He ran his fingers over the soft silk, green as shamrock. He beamed with pride.

Ned sighed. He looked towards the iron bars on the cell door and the inky blackness beyond. His thumb ached so he raised his hand in the dim light to examine the wound. Where the bullet had struck his hand was a puckered, deformed mass of scar tissue, the tip of the little finger on the same hand was very much alike. The back of the hand bore a large, puffy scar where a bullet had gouged across it.

Ned, only a seven-year-old, entered his parents' sleeping quarters. His mother lay in bed. The bedclothes were pulled up to her armpits and in her naked arms she held an infant; pudgy-limbed and pug-faced with a shock of dark hair. Ned looked at the baby with curiosity.

"This is your new brother, Ned."

"What's his name?"

"Daniel. We named him after your uncle."

"When will I be able to play with him?"

"Oh, not for a while yet, he's only just new to the world."

"I hope he can play sport good like me. Jimmy's not good at running games. I'm the best at hop-step-jump at school you know."

"Aye, so Annie tells me."

"Maybe one day Daniel and I will be champions like the sportsmen in the papers?"

"Aye, Neddy, I'm sure one day you'll be in the papers."

At one in the morning Ned closed his eyes and attempted to rest his mind. It was of little use, however, as his mind raced through as many thoughts and memories as possible. Ned shifted on the bed, which creaked unpleasantly.

Night had fallen over the Eleven Mile Creek and Ned and Dan were seated on their mares. Dan leaned over in the saddle to give Kate a kiss goodbye and Ned did the same for his mother who clutched six-month-old Alice tightly.

"Ned, you take care of my boy. See that he stays out of trouble."

"Of course, Ma. No harm'll come to him under my watch, I promise."

"I've a feeling in my bones. I can't tell what it is, but I know that bad times are afoot."

"Don't worry yourself, Ma, I'll get the money for the re-trial from the gold and the whiskey. Proper, honest money."

"No," Ellen stared into the distance, 'it's something else. Like the chill of winter."

"Don't worry, Ma. It will be fine. Ned's gotta get a decent batch of whiskey some time," Dan chimed in.

"Oh, you're a cheeky one Dan Kelly. Stay out of trouble the pair o'ye," Ellen said.

Squeezing their legs into their horses' flanks the brothers rode away towards the Wombat Ranges. On the cusp of his hearing Ned heard Alice whine as she wriggled to be put down. The wind kicked up, sending dust flying towards them.

Ellen drew her shawl tight. "There's something cruel in that wind, my girl."

At two in the morning Ned fell asleep. The guards took the

opportunity to take turns in napping. Ned snored gently, his chest rising and falling beneath the rough grey blanket. In his sleeping mind, dreams devolved into frenetic blasts of colour and sound and then darkness.

At five in the morning, Ned's eyes opened slowly and adjusted to the eerie quiet of the cell. He sat up and rolled out of bed. His crippled fingers locked together as Ned prayed silently by his bed. His lips moved surreptitiously behind the thick moustache and voluminous beard. His prayers complete he opened his eyes and returned to a lying position, his irons clanking softly. He felt a compulsion to look to the opposite wall.

Shadowy figures appeared in the corners of his cell; men made of pure darkness. As he gazed at them, they shimmered and took form. Before him stood Lonigan, Scanlan, Kennedy and Sherritt. None of them spoke, they just stood glowering at him. Ned felt his heart racing, he crossed himself and closed his eyes. Mumbling an approximation of the Lord's Prayer, he opened his eyes again to be met with the scowling face of Sergeant Kennedy floating above him, inches away from his own face before it vanished as quickly as it had appeared. Ned dared not move an inch as he waited for his heart to settle.

***

Clang! Clang! Clang! Chink.

The blacksmith laid down his tools and loosened the iron shackles from Ned Kelly's ankles. As Ned stood up the leather belt around his waist was removed and the irons dragged away. The baggy prison trousers began to slip, but in his weakened state Ned was not fast enough to catch them before they fell. He grunted with frustration and indignity as he struggled to pull the trousers back up to protect his modesty. His legs were no longer muscular and defined but withered looking and spindly.

"Bastard things!" he muttered.

He removed the blue handkerchief from his neck, bunched up the waistband of the trousers and tied the cloth around the bunch as best as he could. The march back to his cell was far easier without the unnecessary encumbering caused by leg irons.

In his cell, he was met by Father Donaghy. A stout middle-aged Irishman with the face of a bulldog and a fearsome glint in his eyes, this was the man who a quarter-century earlier had bathed the infant Ned's head in holy water at his baptism.

"Well, son, it is a pity to see you thus," said the old man in a thick brogue.

"I told you, if ever they got me back in a prison, they'd have to hang me." Ned smiled wryly.

"Aye, but I didn't expect ye'd be lookin' at it as a challenge," Donaghy responded humourlessly. Ned's bravado faded.

"I'm sorry to disappoint you, Father."

"M'lad, you had such a future ahead of you. That damned temper of yours brought you unstuck. I understand. I've been to enough of these to know. It's not me you need to be thinkin' of," Donaghy said gesturing upwards.

"What would you have done in my position?" Ned asked.

"M'lad," said Donaghy, "I'd never have done anything to get into that position in the first place."

His meeting with his religious counsel complete, Ned was marched to the new wing of the prison where the gallows awaited him. As he walked past the tiny garden, maintained by prisoners, he took a whiff of the sweet scent of flowers.

"What pretty flowers." he said to nobody in particular. The walk continued past a wooden handcart. Ned did not know that within an hour it would be used to transport his corpse from the gallows to the deadhouse. The walk led him back inside the gaol and up the stairs to the condemned cell on the middle level. Here he was met by a gathering of priests and acolytes who administered the last rites.

***

As the clock struck ten the Sheriff appeared on the gallows and requested the body of Edward Kelly. The paperwork was checked, and the procedure began. The hangman was roused from the cell opposite Ned's.

He was an old man named Elijah Upjohn, doing time for interfering with livestock. He had white hair cut short all over his scalp, his brow was sloped and deep giving him an ape-like appearance, and his large nose bore a swollen carbuncle on the end. He walked across to the condemned cell holding straps.

"I've come to pinion you," said Upjohn in a slurpy, gummy voice owing to his bad teeth.

"There's no need to pinion me," Ned protested but Upjohn proceeded anyway. Outside, the clock's chimes could be heard fading away into the morning.

Each step across the iron platform towards the gallows felt like an eternity. The strap that pinioned his arms was uncomfortable as it rubbed on his wounds. Each step seemed shakier than the last as Ned struggled to stay upright without assistance. As he walked onto the wooden floor of the gallows, he looked over the railing at the gathering below of fifty men, comprising of journalists, legal professionals and men with social standing. Directly opposite a press artist sketched the scene. Ned positioned himself over the trapdoor and eyed the lever next to the hangman's cell jutting out at waist height.

As Upjohn crouched to strap his ankles together, Ned was asked if he wished to make a statement. He turned to the sheriff impassively.

"Ah, well..."

He trailed off into an inaudible mumble. Upjohn looped the noose over Ned's head and drew the slipknot tight behind the left ear. He yanked the white hood over the condemned man's face and took his position beside the lever. Doctor Barker, the surgeon, reached out to adjust the noose, but before he could Upjohn yanked on the lever with zeal.

In the women's work yard Ellen Kelly dumped a load of soiled sheets into a copper cauldron full of steaming hot water. The quiet industry was interrupted by a loud crash within the main gaol building. Ellen staggered on the spot and clutched her chest. She was unaware that all eyes were on her as she began to tremble. Taking a deep breath, she straightened herself and set about her work washing the sheets. Her lip quivered and tears rolled down her cheeks as she pushed through.

Outside the gaol, beneath the clock, Maggie and Kate began to wail at the tolling of the tenth hour. Ettie Hart collapsed to her knees in convulsing sobs while Kate and Tom Lloyd tried unsuccessfully to remain stoic. The Kelly sisters held each other tight, the onlookers staring awkwardly at the scene.

In the Robert Burns Hotel, Jim Kelly sat at the bar with a whiskey. Next to him Dick Hart and Wild Wright sat with drinks poised. All three stared at the clock on the shelf behind the bar that chimed the hour.

"Well, the poor bastard's out of his misery by now," Jim said regretfully, raising a glass and knocking back the contents in one hit.

In the Benalla police station Superintendent Sadlier examined the Geneva watch that had been taken from Ned Kelly. The long arm twitched to the twelve and he sighed. On his desk were the photographs supplied to the station to help the police identify the gang, for all the good it had done. Sadleir closed the watch and set about filling the bowl of his pipe with tobacco.

At Rupertswood Mansion, Superintendent Hare sat in the garden with his wife, Janet. He heard a grandfather clock inside chiming the hour. He slowly pushed back the sleeve from his injured wrist to examine the wound. It had healed admirably since June, though it still ached from time to time and he still had not regained full movement in his hand. He looked up at a mother bird landing on a branch and prancing about the length to her nest to feed her offspring.

Meanwhile, Ned Kelly dangled seven feet below the drop, unconscious but still more dead than alive, the noose having slipped as he dropped. As the life was strangled out of him by gravity, his body twitched and convulsed, his legs contracted and relaxed as his brain's last impulses surged through his failing nervous system, but he felt nothing. The doctor glared at Upjohn who scratched his scrotum and sniffed the air as he looked down at his handiwork. The onlookers only got a glimpse of the poorly executed man convulsing before they were ushered away, yet several of the men were glued to the spot, shaken to the core by the sudden violence of the execution. Others smirked with satisfaction.

Most were numb. As the audience filed out the officials went about their business. Governor Castieau watched the hemp rope drift as the body at the end of it ceased to move. Another life snuffed out in the name of law and order.

***

After thirty minutes the rope was cut, and the body laid out on the handcart. The smell of evacuation and blood made the process of carting the corpse to the dead house distinctly unpleasant. Once there, the corpse was laid out and stripped. Doctor Barker examined the body, noting the strong chest, the small hands and feet, the myriad scars from his wounds at Glenrowan and the grotesquely broken neck. Blood trailed from the nose and the face was flecked with red from the blood vessels that had exploded from the pressure of the hanging. Despite the horrific signs of the execution the face was placid, a welcome sight to one who had seen his share of horrifically bulging eyes and tongues and faces permanently grimacing in pain from botched executions. He sensed, somehow, that Ned was relieved to have met his end finally.

It was not long before the arrival of Maximilian Kreitmayer, with a kit ready to make a death mask. He and the doctor shaved the bushranger's moustache and beard off before removing the hair. Locks of the hair were taken and sealed in envelopes for interested parties. Kreitmayer bathed the face and scalp in oil before laying a string in the centre of the face. Melted wax was poured over the clean features then reinforced with bandages soaked in plaster of Paris. Once the mould was set, the string was pulled to separate the halves. Satisfied with his work, Kreitmayer packed up his equipment and took his leave.

Following the routine procedures, Ned's body was smuggled out of the dead house and taken to a building close by where medical students went to work on it. They carved into the flesh, pulling out every possible organ, most of which ended up discarded, but a few prize pieces were placed in jars of formaldehyde. His skull was sawed open and the brain fluid drained. The brain was extracted and preserved. It seemed smaller than a man of his size and age should have possessed, slightly shrivelled and under-developed.

What was left of Ned Kelly, once the most feared man in Australia, was dumped in a wooden box and returned to the gaol in secret where it was put in a shallow grave and covered in quicklime. When the body was interred, the flagstones were replaced as if nothing had changed. One of the prisoners given the grim task of performing the burial found himself standing above this infamous man's remains thinking to himself, what a way to go for Ned Kelly.

***

At noon, as Jim was continuing to drown his sorrow in the Robert Burns Hotel, a man entered the bar room dressed in a plaid suit and bowtie. His face was smooth, and his thinning hair slicked down with oil to make it seem more voluminous than it was. He had a strange, young-old face that seemed like it could be anywhere between 25 and 40 years of age. The man made a beeline to Jim and extended his hand.

"Jim Kelly?"

"Yes; what is it?"

"My name is Alfred Burton. I run the Apollo Hall on Bourke Street."

Jim's brow furrowed as he scrutinised his visitor. Realising that there would be no handshake forthcoming, Burton withdrew his hand.

"What do you want?"

"Well, I've been following you through the papers, and of course it has been difficult not to have noticed the rallies. I've been speaking to

Mr. Gaunson, and he suggested I should see you. I want to offer you a chance to tell your own story."

"What does that mean?" Jim asked, growing impatient.

Burton took a seat next to Jim and continued.

"I have a spot open at the Apollo tonight. It would be a good opportunity to talk about your experiences in all of this and thank those who supported the reprieve campaign. Perhaps your sister Kate would be able to attend as well?"

"Kate's not in a good way at the moment. I don't think she would be well-disposed to doping something like that."

"Look, I understand that it's probably a bit hard on the old love, but this is a chance to set the record straight about your brothers. And I might add it's a good way to make some easy money. I reckon there would be a big attendance."

Jim sat in silence for a moment and drank his whisky thoughtfully. He seemed to reach a conclusion in his head.

"Alright. I'll have a word to her. What do you need from me?"

Burton smiled broadly. In his head he was already counting the money.

"Just come to the Apollo Hall at seven tonight. I'll take care of the rest."

Burton grabbed Jim's hand and shook it before taking his leave.

***

That evening at eight o'clock scores of people descended upon the Haymarket Theatre and lined up to pay a shilling to see the Kellys. Some gripped handbills that had been thrust at them by Burton's staff advertising the event. An appearance by Ettie Hart was also billed, but as she was long out of town she was nowhere to be seen. Still, Burton reasoned, two Kellys should be enough to satisfy most curiosity.

Burton himself stood at the ticket booth, taking in the shilling entry fee and allowing the customers to enter. As they moved into the space, at the far end could be seen Jim Kelly dressed in a borrowed suit, looking dour and uncomfortable. Beside him in her dark riding habit with a black veil over her face and a bouquet of flowers in her hand, sat Kate Kelly.

The audience comprised mostly of young larrikins who had come to either rub elbows with notoriety or to get a look at Kate Kelly to see if she was indeed as pretty as they had heard.

A gang of four lads in their teens sat in the front row drinking cheap ale out of clay bottles. One of them, a boy of sixteen with carroty hair and freckles, stood up and instructed Kate to take her clothes off so he could get a better look. A threat from Jim was enough to keep the quartet quiet for a few minutes before they got bored and left.

Over the course of the next two hours Jim and Kate took questions from the audience, though most were either repetitions of previous questions or completely ludicrous. As Kate's voice was far weaker, Jim did most of the talking. He affirmed the family's story about Fitzpatrick trying to arrest Dan without a warrant, even going so far as to state that the trooper had shot himself in the wrist to implicate the Kellys. He spoke at length about the rough treatment the girls had endured at the hands of the police and how it was perjury that landed their mother in gaol.

After repeatedly having to dispel rumours of Ned Kelly's hidden treasure trove, Kate rose to her feet with tears in her eyes.

"Look at me. Does it look like we have thousands of pounds hidden away? I have had to sell almost every piece of jewellery I possessed just to buy enough food to keep us going. We are poor farmers, and we have been bullied to desperation by the police. My brothers were good men, pushed to their limits by the police who have had a down on us for as long as I can remember. If you starve a dog, will he not turn wild with hunger and bite you? Between the police and the squatters, we've never had a chance to get ahead. They've taken everything from us."

The crowd fell into an awkward silence. Unsure what to do next, they slowly began to filter out. Gradually the entire assemblage turned their backs on the pair and left. They had their gawp, leering at the siblings like exhibits in a zoo, and now there were other things to be doing.

Jim and Kate looked at each other with regret. No amount of money was surely worth such a feeling of degradation as this.

Jim sought out Burton and demanded their pay. Burton turned him away and told him to come back the following day once the takings had been counted. Jim threatened to lay the theatre manager out with a punch leading to Burton paying Jim £50 to leave him alone.

Jim and Kate returned to the hotel crestfallen and deeply embarrassed.

***

Months passed and Kate Kelly walked down Bourke Street dressed in her mourning wear. She headed to a building with a flag out the front declaring that within the building was the waxworks. Kate moved through the displays of historical figures immortalised in wax to a room with a sign above the door that read CHAMBER OF HORRORS.

Inside were rows of life-sized statues of infamous bushrangers like Dan Morgan and Captain Moonlite, gruesome and grizzly. At the far end she reached her destination: a display of the Kelly Gang. The dummies of Dan and Steve appeared to be generic characters, not resembling her beloved brother or his mate in the slightest, but the dummy of Joe had been made with the cast of his hands and head taken by the proprietor's wife. The mud and blood encrusted boots taken from Byrne's lifeless body adorned the feet of the dummy. On a plinth next to a fairly reasonable likeness of Ned Kelly in shirtsleeves was a plaster cast of Ned's death mask. The face was smooth and youthful, reminding Kate of how her brother looked when she was tiny, and he was gallivanting around with Harry Power. Kate reached out and stroked it tenderly, the cold, firm plaster being hardly a substitute for the flesh of her departed kin.

A stout, white-bearded man appeared behind Kate and raised his hands in frustration.

"Mein Got! They have taken his coat again," said Max Kreitmayer in his thick Bavarian accent, "Well, I suppose there will be one well-dressed tramp under the Princes Bridge tonight."

Kate looked at the man with confusion. He tugged at the shirt on the Ned Kelly dummy.

"The homeless men sneak in and steal Ned Kelly's coat. Always Ned Kelly's coat, not the others," he paused, "You look rather familiar. Do I know you?"

"I'm Kate Kelly,' said Kate as she pointed to the death mask, "This is my brother."

"Ah! Yes! I see the resemblance. You are much prettier than the illustrated papers portray. I am the proprietor here. What do you think of my display?"

"It's nice to come and visit and remember the boys, although those two on the end aren't right."

"Well, I suppose you would know," replied Kreitmayer.

"I must be going now. It was a pleasure to meet you, Mister..."

"Kreitmayer. Maximilian Kreitmayer." He extended his hand and Kate shook it gently, "Perhaps I should add you to my display, no?"

A few blocks away, Ellen Kelly waited patiently at the huge gates at the entrance to the Melbourne Gaol. Kate, Grace and Jim arrived on a buggy to collect her. As the buggy drew to a halt, Jim leaned over. Ellen barely recognised him as the teenager who she had last seen so many years ago.

"Come on, Ma. It's time to go home," said Jim. Ellen smiled and climbed in, taking a seat next to two potted Cyprus trees and flowers.
"What are these?" Ellen asked.
"The flowers and trees are to put on poor Danny's grave," replied Kate. Ellen stroked a sapling gently. There was one for Dan and one for Ned.

"If we're swift we might be able to make it home in time for tea. Come on, Jim," said Grace, tugging at her brother's jacket. Jim flicked the reins, and the horse took off down the bustling urban thoroughfare far faster than was acceptable. Ellen flew into a panic and swatted Jim.
"Slow down, you devil! I've only just got out of gaol; do you want to put me back in?"

After years of misery, the clouds lifted, and for a brief moment laughter was the song sung by the Kellys.

Epilogue

Following the siege of Glenrowan, Ann Jones struggled to piece her life together again. The day of Ned Kelly's execution she was arrested on a charge of harbouring the outlaws and remanded in Melbourne Gaol as she could not afford bail. Superintendent Sadleir sent Detective Eason to Glenrowan in order to gather any evidence that would incriminate her. The prosecution case was so weak that Jones' legal team did not bother to call any witnesses. She was duly acquitted.

Following this, in 1881, Ann filed a claim to the government seeking £5000 compensation for the loss of her home, business and son at the hands of the police. After a protracted legal battle, during which Detective Ward supplied a good character reference for Ann Jones, the court awarded her £280, plus £25 to cover legal fees. Though it was never stated outright, it was clear that the inquiry board were heavily biased against her from the outset. In spite, Ann refused to accept the money.

Johnny Jones was buried in Wangaratta cemetery in a shared plot with his sister Ann Julietta who had died in 1879. In 1882, Johnny was joined by Jane who died of tuberculosis. After the siege Jane had been in poor health consistently. Ann blamed the police.

When Ann reunited with her husband Owen and son Thomas the family gradually put together a slab hut attached to the parlour chimney of the former inn. Eventually a second inn was built on the site using the original chimneys and exterior lamp. The authorities refused to grant her a liquor license and instead she specialised in selling wine.

Owen Jones died in 1890, but Ann was not a widow for long, marrying former sailor Henry Winstanley Smith the following year. Smith was one of the staff at the new wine shanty Ann had constructed after authorities refused to grant her a liquor licence. The family moved to Collingwood, just outside the city of Melbourne. Life with Smith was harder than Ann had imagined and in 1901, he died after a battle with depression leaving Ann a widow yet again. Still, Ann lingered on for her sons, passing away in 1910.

***

Thomas Curnow was awarded a silver medal by the Victorian Humane Society and £550 of the reward for the gang's capture. Feeling his family had been short-changed, he campaigned unsuccessfully for a greater portion.

He spent the rest of his career as a school teacher in Ballarat. When he died in 1922, he was remembered as "The Hero of Glenrowan".

Even into her dotage, Curnow's wife Jeannie remained paranoid that Kelly sympathisers would seek retribution. Despite this, the family lived a happy, full life.

***

The Reardons remained in Glenrowan after the siege. Michael was hospitalised while he recovered from being shot in the back by Sergeant Steele. His lungs permanently damaged, Michael took a long time to recover and was irreversibly weak ever after.

Members of the police tried to force the Reardons to claim that it was

Ned Kelly who had shot Michael, but the family staunchly refused. In fact, the Reardons' experience of being bullied by the police pushed them to become some of the staunchest sympathisers of the Kellys thereafter.

***

George Metcalfe spent considerable time in hospital recuperating from his eye injury. He applied to the government for compensation and received it, as it was concluded that a police bullet had injured him accidentally. Metcalfe died of peritonitis a few months later.

When the police force's unquestionable guilt in the injuring of Reardon and the killing of Martin Cherry were proven and published in the newspapers, Superintendent Sadleir sent Detective Eason to Glenrowan to try and find anything that would invalidate George Metcalfe's compensation claim against the police for his eye injury, desperate to try and claw back some level of credibility. Eason induced John Stanistreet, Michael Reardon and Alphonso Piazzi to sign a statement that it was really Ned Kelly that had shot Metcalfe with Piazzi's old pistol, and that Metcalfe had lied to gain money from the government.

Though Stanistreet and Reardon had made statements giving their account of the events at Glenrowan publicly and prior to signing the statement, neither of them had previously mentioned Metcalfe or the story of Ned playing with Piazzi's gun, nor would they refer to it in later remembrances. For Piazzi's part, after signing the statement for Detective Eason, his claim for compensation for horses that were shot during the siege was quickly approved and paid out by the police.

***

Hugh Bracken did not remain in Glenrowan. He was quickly

transferred to Benalla and then to Richmond. He was awarded £275.13.9 for his role at Glenrowan from the reward money.

The next few years saw Bracken bouncing around various police stations. At every single one, Bracken was bullied and harassed by his colleagues for not allowing Steele to execute Ned Kelly. Eventually, this led to a nervous breakdown that saw him kicked out of the police force.

The nervous breakdown, combined with the premature death of his wife leaving him as a single father, saw Bracken spiral into depression. Though he remarried and had a second child from this new union, he never regained his mental health and took his own life with a shotgun in 1900.

***

Francis Augustus Hare gradually recovered from his injury and gifted the Clarkes of Rupertswood two trophies from the siege as thanks for their care: Ned Kelly's revolving carbine and Joe Byrne's armour, both of which Hare had arranged to be smuggled from storage before they were to be destroyed on Captain Standish's orders.

He received £800 from the reward money, though the Royal Commission of 1881, upon reviewing Hare's conduct, suggested that he was no longer fit for active service and recommended immediate retirement.

He became a respected police magistrate, dying in 1891 after slipping into a diabetic coma while convalescing in Rupertswood Mansion. Prior to his death he wrote and published a popular memoir in which he recalled his adventures as a policeman, but especially his involvement in the hunt for the Kellys.

***

John Sadleir received £240.17.3 from the reward, but with it he also received a considerable amount of criticism in the 1881 Royal Commission, specifically pertaining to his conduct at Glenrowan. Between Standish, Hare and Assistant Commissioner Nicolson, who had all attempted to obscure their own ineptitudes from the duration of the hunt for the gang, Sadleir had no choice but to cop it on the chin. As a result, he was demoted but remained in the force until 1896.

He resented his punishment and harboured ill-will towards his colleagues and the commission ever after, never missing an opportunity to put down his detractors and laud those who he considered to have been similarly maligned, including Sergeant Steele.

After his retirement, he was engaged with the Society for the Prevention of Cruelty to Children and the Historical Society of Victoria, and wrote a popular book of memoirs. He died in 1919 aged eighty-six.

* * *

Stanhope O'Connor and his wife returned to Queensland as soon as possible after the siege. O'Connor was greatly aggrieved that he was not given special thanks by Captain Standish, or lauded in the press as Hare had been. He quit the police force as a result, but was convinced to return by the chief commissioner in Queensland.

When the reward was divided, he was indignant that his trackers did not receive a bigger portion and refused his reward of £237.15 in protest. His complaints fell on deaf ears. To add insult to injury, the £50 each that his trackers were awarded was given to the Queensland government who refused to pass it on to them. To date, that money has never reached the families of the Queensland native police to whom it was owed.

The final straw for O'Connor was when he attended the Royal Commission in 1881 to tell his version of the events that transpired during the Kelly hunt. The Queensland police force refused to allow him extended leave to do so and rather than return to Queensland without having defended his reputation, he resigned for good. O'Connor eventually became a well-known stock broker. He died in 1908.

***

Charles Frederick Standish retired soon after the conclusion of the Kelly Outbreak, on 11 September 1880, after twenty-two years as chief commissioner. Six months later he was harshly judged in the Royal Commission for his inadequate governance of the police force. It was during this time that his health declined considerably. He continued his residency at the Melbourne Club where he died after a stroke in 1883.

***

Detective Michael Edward Ward was transferred to Melbourne after the Glenrowan siege. He was promoted to the rank of Sub-Inspector before he retired from the police force in 1905, having reached the cut-off age of sixty and the enthusiasm for the work evidently tainted by charges being laid against him earlier that year for being drunk on the job and mouthing off about the quality of the new recruits to the force. He was married twice but left no issue, his only child being an adopted teenage boy named Charles Eustace Hayes, who was an orphan. In his later years he ran a private detective agency, but would frequently visit his former colleagues at the police station. He died in 1921, aged seventy-five, fondly remembered by his peers.

***

Arthur Loftus Maule Steele always maintained it was he alone who captured Ned Kelly. He was taken to court for reckless firing at the siege but was let off. In the Royal Commission, he was recommended for demotion. The recommendation was never enforced. He eventually retired as a wealthy man and became an amateur botanist. The shotgun with which he shot Ned Kelly was one of his most prized possessions, along with the bloodstained cartridge bag he souvenired from the fallen outlaw, and he would often bring them out to show his guests.

In 1906, he complained to the projectionist after a screening of the motion picture The Story of the Kelly Gang as it depicted him being killed during the siege. He was satiated with a season pass for his children as compensation for the error.

***

Senior-Constable John Kelly received £377.12.8 out of the reward money. He continued to climb the ranks to become a sergeant, first class. After Glenrowan, his life seemed to be almost devoid of excitement. He often regretted the loss of life on that fateful June day in 1880, but knew he had done all he could to prevent it. He passed away in 1905.

***

The police constables who served at Glenrowan were given portions of the reward in excess of £100 each. Constable Arthur was frequently bullied by his peers for falling back during Ned Kelly's last stand. Many others were also attacked within the ranks for various reasons. However, the heaviest criticism was reserved for the four constables who had hidden in the bedroom rather than confront the bushrangers on the night of Aaron Sherritt's murder. Armstrong, Alexander, Duross and Dowling were publicly shamed and sacked.

***

Constable Thomas McIntyre's health had deteriorated consistently after the tragedy at Stringybark Creek and he left the police force in 1881. He was not given any portion of the Kelly reward money but did receive a pension.

He moved to Ballarat where he and his wife raised seven children. McIntyre became a journalist, penning his memoirs about his days in the police and his involvement in the Kelly Outbreak as well as writing a great deal of poetry. He died in 1918.

***

Ellen Kelly was released from prison in 1881 and returned home to Greta. For the remainder of her years, she lived in dire poverty and was cared for by her son Jim. She outlived many of her children and grand-children.

Rumours that Dan had escaped the siege and was living abroad induced much distress in Ellen who questioned how her beloved boy could run away and not once make contact with her and allow her to live in squalor. She lived long enough to see the introduction of automobiles and the coming and going of World War One. She died in 1923 at the age of 91.

***

Maggie Skillion struggled after the deaths of her brothers. She tried to make a go of things, leaving her husband Bill Skillion and living with her common law husband, Tom Lloyd with whom she had eleven children.

Maggie died of complications from rheumatic gout in January 1896. Only a few months later, her daughter Ellen followed her, committing suicide after a disagreement with her step-father. They are buried next to each other in unmarked graves.

***

Kate Kelly never fully recovered from the events of 1880. She left home and travelled the country picking up work where she could, usually as a domestic servant. Wherever she went she attracted attention; gossip about her activities was often printed in the newspapers. Thus, she assumed the pseudonym Ada in order to go unnoticed.

She married Brickey Foster and settled in New South Wales. She had six children before succumbing to alcoholism, the same thing that had killed her father. She was found dead near Forbes, floating in a lagoon after having abandoned her infant daughter in a depressive episode. She was buried in Forbes cemetery only metres away from her eldest brother's idol, the bushranger Ben Hall. Her children were collected by Jim Kelly and raised by their grandmother.

***

After the events of 1880, Tom Lloyd tried repeatedly to purchase land to start a farm, but was knocked back due to his troubled reputation. When Maggie passed away, Tom tried to look after the children as a widower, but Ellen Skillion's death threw him into a depressive spiral.

He was rescued from his sorrow by Steve Hart's younger sister Rachel and together they raised a large family that united the Kellys, Lloyds and Harts, but Tom's heart always belonged to Maggie.

He passed away as an old man, but always shed a tear when reflecting on those wild days with his outlaw cousins.

Jim Kelly wasn't out of trouble long. In 1881 he was again nabbed for stock theft with Wild Wright. He eventually tired of his lawless ways and dedicated his life to looking after his mother, just as he had promised Ned.

Jim never married, stating that he would never be cruel enough to inflict his family name and reputation on a woman. He died in 1946 while living with his nephew, Patrick, having become a recluse.

Kate Lloyd was very badly affected by Ned's death and refused to speak of those days. In 1881 she was married and lived a full life. She died in 1936. It was always rumoured that she was Ned Kelly's true love. It was a claim she didn't deny.

Ettie Hart tried to piece her life together after 1880 and some-how succeeded, marrying into a well-to-do family. She settled down but always cherished her memories of Ned and the gang. She kept a secret scrapbook full of articles and poetry about the outlaw days and her love affair with Ned Kelly that would not be discovered until decades after her death.

Dick Hart briefly went off the rails following the siege. In the wake of Ned's execution, he attempted to form his own gang with Paddy Byrne,

Jim Kelly and Wild Wright. With the intervention of Constable Robert Graham and Ellen Kelly, the second Kelly Gang was quickly dissolved.

Briefly he found himself in trouble with the law when a bushranger, who had assumed his identity, began committing crimes. Fortunately, the real culprit was discovered and Dick was cleared of the crimes. This seemed to make him more determined than ever to avoid any limelight and married Sarah Bowdern with whom he spent the remainder of his days quietly, raising their family until his death in 1934.

* * *

Wild Wright never really changed. He always maintained his habits of causing trouble, mouthing off, and spreading lies in an effort to look tough. He continued to be in and out of prison for years until he grew too old for such a lifestyle. For a time, he travelled into the Northern Territory as a swaggie and whenever he was asked who he was he would enthusiastically say "I'm Dan Kelly, the bushranger."

* * *

Paddy Byrne was burdened by what happened at the Devil's Elbow and Glenrowan, as well as the government's clandestine burial of his brother to deny the family an opportunity to give him a proper grave and funeral. Joe was not allowed to be mentioned in the household except for when his mother referred to him as "The Devil".

Paddy became the breadwinner for the family, which was a position that brought with it a level of pressure he could not handle. As much as he tried to balance his duty to his ever-needy mother with having a life of his own, it never worked out and Paddy fell into a depression that saw him take his own life many years later.

***

After the loss of her brother Joe, and her former fiancé Aaron Sherritt, Kate Byrne's behaviour became erratic and unpredictable. When the family had relocated to Albury, she was thrown into a lunatic asylum on the recommendation of her mother after developing symptoms of schizophrenia. Eventually her relatives stopped visiting her entirely and she died in the institution as an old woman, forgotten and alone.

***

Joe Byrne's lover, Maggie, was forced out of her job at the Vine as a result of the police attention her affair with the bushranger had brought.

Unemployed and homeless, she disappeared from history. Some say she sought refuge with Joe's Chinese friends and associates on the Sebastopol flats, where she lived with a man named Ah On before dying of illness only a few years later.

***

Belle Sherritt miscarried soon after that fateful night in June 1880. Many believed it was either due to the stress of her husband's murder, or due to her rough treatment by the police. Afterwards, she was constantly in poor health.

Belle was not afforded a share of the reward for the Kelly Gang, however her father-in-law, John Sherritt, received £42.15.9. This led to a public campaign to petition the government to provide her with a pension due to her husband losing his life in an effort to aid the police. It was eventually successful. This allowed her to continue living in a room in Beechworth while working before she remarried, this time to Michael Murphy, the publican at the Woolpack Hotel in Corowa.

After bearing Murphy four children, he deserted her. He was arrested in 1902. The couple settled out of court and the charges were withdrawn. After that Belle lived quietly and faded into obscurity.

***

Mere days after Ned Kelly's execution, Sir Redmond Barry took ill with pneumonia from which he died. Barry's illustrious career had ended with perhaps his most famous court case. Many chose to see this as Ned Kelly's prediction coming true, and Barry being summoned to a greater court, but real life is hardly so poetic.

He was initially remembered for his great contributions to Melbourne's cultural and educational institutions, but over time these achievements were overshadowed by his role as the nemesis of Ned Kelly. Such is life.

***

Ned Kelly's body remained secretly buried in the grounds of the Melbourne Gaol until the 1920s when redevelopment saw more than half of the gaol torn down to make way for a university. When Ned's remains were found, many of the young men working on the site souvenired bones from the notorious outlaw.

Most of the bones were returned and what was left of Ned was buried in the grounds of Pentridge Prison. It was here that the remains, minus his skull and a number of other smaller bones, were rediscovered and eventually they were moved yet again. This time they were taken to Greta to be buried with his family. In 2013, the earthly remains of Ned

Kelly were finally interred near to his mother and most of his siblings in an unmarked grave, in consecrated ground, as per his final wishes.

***

While many of the people who were involved in the Glenrowan tragedy were forgotten and fact was overtaken by legend, and legend became masked in myths, the bulletproof armour became an enduring symbol of rebellion. While it had failed to protect the gang from destruction, it grew to become something more powerful than Ned had ever imagined as a symbol.

Today, the armour signifies to many, regardless of its true purpose, the values of defying tyranny, the resilient frontier spirit and loyalty to your beliefs and your kin.

More than a century after the Glenrowan siege, Ned's suit of iron plate armour is the prize of the collection of the State Library of Victoria; the institution masterminded by Sir Redmond Barry to elevate the masses. While Kelly and Barry were polar opposites in life, in death they create an unusual alliance in the pursuit of wisdom and an appreciation for the past.

"I do not pretend that I have led a blameless life, or that one fault justifies another, but the public in judging a case like mine should remember that the darkest life may have a bright side, and that after the worst has been said against a man, he may, if he is heard, tell a story in his own rough way that will perhaps lead them to intimate the harshness of their thoughts against him, and find as many excuses for him as he would plead for himself."

EDWARD KELLY, AUGUST 1880

Afterword

This book has been the product of more than twenty years of passion and research. I fell in love with the Kelly story on my first visit to Glenrowan in 1998 on a school camp to Beechworth. Once I got the taste for it, I was snagged, hook, line and sinker. It has finally culminated in this novel, which is a cocktail of historical fact and creative licence I hope invites new perspectives on this incredible saga. It is an attempt to weave what we know to be true into a narrative that fills in the gaps in our knowledge with inspired creative flourishes, and show these historical figures as human beings with passions, beliefs, faults and vices.

I highly encourage people to read further into the Kelly outbreak, and Glenrowan in particular, and make up their own minds rather than relying on wordsmiths, artists and zealots to tell them what their opinions should be. There is something very powerful in this story that 140 years on can still leave us spellbound. Ned Kelly as a figure in Australian culture is chameleonic; adapting to each generation to fulfill whatever role they require of him. While the truth of the man is far removed from the myth, which I have attempted to portray here, there is no doubt that the myth, or the idea of him as a folk hero, has a function in Australian culture and is integral to our national identity in one way or another.

I wish to extend thanks to all those who helped and supported my endeavours to bring this tale to life. In particular I wish to thank Matthew Holmes, whose support and assistance has been invaluable throughout the creation of this text and the publishing of the book itself. Also, Noeleen Lloyd, whose historical knowledge of the story as much as her insight as a descendant of Tom Lloyd and Rachel Hart, were invaluable in ensuring that I was getting the facts right. My various beta readers, whose feedback reassured me that I was doing things the right way over the course of writing and editing the first edition, also deserve my gratitude.

Most importantly, I thank my mother, Angela, whose unwavering support and encouragement has kept me going through the dark times and the light; my son Dash who gives me a reason to get out of bed in the mornings; and my partner Georgina Stones, who pulled me through all the gnashing of teeth and wringing of hands that writing this book induced, as well as encouraging me to push myself into some of the more uncomfortable parts of the narrative that I otherwise would have shied away from.

On a closing note, I want to remind each of you reading this that now a part of the history lives inside you. Nurture it and help it take root. It is only in preserving stories and probing deeper to the core of them that we can preserve our heritage. History, one may muse, is the journey of the ripples on a lake. The role of the historian, academic or otherwise, is to find where and how the ripples began, for it is there that we shall find ourselves. We must also remember that humanity's journey through time is not merely a collection of songs by a myriad of composers, but one long and complex symphony. It binds us to each other and to the land that we stand upon. Open your ears to it and find your voice.

The site of the siege, in 2020 - 140 years later.

Supplementary Material

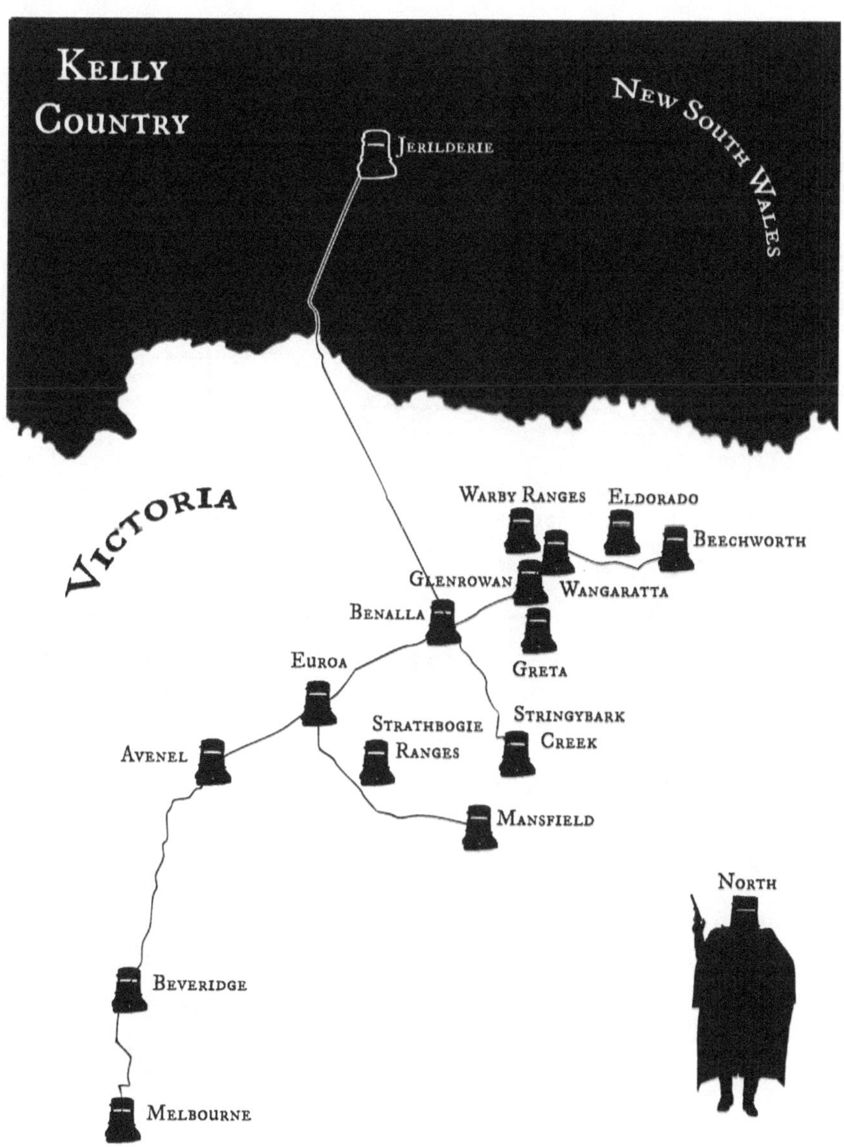

Map of Kelly Country

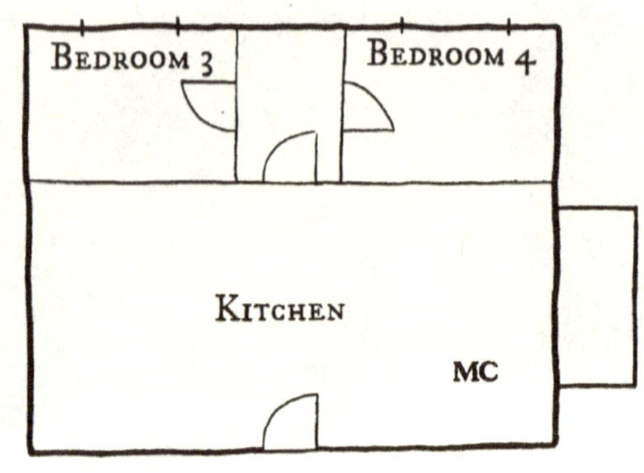

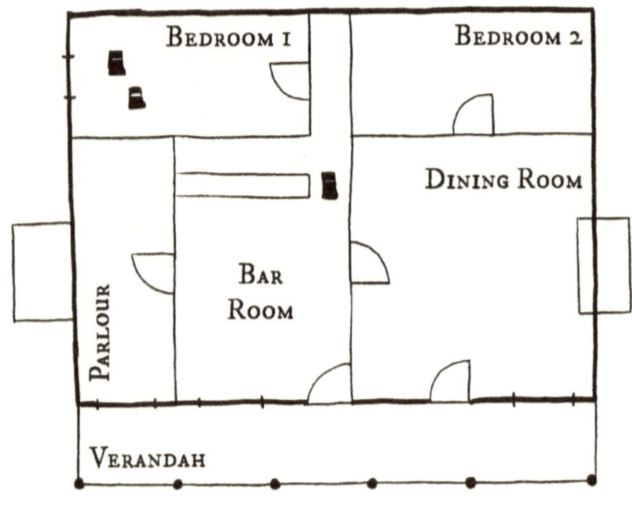

THE
GLENROWAN INN

ANN JONES
BEST ACCOMMODATION

Floorplan of Ann Jones's Inn

The Kelly Gang Armour

[Image: Bird's Eye View of Glenrowan by Thomas Carrington; The Illustrated Australian News 17/07/1880; State Library Victoria]

CONCERNING NED KELLY

The core of the *Glenrowan* story is Ned Kelly. Everything that occurs is either directly or indirectly linked to him and his decisions. Naturally this should position him as the protagonist of the story, though protagonist usually implies that character is the "good guy". As I've discovered, simplistic terms like "good", "bad", "hero", or "villain" are just completely inadequate to describe someone as complex as Edward Kelly.

I was twelve when I first became hooked on the story of Ned Kelly. It was a name I was familiar with, of course, but I knew nothing particular about him until I was in grade six. My Grandma had some time previous to this regaled us with the story of her trip to Glenrowan with her social club. Back in those days she was always on a bus off to somewhere with other old ladies. She brought back with her a flyer from Bob Hempel's light and sound show. All I recall from her recounting of the show was that at some point she went into a pub and the roof caught on fire. I would get context for this statement later. Until I went to see it myself, all I had to connect with "Ned Kelly" was the name written in the style of the Indiana Jones logo and a vague image of a bearded man in a hat.

When I was in grade six, however, our school camp was to Beechworth. This was to be the moment that changed everything. As embarrassing as it is to say now, I found the "animated theatre" in Glenrowan to be tremendously exciting as a kid. Now, keep in mind that I have to this day never left Australia, I've never been to Universal studios or Disneyland, so such a clunky and rudimentary collection of "animatronic" figures was a revelation. Even though the gang in their armour were totally static I remember them being positively alive with motion, guns blazing and the outlaws barking insults at nobody in particular. This really shows the power of imagination I suppose. At this stage the fire segment of the show was out of order as a malfunction had resulted in the shack doubling as the Glenrowan Inn to be burnt severely. I'm sure the irony wasn't lost on Bob Hempel. At the end of that experience I had an image to put to the name and for the remainder of the camp I waited eagerly to hear more tales of Ned Kelly. Visiting places like Harry Power's cell and the Burke Museum really did something to me and I remember the excitement I had at being able to spend my pocket money on a plaster figurine of Ned and a pack of MB Brewery Ned Kelly soft drinks. I couldn't wait to drink my Kelly Kola and Red Ned Portello. I could go for one now, actually. I digress.

When we had to do our Australian history assignments I did a deep dive on Ned Kelly. My favourite book that I came across was the special magazine that was released in conjunction with *The Last Outlaw* in 1980. I kept it hidden in my desk for months and would trace the photographs to do drawings and read with wonder about how the costumes and the sets were re-created. I knew at that point that I wanted to make a Ned Kelly movie. There was something magnetic about this ironclad rebel and the story of his fight against corruption that provided an escape for me at a key transition point in my life. In fact, my last strong positive memories of my father for a fair chunk of time around this period came as a result of things pertaining to Ned.

At the end of the history unit we had to dress up as our chosen historical figure and answer questions as them. I had the best costume, naturally, which Dad had constructed with my assistance. I got details wrong when answering questions and this irked me so much that I spent the next two years trying to learn as much as I could (I'm still learning 20+ years later). Over the next few years, after my parents split, Dad would occasionally take my brother and I to places like Beveridge and Glenrowan to see the Ned Kelly stuff there. It still means a lot to me that Dad would do that and he probably never knew how important those experiences were for me.

Now, all through this time the story had been pretty clear cut in everything I read. Ned was Irish, poor, picked on by the police and fought back against them when they pushed him too far. This was the prevailing depiction of him across fiction and nonfiction alike. I was able to dismiss Edgar Penzig's depiction of Ned as a brutal thug because nobody else was saying the same things in any of the books I read (of which I had surprisingly few to access at the time). But when I read Alex Castle's book *Ned Kelly's Last Days* I had an awakening of sorts. Here was Ned through an objective lens. A viewpoint that pointed the finger at the criminal and the law enforcement equally instead of pushing an agenda to lionise the one over the other. In this text I saw Ned as arrogant, childish and ultimately victim of the machinations of the forces of law and order that would have done anything to make an example of him. This Ned was not a hero or a put-upon victim of systemic bullying like I had believed for so long, but a man with flaws – big flaws – who had been put on trial for putting men to death. Whether it was self defence or outright murder, the fact was that Ned had killed men and the question was whether the trial and Ned's incarceration had been handled correctly from a legal standpoint. When you really look at Ned's own words and behaviour you see moments like his argument with Redmond Barry as less of a battle of wits and more of a petulant tantrum. My opinion of Barry and much if the establishment remained quite low after reading that book, but I began to question who the real Ned Kelly was.

Throughout my twenties Ned took more of a back seat in my life, but he was always there. It wasn't until my own marriage crumbled like a wet cake that he re-emerged. Strangely, there was something stabilising about reconnecting with Ned. The story became something I could share with my son that only the two of us were necessarily interested in. That's when things really took a left turn.

After backing *The Legend of Ben Hall*, and putting my hand up to help out in any way I could on the film to get it over the line, I somehow found myself drawn into the Ned Kelly community. I had not considered myself part of it until this point, though I had interacted with the Iron Outlaw website in the early days (if I'm not mistaken I once wrote that I intended to write a film one day with Ettie Hart as Ned's love interest, because even back when I was a teen I somehow knew that the Kate Lloyd love affair didn't quite make sense to me). It is not an exaggeration to say that I was stunned when Matthew Holmes invited me to work on a Ned Kelly film with him. *Why me?* I thought, but I didn't really question it. Now was my chance to help make the Ned Kelly movie I always wanted to see and I knew Holmes was the man to direct because of how spot on his work with Ben Hall had been. It's like being asked to do the next Star Wars film by George Lucas himself.

The project was invigorating and it was the first time I had felt that kind of energy working on a production. I had written a school play for Montmorency Secondary College as my first writing gig out of high school, which was naturally a very different animal to what I was attempting here, so it was always going to be a big learning curve. We did our "Legend of Ned Kelly" tour around the hotspots in Victoria and that was when I finally met Ned.

Now, I had seen the armour so many times prior to this trip that it was almost mundane by this stage. Yet, when I entered the gallery of the State Library where it was housed behind glass like a sacred object, there he was looking out of the helmet at me. It was a look that seemed to be weighing me up and I can tell you that it was incredibly intimidating. Those dark eyes with heavy brows could look straight into your soul, and that day they did. Had he thought me worthy? Only time would tell.

Over the course of researching for what was at that time a cradle-to-grave of Ned's life, I came to reassess who Ned was. I avoided reading anything that wasn't a newspaper report or a court transcript, or other primary sources, unless I was getting stuck and needed a pointer. I particularly avoided any books that were known to skew heavily one way or another in painting whether he was heroic or evil incarnate – so there was no real reference to Ian Jones or Doug Morrissey at this phase. The picture I began to see emerge was that Ned had the entire gang under his thumb. It wasn't simply keeping them in line, but rather a need for total control. But as time went on and he pressed the thumb harder, he squeezed the others to the point of crushing them. Ned was in it for Ned, and his selfishness created mutually assured destruction, but why?

I spent months looking for the answers to my questions about what motivated Ned. I found him to be domineering, arrogant, brash, and short tempered, yet there was this other side to him that revered women and children, adored horses (not just the ones he stole), was capable of picking up any skills he needed to perform a trade, and was willing to give anyone the benefit of a doubt even when it was obvious that they couldn't be trusted. Who the hell was this guy? What made him tick.

So I started to get a bit Freudian with my thinking (Freud is surprisingly useful when looking at character and motivation). How did his parents shape him? You had Red, an ex-convict who was living in effective exile for stealing pigs and who endured untold horrors in the penal system. He was a quiet man because he didn't want to go back to gaol or put his family in difficulty, yet he probably harboured a lot of ill-will towards the authorities. In comparison you had Ellen, the daughter of a free settler who was feisty, promiscuous, quick to anger and never seemed to think much about consequences. So, how do these manifest in Ned? It seems he took the work ethic and the burden of the tyranny the Irish were subjected to from his father, while his mother gave him his temperament and his passion. Mix it all up and you've got a young man with a victim complex and a volatile temper that sees him pulled up on multiple charges linked to violent assault in the span of a few months. You take this angry kid and chuck him into the lion's den with hardened offenders and it's no wonder that he had such a chip on his shoulder and constantly teetered between toeing the line like his father and biting back like his mother.

Then you look at how this must have informed his relationship with the gang. He demanded respect and compliance – he didn't earn it. You see this in his treatment of Steve at Jerilderie and Dan at Stringybark

Creek. You only hear him talk glowingly of Joe because Joe was a born follower, a man who would do anything if the right person gave him permission. Yet, it was Steve that gathered the information that led to the Euroa heist, and Dan who showed the most competence in keeping crowds under control during the campaigns at Jerilderie and Glenrowan. This demonstrates that to Ned you were only as valuable as the unquestioning loyalty you gave him. It must have blown his mind to learn that Joe had gone against his express orders and murdered Aaron Sherritt. This man Ned had described as "cool and firm as steel", the one member of the gang he never felt the need to bully or put down, was the one who did the most egregious thing in defying Ned's orders while the other two seemed perfectly compliant right to the end. In fact, it is demonstrably true that Dan and Steve felt obligated to stick things out at the inn until the prisoners could escape, while Ned's first instinct had been to abandon the prisoners to their fate after his plan had backfired. This makes Ned's venom towards Dan and Steve after his capture all the more egregious.

Ned was insecure. A life of constant upheaval and misfortune does that to people. But not everyone in that situation becomes a violent criminal. Ned was clearly a far more complex man than anyone writing about him has been willing to admit. I honestly believe that I have done damn sight better than the vast majority of authors in capturing him authentically in text by this point. He is a deeply flawed man. One could even argue he is simply a wounded child in a man's body. But the one thing I have found is that for all his flaws, he is not an evil man. Even the most atrocious crimes can come from a place of good faith. Did Ned Kelly rob banks, steal horses and kill police? Yes. Can this be justified? No. Can they be explained? Of course. There's a big difference between rationalising an action and justifying it. When Ned felt trapped or in danger he responded like a wild animal. He was destined to be a warrior, but it was never clear how it would manifest. Glenrowan was his apotheosis where he both demonstrated his utter failure as a leader and his reckless daring as a combatant. He refused to be led and that's what defines Ned.

[Image: Ned Kelly in chains by Charles Nettleton, 10/11/1880; Papers of Dolia and Rosa Ribush, MS 9298, State Library Victoria]

Aidan Phelan is the writer and historian for *A Guide to Australian Bushranging*, an online resource that has been bringing Australia's outlaw heritage to a worldwide audience since 2017. *Glenrowan* is his first novel. He has also worked as an illustrator and regularly provides illustrations for *An Outlaw's Journal* by Georgina Stones. He is also developing *Glenrowan* as a television mini-series with Matthew Holmes (writer and director of *The Legend of Ben Hall*.) He is also a member of the Australian Crime Writers Association.

Aidan has a Bachelor of Arts and a Diploma of Education, and studied writing and editing at what is now known as Melbourne Polytechnic. He was born and raised in the suburbs of Melbourne and developed a fascination with the story of Ned Kelly on his first visit to Glenrowan as a child. This soon grew to be a consuming passion for Australian history, culminating in the creation of *A Guide to Australian Bushranging*; a repository for the information he has gathered on the subject of colonial banditry, incorporating reviews and articles about the associated popular culture.

www.ingramcontent.com/pod-product-compliance
Lightning Source LLC
Chambersburg PA
CBHW050058120726
47904CB00004B/1140